HÅKAN NESSER

THE SECRET LIFE OF MR ROOS

Translated from the Swedish by
Sarah Death

PAN BOOKS

First published 2020 by Mantle

This paperback edition first published 2021 by Pan Books
an imprint of Pan Macmillan
The Smithson, 6 Briset Street, London ECIM 5NR
EU representative: Macmillan Publishers Ireland Ltd, 1st Floor, The Liffey Trust Centre,
117–126 Sheriff Street Upper, Dublin 1, DOI YC43
Associated companies throughout the world
www.panmacmillan.com

ISBN 978-1-5098-9225-9

Originally published in 2008 as *Berättelse om herr Roos* by Albert Bonniers förlag, Stockholm.

1 3 5 7 9 8 6 4 2

A CIP catalogue record for this book is available from the British Library.

Typeset in Dante MT by Palimpsest Book Production Limited, Falkirk, Stirlingshire
Printed and bound by CPI Group (UK) Ltd, Croydon, CRO 4YY

Visit **www.panmacmillan.com** to read more about all our books
and to buy them. You will also find features, author interviews and
news of any author events, and you can sign up for e-newsletters
so that you're always first to hear about our new releases.

The towns of Kymlinge and Maardam do not exist in real life, unlike the Romanian writer Mircea Cărtărescu whose work is cited at several points in this book.

'All my life I have longed to be alone in a place like this'

Per Petterson, *Out Stealing Horses*
(translated by Anne Born)

ONE

1

The day before everything changed, Ante Valdemar Roos had a vision.

He was walking with his father in a forest. It was autumn and they were holding hands; the sunlight filtered through the lofty crowns of some tall pines; they went along a well-worn path that wound its way between mossy rocks and low, twiggy clumps of lingonberry. The air was clear and bright, with a scent of mushrooms as they passed some spots. He was probably five or six, and could hear birds calling and a dog barking in the distance.

Here's Gråmyren, said his father. This is where we usually see the elk.

It was the 1950s. Father was in a leather waistcoat and a checked cap, which he now took off, letting go of his son's hand to wipe his forehead with the arm of his shirt. He took out his pipe and tobacco and started the filling process.

Look around you, Valdemar my lad, he said. Life never gets any better than this.

Never any better than this.

He wasn't sure if it had really happened. If it was a genuine memory or just an image floating to the surface of the enigmatic well of the past. A yearning back to something that possibly never existed.

On this particular day, more than fifty years later, sitting on a sun-warmed rock beside his car, he shut his eyes and turned his face to the sun, and it wasn't easy to work out what was true and what just seemed to be real. It was August, there were thirty minutes of his lunch hour left. Valdemar's father had died in 1961 when he was a boy of twelve, and his memories often had this sort of shimmer of a lost idyll. He tended to think it wouldn't be so very odd if it had never happened. But his father's words had a genuine ring, and didn't feel like something he'd invented himself.

Life never gets any better than this.

And he remembered the cap and the waistcoat vividly. He was five years younger than I am now, when he died, he thought. He only reached fifty-four.

He drained his coffee and got back behind the wheel. He reclined the seat as far as it would go and closed his eyes again. Opened the side window so the warm breeze could reach him.

Sleep, he thought, I've got time for a fifteen-minute nap.

Perhaps I'll get another glimpse of that moment in the forest. Or perhaps some other lovely vision.

Wrigman's Electrical made thermos flasks. When the firm started in the late fifties and for a decade or so thereafter, its range had comprised a variety of electrical goods such as fans, food processors and hairdryers, but from the mid-seventies onwards it had produced only flasks. The change was made primarily because the founder, Wilgot Wrigman, as good as went up in smoke in a transformer fire in October 1971. That sort of thing can give an electrical company a bad name. People don't easily forget.

But the name lived on; there were those who felt Wrigman's

Electrical had become a recognized brand. The factory was out in Svartö, about twenty kilometres north of Kymlinge, the company had around thirty employees and Ante Valdemar Roos had been its head of accounts since 1980.

Twenty-eight years, to date. Forty-four kilometres by car every day; and if you calculated on the basis of forty-four working weeks a year – for the sake of a pleasing balance if nothing else – and five days a week, that came to 271,040 kilometres, which was the equivalent of roughly seven times round the globe. The longest journey Valdemar had ever made in his life was to the Greek island of Samos, that second summer with Alice, twelve years ago now. Say what you liked about time, it certainly did have a way of passing.

But there was also another kind of time; in fact, Ante Valdemar Roos would sometimes imagine that two vastly differing concepts of time existed in parallel.

The time that rushed by – adding days to days, wrinkles to wrinkles and years to years – there wasn't much you could do about that. You simply had to hang on in there as best you could, like young dogs chasing after a bitch in heat, or flies after a cow's arse.

But the other time, the recurring kind, that was something different. It was slow and long-drawn-out, sometimes coming to a complete standstill, or at least that was how it seemed; like the sluggish seconds and minutes when you were seven-teenth in the queue and waiting at the red light at the junction between Fabriksgatan and Ringvägen. Or when you woke up half an hour too early and couldn't get back to sleep for the life of you – only lie there on your side, watching the alarm clock on the bedside table and slowly getting used to the idea of dawn.

It was worth its weight in gold, that uneventful time, and the older he grew, the more evident that became.

The pauses, he would think, it's in the pauses between events – and as the ice forms on the lake on a November night, if you want to be a touch poetic – that I belong.

I and people like me.

He hadn't always thought that way. Only for the last ten years or so. Maybe it had gradually crept up on him, but there had been one particular occasion when he became aware of it – and put it into words. It was one day in May, five years ago, when the car suddenly died halfway between Kymlinge and Svartö. It was morning, and a minute or so after he passed the crossroads at Kvartofta church. The car ground to a halt at the roadside and Valdemar tried to start it a few times but without even a hint of success. First he rang Red Cow to say he would be late, then he rang the roadside assistance firm, and they promised to be there with a replacement car within the half hour.

An hour and a half passed, and it was in the course of those ninety minutes, as Valdemar sat behind the wheel, watching the birds in flight beneath the clear skies of a May morning, with the light playing over the fields and over the veins on his hands, where his blood pumped round with the aid of his trusty old heart, that he realized it was at times like this his soul made a space for itself in the world and set up home there. At exactly these times.

He didn't care how long it took the breakdown truck to arrive. He was unperturbed by Red Cow ringing to ask if he was making a bid for freedom or what. He felt no need to talk to his wife or to any other human being.

I should have been a cat instead, Ante Valdemar Roos had

thought. Hell yes, a fat farm cat basking in the sun outside a cowshed, that really would have been something.

He thought of the cat again now, as he woke up and looked at his watch. The lunch hour would be over in four minutes, so it was high time to make his way back to Wrigman's.

It would only take him two from this secluded clearing he had found, just off a disused forest track and a stone's throw or two from the factory. Sometimes he came on foot, but he generally took the car. He liked a fifteen-minute nap and it was nice simply to recline the back of the seat and doze off. A man asleep on the ground in a forest glade could have aroused suspicion.

The staff room at Wrigman's Electrical was a bare fifteen square metres in size and decked in dark-brown lino and mauve laminate, and after spending an eternity of lunch hours there, Ante Valdemar Roos had dreamt one night that he was dead and had gone to Hell. It was 2001 or 2002 and the Devil had received him personally, holding open the door for the new arrival with his characteristically sardonic smile, and the space inside had proved to be nothing more or less than the staff room at Wrigman's. Red Cow was already sitting in her usual corner with her microwaved pasta and her horoscopes, and she hadn't even looked up to give him a nod.

From the next day onwards, Valdemar had swapped over to having sandwiches, yogurt and coffee at his desk. A banana and a few ginger snaps that he kept in his top right desk drawer.

And now, at least if the weather was decent, he liked to take the car and get away completely for an hour or fifty minutes.

Red Cow thought he was odd, and she made no secret of the fact. But it wasn't only on account of his lunch habits and he'd learnt to take no notice of her.

It was the same with the rest of them, actually. Nilsson and Tapanen and Walter Wrigman himself. The population of the office; he realized they found him a difficult type, and he'd heard Tapanen use that very phrase when he was on the phone to someone and thought nobody could hear.

Yes, you know that Valdemar Roos is a difficult type, thank goodness I'm not married to anyone like that.

Anyone like that? Valdemar parked in his usual place next to the rusty old container, the removal of which had been under discussion since the mid-nineties. Tapanen was only a couple of years younger than he was and had worked at Wrigman's for almost as long. He had four children with the same woman but had got divorced a while back. He bet on the horses and had been claiming for the last 1800 weeks that it was only a matter of time until he hit the jackpot and bloody well said goodbye to that moth-eaten firm. He always took care to say it in earshot of Walter Wrigman, and the managing director would shift the wad of snus inside his cheek, run his hand over his balding head and declare that nothing would give him greater pleasure. Nothing.

Valdemar had never liked Tapanen, not even back in the days when he still liked people. There was something petty and vindictive about him; Valdemar often thought Tapanen must be one of those people who would desert his comrades in the trenches. He didn't entirely know what that meant or where the image had come from, but it seemed as intrinsic to the man as warts were to a warthog.

But he'd liked Nilsson. The round-shouldered Norrlander spent most of his time out on the road, admittedly, but every now and then he'd be sitting in his place to the right of Red Cow's glass box. He was no more than forty now, and had been even younger when he started, of course; he was quiet and amiable, and married to an even more reticent woman from Byske, or was it Hörnefors? They had five or six children and were members of some free church, but Valdemar could never remember which one. Nilsson had started at Wrigman's about six months before the millennium, taking over from Lasse with the leg, who had died in unlucky circumstances in a fishing accident out Rönninge way.

He had a solemnity to him, Nilsson, a greyish, lichen-like quality that less sympathetic souls, Tapanen for example, would have called dullness, and however much Valdemar would have liked him to, he couldn't recall Nilsson coming out with anything that might have been called a joke, either. It was hard even to say if he had ever laughed in his almost ten years at Wrigman's Electrical.

So it probably said something about Ante Valdemar Roos that he approved of someone like Nilsson. Used to approve of, that is. Before.

That image of the walk with his father still lingered, anyway. The tall, straight trunks of the spruces, the twiggy clumps of lingonberry, the damp hollows with their meadowsweet and bog myrtle. When he was back in his place behind the desk and switching his computer back on, it was as if his father's words were going round on an endless sound loop in his head.

Life never gets any better than this.

Never any better than this.

The afternoon passed in an atmosphere of gloom. It was Friday. It was August. The dog days of summer were still hanging on, the first working week after the holidays would soon be over and the immediate future was set out like a hopelessly ill-laid stretch of railway track: a party at his wife Alice's brother and sister-in-law's in the old part of Kymlinge down by the church.

It was a tradition. The Friday after the second Thursday in August they went for a crayfish supper at Hans-Erik and Helga Hummelberg's. They observed all the usual rituals, donning gaudy little party hats, drinking six different kinds of beer and home-spiced schnapps and slurping crayfish with all the trimmings. There were usually a dozen of them, plus or minus a couple, and for the past three years, Valdemar had fallen asleep on the sofa.

Not as a result of too much strong liquor, but rather from sheer boredom. He could just about bring himself to join in the conversation, produce a sufficient number of witty remarks and show an interest in all sorts of esoteric nonsense for two or three hours, but then it was as if all the air went out of him. He started to feel as out of place as a seal in the middle of a desert. He spent half an hour in the loo, and if nobody noticed he'd been missing he would generally allow himself another half hour a bit later, sitting on an unfamiliar brown-varnished toilet seat with his trousers and underpants round his ankles, wondering how he would go about it if he ever decided to kill himself one day. Or kill his wife. Or run away to Kathmandu. He had learnt to use the so-called children's bathroom in the teenagers' part of the house. They were never home for their parents' parties anyway, and here he could sit undisturbed and unloved under a brooding cloud of pessimism for as long as he wanted.

But there must be something wrong, he'd thought the previous year, something seriously wrong with life itself, if in your sixtieth year or thereabouts you couldn't think of any better solutions than going to a party and locking yourself in the toilet.

So what to do? he thought when the working week came to an abrupt end and he was once again seated at his steering wheel. *What to do?* Slam his fist on the table? Declare his opposition and explain politely but firmly that he wasn't coming with her to Hans-Erik and Helga's?

Why not? Why not tell Alice without further ado that he disliked her brother & co. as much as he disliked rap music and blogs and shouty headlines on newsstands, and that he had no intention of setting foot in their quasi-intellectual drinking club ever again?

As he drove the twenty-two kilometres back to Kymlinge, these questions bounced back and forth in the desolate vacuum inside his head. He knew they were fictional, not real; this was nothing more than the usual litany of cowardly protestations that droned pretty continuously inside him. Questions, formulations and venomous phrases, which never ever passed his bloodless lips and served no other purpose than to make him even more dispirited and melancholy.

I'm dead, he thought as he passed the new Co-op complex out in Billundsberg. In all essential respects there's less life in me than in a plastic pot plant. There's nothing wrong with the others, it's me.

Seven hours later he actually was sitting on the toilet. His prediction had come true in every last detail, with the minor addition of his being drunk. Out of pure boredom and in an attempt to infuse life with some meaning he had downed four shots of schnapps, a large amount of beer and two or three glasses of white wine. He had also told the assembled company a long story about a whore from Odense, but when he reached the punchline he unfortunately found he had forgotten it. Such things happen in the best families, but the woman who was one half of a new couple – a bosomy, dyed-blonde psychotherapist with roots in Stora Tuna – had observed him with a professional smile, and he had seen Alice gritting her teeth so hard that she was white around the jaw.

He had no idea how long he had been sitting on the varnished brown ring, but his watch said quarter to one and he didn't think he'd dozed off. In Ante Valdemar Roos's experience it was well nigh impossible to sleep on a toilet. He pressed the flush as he got to his feet to adjust his clothes. He splashed his face with cold water a couple of times and tried to comb the thin strands of hair still growing sparsely on his uneven head into some kind of pattern. Helped himself to a blob of toothpaste and gargled.

Then he staggered cautiously out of the bathroom and headed for the big sitting room, where Spanish guitar music mingled with loud voices and smooth laughter. Unless anyone else had slipped away to hide, there ought to be eleven of them in there, thought Valdemar; a whole football team of people in various stages of middle age, successful, quick-witted and enjoying their well-earned inebriation.

Suddenly he hesitated. All at once he felt manifestly old, a genuine failure and not remotely quick-witted. His wife was eleven years younger than him, all the others in the gang were between forty and fifty and the psychotherapist could even still be in her thirties. As for him, it was only a few months until his sixtieth birthday.

I've nothing to say to a single one of them, he thought. None of them has anything to say to me.

I don't want to be part of this any more, the best I can wish for is to be a cat.

He looked around the hall. The décor was entirely white and aluminium. There wasn't a single object of interest to him. Not a single damn thing he'd have felt like pocketing if he were a burglar. It was just too pitiful.

He turned on his heel, let himself out quietly through the front door and was met by the cool, clarifying night air.

Never any worse than this.

2

At half past twelve the following day, Ante Valdemar Roos was on the sofa in his living room, trying to read the newspaper. It wasn't going unduly well. The text swam before his eyes. His head felt like something that had been left in the oven for too long. His stomach wasn't in a much better state, and there seemed to be some kind of malignant yellow-flowered coltsfoot clogging the periphery of his field of vision.

His wife Alice hadn't spoken to him all morning, but his younger daughter Wilma had told him – just before the two of them slunk out of the door – that they were going out shopping for a few hours. She was sixteen and maybe she felt a bit sorry for him.

His elder daughter Signe was out on the balcony smoking. Neither Wilma nor Signe was Valdemar's own; they had come as part of the Alice package when they got married eleven years earlier. They'd been five and nine. Now they were sixteen and twenty. There was quite a difference, thought Valdemar. You couldn't say things had grown easier with time. Hardly a day passed without him praying to the higher power in whom he didn't really believe for Signe to stir her stumps and move out. She had been talking about it for three years, but still hadn't got round to it.

Ante Valdemar Roos did have a child of his own flesh and

blood, however. A son by the name of Greger, who was the product of a bewildering first marriage to a woman called Lisen. It wasn't a standard name even then, and he didn't think she had been a particularly standard sort of woman, either. Neither in general nor at any given point in time.

She was dead now. She had died on a mountaineering expedition in the Himalayas two years before the millennium. The idea had been, if he had understood correctly, to reach some summit or other exactly on her fiftieth birthday.

They'd been married for seven years when she admitted having had another man on the side almost the whole time, and they had divorced without much fuss. She took Greger with her when she moved to Berlin, but Valdemar had some contact with the boy when he was growing up.

Not much, but some. School half terms and summer holidays. Some fell-walking and a couple of trips away: a rainy week in Scotland, amongst other things, and four days at the Skara Summerland theme park. Now Greger was entering middle age and lived in Maardam, where he worked at a bank and lived with a dark-skinned woman from Surinam. Valdemar had never met her but he had seen a photo. They had two children and he generally emailed Greger every three or four months. The last time he had seen him was at Lisen's funeral in a windswept cemetery in Berlin. Ten years had passed since that day.

Signe came in from the balcony.

'How are you doing?' she asked.

'Fine,' said Valdemar.

'You look rough.'

'Do I?'

'Mum said you let things get a bit out of hand last night.'

'Pfft,' said Valdemar, and dropped the paper on the floor.

She sat down in the armchair opposite him. Adjusted the towel that was wound round her hair. She was wearing her big yellow bathrobe, which he took as a sign that she had managed a shower before her first fag of the day.

'She says you went missing from the crayfish party.'

'Went missing?'

'Yes.'

He picked up the paper and felt the throbbing in his temples as he bent forwards. The coltsfoot seemed to be spreading luxuriantly.

'I . . . took a walk.'

'All the way from Old Kymlinge?'

'Yes. It was a nice evening.'

She yawned. 'I heard you come in.'

'Oh yes?'

'Only ten minutes after I did, actually. Half past four.'

Half past four? He thought, and a wave of nausea swept over him. Surely that couldn't be possible?

'It takes a while from Old Kymlinge,' he said. 'As discussed.'

'Yeah right,' sneered Signe. 'And then you dropped in at Prince for a few beers. Expect that took a while, too.'

He realized it was true. Signe was as well informed as ever. He had passed a bar on Drottninggatan, seen it was open and nipped inside. He didn't know it was called Prince, but he suddenly remembered sitting at a shiny bar counter, drinking beer. He'd chatted to some woman too, with lots of red hair and a Yasser Arafat scarf, or at least, some kind of check-patterned headgear, and he might have bought her a drink as well. Or two. If his memory wasn't playing tricks, she'd had a man's name tattooed on her forearm. *Hans?* No, *Hugo,* wasn't it? Ante Valdemar Roos groaned inwardly.

'Cilla, my mate, saw you. You were pretty pissed, she said.'

He chose not to comment, leafing through the paper instead and pretending he had no interest in the conversation. Pretending he wasn't bothered.

'And she said you were fifteen years older than anyone else in the place. The hag you were with came in at number two.'

He found the sports pages and started reading the results. Signe went quiet for a moment and sat staring at her nails.

'Mum's a bit fed up, isn't she?' she said, and whisked off into her room without waiting for an answer.

A day like any other, thought Ante Valdemar Roos, and shut his eyes.

In the early afternoon he grabbed the chance of a nap, and when he woke up around four he was surprised to discover that he was alone in the house. Wilma and Signe could be anywhere in time and space, but Alice had left a note on the kitchen table.

Gone to Olga's. Back late. A

Valdemar scrunched up the piece of paper and threw it in the rubbish. He took two painkillers and drank a glass of water. His thoughts went momentarily to Olga, who was Russian and one of his wife's innumerable friends. She was dark-eyed and spoke slowly and mysteriously in a deep voice that was almost a baritone, and he had once dreamt that he had had sex with her. It was a very vivid dream in which they'd been lying on a bed of ferns; she had been sitting astride him and her long black hair had danced in the wind. He had woken just before he climaxed, startled from sleep by Alice turning on the vacuum cleaner half a metre from the bed and then asking him if he was ill or what.

He opened the fridge and wondered if he was expected to make dinner for the girls. Maybe, maybe not. There were certainly the ingredients for some kind of basic pasta dish. He decided to wait and see. One or the other would presumably turn up in due course, and maybe they'd prefer him to give them some cash so they could stuff their faces in town instead. You never could tell.

He found his pools coupon and sank into a chair in front of the TV.

Little did Ante Valdemar Roos think at that moment that his life was about to undergo a radical and fateful change of direction.

This idiotic phrase was to keep popping into his head in the weeks that followed, and every time it did so he would laugh at it, and with every justification.

It was his father who had started with that line of numbers. Before he hanged himself he'd been going to the tobacconist on Gartzvägen in K– and playing the same single line of numbers for eight years. Every Wednesday before 6 p.m., and sometimes Valdemar was allowed to go with him.

Same line? the phlegmatic tobacconist Mr Pohlgren would ask.

Same line, his father would reply.

Most of the people who played, Valdemar had come to understand, liked to try their luck with five or eight lines, or with some little system they'd developed, but Eugen Roos stuck to his single line.

Sooner or later, my boy, he explained, sooner or later it'll win. When we least expect it – all it takes is patience.

Patience.

After his father's death, Valdemar had taken over, and the very first Wednesday after this misfortune he had gone into Pohlgren's, filled in the one line on the coupon and paid the forty öre it cost in those days.

And he had carried on, week after week, year after year. When the pools organizers expanded from twelve to thirteen matches, Valdemar expanded too. From one to three lines. He always hedged his bets on the thirteenth number.

The same line ever since 1953, in other words. Sometimes he wondered if it was some kind of world record. It had been over fifty years now, a considerable chunk of time however you looked at it.

The remarkable thing was that neither he nor his father had ever won so much as a krona. Twenty times he'd got nine right; three times it was ten, but there had been nothing paid out for ten on any of those occasions.

Patience, he would tell himself. If I leave the line to Greger when I die, he'll be a millionaire one of these days.

He dozed off in his armchair for a while, he just couldn't help it. From the twentieth to the forty-fourth minute of the second half, more or less, but he was wide awake for the results round-up at the end. He was still alone in the flat, and as he reached for his pen he thought that if he couldn't be a cat in his next life, at least he could ask to be a bachelor.

And then, as the world went on as usual, as innumerable winds blew from all corners and nothing or everything happened or didn't, the miracle ticked into life.

Match after match, result after result, tick after tick; Valdemar's first thought when it was all over was that he'd been the one supervising the whole procedure. That it was all thanks to him – and his careful supervision. He wasn't in the habit of doing it, and very rarely watched the show these days; he usually made do with checking the winning line on teletext or in Sunday's or Monday's paper. Noting that he'd got four or five or six right as usual, and there was nothing to do but try again.

Thirteen.

He tasted the word. Said it out loud to himself. *Thirteen right.*

He suddenly started to doubt he was awake. Or even alive. The dusky light in the room and in the flat suddenly didn't feel real, but more like a shroud, so perhaps he was actually dead; apart from the TV there was not a single source of light and for the first time he also noticed that it was raining outside in the world and that the sky over Kymlinge was as dark as freshly laid tarmac.

He pinched his nostrils, cleared his throat loudly, wiggled his toes and said his name and date of birth in a clear, firm voice, after which he cautiously drew the conclusion that he was neither sleeping nor dead.

Then they announced the payout.

One million . . .

His headache gave a kick as he opened his eyes wide and leant closer to the TV set.

One million nine hundred and fifty . . .

The telephone rang. Alexander Graham Bell, go and play with yourself, thought Ante Valdemar Roos, and wondered why such a phrase, and in English to boot, should suddenly pop into his convalescent brain, but it did, only to be blown away and forgotten the next moment.

One million, nine hundred and fifty-four thousand, one hundred and twenty kronor.

He found the remote control, switched off the TV and sat stock still in his armchair for ten minutes. If my heart doesn't stop I'll live to a hundred now, he thought.

It was half past nine in the evening by the time Alice got back from her friend Olga's, and Valdemar had totally recovered.

'I'm sorry about yesterday,' he said. 'I somehow had a few shots too many.'

'*Somehow?*' said Alice 'It's pretty simple, you just *downed* them.'

'You could be right,' said Valdemar. 'I drank too much, anyway.'

'Are the girls home?'

He shrugged. 'No.'

'Wilma called my mobile and promised to be home by nine.'

'Did she?' said Valdemar. 'No, they've both been out all evening.'

'Did you deal with the washing?'

'No,' said Valdemar.

'Water the plants?'

'No, not that either,' admitted Valedemar. 'I haven't been feeling great, as I said.'

'I presume you didn't ring Hans-Erik and Helga to apologize, either?'

'You're right,' said Valdemar. 'Another thing I failed to do.'

Alice went out into the kitchen and he followed her because he could see the way things were going.

'I didn't mean to,' he said. 'Not to just walk out like that. But it was such a fine evening and I thought—'

'That story you told, did you think it was appropriate for the occasion?'

'I know I forgot the punchline,' he acknowledged. 'But it is quite funny. It's come back to me now, so if you like—'

'That's enough, Valdemar,' she interrupted. 'I can't take any more right now. Do you really want to stay married to me?'

He subsided onto a chair but she stayed on her feet, staring out of the window. Nothing happened for a long time. He sat there with his elbows chafing the table, his eyes fixed on the pot plant, a droopy little mind-your-own-business, and the diminutive salt cellars they had bought in Stockholm Old Town on a rainy weekend break seven or eight years before. Well it was a cruet set, of course, one salt, one pepper. Alice stood there with her broad fundament turned his way, and it occurred to him that this generously proportioned part of her anatomy was what their whole marriage rested on. It truly was. Admittedly she was only forty-eight, but it wasn't easy to find a new partner when you were twenty kilos overweight, not in these times so obsessed with appearance, superficiality and slimness – and possibly not in any other time, either. He knew nothing frightened her more than the prospect of having to live alone.

The equation had already been written and calculated when they married. Valdemar had been ten years too old but Alice, in return, had been twenty-five kilos too heavy; neither of them had ever voiced this sad truth, but he was convinced she was as conscious of it as he was.

In the cheerless name of this same truth – he had time to note while wearing out his elbows as he waited – Alice had actually shed a few kilos since their wedding, whereas Valdemar had not grown any younger in recompense.

'We haven't made love for over a year,' she said now. 'Do you find me so disgusting, Valdemar?'

'No,' he said. 'But I find myself disgusting, that's the problem.'

He briefly wondered if that was true or just a clever answer, and presumably Alice was doing the same, because she turned round and looked at him with a slightly sad and quizzical expression. She seemed to be weighing up whether to say more but then gave a deep sigh and went out to the laundry room.

Two million, thought Ante Valdemar Roos. If I add on the winnings for the twelve out of thirteens, it must come to over two million. What the hell shall I do?

And suddenly that image of his father in the forest popped into his perforated mind. There he was again, pipe in hand, his face seeming to loom closer, and when Valdemar closed his eyes he could see his father's lips moving. As if he had a message for his son.

What? he thought. What are you trying to tell me, Dad?

And then, at the very moment he heard his wife set the tumble dryer going, he could also hear his father's voice. It sounded faint and distant as it found its way through the noise of past decades, but it was still unmistakable – and clear enough for him to understand without difficulty.

You needn't play that line next week lad, he said.

And you needn't be patient any more.

3

After three weeks at the home in Elvafors, Anna Gambowska knew she would have to run away.

There was no way round it.

She had spent the first week crying from dawn till dusk. Sometimes all night, as well; there was something in her soul that needed the lubrication of these tears to soften it and bring it back to life. That was exactly how it felt. It was therapeutic weeping, designed to heal, even if it had its source in great sorrow.

It was the first time she had thought about her soul in that way. Like a pitiful little plant that had to be watered and nourished before it could cope with life. Before it could grow and take its rightful place in this bare and inhospitable world. But when life grew too hard it was better to let it stay hidden deep down in the frozen ground and pretend it didn't even exist.

A soul deep-frozen in the ground. Or a soul in the deep-frozen ground. It sounded like a grammar exercise from school.

Things had been like this for a while now. All through the spring and summer at least, maybe even longer. Her soul had lain forgotten at the bottom of the frozen pit inside her, and if she hadn't got into the home at Elvafors in time, it could easily have perished entirely.

Thinking that thought made her cry even more. It was as

if her soul could wring nourishment from its own sadness. Yes, that really was how it seemed to be.

It was her mother who realized the state she was in. Anna stole money from her to buy heroin to smoke. It was her mother, too, who saw to it that the authorities were called in.

She stole four thousand kronor. It was beyond Anna why her mother had so much cash at home, and in her first few days at Elvafors, as she thought back over what she had done – referred to in the twelve-step programme as *the ethical collapse* – her soul knotted painfully and demanded a retreat down to the depths. Her mother worked at a daycare centre, four thousand was more than she earned in a week, and she had been saving up so she could buy Marek a new bike.

Marek was eight and Anna's little brother. Instead of a bike it went on heroin for his big sister.

She cried over that, as well. Cried over her shame and her wretchedness and her ingratitude. But her mother loved her, she knew that. Loved her anyway, in spite of everything. Even though she had her own problems to tussle with. When she discovered the money was gone she was livid, but it didn't last. She took Anna in her arms, comforted her and told her she loved her.

Without her mother she would never be able to turn her life around, Anna Gambowska knew that.

Maybe not even with her, but absolutely not without.

She arrived at Elvafors on the first of August. That was eight days after her mother found her out, and it happened to be her twenty-first birthday. They stopped at a cafe on the way and celebrated with coffee and cake. Her mother held her hands, they both shed some tears and promised each other this was the start of a new life. Enough was enough.

I had a huge burden of pain to bear when I was your age, too, her mother had told her. But we can get over those things.

How did you get over yours? Anna asked.

Her mother hesitated. I had you, she said eventually.

So you think I should make sure to get pregnant, on top of everything else? Anna wanted to know.

Just you dare, her mother said, and the two of them laughed so loudly that the serving staff exchanged looks.

It had felt good sitting there in that anonymous cafe, laughing at life in general, thought Anna. It had been a good moment. Simply giving all her troubles and the whole wretched state of affairs a big kick up the backside. Maybe that was the way to get one over on life for fucking things up? Maybe there was no better method than that?

She'd been fifteen when she tried hash for the first time. For the past three years, once she'd decided to ditch upper secondary and found work in a kiosk, a cafe and a filling station instead, she'd been smoking it at least three times a week. And pretty much every day since she left home in February. In April she'd met Steffo and started dealing. He had contacts, he was six years older than her and had moved in with her in May. He'd also got hold of some of the harder stuff: amphetamines and morphine and ecstasy a couple of times. The smoking heroin was the last step, in a way. She'd used it four times and when the intensity of the trips made her cry, it was as if her tears were of pure blood.

Or impure blood, to be more accurate.

Her mother didn't know much about Steffo, only that he existed. Anna had protected him from social services, and from the police, and she wondered where he'd got to since her mother went in and emptied the flat.

But there was no shortage of places for someone like Steffo, she was sure. Beds for the night, as well, it was nothing she needed to worry about.

And she hoped he had found another girl. Hoped it for her own sake. There were things about Steffo that scared her, scared her a lot, which was presumably why she had protected him.

You're mine, he had said. Never forget you're Steffo's now.

He'd also said she ought to get his name tattooed on her leg, the inside of her thigh for preference, but she'd managed to talk him out of that bit. It's a present, he declared, a present from me to you. Oh yes, she really hoped he'd found another girl.

Thinking of Steffo reminded her of all the other questions, too. They were floating around just under her tears and she knew they were looking for answers the way a missing calf looks for its mother.

Why? Why did you want to destroy my life? Why are you deliberately heading straight down to Hell? What's the point, Anna?

She asked herself, and everyone else asked too. Her mother. Social services. Auntie Majka. She had no answer. If there had been an answer, there'd have been no need for a question, she would think.

It was a darkness. A darkness with an enormous force of attraction.

Yes, a force stronger than herself, just like they talked about in their group therapy sessions.

The first time she saw Elvafors she thought it looked like a picture out of a book of fairy tales. It stood beside a round lake with a carpet of lily pads. A grassy slope dotted with gnarled fruit trees ran up to the house, and around it the forest extended in all directions. The building was a charming old wooden place, yellow and white; eight small rooms upstairs, a kitchen and four larger ones downstairs. At right angles to it a smaller building used for the office and overnight accommodation for staff. Up on the forest margins another building: a little red house known as the first gate with a kitchen and combined bedroom and sitting room, for the two patients who had progressed furthest in their treatment. Patients who would soon move on to the last gate in Dalby and from there back into everyday life again.

There were only women here. A supervisor named Sonja Svensson, half a dozen staff, several of them former addicts, and then the patients: young women who were to be saved from the shameful squalor and corruption of alcohol and drugs. Anna was admitted on the same day as an eighteen-year-old girl from Karlstad.

They had come from all over the country, but mainly from central and western Sweden. By the end of the first morning she had learnt their names; it was a fundamental step in the therapeutic process, Sonia had explained, laughing her dry little laugh.

How can we respect each other if we don't know each other's names?

It was all about respect at Elvafors.

At least on paper.

Yet it was the lack of respect that eventually made Anna Gambowska decide to run away.

Surely it was precisely that? she asked herself.

Yes, it was. Precisely that.

*

There was a set of simple rules at Elvafors. When she was admitted, Anna had to sign a piece of paper to confirm that she accepted these rules. The treatment was voluntary but it was paid for out of the social budgets of the local government authorities where they lived. If the centre proved unsuitable, it was of course better to give your place up to someone else in need.

There was no shortage of people in need, heaven knows. The treatment normally lasted for between six months and a year, and the home welcomed continued contact after the patient was discharged. It wasn't unusual for grateful clients to pay visits, Sonja Svensson told them on the very first day. Not unusual at all.

The most important rule apart from that was to have as little contact with the outside world as possible. It was in the outside world that the girls – none of them older than twenty-three, so Anna found it hard to think of them as women – had taken their knocks, it was out there they had their dubious contacts and destructive networks. It was important to break the patterns, both internal and external. No mobile phones were permitted at Elvafors, but everyone was allowed a weekly telephone call – to a family number agreed in advance, usually to a parent. Relatives were welcome to get in touch, but were urged to take a fairly restrictive approach in the number of times they did so. In return, so-called family days were held twice a year.

There were no computers or Internet at Elvafors, except in an inner room of the office, to which the patients had no access.

Radio and TV were provided though, at least some of the channels.

In the first two months, no leave of absence was granted, and if it was agreed to later, the patient and at least one family member took joint responsibility.

All the cooking, washing-up, cleaning and other household

chores were done by the patients themselves. At least twice a week they were taken on outings together, usually to the nearest town of Dalby, eighteen kilometres away. Bowling, swimming or cafe visits were usually on the programme.

Elvafors was remote, and that was no coincidence. When Sonja Svensson set up the home thirteen years earlier, the geographical location had been her top priority.

No disruptive civilization. No dangers. No connections.

As for the actual treatment, it rested on four cornerstones: openness, good comradeship, help to self-help and the twelve-step programme. After breakfast they all gathered in the big room, sat on chairs in a circle and basically talked about how they were feeling. It took the time it took. Then it was time for individual analysis tasks and then they spent a bit of time on the twelve-step programme.

After lunch there would be activities, either an outing or something at the home. On Tuesdays and Fridays a psychologist visited for one-to-one sessions. Sometimes Sonja Svensson also called in her flock for private conversations.

Then dinner, with the work it took to prepare and clear up afterwards, and finally another circle session around ten to discuss negative and positive experiences of the day.

But there was still plenty of time for other things. For being yourself. Reading or writing or watching TV. There was a piano, and Anna had brought her guitar. There was never any question of communal singing, though. None of the other girls seemed particularly musical, but a number of them liked hearing Anna play and she usually had one or two of them sitting in her room for a while.

At least in the early days.

*

Once her week of weeping was over, a sort of calm initially descended. She liked the regular, stress-free pace of the home. Comparing notes with the other girls also seemed worthwhile, if a little intimidating. She soon realized that when it came to harsh and horrible experiences in life, she was something of a novice. Four of them, so half the group, had been through this kind of therapy before. Marit from Gothenburg, already on her fourth course of treatment, was in the habit of saying she couldn't cry any more. That did seem to be the case; she liked laughing and had a loud, boisterous laugh, but it never reached her eyes. It wasn't at all like the laugh Anna and her mother had enjoyed in that cafe.

Two of the others, Turid and Ebba, had been prostitutes, even though they weren't yet twenty, and Marit had been regularly and secretly abused by her stepfather ever since she was twelve.

But, as Sonja Svensson and the rest of the staff were at pains to emphasize, looking back was easy, the trick was to look forward.

While Anna was preparing the salad for dinner one evening, she also heard a more cynical view of the home from Maria, the eldest and most hardened of them all.

They make money out of us, you know that, don't you? she said, glancing over her shoulder to check they couldn't be overheard. Social services pay a thousand a day for each one of us! Sonja and her fella have got over a million stashed in the bank.

Could that really be the case? Maria wasn't known for saying nice things, but perhaps she was right on this subject? This is my last bit of rest, she would declare when none of the staff were listening. When I get out of here I'm going to drug myself up and be dead in two weeks flat, it'll be fucking lovely.

She was twenty-three.

Anna made various other observations too, it was unavoidable.

That she seemed to be an odd fish in this world, too, for example. As she always had been. None of the other girls read books. And when she told Ludmilla, who was twenty and from Borås, that she wrote poems, Ludmilla suddenly lost it and called her a fucking cow, just trying to make herself seem special.

She brought it up at the morning meeting the next day. Explained that she'd been upset by what Ludmilla said, after which they all sat there on their hard chairs trading insults for nearly an hour. Sonja Svensson wasn't with them; instead they were in the hands of a woman called Karin, who tried ineffectually to calm things down.

Afterwards it didn't feel as if anything much had been resolved and the next day she was called in for a private chat with Sonja Svensson.

There's no need to bury your nose in a book all day, Sonja said. You've got to make an effort to fit in.

But I like reading, Anna had explained.

That's part of your wider set of problems, came the answer. You withdraw. Guitar and poetry and all that stuff. Tomorrow we're playing football in the sports hall at Dalby school, you need more of that kind of thing in your life.

She'd laughed her dry laugh and sent Anna out of her office.

What did she mean by that, Anna had wondered. Was she serious? What was wrong with music? Poetry and books couldn't be any kind of problem, surely?

*

From that day on she was always careful to shut the door of her room. When she was playing the guitar or writing or lying on the bed to read. So she didn't disturb anybody or come across as stuck-up. But clearly that wasn't the right approach because one evening when they got back from swimming in Dalby Sonja informed her she had taken the guitar and locked it in the office.

You can manage without it for a week, she said. It'll do you good.

At the meeting the next morning, Anna said having her guitar confiscated made her feel really upset and indignant. Sonja Svensson didn't give any of the other girls a chance to comment; she just said this wasn't the time to discuss the matter and moved on to the other girls and how they were feeling.

That evening she had a phone call from her mother. So as not to worry her, Anna didn't bring up the guitar incident. She just said everything was OK, she was feeling better and better, and she was in the middle of writing a long letter to Marek. Her mother said her brother had got his bike after all, but that she wasn't feeling great because her knees had started playing up again. She might have to go off sick, and if there was one thing she hated it was having to take time off sick.

That night Anna lay awake for several hours and cried a new sort of tears. At first she couldn't work out what was new about them, other than that they didn't feel the same as usual.

But then she understood.

She wasn't crying for herself and her poor ragged soul, she was weeping for the world.

For the state of things generally. For life itself, the blinkered outlooks, the stupidity and lack of compassion – and for guitars that were shut up against their wills in rank-smelling offices because they were part of someone's wider set of problems.

Not everything about Elvafors was bad, and Sonja Svensson had no doubt set the whole thing up with good intentions, Anna could see that. But the more distance she put between herself and the drugs, the more obviously the cracks showed. No one on the staff had any professional training; they were all former addicts or friends of Sonja's. Two of them were even related to her in some way. No dissent was tolerated; on issues of treatment it was always Sonja who knew best. Of course she always made things sound as if they were in your own best interests and as if everyone was part of the decision-making process. But that was far from the case; it was Sonja who decided and everything had to be done as a group. If you didn't want to join in – didn't feel like watching that reality TV show or playing that game of ludo – it was considered abnormal behaviour and an indication of relapse. Not into addiction, perhaps, but into the patterns that could lead to it, which consequently had to be broken. It was terrorization by majority, thought Anna, but presumably that couldn't have been the original intention.

And a thousand kronor per person per day? Eight thousand every twenty-four hours, which would grow into an enormous sum in just a few weeks. The programme couldn't possibly cost the home that much, so maybe there was some truth in what Maria had said, after all?

In August, Ludmilla absconded while on weekend leave of absence. A few days later Sonja reported that she had been found naked and unconscious in a ditch on the southern outskirts of Stockholm. She had been raped and had taken an overdose, and her condition was critical.

Sonja told them this at the meeting after dinner. There was something in her voice as she said it. In the details. Anna looked round at the other speechless girls and wondered if they had detected it too.

That little hint of . . . well, what was it? Satisfaction?

But the others just looked shocked and scared.

She felt the same way herself, and that was presumably the point.

The point? she asked herself as she lay in her bed fifteen minutes later. What was the damn point?

And that was the evening when it first came home to her that she didn't want to be there any more.

4

Coming out of the branch of Swedbank on Södra torg in Kymlinge late on Thursday afternoon, Ante Valdemar Roos was momentarily blinded by the sun, and he took this as a sign. He was in synch with the powers above, his life was bubbling like a newly opened bottle of champagne, and he felt he could have danced across the square.

Or at the very least made one of those elegant leaps into the air and clicked his heels together, like that woman on TV whose name he had forgotten. Bloody hell, he thought. I haven't felt this full of life since . . . well, since when? He did not know.

Since he had proposed to Lisen and she had accepted, maybe? Though she was already pregnant so her answer wasn't that surprising when it came down to it.

But when he counted newborn Greger's toes, found that there were ten and that the boy was in all likelihood completely healthy, well, that had been a great and powerful moment. He had felt that same fizzing sensation in his body back then.

The same zest for life. The same urge to steam ahead and get things done.

It had all gone without a hitch. He now had 2,100,000 kronor in a brand new account. On the twenty-fifth of every month there would be an automatic transfer from there to his ordinary current account of 18,270 kronor, the exact sum that normally came in from Wrigman's Electrical after tax at source had been taken off. If he just let it run, it would last for 120 months, not counting the interest that would accrue.

Ten years. Christ almighty.

But he wasn't intending to let it run for that long. Not really. In a few years' time he would start to draw his rightful and hard-earned pension. Alice wouldn't suspect a thing. Wouldn't have the foggiest idea. She had her own card for his account, and as long as the money flowed in at its usual pace, there wouldn't be the least call for her to check on anything. She didn't know any of his work colleagues and he couldn't remember ever being on the phone to any of them from home. Not in all the time he and Alice had had the same number, which was maybe a bit odd.

And he never rang from work, nor did she call him there. Possibly one or other of the daughters had on occasion needed to reach him in work time, but always on his mobile. He had once shown Alice where the factory was, when they happened to be passing, but that was all. The girls would never find their way there, even with map in hand. He smiled and strode straight past the shop that had sold him his pools coupon without going in. Good luck, you poor sods, he thought. It's all about being patient.

So the way he'd planned it, one of his millions would stay untouched. It ought to last until he started drawing his pension. At sixty-three or sixty-four, that would be about right. Or maybe sixty-five if the fancy took him; he was feeling so alive at this moment that he could easily reach a hundred.

But as for the other million, he was going to splash out. Very quietly, discretion guaranteed.

And he knew how he was going to use it; it hadn't taken much soul-searching before he came to that decision. Scarcely any, but there would be time for that in due course. First he had to deal with Walter Wrigman.

As he crossed the Oktober footbridge over Kymlinge river, he noticed to his dismay that he was whistling.

I've got to calm down, thought Ante Valdemar Roos. Make sure I keep a low profile. Lie doggo. What is it they say these days – eat crow? No, that can't be right.

It was all the same to him, anyway, and haste was a concept the good Lord hadn't seen fit to create. He put his face into neutral and turned his steps heavily for home.

'What do you mean?' asked Walter Wrigman the next morning, pushing his glasses up onto his bald head. 'What the hell are you saying?'

'I quit,' said Valdemar. 'I've had enough.'

Walter Wrigman's jaws ground on empty for a few moments, but no words emerged from his mouth. His glasses slipped back down and landed with a smack on the bridge of his nose, where there was a deep, mauvish notch expressly for that purpose.

'I'm handing in my notice,' elaborated Valdemar. 'I'd like to leave right away, if that's all right, but I could stay another week if you think it's necessary. No need for any severance payment.'

'What . . . what are you going to do?' asked Walter Wrigman, his voice squeaky with surprise.

'I've got a few plans,' said Valdemar.

'How long have you been considering this?'

'A while,' said Valdemar. 'I should have thought Tapanen could take over my responsibilities.'

'It's a very awkward time,' said Wrigman.

'I wouldn't say so,' said Valdemar. 'We haven't got many orders in the book. I suppose you'll have to appoint somebody younger in due course.'

'Well I'll be damned,' said Wrigman.

'I don't want cake or flowers or any of that crap,' said Valdemar. 'I thought I'd stick around this afternoon and pack up my stuff, if that's all right with you.'

'Well I'll be damned,' Wrigman said again.

You're no bloody charmer yourself, thought Valdemar, extending his hand.

'Thanks for the past twenty-eight years. It could have been worse.'

Walter Wrigman shook his head but did not take the outstretched hand. He just sat there in silence, chewing his lower lip.

'Go to hell,' he said eventually.

Thought as much, Ante Valdemar Roos observed to himself. You bastard.

Before leaving Wrigman's Electrical for the last time, he took his car and went up to his lunchtime glade in the woods. He switched off his engine, wound down the side window and reclined the back of his seat.

He surveyed the scene. The fields, the stony, juniper-clad slope, the edge of the forest. The light was different now, it was nearly five in the afternoon, and he realized he had never seen it at this time before. He had always been here in the middle of the day, between twelve and one, and it suddenly seemed to him to be a different place entirely.

The spruces weren't in sunlight as they usually were, the field had a deeper hue and the junipers looked almost black.

That's how it is, thought Ante Valdemar Roos. Time and space only intersect at the same point once a day. An hour one way or the other means a completely new intersection, that's just the way it is.

Yes, that's how it works, this relationship between time and objects, he continued his philosophical train of thought. The world about us and the thing that cuts clean across it. So there's no need to move for life to change around you, life takes care of that all by itself. All you have to do is sit there on the spot. That's the fact of the matter.

And he realized that this truth in some obscure way – which he still didn't fully understand, but one day would – was bound up with what his father had said in the forest.

Life never gets any better than this.

That day and that moment which quite possibly hadn't happened at all.

As he stepped through the door he could immediately tell that both his stepdaughters were at home.

Their rooms were off the hall, one on either side; both had left their doors ajar, and from Signe's side boomed a kind of music he had an idea might be called techno. It sounded like something electronic that had got stuck in spite of its sluggish tempo; she played it loud because that was how it was meant to be; they had discussed the finer points of this on more than one occasion. From Wilma's room came gales of laughter from some kind of talk show. Like Lennart Hyland's classic show but louder and more vulgar, in Valdemar's opinion. Body weight and incest and a whole lot more besides.

He dodged through the crossfire and reached the living room. Here, too, the television was on, but no one was watching so he retrieved the remote from the floor and switched it off.

Alice was in red tracksuit bottoms, lying on a yellow rubber mat in the bedroom, doing sit-ups. She put him vaguely in mind of a tortoise that had ended up on its back and was trying to lever itself up with its back legs. Unsuccessfully. He saw she had earphones in and didn't try to engage her in conversation. In the kitchen there was a pile of ingredients that were presumably destined for a wok: vegetable stir-fry with chicken and rice, he surmised. He wondered for a moment whether to start chopping, but decided to await further instructions.

So he sat down at the computer instead. It was on; clearly one or both of the girls had been chatrooming this Friday evening, or skyping or facebooking or whatever it was, because a message with a border of red hearts was flashing at him from the screen – *I've got the hots for you, sweetie pie, you're so cute!!!* – and he was pretty sure it wasn't for him. He closed five or six programs and opened his email. He had no new messages, that made it ten days now, and he momentarily asked himself why he'd bothered getting an email address. Maybe he could ask to get some of that spam everybody talked about? Signe came into the room behind his back.

'I need five hundred kronor.'

'What for?' replied Valdemar.

'I'm going out tonight and I'm broke.'

'You'd better stay at home then,' suggested Valdemar.

'What the hell is up with you?' said Signe. 'Are you crazy?'

He took out his wallet and handed her a five hundred kronor note. 'What happened to your wages?'

'I've left that stupid boutique.'

Aha, thought Valdemar. You didn't last more than a month there, either.

'So you're looking for another job at the moment?'

She pulled a face.

'Will I see you at Prince tonight?'

She tucked the banknote inside her bra and left him. He switched off the computer and decided to take a shower.

'There's nothing wrong with Signe,' said Alice four hours later, when the house had subsided into relative calm. Both daughters had gone out, and the only sound came from the dishwasher and the washing machine, grumbling away in their usual keys from their usual places. 'It's just her age.'

Högerberg next door, too, helping his six-year-old with her piano practice, he noted. That was something else he could hear. Shouldn't six-year-olds be asleep by this time? he wondered. Alice was on the sofa, browsing through a book on GI foods, whatever they were. He was in one of the two armchairs, doing his best to stay awake while he waited for the start of the film they'd decided to watch. The programme guide described it as an American action comedy. TV3, so he wondered how many commercial breaks there would be, but realized he would never know the answer, because his aim was to nod off as soon as the wretched thing started.

'You're right there,' he said, the second before he would have forgotten what they were talking about. 'I expect she just needs a bloke and a job.'

'What do you mean by that?' said Alice. 'A bloke and a job?'

'Well,' said Valdemar, 'I suppose I mean more or less that . . . a bloke and a job. A job, at any rate.'

'It isn't easy being young these days,' said Alice.

'It's never been easier to live today than in the whole history of the world,' said Valdemar. 'Not in this country, anyway.'

'I don't know what's got into you,' said Alice. 'The girls say the same thing. You've got so snotty recently. Wilma told me today she barely recognized you.'

'She said that?'

'Yes.'

'But I've always been like this,' said Valdemar with a sigh. 'I'm just a grumpy old man. That's what we're like.'

'It's nothing to laugh about, Valdemar.'

'I'm not laughing.'

'They're at a sensitive age, Valdemar.'

'I thought they were different ages?'

'It's time for the film now. Can you put the TV on and stop being so mean, Valdemar?'

'Sorry, Alice love, I honestly wasn't trying to be.'

'Well forget that now and put the telly on so we don't miss the beginning. And help me eat up this chocolate, it really isn't very nice.'

He pressed the button and sank deeper into his armchair. Glad she's started talking again, he thought. Because that was how it was: it didn't matter what she said, as long as she didn't punish him with silence. He yawned, felt stirrings of heartburn from the stir-fry and wondered if he could be bothered to get up for a glass of water.

But it was after ten and fatigue overcame him before they were even halfway to the first advert break.

If you wanted to count optimistically you could say Ante Valdemar Roos had one good friend.

His name was Espen Lund, he was the same age as Valdemar

and he worked as an estate agent for Lindgren, Larsson & Lund on Vårgårdavägen in Kymlinge.

Espen Lund was a bachelor and they'd known each other since upper secondary. They didn't meet socially any more, not since Valdemar had gone and married Alice, but there had been a period between Lisen and Alice – fifteen or twenty years, in fact – when they had quite a lot to do with each other. Mainly sessions in the pub, but also a few trips to football matches and trotting races. Espen was an inveterate sports fan, both as a spectator and a betting man. He could name all the male gold medal winners from the Melbourne summer Olympics onwards, and had always laughed at Valdemar's ridiculous three-line system – but that wasn't why Valdemar rang his number on the Sunday night.

He had waited until he was alone in the flat. Alice and Wilma had just gone off to the Zeta to see a Hugh Grant film. Valdemar loathed Hugh Grant. Signe, meanwhile, was exhibiting all the signs of having found a new boyfriend on Saturday night and there'd been no word of her for twenty-four hours.

'Can I trust you?' said Valdemar.

'No,' said Aspen Lund. 'I'd sell my own granny for a tin of snus.'

That was a typical Espen Lund joke. Or Valdemar hoped so, at any rate. Espen generally said the exact opposite of what was expected of him – in his private life, that was, not his professional one, where he was always obliged to say exactly what was expected of him. He claimed that this dull fact explained the phenomenon. If you said it was nice weather, Espen Lund would retort that he was fed up with all this damn rain and wind. If you said he was looking well, he would spin you some tale of just having been diagnosed with a brain tumour and given two months to live.

'I could do with your help,' explained Valdemar.

'That's bad luck for you,' said Espen.

'I want it dealt with smoothly and no one else is to know.'

There was the sound of coughing on the line and Valdemar could hear Espen lighting a cigarette as an antidote. 'All right,' he said at last. 'Let's hear it.'

Good, thought Valdemar. We're past the joking stage.

'I'm hunting for a new house.'

'Thinking of getting divorced?'

'Of course not. But I need a little house where I can go to keep out of the way . . . for a project.'

That last bit came to him out of thin air. Project? he thought. Well, why not? That could mean any damn thing at all. Even sitting on a chair and observing changes in space and time.

'What sort of thing did you have in mind?' said Espen Lund.

'A place out in the woods,' said Valdemar. 'As far off the beaten track as possible. But not too far from town.'

'*How* far from town exactly?' asked Espen.

'Twenty kilometres maybe,' said Valdemar. 'No more than thirty, I'd say.'

'Size?' said Espen.

Valdemar thought about it. 'Small,' he said. 'I only need some little shack. A crofter's cottage or something along those lines. No home comforts required, though I wouldn't object to electricity and water.

'Mains drainage?' asked Espen.

'Wouldn't hurt.'

'Price bracket?'

Valdemar could hear him starting to chew on something.

A throat pastille, probably. Espen Lund got through two boxes a day on average.

'Hmm,' he said. 'I'll pay whatever it costs. But nothing too exorbitant, of course.'

'Have you come into some money?'

'I had a bit put by,' said Valdemar. 'But it's important, see, that Alice doesn't find out about this. Or anybody else. Is there a way of making sure of that?'

'The purchase has to be formally registered in the normal way,' said Espen. 'But that's all, there's no need to advertise the fact. Oh, and you'll eventually have to declare it on your tax return, of course.'

'I'll cross that bridge when I get to it,' said Valdemar.

'Hmm,' said Espen. 'Tell me, is there a woman in the picture?'

'Not at all,' said Valdemar. 'I'm too old for women.'

'Don't say that. Have you got Internet access?'

'Yes. Why do you ask?'

'You can go onto our website and have a look for yourself. Everything's on there and I think there might be a couple of properties of interest. Smart idea to buy in the autumn, too, it's a hell of a lot cheaper.'

'Yeah, that doesn't surprise me.'

'Well you have a browse on the web and if you find anything you can give me a ring. Then we'll go out and take a look. Or maybe you'd rather go on your own? How does that sound?'

'Great,' said Valdemar. 'And not a word. Behave yourself.'

'Nothing could be further from my mind,' said Espen Lund. He gave him the website address, and then they ended the call.

*

Once in bed he found it hard to sleep.

Alice was lying on her back beside him, breathing in her usual slightly laboured way. She had mastered the difficult art of falling asleep as soon as her head hit the pillow. Valdemar, on the other hand, found it easy enough to drop off almost anywhere – and at any time of day – but when it came to the crunch, when he finally got under the covers and put out the light after a long and futile day, he quite often found himself having trouble.

Like a cork that wants to sink but can't, he would think, because that was more or less how it felt. Sleep was down there in the depths, a good invigorating sleep, but up on the bright and wakeful surface, Ante Valdemar Roos floated around at a loss.

On this particular evening he had every excuse, of course. Tomorrow would be the first day of the rest of his life, just as that daft sticker had said back in, when was it now, the eighties? The rest of my life, he thought. How would all those days turn out? He remembered Alexander Mutti, their stoical philosophy teacher in upper secondary, trying to hammer his golden rule into their long-haired heads.

You are the only one who can create meaning in your life. If you put the decisions in other people's hands, that's still *your* decision.

Espen? he unexpectedly found himself thinking. Has he got his life in his own hands?

Maybe, maybe not. Going to the pub, watching football, losing money on gambling. Reading Hemingway, because he did that, too, the same books year out and year in. Trekking round showing houses and flats to pernickety prospective buyers forty to fifty hours a week.

Was that worth having?

Possibly to Espen, in spite of everything, thought Valdemar. To him, but not to me.

So what do I want to do?

What the devil is it you want to wring out of your remaining years here on earth, Ante Valdemar Roos?

The question spooked him a bit, he had to admit. Or perhaps it was the answer that was causing this pressure in his chest.

Because there was no answer. Or none that sounded remotely sane, anyway.

I want to sit on a chair outside my house in the forest and look about me. Maybe take a walk now and then. Go inside if it gets cold.

Light a fire.

Could that be the point of it all? But how the hell would it look if everybody just sat on chairs gawping around and then lighting a fire?

Oh well, thought Valdemar, that's not my problem. I'm definitely not like other people, but I hope all the same that I have a hint of goodness to me, somewhere deep inside.

Just a few grains.

He didn't know where that bit about goodness had popped up from, but after this summing up of the situation it only took a few minutes for him to fall into a deep and merciful sleep.

5

Monday started with a few light showers; both Alice and Wilma had their jackets on as they left the building and trudged off, but by the time Valdemar crossed the street to the parking area at the back of Lily's Bakery, the sky had stabilized. A uniformly pale-grey paste stretched from horizon to horizon, the temperature seemed to be around the twenty mark and he was pretty sure he wouldn't need the thick jumper he'd brought with him in his bag.

It didn't look as though there would be any more rain, either, and the mild breeze was blowing lightly from the south-west. As he unlocked the car he felt that flutter run through him again, like the one that had hit him as he came out of the bank and made him want to dance in the square. Something's happened to me, he thought. What were they called, those plants whose seeds could only start to grow after an all-consuming forest fire? *Pyrophytes*, wasn't that the name?

Well I'm a pyrophyte, a human one, thought Ante Valdemar Roos, that's where the problem lies. I only wake up every hundred years or so.

He drove north to the Rocksta roundabout, the same old road he had been taking for twenty-eight years, but instead of going straight on, he turned left, to the west, and this insignificant little novelty made him shout 'Whoopee!' out of the half-open window. He just couldn't contain himself, the sense of well-being was simply overflowing from inside him.

He regained his self-control and checked the time. It was exactly half past eight, as it always was when turned off the Rocksta roundabout. But the traffic was lighter here on the 172, he noted; considerably lighter than it usually was on Svartövägen. Most of the traffic here was on its way into the town, too, only the odd vehicle was heading away from it.

Like him. Heading away.

At Flatfors he came out by Lake Kymmen and a few kilometres later, in Rimmingebäck village, he stopped for petrol at the Statoil filling station. He bought a few supplies, too; a plastic-wrapped beetroot and meatball sandwich, a bottle of Ramlösa mineral water and a bar of chocolate. He had his usual packed lunch in his bag of course, but you never knew. Perhaps the bracing effect of being outdoors all day would give him more of an appetite than normal.

Before setting off again, he got out the maps. The one he kept in the car and two he had printed off the Internet. Some of these places ought not to be too difficult to find. The first was called *Rosskvarn* and was right out by the banks of the Kymmen – on the north side, about fifteen kilometres from town, if he'd estimated correctly. Rather open country perhaps, and he assumed there would be neighbours.

He was pretty sure his second destination, called *Lograna* in the estate agents' description, would be of more interest, but he'd still decided to swing by Rosskvarn first and take a look.

He had time, after all.

He had all the time in the world, did Ante Valdemar Roos. And as he started his car for the second time on this historic morning, he caught sight of his face in the badly adjusted rear-view mirror and found that he was smiling.

No one, he thought, not a single goddamn soul in the whole world, knows where I am.

And somewhere in the region of his larynx, where all strong feelings take their nourishment and find expression, he felt the vibration of something that must have been happiness.

His hunch proved to be more or less right.

Rosskvarn was a house located on a long incline down to the lake, which was about a hundred metres away and visible through a sparse curtain of broadleaf trees. A flock of sheep was grazing nearby and a sharp sound that could have been a moped cut through the surroundings. Or perhaps it was a saw blade. There was nothing wrong with the house itself, thought Valdemar as he drove slowly past, but it was right on the road and there were at least three other properties in view. He didn't even get out of the car but just drove on by, and a few minutes later he was back out on the main road.

He looked at the clock. Only ten past nine. He decided to go straight on to Lograna. It was another twenty to twenty-five kilometres' drive away, first on the 172 and then, just before Vreten, taking the 808 north towards Dalby. He had forgotten to reset the meter when he left home, but on the map he had estimated the total distance to be thirty-five to forty kilometres from central Kymlinge.

A bit further than I'd like, he thought, but of course it wasn't the distance that mattered. No, it was the location that was all-important, as he'd said to Espen Lund. Hadn't he? Be that as it may, thought Valdemar, I'm prepared to buy any old hovel as long as it's in a place where I'll be left in peace.

It struck him that there was an assurance to his thoughts this morning that he wasn't really used to. A kind of power. But considering the circumstances it was probably not that surprising or worrying. Money talks, as someone had hissed out of the corner of his mouth in a gangster comedy he and Alice had watched on TV a few days before. Right at the start of the film; he didn't recall anything of the subsequent plot.

There were only two poor-quality pictures of Lograna on the website, one of the interior, the other taken outside, and they hadn't told him much. The description just said 'summer cottage'; the asking price was only 375,000, barely half of what they wanted for Rosskvarn. He presumed it was because there was no lake nearby.

No more than twenty minutes later, just after the knot of houses at Rimmersdal, he reached the Dalby turning and the road narrowed, but at least it was made-up. He started to fancy a coffee and realized it was nearly time for the daily coffee break at Wrigman's. Quarter to ten. It was not surprising he had developed an internal clock after all these years.

Not in the least surprising. I've ruined my life in that thermos shithole, thought Valdemar Roos. Hope it's not too late to repair myself.

He almost missed his next turning, but that wasn't particularly surprising either. It came straight after a right-hand bend – with dense spruce forest growing unthinned on both sides – a little track with a peeling, rusting sign that said *Rödmossen*. He turned into it and stopped the car while he checked the map and route instructions. He was right: this was the way, along what was now a dirt road, and so narrow that he'd need to think carefully if he met any oncoming traffic. After about 700 metres he would come to another road off to the left, just after a little field.

No sign, just a narrow forest track, and a further 500 metres or so. That was where he would find it. *Lograna*.

Ideal, thought Valdemar. This seems absolutely bloody ideal.

He met no other vehicles and had no need to look for passing points on the 700 metres to the next crossroads, and now he came to think of it, he'd seen no other cars for a long time. Ten or fifteen minutes, surely? To think that Sweden could be so empty, even though they weren't in the wastes of Norrland.

And so full of forest. He remembered Storm Gudrun, which had swept in a few years before and inflicted such losses on the forest owners. Round here, most of the trees seemed to have emerged unscathed, but then they were rather further north than the most badly affected areas.

The forest track along which he was now bumping cautiously was clearly not much used. A flourishing strip of grass ran down the middle; he could hear the rasp and whisper of its coarse blades on the chassis of the car. First-rate forest on either side, he noted; there had been some felling in a few places, but only for thinning purposes, and there was a neat stack of logs at the side of the track. He drove past it and felt the excitement and anticipation ticking inside him.

Round a rocky outcrop, and here it was a bit more open, here it would be possible to climb up and survey the landscape, he thought. Then a long right-hand bend, slightly downhill, followed by a final little jink to the left.

There it was.

I'll take it, he thought, before he had even switched off the engine and got out of the car.

For the first half hour he just sat there and looked. Listened, breathed in the scents. Folded his hands and felt his senses rousing. The pyrophyte seeds within him began to peck open their casings.

He was sitting on a chopping block. It was low and axe-scarred and stood beside a small outbuilding that had a considerable amount of wood stacked along by its wall.

He had a cup of coffee and a few mouthfuls of mineral water, and slowly munched his way through the meatball sandwich.

After a while he started crying. It was something he had definitely not done for twenty years and at first he tried to fight it, blowing his nose resolutely into his fist and wiping his eyes dry on the arm of his shirt.

But then he let the tears flow.

Well here's me, crying, he thought, and for a long time that was the only thought his head had room for.

Well here's me, crying.

Then he remembered something he had read in a book many years ago; it wasn't one of his usual novels, convoluted or otherwise, but a book of travel writing. He couldn't recall the author's name, but it was definitely a British writer and the subject was the Aborigines, the indigenous population of Australia. The book said they saw life as a long journey on foot, and that when they felt the end was near, it was crucial to find their way to the place they were going to die. The predestined place.

Song Lines, wasn't it called, or something like that?

Lograna, he thought. How strange to find my way here now and not before.

It wasn't large. Just an insignificant cottage with stone-built foundations and a tiled roof. It looked pretty much like all the other cottages in the country. The wood was painted the traditional red ochre, with white corners, rather knocked and scuffed in places. A living area and a kitchen, presumably, possibly a little room off the kitchen as well. To one side, the south as far as he could judge, a field of about the same size as the house plot had once been cultivated, but it was choked with birch and aspen saplings that had grown to head height. On the three other sides, and beyond the field, it was all forest. Mostly spruce and pine, but also a few birches and possibly some other kind of broadleaf tree. Right on the edge of the plot, on the northern side, there was an earth cellar.

And then there was the ramshackle little outbuilding by which he was perched, with the compost toilet at one end. That was the lot.

He wondered how long it had been on the market. It didn't look as though it had been lived in for many years, that was certain. There was a cable running from the road into the brick chimney, so he assumed there was electricity. Or perhaps it was an old telephone line, he couldn't tell. A pump in the middle of the garden indicated that this was the source of water. There was no mains water supply.

A deep-drilled well? That was an expression he had heard. Hope the water's drinkable, he thought, noting that his tears had dried up and he was already busy making plans.

He was gripped by a sudden fear. Just think if someone else had already gone and bought it. Just think if he was too late. He leapt to his feet and fished his mobile out of his pocket, only to find there was no reception.

Bound to be patchy out here. Calm down, he told himself. Who but someone like me is going to want to own a place like this?

Someone like me? There aren't that many of us.

But still, maybe one or two. Best not count on it yet.

*

He made a careful circuit of the house, peering in as best he could. He tried the door, too, but it was locked. There were only four windows, and three of those had their blinds pulled down – but the blind in the fourth one had clearly not stayed down. By pressing his face to the glass and shading his eyes with his hand, he could make out a few things inside.

A table with a crocheted cloth, and three chairs.

A chest of drawers.

A bed.

A picture and a mirror on the wall, and a doorway out to what must be the kitchen.

A chimney breast with a fireplace. The place didn't look so awfully shabby after all. And none of the window panes were broken. The roof tiles seemed to be in reasonable condition, too, though perhaps one or two of them could do with replacing.

He went over to the pump. He pumped the handle up and down a couple of times. There came a screech and a growl and a wheeze from down in the depths; the thing very likely hadn't been touched for a long time and he knew pumps liked to take their time.

Though he had no idea where he had come by this knowledge.

Pumps that liked to take their time?

He lingered in the long grass, surveying the scene again, looking in all directions. He closed his eyes and listened as intently as he could.

The faint soughing of the forest was the only sound. Almost like the sea, but far, far away.

The scent of grass and earth. And of something that must simply be forest. A sort of general forest smell. All at once the sun broke through, he opened his eyes and was forced to squint.

He went back to the outbuilding and found he could open the door. It only had a basic hook and eye latch. Inside it was crammed with old junk and there was a smell of damp and mould. He came across an old folding chair, which he put up by the wall outside.

He turned his face to the sun.

Shut his eyes again and heard his father's voice through the years.

Never any better than this.

An hour later he was standing on top of the little rocky outcrop he had passed on the road. It was a good vantage point and he could see in all directions, not huge distances, but still. There wasn't a single building for as far as the eye could see. Lograna was sheltered from sight by a little ridge; open fields were only visible in the distance if he looked north, and they must have been a good two kilometres away. As for the rest, it was forest and more forest.

And just as he had hoped, his mobile worked up here. He rang directory enquiries and asked to be put through to Lindgren, Larsson & Lund.

It was Lindgren who answered, and told him Lund was out with clients.

He asked for the mobile number and rang it at once. Espen Lund eventually answered.

'Lund. I'm a bit tied up.'

'Valdemar here,' said Valdemar, sitting down on a tree stump. 'I want to buy Lograna.'

'Sorry my friend,' said Espen. 'We sold it this morning.'

Ante Valdemar Roos slumped forward and landed on his knees in a scrubby pile of twigs. He was aware of the blood rushing out of his head and his field of vision rapidly shrinking at the edges.

'Not possible . . .' he blurted. 'Not—'

'Only joking,' said Espen. 'You're the first person to show an interest since last spring.'

'Christ,' gasped Valdemar, hauling himself back onto his tree stump. 'But thanks.'

'The problem is the old dear won't bring the price down,' Espen continued blithely. 'You're going to have to fork out three hundred and seventy five.'

'That's no problem,' said Valdemar. 'No problem at all. When can we do the deal?'

'Keen as a randy tomcat,' said Espen. 'Can you come in tomorrow morning . . . no, you'll be at work of course.'

'I can take a couple of hours off,' Valdemar assured him. 'What time?'

'I'd better have a word with the old dear first. But if you don't hear from me, assume ten o'clock.'

'I want . . .'

'Yes?'

'It's what we said about discretion.'

Espen paused and coughed a couple of times. 'Don't worry,' he said finally. 'Lindgren and Larsson will both be out at that point. It'll just be you, me and the little old lady.'

'Great,' said Valdemar. 'What . . . what's her name?'

'Anita Lindblom, believe it or not,' said Espen Lund. 'Just like the singer. But it isn't her; this one's over eighty-five. She's only got one arm, by the way. God knows why, but these things happen.'

'Such is life,' said Valdemar, referencing the title of the singer's biggest hit.

'Well put,' said Espen.

When the call was over, he checked his watch. Quarter to one. High time to get back to the cottage and have lunch.

As he climbed back down towards the road, he felt as though his whole body was singing. Almost like Anita Lindblom.

6

In the late evening of 28 August, Freedom was ablaze.

It was a little white-painted construction, something between a gazebo and a play house, over by a lilac hedge about ten metres from the edge of the lake. It really only consisted of a wooden floor and roof, held together by four thick wooden uprights, one at each corner. Two low benches facing each other and a simple table between them. The girls would sit out there and chat and smoke. Anna didn't know where the name had come from; it was known as Freedom and that was that.

All the girls at the centre smoked; drug abuse was pretty much unthinkable if you hadn't started on tobacco first. Anna remembered how it had been at secondary school when the senior management decided to register all the pupils who smoked; they sent a letter home to the parents, pointing out that their kids could well be in the so-called risk zone. It created a hell of a fuss. Infringements on personal liberty, fascist-style behaviour, unfounded accusations; some of the smokers were members of the Social Democrat Youth League and had been on courses about their democratic rights. It had led to a half-day school strike.

But the poor principal had been right in a way, Anna had thought afterwards. Young people who didn't start to smoke didn't start using drugs, either.

Though of course there were people who smoked without moving on to the harder stuff. Plenty of people, in fact most, to be strictly accurate.

At any rate, smoking was allowed at Elvafors. Outside, and in the shelter of Freedom; attempting to get the girls off drugs and tobacco at the same time would have been a step too far. One thing at a time, first the major problems, then the minor ones, Sonja Svensson was in the habit of saying. She didn't smoke herself, but a number of the staff did, and as far as Anna knew, none of them thought there was anything wrong with that.

She didn't think so herself, either, except for the cost of the habit. The home gave them weekly 'pocket money'. Two hundred kronor; learning to handle their own finances was a fundamental requirement for getting their lives in order. All the girls, without exception, had debts: letters from debt-collecting agencies and piles of unpaid bills. In the first few weeks, Lena-Marie, a cousin of Sonja's who had some form of training in economics – or at any rate had studied the subject for two years in upper secondary – had one-to-one sessions with everyone to try to sort out that particular messy corner of their messy lives. The eventual intention was for the girls themselves to contact those they owed money to, in order to set up some kind of repayment plan. It sounded breathtakingly difficult, Anna thought, and all the others thought so too.

Anyway, more than half their pocket money went on cigarettes, that was just the way it was.

But it wasn't carelessness with cigarettes that burnt Freedom to the ground. On the contrary, by the next morning everyone knew someone had set it alight.

*

It was Conny, Sonja's husband and the only one of his sex who ever set foot in Elvafors, who found an empty petrol can behind a shed. The can had come from inside the shed, where an assortment of supplies for the home was stored: tools, bumper packs of toilet rolls and so on.

The door hadn't been locked; it hardly ever was because there was nothing inside that anyone would want to steal. Anyone at all could have sneaked in around 11 p.m. – the fire had started about fifteen minutes later – taken the petrol can, poured the contents over Freedom and set light to it. Conny was a volunteer firefighter and had seen a thing or two, and he was in no doubt that was how it started.

That meant one of the girls. In theory, of course, it could have been some passer-by, but only in theory. Sonja Svensson dismissed that alternative more or less out of hand. What motive could an outsider have for setting fire to Freedom?

She did not venture into what motive any of the girls could have for the same thing. At their meeting after breakfast she made a stern speech and told them that unless the culprit came to her in the course of the day and owned up, they would all suffer for it.

If no one took their individual responsibility, the whole group would have to do so, said Sonja. That was a simple rule, which applied in life as much as at Elvafors.

That afternoon, Anna was down by the lake smoking with Turid, a girl from Arvika who was currently living at the first gate, and asked her if she thought the police would be called in.

'The police!' scoffed Turid. 'Not on your life! Sonja's scared shitless of anything that could give Elvafors a bad name, don't you get it?'

'Why?' asked Anna.

'Because if social services get the idea things aren't working here, they'll stop sending people. We're worth a thousand a day, remember that. And it's not exactly fully booked.'

Anna thought about this and nodded. She was right, since Ludmilla made off there had only been five girls in the big house, and there were spaces for another four. And rumour had it that Turid and Maria would soon be moving to the last gate in Dalby.

'They must be a bit short of junkie bitches in this country,' she said, trying to joke.

'Like hell they are,' said Turid, who virtually never laughed at anything. Anna thought that with her background it was hardly surprising. 'But they probably don't think it's worthwhile spending money on people like us. Better if we die young and aren't a burden on society.'

Anna felt a lump in her throat and swallowed it.

'Who do you think started the fire?' she asked.

'Well who the fuck do you think?' said Turid, throwing her cigarette butt out into the water. 'Mad Marie of course, the crazy cow. Everybody knows that.'

'Marie?' said Anna in surprise. 'Are you sure?'

'I saw her,' said Turid, turning her back on Anna and setting off up to the house.

Marie? thought Anna, the lump in her throat returning. Why would Marie set fire to Freedom? If she had had the choice of which of the girls to confide in – or eventually to share the first gate with – she would have opted for Marie. Without much hesitation. She liked her, and that was just the way it was. You simply liked some people and not others. Anna would never grow fond of someone like Turid even if she practised all her life.

Marie was Korean by birth and as pretty as a doll. She had been adopted by Swedish parents when she was two or three. She didn't know what day or year she had been born. She was quiet and friendly, but had been abused by boys and by an uncle on her mother's side; she had a child, but custody of it had been taken away from her. When she came to Elvafors – a few weeks before Anna arrived – she had found God. So she claimed, anyway, in her quiet and unassuming way. And Anna had seen her reading the Bible.

Why on earth would Marie set fire to Freedom?

But it struck Anna that she didn't really know her. In fact it struck her that she didn't really know any of the other girls. Any one of them could say absolutely anything about any other girl and Anna wouldn't know if it was true or not.

And this was largely her own doing, she realized that. As she slowly followed Turid up to the house, she started thinking about a comment made by her cousin Ryszard, who lived in Canada and did his best to look like Johnny Depp, that summer, the only time they had met.

But you're a loner, Anna, that's just the way it is. You and your fucking soul, you two always have so much to talk about that you've never got time for anyone else.

He'd said it in English, because he couldn't speak Polish any more.

You and your fucking soul, Anna.

Was he right? Well yes, she silently admitted to herself. Maybe he was.

And maybe you could equally well swap one letter in the word *loner*, too.

Loser.

*

That evening Sonja came to her room and told her she had a phone call, on the phone in the office.

It was her mother. Anna could instantly tell from her voice that there was something wrong. Something that for once had nothing to do with Anna herself.

'I can't come and see you next week.'

It had been agreed that she would come on a half-day visit the following Friday. To get an update on how things were going for Anna, see what progress she had made in her first weeks at Elvafors and have an opportunity to spend some time with her. It wasn't one of the family days, but it was usual for a parent or other close relative to pay a short visit after about a month.

'Why not?' said Anna, giving an involuntary little sob. She hoped her mother wouldn't notice it.

She didn't. 'Mum,' she said. 'Your gran, that is, is sick. I've got to go to Warsaw and look after her.'

'Is she . . . is it . . . ?'

'I don't know,' her mother said. 'No, she isn't going to die. It didn't seem quite that critical. But I still have to go. Wojtek says he can't cope with her any more and I'm off work with my knees anyway. I'm afraid I've no choice, Anna, you'll have to forgive me.'

'Of course I do. What about Marek, though?'

'He can go and stay with Majka and Tomek for now. And Anna?'

'Yes?'

'I promise I'll come and see you the minute I get back.'

They talked for a few more minutes before they rang off, Anna fighting back her tears the whole time. But she managed it; the last thing she wanted was to give her mother more of a guilty conscience than she already had. After the end of the call she sat there for a while in the dusky office, trying to regain her composure. Trying to understand why she suddenly felt so forlorn. Of course there were lots of contributing factors: Freedom burnt to the ground; Turid's assertion that it was Marie who set it on fire; her poor mother and grandmother and little Marek; the hopelessness of life in general – despite the fact that she had got her guitar back – yes, there were a lot of things.

And one more; it only occurred to her afterwards, as if she hadn't really wanted to acknowledge it. But perhaps it was this that felt the hardest of all.

Her mother hadn't been sober. She must have downed four or five glasses of red wine before she rang.

Her too, thought Anna as she cut across the open area between the buildings. I've got it from both sides.

She got to bed a while later, and lay awake for a long time, thinking about her family. She lay on her side, staring out of the window, over to the edge of the forest on the other side of the road and the odd star or two starting to shine above it.

Her family and her life.

The fact that so much could happen from one generation to the next. That it went so fast. Her mother's mother, who was now seriously ill, had been born in 1930 in the little Polish village a few dozen kilometres south of Warsaw where she still lived. Anna had been there twice, and both times it had felt like travelling to 1930 and even further back. Another time and a completely different life. She had only met her grandmother five or six times all told, and each time she had felt there was something a bit scary about her. She sort of reminded

Anna of the Groke in the Moomin books. There was something wrong with her head, too, with her mental health, but her mother had said no more than that.

And now she was evidently in a hospital in Warsaw. And had a granddaughter confined to a clinic for female addicts in some little dump of a place in Sweden – a country she liked less and less each time she was obliged to visit it. It had no religion and no honour, she would say. God had abandoned it. And the dump where her granddaughter was held captive was even smaller than that Polish village, in fact.

Held captive? Anna shook her head and tried to laugh, but nothing came.

Anna's mother had come to Sweden in 1984. When Anna was born in 1987, her father Krzysztof was with another woman. But the divorce didn't happen until Anna was six. For some reason, her mother had never really been able to explain it. Be that as it may, by the time Krzysztof was forty he'd had children with four different women, all of whom had moved to Sweden from Poland in the 1980s. All living in or around Örebro or Västerås. He was a handsome, weak man, and women liked drowning in his melancholy eyes, so her mother had once said. For his part, he was drowning in booze.

Born with the soul of a great artist, was another thing she said. But sadly devoid of all talent.

Maybe I'm the same, thought Anna. With my guitar and my pathetic bloody songs.

Marek, her little brother, had a different father by the name of Adam; another unreliable man, according to her mother. That seemed to apply to all the men in the Polish-Swedish environment in which Anna had grown up. It was the women who were the strong ones, holding together families and networks, caring for the children and getting on with life. Somehow. The men drank, were profound and misunderstood, and talked politics.

But Anna hadn't been strong, and she wondered how her mother was actually coping as well. She couldn't stop worrying about that inebriated voice on the phone.

And if her mother hadn't the strength, however was she to find hers?

Swedish or Polish, it was all the same. When she was unhappy at upper secondary before she finally dropped out, she had liked to blame her double identity. But later, and in the name of honesty, she realized that had just been a cowardly cop-out. Sweden and Poland weren't *that* different. You couldn't tell where she came from just by looking at her, for example; she could just as well have been born to 100 per cent Swedish parents in Stockholm or Säffle.

Her life was in her own hands, that was the fact of the matter. If she wanted to throw it away, that was her own choice – just as they always said when they were sitting round in the circle, analysing their shortcomings. It wasn't circumstances that things depended on. It was oneself.

So damn easy to say, so hard to live by.

Unless you followed the twelve-step programme, that is. That was the salvation. A power greater than myself . . .

Then Steffo popped into her head. That was another sort of power.

How the hell could she have let someone like Steffo into her life? That was the most disagreeable question of all, the one she loathed most and wouldn't touch with a bargepole. She had never been anywhere near falling in love with him. She hadn't even thought him particularly fit.

Though the answer was simple. He had kept her supplied with drugs, and that made him more important than everything else. It was the same with the other girls; this was the pattern you inevitably ended up in if you were drug-dependent and a member of the so-called weaker sex. All the girls at Elvafors had been with men who were total bastards, all as evil and egoistic as each other. Steffo perhaps wasn't the worst; they had only been together a few months and of course she didn't know how things would have developed if they'd gone on.

But he was certainly evil. One episode suddenly came back to her, and on reflection she realized that it said a good deal about him.

It was something he'd told her. He'd been to see some kind of psychologist, a woman for whom he clearly had nothing but contempt. She had talked to him about empathy, and the ability to appreciate how others feel and think when faced with certain things.

Children who hurt animals, for example, she had evidently said, don't always understand that the animals can feel pain. And there are people who don't understand that sort of thing later in life, either.

Do you think I'm that kind of person? Steffo had asked the psychologist. She'd answered that she hoped he wasn't.

Then Steffo told her she was quite right about that, because when he was twelve and broke the wings of his sister's two little canaries, he had certainly known it was hurting them.

That was the whole fucking point.

He had laughed as he told Anna about it. As if he was proud of it. Not just what he'd done to the poor birds but also what he'd said to that stupid psychologist.

She felt goose bumps on her arms just thinking about it.

That's how it is, she thought. As the toxins clear from my blood, it starts to hit me how scared I am of him. In reality.

Never again. Anything rather than having to see Steffo again.

None of the girls had owned up to setting fire to Freedom.

Sonja informed them of this at the meeting the next morning. But they were still going to get to the bottom of it. As long as the other girls decided to cooperate.

And they had all agreed to follow the twelve-step programme and the Elvafors rules, hadn't they? Surely every single one of them understood – deep inside – that this was the only way out for them from the hell in which they had spent their recent years?

Anna didn't get what she was talking about. What had the twelve-step programme got to do with the fire? What did Sonja mean by saying that they'd either cooperate or founder?

That was what she actually said. *Cooperate or founder.* Anna looked around her and saw that the other girls looked just as baffled as she felt. Except possibly Turid.

But afterwards it was only Anna who was asked to stay behind. The others got up, put their chairs straight and went out for a smoke. Anna sat there waiting for what Sonja was going to say to her this time.

This time. That was how it felt. She registered that she wasn't surprised, and she didn't have long to wait to find out what was going on.

'I know that you know who set fire to Freedom,' said Sonja. 'Why don't you tell me?'

'You don't know that at all,' said Anna.

'There's no need to lie,' said Sonja. 'Tell me the truth now, otherwise you'll only make things worse for yourself.'

'I'm not lying,' said Anna.

'One of the other girls said that you knew. That you told her.'

Then she realized what had happened.

Turid.

How the hell . . . how the hell could she? First she'd grassed on Marie to Anna, then she'd . . . well, then she'd told Sonja that Anna knew who the guilty party was.

That was it. That must be how it had happened, and Turid . . . yes, presumably Turid was capable of just that sort of spite and calculation. Anna shook her head and wondered what sort of person she was. Why would anyone do such a thing? Was she trying to get at Marie? Maybe at Anna herself, too? Why? Was it just because Marie was pretty and everyone liked her?

She thought about it. Yes, that would be enough. Turid wasn't particularly attractive, carried a bit of extra weight around her middle and had already developed the bad skin typical of addicts. As far as Anna knew, no one liked her very much. Was it as simple as that?

Yeah, she thought, it probably was as fucking banal and simple as that. Twenty-two and already bitter. Maybe it was actually her who'd started the fire?

'I'm waiting,' said Sonja. She'd crossed her arms on her chest and was rocking in her seat. She looked mightily pleased with herself and her approach, hard but fair. Anna felt a sudden urge to spit at her but held back.

'I'm sorry,' she said, drawing herself upright, 'but I'm afraid someone's deceived you. It wasn't me who set Freedom on fire and I've no idea who did.'

'I know you're lying,' said Sonja Svensson.

'You can think what you like,' said Anna. 'Can I go now?'

'You can go,' said Sonja. 'It's unfortunate you refused to cooperate. Unfortunate for you.'

When she got out into the open air it had started raining. The other girls had finished their smoking break and were on their way in again. Marie was the only one she was able to make eye contact with. She looked on the verge of tears.

Right, thought Anna. Why should I stay here? My soul's already trying to bury itself again.

7

On the remaining four days of the week, even Friday, Ante Valdemar Roos drove the thirty-eight kilometres between Fanjunkargatan in Kymlinge and Lograna. There and back every day. He spent eight hours round and about the cottage, but not inside it – although on the Wednesday, when they signed the contract in Espen Lund's office in town, he only fitted in five hours. The contract set a date of 1 September for him to take possession of the property; Anita Lindblom wasn't going to compromise on principles just for the sake of it and had no intention of handing over the keys early.

He made the most of these warm and pleasant late summer days to either take walks in the surrounding forest or sit on his chair by the wall of the outbuilding with the sun on his face. He drank coffee from his thermos and ate his sandwiches, one cheese and one salami, as he pondered on the directions life could take you in.

And he didn't mind which. Whether he was sitting there against the red-ochre wall of the shed, or out walking – beneath the stately pines towards the Rödmossen road, heading south through boggier areas of spruce trees and coppice shoots, or up to the higher ground in the west – he could feel something insistent within him.

Yes, *insistent* was the right word, thought Ante Valdemar

Roos. Almost like insemination, and becoming aware of a space inside him filled with new life. Pregnant, you might say. At his advanced age, certainly not a moment too soon.

It does happen sometimes, he thought with a smile, an inward chuckle. Even that sort of truly remarkable thing can happen to us pyrophytes and such is life, as I may have mentioned.

He had bought himself a detailed map of the district. A so-called Green Map, with a scale of 1:50,000, on which he could see all the features in the landscape: forest, open fields, settlements right down to individual farms and houses. Roads, paths, watercourses and contour lines. He couldn't remember poring over a map like this since the obligatory autumn orienteering runs during his time in upper secondary at Bunge high school.

He checked the map against reality, too, confirming with pleasure that Lograna was just as isolated as he had thought. A little black dot in a great big forest. The nearest property was more than two kilometres away, and it was Rödmossen, the name he had seen on the rusty signpost out on the Dalby road. He had walked there through the forest one morning and stood observing the property from the edge of the trees, just an ordinary farm as far as he could see, with a house, a cowshed and some kind of machinery store. The fields around had just been harvested, except on the western side where about ten cows were grazing. Two dogs barked from a kennel.

The narrow and uneven track leading past Lograna itself continued in an extended u-shaped curve and emerged back onto the Rödmossen road about a hundred metres from the farm, and apart from his own house he only came across one other building along the forest track: another old crofter's cottage about the same size as Lograna, but in a considerably worse state of repair. It lay a kilometre to the west, further into the forest; half the chimney had fallen in, sheets of hardboard had been fixed over the windows and he doubted anybody had set foot in it for the past twenty-five years.

There weren't many other roads. One day he tried to walk south in a straight line to hit the 172, the main road between Kymlinge and Brattfors, hoping to come out somewhere around Vreten. It ought to have been about two and a half kilometres, according to the map – but the going was far too difficult: untamed thickets and areas of wet bog, and he had to turn back after an hour.

On the Tuesday and Thursday he took two walks a day. A longer one in the morning and a shorter one in the afternoon. I'm taking control of my landscape, he thought. This is what people do, it's the nub of everything and it's what I've been missing.

Every day he also slept for a while, twenty to thirty minutes in his chair after lunch; he found it a bit tricky orientating himself at the moment he woke up after these naps, but it passed. By Friday he knew where he was the moment he opened his eyes.

Lograna. His place on earth.

On Friday he didn't go for an afternoon walk. He stayed in his chair instead, thinking about one thing and another; he did that while he was in motion too, of course, but that day there was something very special about just sitting there with the comfortably warm sun on his face, doing nothing but breathing and just being.

No aim in view. If the apple trees or currant bushes or pump had the gift of speech, we could have a little chat, he thought.

Not that he felt the need, but it would have been interesting to hear what they had to say. Maybe they could have taught him a thing or two. He took the opportunity of sampling the apples, too, but they were sour and hard. Some winter variety, he supposed; perhaps you were supposed to pick them, store them in paper bags and save them for Christmas. He remembered that kind of thing happening in his childhood in K–.

His thoughts had a tendency to take him backwards, but occasionally they also took him forwards. Overall he found himself positioned at a harmonious intersection between the present, the past and what was to come, and he imagined this had to do both with his age and with the new circumstances in his life.

The here and now. What lies ahead. What has been.

It all weighed equally. And what was more, it seemed whole and indivisible in a way he hadn't experienced before. A sort of trinity, or near enough.

His women, he thought about them too. Lisen and Alice. They both existed, not only then but now and in the future. His thoughts of them, that is. Admittedly Lisen was dead, that was undeniable – but on closer consideration he was disposed to consign them both to the past. Not just Lisen, but also Alice. Both she and her daughters were entirely out of place in his new existence in Lograna. Incompatible, in the modern parlance. A word that had often struck him as sounding like some kind of preliminary stage of incontinence.

There were so many ill-judged words nowadays. What was wrong with not getting along and having a weak bladder?

His thoughts seemed somehow unfettered, fresh and daring,

particularly as he closed his eyes after he'd finished his coffee and waited for sleep to claim him.

I ought to tell Alice to get lost, for instance. The thought suddenly came into his mind. Just like I told Wrigman to get lost. And if they hadn't had such idiotic trolleys at the super-market I wouldn't have been lumbered with her at all.

Or she with me, more to the point.

This was the way it had happened. One Friday twelve and a half years earlier, he had been pushing his trolley through the ICA Express store at Norra torg in Kymlinge, and as he turned right into the soup and sauce aisle, a woman careered straight into him. She came from the left, going far too fast, and their trolleys got caught in each other.

The staff said they simply couldn't understand it, nothing like that had ever happened before. Her broken eggs ran all over his chipolatas and it took almost half an hour before they managed to untangle the trolleys. By that time Valdemar and Alice had started to chat; they were both without partners, it transpired, and one thing led to another and eight months later they got married in Holy Trinity Church. Neither of them was particularly religious, but Alice insisted on a church wedding. The last time she'd made do with a civil ceremony and just look how that had turned out.

As for Lisen, Valdemar had virtually forgotten how they first met. He thought they had probably slowly floated together like two rudderless jellyfish, in the late-sixties sea of love, peace and understanding. And what on earth had all that been about? Anyway, they had sex for the first time on a patch of grass in Gothenburg after an outdoor concert featuring some English band and a couple of home-grown ones, and

Lisen got pregnant so they moved in together. Then she had a miscarriage, but since they were already a couple they continued on the same track and Greger came into the world a couple of years later.

Did I really experience all that? was a thought he liked to return to. Is that my life?

It didn't feel that way, not in either case. But if it actually was, then it still couldn't have been his real purpose, could it?

So what *was* his real purpose?

This was a fine thing to be asking himself at the age of almost sixty, of course. People generally got such questions out of the way before they left college or while they were doing their military service, and could then devote themselves to more sensible matters for the rest of their lives. Home, work, children and all that.

Or so Ante Valdemar Roos assumed. He had never asked his women, neither Lisen nor Alice – nor his son or stepdaughters for that matter – what answer they would give to the purpose question.

And he had a fair idea that Alice, at least, would be furious if he did.

You're nearly sixty, he assumed she would say. Just listen to yourself.

No, when it came to existential quests he was sure it would be more rewarding to address himself to the pump, the apple tree and the currant bushes.

His father would certainly have agreed. Before he hanged himself he had worked as warehouse foreman at a shoe factory. It was a job as good as any other, but Eugen Sigismund Roos's soul was not to be found amongst the shoes.

That was what his elder brother Leopold said at the funeral. Valdemar could still remember it word for word.

You were a great man, my dear brother Eugen, and far too great for your surroundings. And your soul did not fit into Larsson's down-at-heel shoe factory, no, we must look for your soul in other places entirely.

In the sighing of the forests, the surging of the streams, the incurable solitude of the human heart. Where it has now found its final abode.

Back then, when he was only twelve, Valdemar had thought *the sighing of the forests* and *the surging of the streams* had such a lovely ring to them and it had irritated him that *the incurable solitude of the human heart* didn't sound anywhere near as good, or fit in properly with the rest. Surely Leopold could have tried a bit harder and made his ending better?

But as he grew older he tended to the view that the incurable solitude of the human heart was something that simply did not fit with anything else, and that had been the whole point.

Leopold had died only a year after his younger brother, and Valdemar had never had a chance to ask him.

He'd had no chance to ask his dad Eugen either, of course, about what was important and what wasn't. That was a shame, because Valdemar had a distinct feeling his father had known a good deal about that. The fact that he had decided at the age of fifty-four not to go on living was a sign of just that: of having gained insight into certain things.

Life can never be any better than this.

He remembered an episode from when they lived out on the west side of town. It was before the fire in the basement, so he must have been seven or eight.

He'd been outside playing, maybe kicking a ball around in the park with the boy next door, and had come into the kitchen – dusk was in the air both indoors and out and his father was sitting at the kitchen table. A bottle and a glass stood on the checked oilcloth in front of him, so he had presumably taken a drink or two, and he was sucking on his crooked pipe.

Blue twilight, lad, he said. I expect you know why twilight's blue?

Valdemar had admitted that he did not.

Because it's grieving for the day, his father had explained, blowing out a cloud of smoke. The same way a man can grieve for a woman he's about to lose.

You could hear in his voice that he was a bit drunk, but he didn't normally come out with odd statements like that, even then. Valdemar didn't know how to reply, and in fact he didn't need to say anything, because just then his mother came into the kitchen.

The strange thing was that she was naked.

You could have told me the boy was home, she said to her husband, but he just smiled and squinted at her through screwed-up eyes, his pipe dangling from the corner of his mouth.

But she didn't make any attempt to cover herself, just wandered round for a while, apparently looking for something in cupboards and drawers; her breasts swung softly and attractively and the gingery bush of hair between her legs looked like . . . well, the very opposite of blue twilight.

It was his father who put that into words too, of course it was.

What you see there, lad, is the very opposite of a sad

blue twilight, he said, pointing with the stem of his pipe.

Valdemar didn't answer that, either, and his mother went over to his father and hit him. It wasn't a full box round the ears, but it wasn't just a friendly pat, either, when her half-clenched fist made contact with the back of his neck, and afterwards, when she had left them alone in the kitchen again, his father had sat there for quite a while, massaging the spot where the blow had landed.

He made no further comments to Valdemar, either. He poured himself another shot and just carried on staring out of the window. It turned bluer and bluer outside. *Never any better than this?*

What helped to fix this episode indelibly in Ante Valdemar Roos's mind was, he supposed, that this was the only time in his entire childhood he saw his mother naked.

And he couldn't for the life of him work out what had preceded the short scene in the kitchen.

Neither then nor later. His father had been fully dressed and it was hard to imagine his mother had just had a bath. They had no access to a shower in those days, and only took a bath once a week, whether they needed it or not, and his parents always had theirs on Saturday nights, after he was in bed.

But his tipsy father at the kitchen table, talking about blue twilights and the grief of losing a woman, his mother's naked-ness, her gingery opposite and the punch to his neck – much later, Valdemar would sometimes think that if only he had been able to interpret that remarkable scene from his child-hood, he might have managed to handle his own life with significantly greater success.

And now, as he sat outside his barred and bolted cottage in the depths of an unfamiliar forest, half a century had passed since that day in the kitchen. Where had the years gone?

He had always finished at Wrigman's Electrical at half past four – he presumed he had occasionally worked overtime, but very rarely and then only for an hour or two.

On these first days he also got into the habit of leaving Lograna at the same time. Each time it was with a touch of blue melancholy in his breast, but he could bear it. He knew, after all, that he would be back the following morning.

Except on the Friday. It was with an unmistakable lump in his throat that Ante Valdemar Roos got into his car and left Lograna on Friday 29 August. The imminent weekend appeared to him in prospect interminably long and depressing, and he couldn't help wondering how things were going to be in future.

Would he ever be able to spend a night out here? Would he ever wake up at dawn to the chatter of the birds, light the stove and put on his morning coffee?

Well, he'd cross that bridge when he came to it, he thought. It was sometimes a useful skill to be able to put things off for a while – not all decisions had to be made here and now – and on Monday 1 September, just after nine o'clock in the morning, Ante Valdemar Roos put the key in the lock for the first time and took possession of the crofters' cottage of Lograna.

8

In the week that had elapsed since he signed the documents and became a smallholder, not a drop of rain had fallen, and this Monday promised another day of glorious weather. Not a puff of cloud in the sky, and having picked up the keys from Espen Lund, he was driving the now pretty familiar forty kilometres westwards when he caught himself singing.

The old Anita Lindblom song, 'Such is Life', seemed to have stuck in his mind, which wasn't so very odd in the circumstances. He remembered Uncle Leonard once declaring – when he'd had a few too many, presumably, and Valdemar couldn't have been more than nine or ten – that life, life itself, contrary to what many people believed, didn't go on the whole time. A couple of hours a week, that was about what you could count on, fourteen days a year if you added it all together, whereas all the other time, the wretched grey and sticky mass of it, was something else and totally different. Like porridge going cold as you waited for your coffee, or a persistent state of constipation.

But what matters, Uncle Leopold had stressed, tapping Valdemar's chest with his nicotine-stained index finger, what matters is knowing when it starts. And keeping up when life really gets going. Otherwise you can miss out on the whole lollipop. By God you can.

★

The door gave a squeal of complaint as he attempted to open it. Over the years it had clearly warped and it caught on the floorboards inside so he had to put his shoulder to it and give it a real shove. This was only to be expected, of course.

But in all other respects, everything looked fine. A little hallway, a kitchen and one bigger room. That was it. Wide floorboards, painted grey. A couple of rag rugs. Light brown walls. An old iron range in the kitchen, but also two electric rings. A small fridge, a table and two kitchen chairs, a sink and draining board with an overhead cupboard. The living room, which until now he had only seen through the window, featured a fireplace, a bed in an alcove tucked behind it, a table, three upright chairs, one basket chair and a sideboard with a little bookshelf on the wall above it.

On the walls hung not only the mirror but also two small pictures that appeared to him to be original oil paintings, both of them nature scenes. One a meadow in winter with a hare, the other a reed-edged shoreline and some grazing cows. The kitchen walls were adorned with a clock that had stopped at a quarter to four, a 1983 calendar from Sigge & Benny's Car Repairs Co. Ltd., and an embroidered wall-hanging with the motto 'Live for one another'.

All the contents were included in the contract of sale. Widow Lindblom had no interest in coming out to Lograna to rummage around. Ah yes, thought Ante Valdemar Roos, surveying the room, what more could a person need?

He tried the basket chair. It creaked.

He tried the bed. It was silent, but a bit lumpy.

He let up the blinds and opened the windows to air the place. The windows initially stuck but eventually opened without too much trouble, in both the kitchen and the living room. His nose told him there was a slightly stuffy smell, but that was all. Nothing rotting. No mouse droppings. He opened the door, too, so the wind could blow through more easily.

He sat down at the kitchen table, unscrewed the top of his thermos and poured his coffee.

Never any better than this. He could feel the tears rising in his throat, but when he took a bite of his cheese sandwich they subsided again.

He spent the rest of the day being practical. He did a quick inventory of household utensils and other useful items. In the drawers, kitchen cupboards and sideboard he found most of what one might need. China, cutlery, saucepans and a frying pan. Sheets, blankets, pillows. He sniffed all the fabrics and they needed airing, of course, but he thought that was all. Not that the idea was for him to spend the night here anyway, but it might be nice to stretch out on the bed for a while during the day, too.

Though the very thought of not being able to spend a night out here made him feel sad again, and he realized he would have to come up with some solution to the problem. Preferably in the not too distant future.

For the night is mother to the day.

The electricity hadn't yet been reconnected, but a man was due on the Tuesday to sort it out. This was something Espen had arranged, not because it was strictly part of his estate-agent duties, but because he was a decent guy. Valdemar contemplated trying to light the range, but decided to put it off for a couple of days. He realized it was going to be a delicate operation – there could be birds' nests and Lord knows what else in the chimney after all these years.

He didn't take his walk in the forest on this first day, but allowed himself his usual nap outside in the sunshine after lunch. He awoke at quarter past one with a slight backache and decided to get himself a more comfortable deckchair. He added this article to the list he'd already started, and as there were various items he needed to buy he left Lograna a bit earlier than usual, so he would have time to do at least some of his shopping before it was time to get back to Alice and the girls.

Maybe not the deckchair today, it could be a bit tricky to get into the car, but a few carrier bags' worth of general necessities could easily spend the night in the boot. Alice had her own car so there was no risk of her catching him out.

No risk at all.

The electrician turned up on Tuesday afternoon, a surly, long-haired young chap who tinkered around in the fuse box for a while, took his payment and drove away. Valdemar checked that the lights worked in the kitchen and living room, and that the electric hotplates worked. He switched on the fridge, and it awoke with a growl of surprise but gave every sign of being in good health.

Then he turned his attention to the pump. He had already tried to pump up some water the week before, but without success. He remembered having heard that you needed to add some water from the top to get old mechanisms like this one started, so that was what he did. He carefully poured some in from the can he had filled at the Statoil petrol station in Rimmingebäck, and it only took a couple of litres before he could hear something happening down below. The screeching noise took on another, deeper pitch and after a mere twenty or thirty pumps of the handle, the first drops emerged.

And soon it was in full flow. To start with the water was browny-black, but it soon turned a slightly lighter brown and faded to dirty yellow before finally running clear and transparent. He cupped his left hand, still pumping with his right, let it fill and then tasted the water.

Earth and iron, he thought. Maybe some other mineral as well; it wasn't like the water in town, because this had a taste. But he didn't dislike it. And it was cold and clear.

He gulped down a few handfuls. There's no doubt about it, he thought. This is water that quenches your thirst. He felt something stirring inside him at this thought, a string starting to vibrate with a base note so low and melodious that he realized it must be linked to life itself. He took the two buckets he had bought, filled them and carried them into the kitchen.

There we are, he thought. Time to tackle the range.

It took a while. But not all that long, in fact; he'd been afraid he might have to get up on the roof – and there was a serviceable ladder out in the shed – but there turned out to be no need. When he lit the first sheets of newspaper he couldn't detect even a hint of a draught in the flue, but he used a broom handle to dislodge a compacted lump of something fairly unidentifiable – conceivably an old abandoned wasp's nest –and before long fires were burning merrily in both the kitchen range and the living-room fireplace. He washed himself clean of soot and emptied the pail of dirty water through the kitchen window. Out in the yard a bit later, seeing the smoke curling from the chimney and evaporating in the bright autumn sun, he was put in mind of his father's pipe.

And he wished that he were a smoker himself. Wished that right now, at this very moment, he could have taken tobacco and pipe out of his trouser pocket, filled the pipe and lit it. There was something about that careful sequence of hand movements that felt so strangely genuine and complete. As if he had already inherited them in his hands and was therefore in harmony with something vital and yet mysterious at the same time.

He had no idea where these thoughts came from, but he decided that if they started to recur, he would make sure he took up smoking a pipe. It was never too late in life to start appreciating tobacco; on the contrary, by starting at such an advanced age one ran considerably less risk of falling prey to any of the well-known harmful effects. No risk at all, really.

Naturally, Ante Valdemar Roos had smoked a cigarette or two in his youth, but he'd never gone in for it seriously.

It was the same with drinking. The alcohol thing, getting smashed, had never really appealed to him. His over-indulgence at that unbearable Hummelberg crayfish party the other week genuinely was a one-off.

No, it is as it is, he thought as he stood out there in the long grass, watching the wisps of smoke spiral upwards on their journey to higher strata of the air. There are a lot of things in my life I haven't taken seriously.

Not as I should have done and not as I intended to.

On the Wednesday he didn't make himself a packed lunch. He simulated the usual rituals in the kitchen at home in Fanjunkargatan so as not to arouse any suspicions, but as soon as Alice and the girls had left the house he stopped. He took his usual bag with him, all the same, but didn't put anything in it until he got to the little ICA in Rimmersdal. He bought coffee, butter, bread and some salami and cheese. A box of eggs, too, plus salt, pepper and a bit of fruit, and as he paid and thanked the friendly woman at the checkout, he thought he could sense a kind of mutual understanding in her warm smile.

I'm sitting here and you're standing there, she seemed to want to say. I can see from your look that you're on your way into a good day but it'll be nice to see you back again sometime soon, I shall be here tomorrow as well. And all the other days.

She seemed about Alice's age, but she wasn't at all the same type. She looked as though she could have come to Sweden from another country, with her dark, medium-length hair and lively brown eyes. Next time I come in here for my shoppping I shall have a little chat with her, Ante Valdemar Roos decided.

I shan't say much, just something about the weather, or Rimmersdal. Ask her if it's a nice place to live, perhaps.

And how about you? she would ask. Have you just moved to Rimmersdal?

I've got a place a few kilometres from here, he would be able to answer. But this is a well-stocked shop, so you'll be seeing me a fair few times, I expect.

She would give him a smile and say he was always welcome.

Always, maybe there'd be some kind of hidden meaning in that.

He'd bought a crossword-puzzle magazine in Rimmersdal, too, and in the afternoon he lay down on his bed and dived in. For the first time in several weeks it was overcast, and just before half past twelve it started to spit with rain. But he'd taken an hour's walk in the forest that morning and felt entitled to rest indoors. A strangely pleasant sensation came creeping over him as he lay there trying to solve the crossword compilers' ingenious inventions. He wasn't a crossword devotee, but nor was he a complete beginner. Along with Nilsson and Tapanen, he had occasionally come to the aid of Red Cow when she got stuck on a clue in the lunch room at Wrigman's.

But Wrigman never joined in. He wasn't a man of words, experienced some difficulties with spelling and had an everyday vocabulary that would have fitted on the back of a sticking plaster. And anyway, Red Cow had started paying more attention to horoscopes than crosswords, and seldom required any assistance nowadays.

How pleasantly far away it all felt. How strange and distant. And this very moment, what was actually happening, felt correspondingly agreeable and present. Here I am in my cottage, solving crosswords, thought Ante Valdemar Roos. In the middle of the afternoon, in my sixtieth year. In a minute I shall take a nap, then I'll light the range and make myself some coffee.

It's four hours until I've got to be back.

Tomorrow I shall buy two new pillows and a blanket, he declared to himself. Maybe a little radio too; if I'd had one of those, I could have listened to the lunchtime news programme.

He thought for a while about the notion of different sorts of time – the sort that just went ticking by and the sort that could stop and give a person a bit of breathing space – and about what Uncle Leopold had said on the subject, but before he got very far with his reflections he had fallen asleep and started dreaming about the Bodensee.

He did this occasionally. Not often, but every now and then; four or five times a year perhaps. The time between the dreams was gradually lengthening, of course, a longer space of time between one Bodensee and the next as the years went by. Back then, when it happened, the images and the dream had recurred at much shorter intervals than they did now.

It was summer 1999, they had been married for two years and the Hummelbergs had offered to look after the girls. Valdemar and Alice drove down to Bavaria on their own, planning a couple of detours into Switzerland and Austria while they were about it. They'd see how things went; they hadn't booked anything in advance and the whole trip was meant as some romantic little adventure, or at least that was how Alice had visualized it. A week, or even ten days if they wanted – the Hummelbergs had assured them that would be fine.

They checked into a little hotel in Lindau, and spent the afternoon sauntering round the picturesque town before having dinner at a posh restaurant with a view over the lake and the beautiful Swiss mountain scenery on the other side. Alice was unquestionably the youngest woman in the whole establishment; they hadn't realized Lindau was a destination favoured by retired people, but they were very aware of it now.

Something went wrong. Perhaps Alice had a bit too much to drink; it was a seven-course menu with a different wine to accompany every dish served. They must have spent three hours eating and drinking and by the time they came out onto the paved promenade along the shore, a magnificent full moon had risen over the lake. Valdemar thought the whole thing looked like some third-rate kitschy painting, but he held his tongue, and Alice instantly fell into some kind of romantic trance. She kissed him passionately and wanted them to make love at the water's edge. They'd done that in Samos once and very memorable it had been.

This time Valdemar didn't think it was such a great idea. Admittedly there weren't many people about; most of the pensioners had presumably gone to bed and various bushes could have provided cover, but even so. There was actually quite some difference between a remote Greek beach and the Bodensee. It might even be illegal.

He pointed this out to Alice without being too blunt or brusque, but she took it the wrong way. She burst into tears, claiming that he didn't love her any more, that she was married to an unromantic and impotent ass and that she didn't want to go on living. Then she stripped off to her bra and pants, folded her clothes neatly on a rock and threw herself into the water.

Valdemar's first reaction was to pinch his nostril to make sure he wasn't asleep and dreaming. This was something he'd learnt from Uncle Leopold as a young lad. Your standard dimwit pinches their arm and thinks that will wake them up, he explained, but those of us who go for the nostril, between thumbnail and index finger, we know for sure. Nobody, not a single bugger, can sleep through a pinch like that.

He wasn't asleep. He was standing on the edge of the Bodensee, watching his generously proportioned wife swim out across the moonlit water. Calmly and deliberately, by the look of it, doing a powerful breaststroke. He tried to decide how he actually felt about this and came to the conclusion that he was utterly nonplussed.

What should he do?

What was she expecting him to do?

Was there a correct way of handling situations like this one?

As he stood weighing up these questions, his wife made steady progress out into the lake. It was too late to swim out after her, at any rate, Valdemar thought. And if he were to try to call her back, he would really have to raise his voice for her to have any hope of hearing him – and a shouting man at the water's edge only about thirty metres from the nearest restaurant, where he could see diners still seated at their tables, would undoubtedly attract attention.

He decided to go back to the hotel. It seemed the neatest solution, at least for him. But he still didn't want to abandon his wife to her fate, just like that, and he felt he ought to let her know what he was doing. He thought for a moment, then cupped his hands to his mouth and shouted as loud as he could:

'Alice, I need the toilet! I'll come back down in a little while and see how you're getting on!'

He hadn't been back in their room for more than ten minutes before she turned up. She had put her clothes on again but not bothered to dry herself first, and the water had soaked through her skirt and blouse. Her hair was hanging as sadly and limply as sea grass washed ashore, and her pale suede shoes were muddy. The areolae of her heavy breasts were clearly visible through the her wet bra and blouse and seemed to be glaring at him like two angry hamburgers. The thought ran through Valdemar's mind that his wife really did look as if she'd drowned.

She planted her feet steadily in the middle of the floor and gave him a dark look; her mascara had been washed off by the waves, but not all of it, and her right eye looked like a fresh bruise while the left had lost its false eyelash. She seemed generally off balance.

Once she'd finished glowering at him she kicked off her shoes, threw herself onto the bed face down and began to sob.

Valdemar hesitated for a few seconds. 'There there,' he said, stroking her back a bit clumsily. 'Let's have a game of Yahtzee and forget all about this.'

That made her stop. She pushed herself up onto her elbows, looked at him with her lopsided eyes and an expression he had never seen on her face before, and then punched him hard on the nose.

He was bleeding like a stuck pig. He had to stem the flow with a pillowcase because Alice had dashed straight into the bathroom and locked the door – and when things eventually calmed down, it struck Ante Valdemar Roos that their room looked as if someone had been murdered there.

That was what had actually happened. Whenever Valdemar dreamt about that unforgettable evening, however, the scenario tended to vary.

Sometimes he would heave himself into the water after his wife. Sometimes he would enlist the aid of some passing tourists, who invariably soon proved to be old enemies or military service pals of his or – more rarely – teachers he'd had at Bunge high school forty years ago. Once he dreamt he had run halfway round the Bodensee to receive Alice on the other – Swiss – side.

But however the film of his dream played out, one thing remained the same.

It never ended happily. Whatever he did, it always ended up at the moment where she whacked him and the blood spurted from his nose.

That was the point at which he normally woke, too, but on this particular day the dream was interrupted when they were still down on the shore. For some reason he was the one who had stripped off this time; he was stark naked and standing up to his knees in the cold waters of the Bodensee, staring up at the exceptionally large moon – it seemed to be giving a worried smile, but also detaching itself from him in some way – when his mobile phone rang.

It was Wilma.

'Are you at work?' she asked.

Valdemar looked around the room. Perhaps the signal wasn't quite patchy enough. He sat up, swung his legs over the side of the bed and yawned. 'Of course,' he said. 'Where else would I be?'

He looked at his watch. It was half past two, so that was entirely correct. Where would he be if not at work?

'What do you want?' he said. It was rare for any of them – his wife or the girls – to ring him when he was at Wrigman's, but on the few occasions when it did happen, it was always on his mobile. He didn't think Alice had the factory number written down or saved in any phone, and probably neither Wilma nor Signe could remember where he actually worked. As previously mentioned. Just now he had every good reason to be thankful things were that way. He gave a sigh of satisfaction.

'I'm planning to sleep over at Malin's tonight,' Wilma told him.

'The best thing would be to talk to Mum about that,' said Valdemar.

'I can't get hold of her.'

'Well I think you ought to carry on trying until you do.'

'I can't do that,' said Wilma.

'Why not?'

'Because we finish in quarter of an hour and Malin's dad's coming to pick us up.'

'Are you calling me in the middle of your lesson?' asked Valdemar in astonishment.

'It's only a supply teacher,' declared Wilma. 'I'm nearly out of battery. So you'll tell Mum I'm staying over at Malin's, then?'

'Wouldn't it be better if—?'

'Don't make such a big deal of it,' said Wilma. 'Bye then, got to go.'

Ante Valdemar Roos pressed the relevant button and put his mobile away. He got to his feet and went over to the window. He rubbed his eyes.

There were two deer standing outside. The rain had stopped and the sun was starting to break through the clouds.

Oh my Lord, he thought, and pinched his nostril. Please let me never lose this.

9

It took her a week to leave, she wasn't really sure why.

On the other hand, once the decision was made, there was no hurry. Just as well have a good rest first; get rid of the cold she'd been nursing and pluck up courage.

Maybe she also had some idea of getting to the bottom of the whole Marie and Turid and burning down Freedom thing, but nothing happened. The whole thing fizzled out. Sonja didn't get back to Anna about it individually, or bring it up in any of the group sessions, so whoever did it, she got off scot-free.

Assuming it actually was one of the girls. Anna found it hard to believe, but who else could it have been? Anyway, the matter had now been set aside, and it was time for her to do the same with Elvafors itself.

She was rather sorry she wouldn't be able to take everything with her. She had arrived by car with her mother, but she would be leaving on foot. Her rucksack and her guitar, that was all she could possibly carry. Late on the Friday evening, when she hoped all the others would be asleep, she did her packing and weeded out everything she thought she could manage without, or was not too emotionally attached to.

The problem was that she had no plan. She had no way of judging what might come in useful, and she didn't really want to leave anything behind. She even felt sorry for her old wellies, which were far too big and unwieldy to fit in. It was hard to discard books too, even though she'd read them all, some twice, and would no doubt be able to get new copies at some future point if she felt an urge to read them again.

Finally she was ready. Her rucksack was bulging and quite heavy, but she could carry it. Six books, one jacket, her boots and two thick jumpers she didn't like would stay at Elvafors. They would be all that was left of her when Sonja or someone else looked into her room tomorrow morning to find out why she hadn't come down for breakfast.

She hadn't told anybody she was planning to go, but she thought Marie had a fair idea, even so. So she, at any rate, wouldn't be surprised. They'd been sitting down by the lake smoking and having a long chat that afternoon. Marie had been feeling quite down about the unspoken accusations that she was the one who started the fire, plus various other things. She felt the other girls were against her, and not just Turid. It had always been like that, she claimed. Ever since she changed to a new school and a new class at the start of secondary, it had been impossible for her to form friendships with other girls. Even though there was nothing she wanted more than to have a best friend.

Then things had gone the way they'd gone. She'd always been popular with the boys, so she turned to them. She learnt to smoke, drink and smoke hash. Learnt what it was they wanted from her. Her soft, pretty face, her submissiveness, her pussy. She had lost her virginity the autumn of the year she'd turned fifteen, and by the end of the following school year she'd had sex with ten different boys. Or men; the eldest had been over thirty.

Anna had no difficulty seeing where the problem lay.

'You're too pretty and you're too nice,' she said. 'It's a hopeless combination.'

'Do you like me?' Marie had asked her with an innocent look.

Maybe rather too naive, as well, thought Anna, giving Marie a hug. And too weak, above all, far too weak. But where on earth were people like Anna and Marie to find strength in a world like this one?

'I'd like you to be my friend here at Elvafors,' Marie had said to her. 'I think you're the nicest person here.'

But she hadn't even been able to promise her that. To be her friend. She had made herself say something vague and non-committal and then they went back up to the house to start preparing the meal.

But perhaps she'd known.

If not, she'd know tomorrow.

That's to say, today.

She had set her alarm for half past four, but woke of her own accord three minutes before it went off. She dressed quickly and stole downstairs with her rucksack and her guitar in its soft black case. Nobody heard her and by quarter to she was out on the road. She stopped for a few seconds, adjusted her rucksack and looked back at the yellow building, huddling there in the dew and a morning mist that crept up from the lake.

She gave a shiver and swallowed a couple of times in an effort not to start crying. What lies ahead for me? she thought. What the hell am I doing?

Surely any idiot can see this is going to end badly?

But she still started walking.

To the left. South, not towards Dalby. She knew Gothenburg was only a hundred kilometres away, or a bit more, and even though it wasn't a consciously formulated decision, this was presumably what sent her in that direction. She had only been in Gothenburg twice in her life, both of them before she reached her teens, both times to visit the Liseberg amusement park. But Gothenburg was a big city, and big cities meant opportunities.

Positive and negative ones, there was no point deceiving herself. If she wanted to fall back into all that again, there was no place to be more confident of doing it than a big city.

That was just a matter of fact, but for now she was far away from anything remotely like a town. She trudged along a narrow road that wound its way through dense forest. Uphill, downhill, round bend after bend, spruce and pine, hardly any straight stretches and after half an hour she hadn't passed a single house or a single opening to a wider vista.

And not a single vehicle in either direction. A loop was going round and round in her head, two lines from a song she had been struggling to write over the past few evenings.

Young girl, dumb girl, dreaming in the grass
Sad girl, bad girl, wannabe a dead girl

She found she was walking in time to it, too. Sometimes she changed *wannabe* to *gonnabe*, she couldn't decide which sounded better. Or worse, rather. It was a rubbish lyric, she knew that, but she had a loop of tune she didn't think was too bad. And she needed something mechanical to fill her head with so she wouldn't have to think about the fact that she was already feeling sweaty and thirsty, even though it was overcast and not particularly warm.

And she was tired. It had been one thing to stand in her room and test out the rucksack, an entirely different matter to have it on her back as she walked.

Young girl, dumb girl . . . she had a hundred and twenty kronor in her purse and six cigarettes left in the packet. After exactly an hour she sat down on a rock at the side of the road and smoked the whole of the first one. She took a break from the rucksack, too, and halfway through the cigarette she began to curse herself for not even bringing a bottle of water with her. How stupid could anyone be? More than anything she would have liked a cola and a . . . a big soft bed to snuggle down into.

Never in my lifetime, she suddenly thought. If I ever do get to sleep in a bed again, it'll be lumpy and have dirty sheets that loads of other people have already slept in, and they'll have finished up the can of cola, too.

Home? she pondered. It would be nice if that word had actually had some meaning, some content. The flat where she had been living for the past six months had gone back to its previous owner and her few possessions had been put in a storeroom, her mother had seen to that. I wish I had something to run away *to*, she thought. Not just *from*.

And where am I heading? Am I going to try hitching a lift or shall I just carry on walking and walking until I'm picked up at sunset by a knight on his white steed?

Or by the police? Exhausted and unconscious in a ditch.

That seemed a heck of a lot more likely. But she knew it was better to walk than to sit still. Movement kept the tears and the dejection at bay. As did those lines . . . *Sad girl, bad girl* . . . even the rubbing on her shoulders and the thumps in the small of her back were useful, because they distracted her thoughts from the desperate situation.

From the swamp of self-pity, as her mother was fond of saying. She knew a thing or two about life, her mother, there was no doubt about that. The sort of thing you generally felt happier not knowing.

She shouldered her rucksack again, retrieved her guitar and carried on walking. In an hour's time it'll be seven, she thought. By then I'm bound to have come to a petrol station or a cafe. And then I'll be in better shape to make a decision.

But it didn't turn out that way.

Just after she had passed a derelict farm and had felt the wind turn colder and a few raindrops blow against her cheek, the first car of the morning came along.

It was going the right way and almost unwittingly she raised her hand. Not much; it wasn't a proper lift-thumbing gesture, more an ambivalent wave with no definite intent.

The car was a blue Volvo, neither very old nor very new. A man of around fifty was behind the wheel; she glimpsed his face as he drove past. Or perhaps he was actually older, she was useless at judging people's ages.

He pulled in about ten metres in front of her. He opened the side window and stuck his head out.

'And where are you off to, little lady?'

Her first instinct was to ignore him. His face was a bit puffy but he wasn't exactly unkempt. Glasses, short, mousy hair, a shirt and leather jacket. As she came abreast of the car he looked her up and down, appraisingly she felt, before he looked her properly in the eye.

You have to look people in the eye first, her mother was in the habit of saying. Once you've done that you can look wherever you like.

'Jump in and I can take you part of the way.'

'Thanks, but—'

'I'm only going to Norrviken but it'll save you a few kilometres at any rate. Well?'

He revved the engine a touch and she realized she'd got to make up her mind. She was the one who needed help, not him.

'OK.'

She went round the car, opened the back door first and put her rucksack and guitar in the car. A scruffy old brown bag was already lying there. He reached across the passenger seat and opened the door for her. She got in and fastened her seatbelt; he sat still for a moment, looking at her from the side. Before nodding to himself, letting out the clutch and pulling away.

'Do you play?'

'What?'

He gestured towards the guitar in the back seat. 'That.'

'A little. I'm learning.'

'I played in a band once.'

'What did you play?'

'Drums. I was the drummer.'

His fingers tapped a drum roll on the steering wheel. 'You're one of those Elvafors girls, aren't you?'

'Elva . . . what makes you think that?'

He gave a laugh. 'On the run, eh? Yeah, well, it's not that bloody hard to work out. Have to say I didn't think your lot were such early birds. So what made you run away? Don't worry, I'm not going to report you.'

She thought quickly. Realized there was no point denying it. If he knew what sort of place Elvafors was, and presumably everybody in the district did, then it wasn't difficult to draw the right conclusion.

'I'm on my way home. It's voluntary, staying there, and it didn't suit me.'

'So what does suit you then, little lady?'

He patted her twice on the thigh and then shifted his hand back to the wheel. She gave a shiver and all at once it hit her: was it going to happen now?

The worst of things.

This had never happened to her before. She'd had sex with boys when she didn't really feel like it, of course she had, but she'd never actually been raped. Those little pats sent shudders through her and she felt her whole body tense. That sort of sensation, anyway. RLH, she thought. That was Rule Number One she had learnt from the self-defence girl who came to talk to them at school.

Run Like Hell.

That was all well and good, but what if you were sitting in a moving car.

'How would you like to earn a bit of cash?'

He said it in a completely neutral tone. An innocent work question, as if he were asking her to take on an extra washing-up shift in a cafe. Or deliver some newspapers.

But he didn't mean either of those things, she was pretty sure of that.

'Could you stop please, I want to get out here.'

He didn't seem to have heard her.

'Five hundred for a half-hour job, what do you say?'

'No thank you. Please be nice and stop.'

'I can be nice all right, but I'm not stopping till I feel like it. I bet a girl like you has seen a thing or two, eh?'

He accelerated slightly. She dug her nails into the palms of her hands and bit the inside of her cheek. She decided to keep quiet.

'Just a little photo job. I've got a camera in the back. I won't touch you.'

She cast a glance at his powerful hands on the wheel. She could see she would have no chance against him. He was burly but not fat. At least fifty, as she'd thought, so perhaps she could outrun him, but there was no way she'd get the better of him if he caught her. And would she just have to leave all her stuff behind? Forget it, she told herself. She wondered if the camera story was true. Could it really be that he only wanted to see her in the nude? That he was one of those types who just liked a good gander?

She took a deep breath and gave him a sideways look. He gave her one back and pulled one corner of his mouth into a sort of grin. She could see that his teeth were quite white and even. So at least he wasn't a slob, but then she knew that already.

Just a creep. A middle-aged, fairly well-off creep. Maybe he had children older than she was. Maybe he had a wife and a detached house and a neat and orderly life.

Sad girl, bad girl, she thought. How the hell could you have been so stupid as to get into this car? You've been away from Elvafors less than two hours and you've already got yourself into a mess.

One hell of a mess, at that.

'So is that a deal?' he said.

'Stop the car and let me out,' she said. 'I'd recognize you and I know your number plate.'

Even as she said it she realized it was very probably another mistake. If he really did assault her, he'd also have to kill her. *Gonnabe a dead girl*, that worthless lyric suddenly felt painfully real.

'Rubbish,' he said. 'You're running away, I just want to take some photos of you. You'll get five hundred kronor, and I expect you've a use for it, haven't you?'

Well she hadn't scared him, that was one thing. On the other hand, he was showing no signs of stopping or slowing down . . . he sat there calmly with his hands on the wheel, keeping his eyes on the road but occasionally glancing in her direction.

'Can I see the camera?' she asked after a silence of half a minute or so.

He reached over to the back seat and delved one-handed into the brown bag. He brought out a system camera that looked pretty old. But also professional, so perhaps he was genuinely some kind of photographer. He passed the camera to her and at the same time reduced speed and turned off to the right, onto a track through the forest. It wasn't much more than two wheeltracks with a line of grass along the middle. She could see it would be possible to open the door and leap out without hurting herself too much, but what was she to do then? If she ran into the forest and he didn't bother to chase her, she would lose her rucksack and her guitar.

And the purse with her collected fortune of a hundred and twenty kronor was in the rucksack, too.

'Stop,' she said for the umpteenth time, and this time he obliged. They hadn't gone more than a hundred metres when he drove into a little clearing between four pines, where he turned the car so it was pointing back towards the road. She tried to open the door but couldn't; some kind of central locking of course, but she hadn't reckoned on that, either. He produced his wallet from his inside pocket, extracted a five hundred kronor note and put it on top of the dashboard.

'There we are. Get out now and take your clothes off. I'll sit here and wait, and this is yours once we've finished. Twenty minutes, it won't even take you half an hour's work.'

She thought about it.

'I want you to get my things out of the car first,' she said. 'I'm not getting back in that car with you afterwards.'

He nodded. 'I'll fetch them out while you take your clothes off.'

He pressed a button and unlocked her door. She opened it, put one foot on the ground and then took a decision that she found hard to rationalize afterwards.

She still had his camera on her lap. Before she got out of the car she took the weighty object in her right hand and pretended to pass it over to him, but then slammed it into his head with full force instead.

The blow struck his right temple at an angle, she heard his glasses smash and the air suddenly seemed to go out of him. Like a deep sigh, a strange, ominous sound. He fell backwards against his seat and the side window and slumped there with his mouth hanging open and blood pouring down the side of his face, over his leather jacket and onto the car seat. His hands rested on his thighs in front of him, twitching slightly.

For a moment she thought she was going to faint, too, but she clambered out of the car, opened the back door and got her things. She pulled on her rucksack, picked up her guitar and started to run. Straight into the forest.

It wasn't easy. Several times she was almost tripped up by undergrowth and tussocks of grass, but she didn't look round.

Her heart was thudding in her chest and she was gasping for breath, but she didn't stop. She couldn't find a proper path but kept on running, staggering along until she simply couldn't go on. She sank down behind a mossy rock and waited. The thought went through her mind this must be how a hunted animal felt, this must be exactly what it was like to be some other creature's prey.

She sat there for several minutes. If he comes, he comes, she thought. I can't run any more. Not a single step, so if he turns up, that's that. *Young girl, dumb girl.*

Her pulse finally sank to below a hundred and she felt able to bob up and peer round the rock. She looked back in the direction from which she had come.

Her view only extended about twenty or thirty metres but there was no sign of life to be seen. Birch shoots, rocks, scrubby bushes, not a particularly beautiful forest, only a few tall spruces and pines. Maybe it was an old felling area? She held her breath and listened. The sound of the forest, almost like a kind of breathing, and nothing else.

She surely couldn't have . . . ? Surely she hadn't . . . ? She couldn't really take in the thought, but eventually she was able to put it into words.

Surely he couldn't be dead?

She sank down with her back to the rock again and a feeling of weakness came washing over her. Her field of vision started to shrink, yellow flecks danced at its periphery and again she had that momentary sensation of being about to pass out. Or throw up. Or both.

Just think if she had killed another human being.

Taken his life.

He had lived on this earth for fifty or fifty-five or sixty years, every day and every hour of all those years he had been alive, but then he'd crossed paths with an Elvafors girl on the run. Picked her up in his car and now he was dead.

She didn't know his name. Maybe he'd only wanted to take pictures of her, when it came to it. Maybe he wouldn't have touched her, just as he said.

And whatever would the police think when they found him? What would his wife and children imagine, if he had any? Could it all even lead to . . . ?

Her thoughts were interrupted by a sound. A car starting and driving away. Dear God, hadn't she got any further away than that? It only sounded about fifty metres away. Had she run round in a circle?

She heard the sound die away. It must . . . it must surely have been him? There couldn't have been another car that close by. She hadn't seen a single vehicle all morning, apart from that Volvo.

She noticed it had stopped raining. Or perhaps it had never really started? She couldn't recall him having the windscreen wipers on. Or had he?

Why the hell am I wasting my time thinking about windscreen wipers? she wondered. I must be losing it.

She fought down the tears by lighting a cigarette. She checked her watch as she did so and found it was exactly seven.

That had been her plan, hadn't it? A fresh fag and some fresh decisions.

Though she hadn't really visualized it like this. Instead of that service station or cafe she was in something approaching a state of shock behind a boulder in the forest and had just avoided being raped.

Just avoided being a murderer.

So, thought Anna Gambowska, inhaling deeply, this hasn't started very well. Not very well at all.

A short while later she was back at the place where he'd parked the car. The car had gone; just as she'd thought, he must have come round and driven off. Dazed and bloodied but still alive. Thank God.

Thinking about it, she felt she could understand his reaction. You would, wouldn't you? You'd give up, call it a day, rather than plunging into the forest to look for a crazy Elvafors girl who was clearly a danger to anyone she met.

She shook her head and started her trudge back to the main road, trying to keep her spirits up. After all, she thought with a kind of desperate optimism, I did handle that pretty well, all things considered.

I taught him a lesson he won't forget and kept my dignity too. That was the way to look at it, of course. When she emerged onto the road again, she did not stop. She just straightened her rucksack and went on heading south. Or west or whatever it was. The song lyric resurfaced as soon as she settled back into a steady pace, but she changed it a bit. Or rather it changed itself; clearly she felt she'd had enough death and misery for one day.

Sad girl, bad girl, gonnabe a good girl.

Yes, it was better like that, much better.

But tiredness was setting in. She hadn't gone more than a few hundred metres before she realized she needed a proper rest. A chance to eat and drink something, too, but above all it was the fatigue, which was starting to feel like a lead weight inside her. If I can just sleep for a couple of hours I'll be able to cope much better with things, she thought, glancing up at the sky. The clouds were gathering. It was undoubtedly going to start raining again very soon.

Indoors, she decided. I've got to get indoors somewhere. Or under cover at any rate; if I doss down here in the forest I'll wake up with pneumonia.

She came to a turning off to the right. *Rödmossen*, said a peeling little sign sticking up out of the ditch.

She turned along the narrow track without really knowing why.

10

Thursday passed, and Friday.

Then it was the weekend, which lasted for centuries. Never in his life had Valdemar Roos experienced anything so horribly protracted and pointless.

After morning coffee on Saturday, and after he had explained several times that he happened to step on his glasses in the shower and break them, the day fell into three parts.

First they went to the Co-op superstore in Billundsberg and bought all the essentials at a cost of about two thousand kronor. It took three hours. Then they went home and started chopping up and preparing all these essentials in various ways. That took almost as long again.

Then they showered and got themselves ready. This took Valdemar fifteen minutes, and Alice an hour and a half. Valdemar fitted in a ten-minute nap.

At seven, the doorbell rang and Alice's old friend from college days, Gunvor Sillanpää, and her new partner Åke Kvist made their entrance.

Then they socialized and consumed the variously prepared ingredients – plus a selection of wines and spirits – for four hours and forty-five minutes. The evening's conversation was structured around the four pillars of clay pigeon shooting, the TV programme *Who Wants to be a Misanthrope?*, personality disorders and the general burden of taxation, and it was quarter past one by the time all the washing-up and clearing away was done. Valdemar had heartburn when he finally collapsed into bed and neither of the daughters had been seen in the house since four in the afternoon. One of the new set of matching Kosta-Boda glasses had got broken.

'What did you think?' Alice wanted to know.

'About what?' asked Valdemar.

'About him, of course,' said Alice.

Valdemar thought.

'He was a bit short.'

'Short?' said Alice, switching on the bedside light she had just turned off. 'What do you mean, he was short? What does a person's height matter?'

'All right,' said Valdemar. 'No, you've got a point. He was just about right.'

'I simply don't understand you,' said Alice.

'It was interesting to learn so much about clay pigeon shooting,' said Valdemar. 'I had no idea so many people went in for it. And I'm sure it's an advantage not to be too big when you have to . . .'

He stopped talking when Alice raised herself up on one elbow and glared at him from a distance of twenty centimetres. 'Do you think you're being funny, Valdemar?'

'No, I'm just trying—'

'Because I don't think so.'

She turned her back on him and put out the light.

Tomorrow's Sunday, thought Ante Valdemar Roos. Tomorrow I'll have to be very careful what I say.

★

On Sunday they went to Västra Ytterboda and visited Alice's father Sigurd, who was in a nursing home there. It was his eighty-sixth birthday, but he was as oblivious to that as to everything else. He didn't recognize Alice but he instantly identified Wilma – bribed into coming by the promise of an iPod (some new kind of music gadget everybody had nowadays) for her birthday (which was in about a fortnight's time) – as Katrina from Karelia, a woman he'd been mad about in his youth. She wasn't Alice's mother, who had died a number of years before. Oh no, Katrina was a much better woman. Of an entirely different calibre, declared Sigurd loudly about thirty times in the course of the hour they spent with him. He also tried repeatedly to squeeze Wilma's breasts, but his decrepitude and Wilma's demonstrative unwillingness thwarted his efforts.

'I'm never going to come and visit that disgusting old man again,' she said once they were back in the car.

'He's your grandfather.'

'I couldn't care less,' said Wilma. 'He's a perverted old weirdo.'

'But you can't help feeling sorry for him,' said Alice.

'I feel sorry for anyone who has to be near him,' said Wilma.

Valdemar hadn't uttered a word during the visit and he held his tongue now. He maintained the same silence throughout the long 130-kilometre drive home.

I'm in internal exile, he thought.

I've got to find some excuse for getting away at the weekends, too, was his next thought. I can't stand this.

Before he went to bed that night he had a long soak in the bath and did some thinking. He had locked the door and lit a candle in the holder on the wall; the flicker of its flame cast lovely dancing shadows over the Italian tiles Alice was so proud of, but what preoccupied his mind above all else was provisions.

The provisions he would buy the following day. What he would stop and buy at the little ICA store in Rimmersdal with the nice cashier. He tried to make a mental list and memorize it: coffee, filter cone, filter papers, milk, sugar, salt, black pepper, bread, biscuits, crispbread, butter, cheese, fruit, chipolatas, eggs, tinned foods, yogurt, toilet paper . . . It would be ideal, he thought, if he could get by with shopping once a week, on Monday mornings, and then make his stores last for five days. In his mind's eye he could see a series of little conversations with that cashier with the dark eyes, and it wasn't hard to imagine the contact between them being reinforced, each Monday meeting more than just an encounter between a cashier and her customer. Until one day she would confide in him, tell him a few details about her own life, which was definitely not the most comfortable, and no wonder with a bastard like that for a husband, and Valdemar would say he understood her, he had lived a limited life like that once, but there was no need to believe it would last for ever, it just took patience and eventually, in a year or so, or maybe just a few months, he would ask her if she felt like coming with him to look at his place in the forest. At first she would hold back, for a week, a month perhaps, but in the end she would say yes of course, why not, nothing ventured nothing gained, and he would agree and say that was exactly how life worked. And she would step out of her seat at the till and go with him, and he would hold the car door open for her and together they would go out to Lograna and when she saw it she would be struck dumb at first, but after that she would put her hands to her mouth, and then place one of them on his arm and say that . . . that all her life she had been longing for a place like this. And then he wouldn't be able to control himself any longer but would . . .

He was roused by a banging on the door. The water was cold and he realized he'd been lying there dreaming for a long time.

Signe shouted something, he couldn't make out what.

'I'm in internal exile,' he called back.

'What?'

Valdemar stood up and got out of the bath. 'I said I'll only be a couple of minutes.'

'I need to get in.'

'There's another bathroom, if you ask your mum I'm sure she'll be—'

'I don't want the loo. How can you be so dim? I've got some things in the cabinet.'

'Five minutes,' said Valdemar.

'Fucking hell,' said Signe.

He heard her moving away as he pulled the plug out and started drying himself. He blew out the candle so he wouldn't have to look at that flabby white body in the mirror. The human race would feel better if everyone was blind, he thought.

'Valdemar, there's something I've got to ask you,' said Alice once they were finally in bed on Sunday evening.

'Oh?' said Valdemar. 'What sort of thing?'

'You seem so different. Has anything happened?'

'Not as far as I know. I think everything's just the same as usual.'

'The girls are saying it too. They hardly recognize you.'

'Recognize me?'

'Yes, that's exactly how Wilma put it. It's as if you're hiding something, Valdemar.'

'What on earth would I have to hide?'

'Only you can know that, Valdemar.'

'Alice, I honestly have no idea what you're talking about.'

She lay there in silence for a while. Put her mouth guard in and then took it out again.

'We don't talk to each other any more, Valdemar.'

'We never really have, have we Alice?'

'Is that supposed to be funny?'

'What?'

'Us never talking to each other. I don't know why you say things like that. What's it meant to achieve?'

'It's not meant to achieve anything. But it's the same with everything I say, or ever have said. None of it has achieved anything. So there isn't really any change to speak of.'

Alice turned her head. He could feel her gaze heating a patch on his left temple and he began to suspect he had said something slightly ill-considered. Two or maybe three minutes passed without a word from either of them; to have something to occupy his brain, he started going through his provision list in his mind: coffee, filter cone, filter papers, milk, sugar, salt, black pepper, bread, sweet biscuits, dry biscuits, butter, cheese . . .

'I think you're depressed, Valdemar,' Alice finally said. 'I actually think you're having a classic bout of depression.'

He broke off his provisioning and pondered this. Maybe it wasn't such a stupid idea when it came to it.

'You know what, Alice?' he said. 'Now that you say it, well . . . I have been feeling a bit out of sorts recently.'

'There we are,' said Alice. 'That explains things. You'll have to start taking something for it tomorrow.'

She inserted her mouth guard and put out the light on her side. Valdemar picked up the book he had on his bedside table, a novel by a Romanian author that he'd been reading for two months. He was a bit unclear what the book was about but his reasons for carrying on with it were twofold: partly he didn't like leaving books unfinished, and partly he came across occasional sentences in the text that seemed to him extraordinarily true. As if the author had in some strange way been addressing him directly, and him alone. This evening he had not read more than half a page before he found the following:

Like a pore that happens to arise in the hard ivory surrounding one's inner reservoir of living light, a winding pore akin to the passages of a wood-eating beetle, so a tunnel can suddenly open up to the eye, into the immortal fire within, as one circles in dreams and fantasies around and around the great Enigma.

How can any individual have that thought? wondered Valdemar. And find a way of putting it into words? . . . *the hard ivory surrounding one's inner reservoir of living light,* how could anyone come up with something like that? He had found the book in a wire basket in Åhléns' department store at the start of the summer, for the knock-down price of twenty-nine kronor.

He reread the sentence three times and tried to memorize it, then he had a sudden brainwave and added an item to his shopping list: a notebook.

Every day I spend at Lograna, he decided, I shall write a sentence like that. Weigh every word and craft a genuine thought about life and its terms and conditions. Enter it with its day and date in a book – that is, an ordinary lined notebook with soft black covers, the sort that would doubtless be readily available in ICA in Rimmersdal.

Pleased with this decision, and with the fact that it would finally be Monday morning when he woke up, he laid the Romanian aside, switched off his light and did his best to fall asleep.

The final time he opened an eye and looked at the clock the display had dragged its way to 01.55.

11

Alice had not forgotten the depression diagnosis overnight. But she had revised the treatment programme.

'I think it would be a mistake to start on any pills just like that,' she declared once Valdemar had sunk onto his chair at the breakfast table and taken refuge behind the morning paper. 'I'll make you an appointment with Faringer instead.'

'It won't be necessary,' said Valdemar.

'It will be necessary,' said Alice.

'It'll pass of its own accord,' said Valdemar.

'There's no way of judging that for yourself,' said Alice.

'What's necessary and what's there no way of judging?' asked Wilma. 'Who's Faringer?'

Valdemar squinted over the top of his paper. Wilma both looked and sounded full of bounce, considering it was a Monday morning. They didn't usually get a single word out of her at this time of day.

'Don't you worry about that, darling,' said Alice. 'Did you see if Signe was up?'

'How am I supposed to know?' said Wilma. 'She's not in her room, anyway.'

'What do you mean, she's not in her room?' said Alice, squeezing a generous squirt of cod roe from its tube into her boiled egg.

'That she slept at Birger Butt's, for example,' said Wilma.

'Don't call him that,' said Alice. 'What's he actually called? He must have a proper name?'

'Not that I know of,' said Wilma. 'Everybody calls him that. Or Birger the Bum.'

'Dear me,' said Alice. 'How can they . . . I mean, why?'

'He won a competition a while back to find the cutest arse in town. Though I'm sure he bribed the girls on the judging panel. You can ask Signe when she gets home if you're interested.'

'Wilma, please,' said Alice. 'That's enough. Aren't there more important things to talk about?'

'Yes, the money on my bus pass has run out,' said Wilma. 'And I need five hundred for those trainers. I've got to nip in and buy them on my lunch break today.'

Ante Valdemar Roos raised the newspaper and concluded that Dr Faringer had somehow dropped off the day's agenda.

Fifteen minutes later he was alone in the flat. He dutifully made himself some sandwiches – as Alice had bought a new kind of health-food loaf that she was very keen to hear his opinion on – packed them up and put them with the empty thermos and a banana in his brown leather bag, the one he had been using ever since 2002, when he got it as a present from his stepdaughters. He re-taped his glasses, and would of course have to get round to taking them to an optician for repair, but it could wait a few days. He asked himself if he ought to write down all the things on his shopping list for Rimmersdal or could rely on his memory, and decided on the latter. If he forgot anything essential he could always drop in some other day this week – it was sure not to be a wasted move in his game of chess.

He wondered what her name was, his cashier. Maybe he

ought just to ask her straight out, but it was hard to know how she would take it. It would probably be more sensible to wait a few Mondays.

He got away almost ten minutes earlier than usual, experiencing even as he crossed the courtyard to his car a sensation of being filled – in both body and soul, it truly wasn't easy to separate them on a morning like this – with lightness and elation, and he tried to remember those words . . . *a tunnel into the immortal fire within* . . . well yes, that wasn't a bad description of the situation. Deep inside him, in a room that had lain shut and barred for so many years, a door was gradually being opened . . . on reluctant, rusty hinges, certainly, but with dogged and irrepressible effort: a door which had also been lying there unexploited all this time, through all these days and wasted years . . .

With these remarkable thoughts he sank into his seat behind the steering wheel and reminded himself that whatever else he might forget on his Rimmersdal shopping list, he must be sure to get that black notebook. He couldn't really explain to himself why it had to be black, but it was vital that it should be, nonetheless. Certain thoughts and certain phrases simply will not let themselves be randomly framed and captured, he thought, and they were precisely the kind of words he intended to catch and pin down. Words thrown up by his immortal fire, nothing more and nothing less, to land between soft black covers, that was most definitely how it was.

How it would be, anyway.

Life never gets any better than this. That was the first thing he would write down, that would be the nub of it all. Perhaps he could add that you had to stop, because if you didn't stop and slow the pace, as it were, you would never notice that moment when it was at its very best.

He gave himself a serious smile in the rear-view mirror, started the car and backed out from his parking space. He wound the side window as far down as it would go and drove out onto Regementsvägen; late summer still hung in the air, his thin hair was slightly ruffled by the warm wind and for some reason the name Lucy Jordan came into his head. Who the merry hell was Lucy Jordan?

But she sank back into the anonymous well of oblivion; as he turned onto the Rocksta road he noted that the sun had just climbed over the forest edge up on Kymlinge ridge, setting the newly replaced copper roof on the Johannes church aglow. Birds went sailing across the recently harvested cornfields and the skirts of a young girl pedalling her bike along the edge of the road billowed out.

Never better than this.

There wasn't just one sort of black notebook at ICA in Rimmersdal, there were two. One in A4 format, one in A5, both the same make, with the same soft covers, and after some hesitation he chose the smaller variety. Modesty is a virtue. As soon as he entered the store he could see the cashier was there; he saw her, but she didn't see him, because she was sitting with her back to him, dealing with a customer.

After twenty minutes of sauntering round the shelves he was done; the shop was almost empty, with only a couple of stooped, elderly women moving in a slow and stately fashion like two sorrowful celestial bodies between the almond cakes, the special-offer coffee and the herring fillets. Ordinary people were at work, of course, thought Valdemar; these were the hours of the day when the unusual people made the most of it.

I'm an unusual person, thought Ante Valdemar Roos. An interesting person, that's doubtless precisely the thought now going through her head as she catches sight of me.

'Good morning,' she said with a smile.

'Good morning,' he said back. 'Yes, it really is a good morning.'

She gave a laugh and started passing his groceries in front of the scanner. Valdemar unloaded his basket in a slow and stately manner, making an effort not to go too fast, trying to match his pace to hers. As if they were in effect work colleagues, he thought. As if they were at the same conveyor belt, carrying out the same manual operation they had carried out day after day for many years. Hardly surprising if people develop a certain rapport in such conditions. Nine out of ten romances start at a place of work, so he had read in the paper fairly recently.

'Is that all?'

'Yes, thank you, that's great.'

She smiled again as he handed over his money. He gave her a friendly nod and took his change. His hand happened to brush hers, which felt warm and gentle. He started packing his groceries in one of the two paper bags; she seemed to hesitate for a second, but then came round from her seat to help him pack the other. There were no other customers queuing, after all.

'Thank you,' he said. 'That's very kind of you.'

'I need to stretch my back a bit,' she said, and he could hear her accent quite clearly. 'I sit here all day, it's not good for me.'

'I know that feeling,' he said. 'Fresh air and movement are what the body needs.'

He stretched a little as he said it and she laughed again. 'You're so right,' she said. 'Air and movement . . .'

Once his bags were full he nodded to her again. 'It's a lovely day out there.'

She sighed and gave a little shrug. 'I know. I went out for a long walk yesterday afternoon. It's such a nice time of year. I love autumn best of all.'

'You're quite right there,' said Valdemar. 'I'd be happy to have autumn all year round.'

One of the old women had finished rotating round the shelves and had reached the checkout; the cashier went back to her seat and gave Valdemar a final smile.

'Have a nice day.'

He left the shop, Anita Lindblom singing in his chest as he went. Her dark, sensual voice wasn't unlike the cashier's, in fact. It was remarkable the way things came together sometimes.

No, thought Ante Valdemar Roos, it's not the coming together that's so striking, it's all to do with the observer. You have to have all your senses wide open and discover all the correspondences surrounding us and bombarding us every single minute. That's how the land lies.

He loaded his bags of shopping into the boot, took out his notebook and wrote down that last thought.

Rimmersdal, the morning of Monday 8 September:

To observe the correspondences presenting themselves to us every single minute, that is what it means to live.

Perhaps not exactly the right words, not quite as apt as he had hoped, but it was captured in the moment and that counted for a lot.

He put the notebook back in the bag, started the car and continued his journey to Lograna.

★

As soon as he got out of the car he had a premonition.

Or perhaps he didn't, perhaps it was just something he liked to imagine in retrospect. But when he got to the cottage, put his hand up to feel for the key in the gutter and discovered it wasn't there, it was a sign that allowed for no misinterpretation.

Something had happened.

He cautiously pushed down the door handle. The door was open. Had he forgotten to lock up on Friday?

It didn't seem possible. He was convinced he had tested the door several times before reaching up to put the key on the far left-hand side, under the eaves; this had already established itself as a ritual in the few days he had spent at the croft. But naturally it was impossible to remember whether he had actually done it on Friday as usual; it wasn't that easy to distinguish one day from another, when it was exactly the same action, with exactly the same familiar movements on each occasion – but it seemed highly unlikely that he would have neglected such a crucial part of his routine. Particularly on a Friday, when he knew the house would be unguarded over the weekend.

Unguarded? As if anyone would bother about a cottage that had lain untouched for decades.

Of course I locked the bloody door, he muttered, and stepped into the kitchen. Of course I did.

The key was in the middle of the kitchen table. Threaded on its shoelace with the little block of wood bearing the name Lograna in curlicued, old-fashioned lettering.

In the middle of the table? Could he really have just left it there and forgotten to lock up?

He set his bags down on the floor and went into the living room.

One window was open, and a rucksack was propped against the chimney breast. On the bed there were a few items of clothing and a guitar.

Someone had been here.

Someone *still was* here. What the devil? thought Ante Valdemar Roos. What . . . what's the meaning of this? He suddenly felt dizzy and leant his hand against the chimney breast.

It was warm. Someone had lit a fire.

He looked around him. On the table were a paperback book, lying open, face down, a notepad and two pens.

An empty coffee cup.

Who? thought Valdemar. Why?

The questions bubbled up inside him and the dizziness still hadn't entirely gone. He pulled out a chair and sat down. He rested his head in his hands, shut his eyes and tried to concentrate. *Somebody* was here in the house. *Somebody* had got into his Lograna, taken it over, and now . . . well, what? thought Ante Valdemar Roos. What on earth does this mean? What shall I do?

Who?

And, above all, *where*? Where is he now?

Something akin to fear took hold of him. He got to his feet, went to the kitchen, came back to the other room again, looked out of the window.

Where was the intruder right now?

Whoever he was, he wasn't in the house. Evidently he had popped out for some reason. The open book, the coffee cup, the notepad . . . every indication was that he would soon be back. Or . . .

Or had he simply fled into the forest when he saw Valdemar's car?

He went to and fro between the living room and kitchen for a good while, trying to decide what he thought. Was he the one who had scared away the uninvited guest – whoever he was – or had he just left the house temporarily to return any minute now?

There's nothing to do but wait and see, thought Ante Valdemar Roos. Either he would come back soon or he would decide to keep away.

He returned to the kitchen and started to unpack his purchases from the ICA in Rimmersdal. Once he had finished he went outside and looked around. No sign of the trespasser – he filled a bucket with fresh water at the pump, went back indoors and put some coffee on.

Nothing to do but wait and see, he repeated silently to himself. He noted that the slight sense of unease, or fear, was receding. With every passing minute it seemed clearer that he himself had scared the visitor away – and presumably he had nothing to fear from such a visitor.

However he twisted and turned this line of argument, he couldn't find anything wrong with it. Nothing to fear.

What did seem a little strange, however, was that he felt no anger. He wasn't nursing any immediate grudge against whoever had illicitly gained access to his Lograna. Surely he should at least have been feeling rather indignant? Furious, in fact?

But that wasn't the case.

And out of some kind of respect for this stranger he decided not to start rooting through his possessions – hunting for something that might offer a pointer to his identity. The paperback on the table was called *The Mournful Knight*, written by someone called Barin. The notepad was closed, and he didn't open it.

Instead he took his sandwiches and a cup of coffee and went out to sit in his chair by the wall of the outbuilding. He turned his face to the sun and felt a pleasant drowsiness come creeping over him.

What happens, happens, he thought. Haste is a concept the good Lord didn't see fit to create.

The day passed.

In view of the uninvited guest, Valdemar decided to cancel all walks in the forest. He stayed in either the house or the yard and garden all morning; the weather was agreeably warm, probably around twenty degrees – he made a mental note to buy a thermometer as soon as he could – with alternating sun and cloud, and only a light wind to be heard in the treetops. He occupied himself by doing crosswords, lighting the fire in the kitchen range, tidying up the plot; he spent a while in the outbuilding looking for a lawnmower or at least a scythe but found neither and wondered whether he ought to go to a hardware store one day soon and equip himself with the most basic garden tools. A rake, a spade, an axe, a saw.

And a scythe, as he'd already said – there was an attractively primitive power in both the word and the object. Not to mention the snath to go with it. But perhaps scythes and their handles weren't available any more. It was the same with some species of animal, there simply wasn't room for them all; when the mobile phones arrived, the scythes disappeared. It was a shame, but hardly unreasonable.

A pair of work gloves was a must, at any rate; they would definitely come in handy. At the same time he was aware that much of this was actually unnecessary. It was the enduring cultivator in him insisting on these things, but such orations did not go unchallenged. Not at all. The grass was welcome to grow as it wanted, thought Valdemar, and the currant bushes and trees as well, but he realized that the woodpile, which thus far looked relatively inexhaustible, could not last forever. There was something rather attractive about the idea of chopping wood, too, positioning the length of log on the block and then splitting it with a well-aimed blow.

Straightening his back when the work was done, squinting up at the sky to assess the weather, and lighting his pipe.

There was that pipe image again. Ante Valdemar Roos made a preliminary decision that the first work tools he had to acquire were a pipe and a packet of tobacco. Maybe as early as tomorrow, at ICA in Rimmersdal.

Did they sell pipes in ICA shops? He was not at all sure, but he could always go in to enquire. There would be no harm in that.

Around noon he ate his lunch. Macaroni and sausage. And once he'd washed up he decided to take a nap in bed. He moved the guitar and items of clothing first, and it was only then he realized the intruder must be a woman. A thin sweater tossed down on top of a pair of panties, and some socks that definitely wouldn't fit a pair of male feet.

A woman? He lay down on his back, clasped his hands behind his neck and tried to examine this new and unexpected factor in the equation.

All morning he had been assuming the uninvited guest was a man. In Ante Valdemar Roos's world, women didn't lurk about the forest or force their way into remote cottages, that was the fact of the matter. It was a phenomenon with exclusively masculine overtones, the sort of trick pulled by fugitives and homeless poets and other castaways of the male persuasion, but not women. Perhaps it was prejudice on his part, but he couldn't shake off his spontaneous surprise. A woman?

Who was she?

What was her background and motivation?

How old might she be?

Although the answers to these questions – or at least some hints leading in the right direction – were no doubt to be found in the bulging, dark blue rucksack, or in the notepad still lying on the table, he stopped himself from looking. Respect, he thought. You always had to show respect to other people, even in circumstances like these.

You don't go rummaging in someone else's rucksack even if that someone is a trespasser.

Possibly that someone had a good and respectable reason for their actions, you never knew, and in that case Valdemar could find himself in a corner feeling very shamefaced.

I'm a gentleman, he thought. And a gentleman doesn't take liberties that go beyond the bounds of decency. That's that.

Satisfied with these simple deliberations and conclusions, he fell asleep.

He woke up to find it was half past two. He had been asleep for over an hour. The window was still open and he could hear the cooing of a wood pigeon outside. The intruder woman hadn't been in the house while he was asleep. If she had been, she would naturally have seen that he was asleep, gathered up her things and made off. There was nothing to indicate she was anything other than a very timid creature, and keen to avoid any contact with him in all circumstances. She had now been keeping out of the way for nearly six hours; he assumed she was somewhere out in the forest, probably quite close to the house, so she could keep an eye on what he was doing. Keeping her distance as a precaution, thought Valdemar, sitting up. So she could make a run for it and get safely away if he decided to go out and look for her.

But he didn't intend looking for her. He was sticking to his gentlemanly decision not to disturb her in any way, and as he made his afternoon coffee, he found he could perceive her presence.

Exactly that. *Perceive* it. There was a difference between taking in reality via one's usual senses – sight and smell, hearing, taste and feeling – and merely perceiving it. It was like a sixth sense, an extra organ being connected, a sort of cautious tentacle reaching out into its surroundings and registering even the smallest and most timid tremor.

A presence, for example.

As he drank his coffee he took out his notebook and tried to encapsulate that very feeling in words. But try as he might, the right formulation eluded him. He was also starting to find it hard not to take a look at the other pad of paper – *her* notebook – but he resisted the temptation and kept the impulse in check.

What he eventually wrote was:

Lograna, the afternoon of 8th September:
I have a visitor. A woman with a guitar, but I still cannot tell what it means or where it might lead in due course. Little can the pawn know the intentions of the grand master.

He didn't entirely understand that last bit himself. But he let it stand; it had occurred to him spontaneously and perhaps one day he would fathom what it meant. It could happen that words preceded meaning – he had read that somewhere, he couldn't remember where, but perhaps it was his Romanian author again.

Before he got into the car for the drive back to Kymlinge he considered whether to leave some kind of message for her, but it was hard to find the right tone for that, too, so he left it.

He locked the door and hid the key in its usual place up in the gutter.

To be on the safe side he left the window catch unhooked and dangling, so it would no doubt be possible to get back in that way if one needed to.

12

She counted to 200 once the car was out of sight and only then did she dare to leave her hiding place.

It wasn't much of a hiding place, anyway; if he had started looking for her he would certainly have found her without any problem. A few low and bushy spruce branches, a mossy rock, a fallen tree trunk. She had spent the last three hours there, after initially wandering about the forest in a state of indecision and semi-panic. In the end she lay down on the ground behind this scant cover. It was no further than thirty or forty metres from the house and she could keep an eye on both the door and the car.

Well, what had she expected? That was the question whirring away in her head the whole time. *What had she expected?*

That she would be able to stay here undisturbed for as long as she liked?

That no one ever came to this little cottage? That it had no owner?

How stupid can you be? thought Anna Gambowska. I'm definitely losing it. *Dumb girl.*

She had gone a little way into the forest to relieve herself, it was as simple as that. She didn't like the compost toilet – it had a horrible smell and she thought it was gross. She'd rather answer the call of nature in God's free air, even if that wasn't exactly enjoyable either.

And as she was crouching there with her trousers down, he turned up. She heard the car first, then she saw it, and finally she saw the man get out and go into the cottage with two heavy bags.

Fuck, had been her first thought. I've had it now. He'll ring the police, and I've been so stupid that I'll lose my guitar and all my stuff.

Including the 120 kronor in her purse. Anna Gambowska, you're a mega loser, she'd thought, and there's no point trying to tell yourself any different. Anybody could have worked out that things would end up like this.

But she had still loitered near the house. Sandals without socks, jeans, a T-shirt and a thin cardigan, that was her entire kit. What point was there in setting off into the world with just those? On the run from a residential treatment centre.

No point at all, even she knew that. So the only solution was to hang about and see what happened. How things developed. Would a police car arrive? She hadn't broken in, after all. She hadn't broken anything, of course, or done any damage, but even so. When she found the house the day before yesterday she had been utterly exhausted, and it was a childish thought that made her feel for the key up in the gutter above the door. Only because that was where Uncle Julek used to keep the key to his house in Kołobrzeg, right by the sea; she had spent a few weeks there over a couple of summers when she was around ten or twelve, and this place reminded her a little of Julek's house. Or she imagined it did, and that must have been what prompted her to look for the key there.

Or perhaps God had decided to help her onto the right track.

The first thing she did was to sleep for five hours. When

she woke up it was already late afternoon and she was ravenous, so she struggled with her conscience for half an hour and then helped herself to the food she found in the fridge and larder. She remembered a fairy tale she had read as a child, where it said that anyone who steals to satisfy their hunger cannot be counted as a thief.

She found bread, butter and cheese. Coffee and crispbread, jam and biscuits. A few packets of soup and a dozen assorted tins. There was no water in the house, but she located the pump outside.

I'll eat my fill and stay the night, she thought, but waking up on Sunday morning to the birds chirruping and the sun shining in her eyes, she changed her mind.

There's a meaning to my finding my way here, she told herself. I came to this little cottage because I'm going to stay here for a while, that's how it feels.

Stay here and decide what to do with the rest of my life.

She had only smoked three cigarettes on the Saturday, so she had three left. One a day, she decided, which felt almost heroic, and as she sat in the chair by the outhouse wall and smoked her Sunday evening cigarette, she felt she could be happy in a place like this.

This is all I ask, she observed to herself. For now, at any rate. To be left in peace on my own in a little house out in the forest. Read, play the guitar and sing, go for a stroll if the weather's nice, why shouldn't a person be able to live in that simple way?

Young girl, dumb girl . . . no, she didn't actually feel young or dumb. Mature and sensible, more like. Once darkness had fallen on the Sunday evening and she had got the stove alight, she wrote a few new lines, finding a simple tune for them almost at once. She played it a few times and felt that if there really was a God in Heaven, as she believed deep inside her soft soul, then He was listening and giving her a kindly nod to show he thought it sounded all right.

> *House in the forest*
> *Heaven on Earth*
> *Soul is a phoetus*
> *Waiting for birth*

The tune was clearly better than the words, and she wasn't sure how to spell or say *phoetus*. But she knew what it meant, and once she had settled down in bed she thought that she wasn't really much more than one of those half-formed creatures – childish and undeveloped with its hands between its knees – but just as she was falling asleep, God told her that this was a mistake that many people unfortunately made.

He said it was this very simplicity and purity that was gradually being lost to the world. And for that reason, it was important to nurture it.

And then it was Monday. A sandwich, a cup of coffee, relieving herself in the woods – and then seven hours' waiting, that was what this day had offered her so far. Hunger had clawed at her as the afternoon dragged by and all she had been able to find to keep it at bay were bilberries. She had always loved bilberries, but they weren't exactly filling.

But apart from the hunger and the fact that she was slightly underdressed she had nothing to complain of. That was the way of the world, she thought: the body's needs first, then the soul's.

But as she came stumbling back down to the house, she felt as if her legs would barely carry her. If she had any thought in her mind at all, it was to have a drink of water and grab some crispbread or whatever she could find. Pack her things and get out of there.

At least he hadn't taken them with him, neither the guitar nor the rucksack. She had seen that from her hiding place behind the earth cellar. She wondered who he was, as she had been doing all day. Was he a baddie or goodie? A kind person or like that creep in the Volvo? The one she'd nearly killed.

Maybe he'd only pretended he was leaving? Maybe he'd work out what time she might risk returning to the house and come back? Was he hiding somewhere up in the forest, watching her?

He'd put the key in the same place where she'd found it before. Why? Why hadn't he simply taken it with him?

Her head was buzzing with anxiety and questions, but first she had to deal with her hunger and thirst. As she'd known she would. If he came back and caught her, well, she'd have to cross that bridge when she got to it. Tell him the truth and hope he would understand.

The rucksack was beside the bed. The guitar too; he had folded up its soft case and the clothes she had left behind and put them all on a chair.

Her book and notepad were still on the table; he didn't seem to have touched them. Or to have gone through her things.

That was odd. Or was it? Her purse was in the outside pocket of her rucksack and she couldn't tell if he had looked in it or not. Shouldn't he at least have tried to find out who she was?

Had he done that? Had he taken out her ID card, called the police and reported everything to them?

Maybe there was an alert out for her? Maybe they were looking for her?

But that was nothing new, was it? Sonja Svensson at Elvafors surely wouldn't have wasted any time in contacting the authorities on Saturday, as soon as somebody realized she was missing.

Yet for some reason she had a feeling Sonja hadn't done so. She didn't really understand where this feeling had come from, but it wasn't something she felt like wracking her brains about right now. The priority at the moment was to get some food inside her.

She devoured several crispbreads and slices of bread with liver pâté and drank half a litre of water. She put on her socks and trainers and a thicker jumper. It hadn't exactly been cold in the woods, but she'd barely moved for several hours and felt chilled through.

Why aren't I getting out of here? she thought, slightly annoyed with herself. Why aren't I packing up my stuff and making myself scarce before it's too late?

Why am I being so slow?

I'm an intruder in this house, who's spent two nights here and taken some of his food. Now he's found me out yet here I still am, waiting to be caught like some stupid mouse in a trap.

She shook her head at her own indecision. Then checked the time. It was almost six, the sun had sunk below the line of trees to the west and the whole area round the cottage was in shadow.

Coffee, she thought suddenly. Coffee and a cigarette.

She laughed as it struck her that her mother would have thought exactly the same thing. And said it, too.

Coffee and a fag first, Anna, she would often declare. No making important decisions on an empty stomach.

She went outside with her cup and her last but one cigarette, and stood in the long grass as she sipped, smoked and listened to the faint whisper of the forest around her.

He won't come back, she thought. Not today, it's been an hour since he went. I'm safe here until tomorrow.

She realized this was wishful thinking. She didn't feel like packing her things and leaving, that was it, of course. Setting off to trudge along the dreary road with her overloaded ruck-sack and unwieldy guitar. It would be dark in a couple of hours' time.

She thought back to Saturday. There was something that had led her to this place, she hadn't imagined it, had she? First when she left the main road at the Rödmossen sign and then when she turned along the narrow forest track, so exhausted she could barely see straight. When she caught sight of the house it had felt as though . . . well, what? As though she was some poor girl in a fairy tale? Who had been forced to leave home by two wicked stepsisters or something, and who was all alone and abandoned on her path through the big, dangerous world.

But under the protection of God, and it was His finger that had pointed out this house to her.

There were other fairy tales, too. The kind about witches who lived in remote woodland cottages like this one, and those tales never ended happily.

Nor had she been driven out by any stepsisters, she had to admit. She was on the run from a home where social services were paying a thousand kronor a day for her to be properly looked after while she found a way out of her drug addiction. That was what her fairy tale looked like, and she would do well not to forget it.

She gave a shiver, took the final drag on her cigarette and stubbed it out. She went back indoors, realized she was fighting back tears, and made another cup of coffee.

She sat down at the table in the main room and put her hands together. She tried to pray to God, but felt fear and forlornness swelling inside her instead.

And then Marja-Liisa came into her head. And Steffo. Which didn't help matters at all.

A few weeks after he moved in with her, she met Marja-Liisa. It was in the town park, in the evening after one of those carefree days that were the addict's *raison d'être*. That was an expression she'd learnt in one of the few French lessons she'd bothered to attend at upper secondary – *raison d'être*, reason for existing. She and Steffo and a few other people had been smoking all afternoon and having a few beers, but once they were at the park, Steffo left the gang to go and do some business.

That was the way he put it. Business, but there wasn't much doubt what he meant. Soon afterwards, two giggly girls came along and sat down nearby, and one of them was Marja-Liisa. She was as delicate as a baby bird and her face was all eyes. But she couldn't stop giggling and was clearly a bit high. For some reason, Anna started talking to her, and it soon came out that she was one of Steffo's former girl-friends. Once it emerged that Anna was living with him, Marja-Liisa's giggles died away. She turned serious and seemed on edge.

'Christ,' she said. 'Christ, you be careful.'

'Why?' Anna asked her. 'What do I need to be careful about?'

'Where is he now? He's not coming here, is he?'

Anna told her Steffo had just left and would be gone for a while. Marja-Liisa hugged herself, her thin body cold although it was a warm, early summer's evening and she was wearing a thick jumper.

'You shouldn't have shacked up with him,' she said. 'He's fucking sick. He tried to kill me.'

'Kill you? What are you talking about?'

'I'm telling you, he tried to kill me.'

'Why?'

'Because I went out with a couple of my girlfriends instead of being with him. We had a few bottles of wine and when I saw him later that night he beat me up and left me for dead. An old man with a German Shepherd found me in the bushes and I was in hospital for two weeks.'

Anna stared at the terrified bird girl. 'But . . . I mean, you must have reported him, right?'

But Marja-Liisa just shook her head.

'Didn't dare. If I'd reported him he would have done me in for sure. You've got to watch out – Steffo isn't right in the head.'

Then she stood up and walked away.

She had trouble getting Steffo out of her head for the rest of the evening. He was there inside her like a painful, unlanced boil, fuelling other dark and brooding thoughts, which she soon identified as the classic craving for drugs.

They had talked about that at Elvafors. The craving for drugs; whatever you did, however you behaved, sooner or later it would resurface. And it was hard to handle. In actual fact it was the worst and most insidious thing of all, everyone was aware of that, but Anna hadn't felt it in earnest in the four weeks she had spent at the place.

Only now. But you had to acknowledge it. Talk about it, look it in the eye and fight it . . . a force stronger than yourself.

But who could she talk to? What had she got to fight with? Alone, on the run, in a stranger's cottage in an unfamiliar forest?

Don't feel sorry for yourself! she thought, straightening her back. Don't sink down into the swamp of self-pity, do something!

She gave a laugh. The only drug in her possession was one miserable cigarette, so at least she was out of range of any immediate temptation. That was always something.

She went out to the kitchen and looked in the fridge. It was pretty full; he had stocked it with a variety of items. If she stayed the night and left early tomorrow morning, she'd be able to have a decent amount to eat first.

But what did it tell her, the fact that he'd stocked up on food?

The answer was so obvious that not even she could avoid seeing it.

He was planning to come back. If not tonight, then in the morning. You don't put cultured milk and butter and fruit and bread in your fridge and larder unless you're intending to eat it.

Lucky he hadn't laid in any beer or spirits, she thought. If he had, she would have drunk the lot, and then she'd have been on her way down into the abyss again.

What sort of person was he?

She always found it hard to judge ages and his was no exception. She'd had quite a clear view of him when he arrived in the morning and later in the day when he was out in the yard. Fifty, perhaps? Or sixty? Two or three times as old as she was, at any event. Oh well, age didn't really matter, and she didn't think he'd looked particularly threatening.

But then she'd thought that about the Volvo man, too.

Did he realize she was just a young girl? He didn't seem to have gone through her things, but he might have worked it out, even so. He must have seen her knickers. And her guitar; old ladies didn't tend to tote guitars round with them, did they?

What if he was the Steffo type, but thirty years older?

No, thought Anna Gambowska, deciding to light a fire instead. I've got to stop being scared of everything. If I'm to get through this, I can't keep meeting trouble halfway.

Just after ten, she went to bed. She lay under the blanket fully clothed, and had her rucksack packed and ready, her guitar in its case. If she was forced to run for it, at least she wouldn't have to scramble to gather up her possessions first.

Before she fell asleep she sent up a prayer to the benevolent God who had helped her so far. What she asked for was a good night's sleep, so she could resume her trek in reasonably good shape the next morning.

And to be left alone for the night. She had locked the door and left the key in the lock on the inside; not that it was much of a protection, but still.

Have trust, she thought. Trust was a word she liked very much, and she kept it in her mind until the moment she fell asleep.

She had resolved to wake up at half past six, and she did. Her internal alarm clock worked as usual.

She went outside to pee. Then she had a wash and cleaned her teeth at the pump. Made some coffee and ate a couple of slices of bread with toppings from the fridge. The weather was as fine as the day before: a blue sky with a few wisps of thin, high clouds. She'd brought her rucksack and guitar out of the cottage, but instead of picking them them up and setting off, she took an entirely different decision.

She stowed her luggage behind the outbuilding. In the tangle of undergrowth and nettles growing there, it was well hidden from the eyes of the world. After that she went into the cottage and sat down at the table with a pen and a sheet of paper torn out of her notepad.

She wrote a message and left it in the middle of the table.

Thank you. My name is Anna.

Then she filled a plastic bottle with water, made some sandwiches, took an apple and a banana and went out into the forest.

13

'I've booked you an appointment with Faringer.'

'I don't need an appointment with Faringer.'

'You're in no state to decide that, Valdemar. You'll have to trust my judgement.'

It was on the tip of his tongue to say he'd never felt better in his life, but he kept quiet. It could have led to misunderstandings. She might have started thinking he wasn't just depressed but had developed manic-depressive tendencies, or worse.

'When?' he asked.

'Thursday of next week,' she said. 'That was the earliest they had. People's health is really going downhill.'

'Maybe it would be better if he devoted his time to someone who really needs help?'

Alice took off her reading glasses and sucked the end of one of the arms thoughtfully. 'What's up with you?' she asked. 'Something's not right, I can sense it all the time.'

'Rubbish,' said Valdemar.

'Is it something at work?'

'Of course not.'

'You never talk about your job.'

'You never ask about my job, Alice dear.'

'That's got nothing to do with it.'

'Hasn't it? Well anyway, everything's just the same as ever at work. Isn't it time you were going? It's quarter to eight.'

'We've got to talk to each other, Valdemar.'

'Can't it wait until next week?'

'What are you saying? Just listen to yourself, the way you sound.'

'I've always sounded like this, Alice. Are you sure you're not the one who's changed?'

She seemed to consider this for a moment but then she sighed heavily, stood up and left the breakfast table.

He would really have liked to go into Wettergren's tobacconist's to choose himself some tobacco and a pipe, but they didn't open until ten. But he was able to buy a curved-stem cutty and a pouch of Tiger Brand in the video shop in Selanders väg.

Imagine Tiger Brand still being around. His father hadn't smoked that brand – he'd preferred old Greve Hamilton – but he had always spoken of it with respect, Valdemar could remember that. Tiger Brand and Skipper Shag and Borkum Riff. What a ring they had to them, those names. Where had all the sonorous old names gone?

He'd been hoping to get his hands on a classic Ratos pipe, or a Lillehammer, but the girl in the shop just shook her head. If his newly acquired cutty had a name at all, it seemed to be *Prince*, but the lettering on the stem was hard to decipher. It could equally well be *Pince-nez*. But they were spectacles of some kind, weren't they?

What the heck, thought Valdemar, if it doesn't taste good I can always promote myself to something better from Wettergren's in due course. He decided not to spend any more time in Kymlinge laying in unnecessary supplies. He'd be better off checking what ICA in Rimmersdal had to offer him, and then top up in town later in the week.

Of course there were also voices in his head telling him to stop wasting time. To get straight out to Lograna and see how his mysterious visitor was doing. Curiosity had been ticking away inside him the previous evening and all through the night, with the same questions in his head whenever he happened to wake up.

Who was she?

What had made her decide to spend the night in his cottage?

Would she still be there today?

He realized he was worrying that she might already have left. Yes, he really was. Worrying that she'd never pop up in his life again and that he'd never get an answer to his questions.

That she'd vanish like a footprint in water.

He decided he'd write that down. No, not water, wet sand was better.

Some people and some events vanish like footprints in wet sand, that was the best he could come up with. He felt he'd like to add something about the tides washing things away, too, but for some reason he couldn't find the right words.

ICA Rimmersdal did not stock saws, axes or scythes.

But it was able to provide him with a hammer, a frying pan, a large saucepan, a washing-up bowl, soft soap, washing powder, a scrubbing brush, tooth mugs, a draining rack, a paraffin lamp and some pork chops.

And a cashier.

'My name's Valdemar,' he said as she handed him his change. 'In case you were wondering.'

'Valdemar,' she said slowly, with a cautious smile, as if sampling a chocolate. A chocolate with a new and slightly surprising centre. 'That's an unusual name. Mine's Yolanda.'

'Yolanda?' said Valdemar. 'That's not particularly common either, is it?'

'Not in this country,' said Yolanda. 'But where I come from, lots of women have the name Yolanda.'

'Really?' said Valdemar. 'And what country's that?'

'It was called Yugoslavia when I left it,' she said, looking suddenly sad. 'I'm half Serb, half Croat.'

'I understand,' said Valdemar, because he did. 'Hmm, life doesn't always turn out the way we imagined it would.'

She gave no reply, but smiled her warm smile at him and started dealing with the next customer.

Yolanda? he thought once he was out of the shop. Yolanda and Valdemar. It sounded beautiful, almost like a pair of lovers in some old tale. Or in a chapbook of old ballads.

Valdemar and Yolanda. It had a ring to it.

He read the message and tried to identify the emotion running through him.

A sense of regret? Of loss?

Nonsense, he thought. You can't feel the loss of something you've never had.

Or could you, in actual fact? Was it some sort of bitter truth about life, that you perpetually went round with some un-specified sense of loss in your breast? A yearning for something you could only sense but not really see.

No, decided Ante Valdemar Roos, things simply couldn't be that bloody bad.

Disappointment, then? Yes, that was more like it. It was a

simple, more manageable feeling. The unknown woman had been in his immediate vicinity – and in his consciousness – for twenty-four hours, and now she was gone. Little wonder things felt a bit empty. A . . . a parenthesis with nothing inside it, he thought, something that had finished before it had even begun.

He sat down at the table and wrote down the words he'd devised in the car that morning.

Lograna, the 9th of September
Some people and some events vanish like footprints in wet sand.
A few minutes later, he added:
Some lives vanish that way, too.

Then he sat there for a while, thinking about how close together expectation and disappointment resided in the soul. Like two neighbours – or even a pair of twins – who could never quite bear to close the door between their rooms.

And pondering how readily thoughts turned inwards instead of outwards. The idea of getting this place hadn't been to create more time for brooding about his inner self. Quite the opposite, in fact; the whole point had been to observe and think about the world around him. To walk in the forest. Listen to the wind in the trees, see animals and plants and birds; to come home, make a fire, eat his fill, have an invigorating sleep – these were the components that were to build meaning into life. To be part of all the rest, as it were.

That was it, he thought. *To be part of.* It was so obvious there was no need to write it down.

Thank you. My name is Anna.

He folded up the sheet of paper and slipped it into the back of his notebook. Then, taking his pipe, tobacco and matches, he went out into the forest.

★

First he walked south, then west and then veered slightly northwards, and an hour later he was up on the little ridge with its sparsely growing birches and a view over the house and land at Rödmossen. He sat down on a fallen tree trunk and prepared for his smoke. He filled the pipe with clumsy, inexpert fingers, pressed the tobacco down with his thumb as he remembered his father doing, struck a match and sucked on the pipe. Getting it to light was easy and he just puffed out the smoke to start with, but eventually he risked drawing it into his lungs as well.

It felt like a kick in the chest and for a few seconds everything went black. Whoops, he thought when he had recovered a little. Well blow me down, this is going to take some practise.

It didn't taste too bad, as long as he was careful not to inhale too much at a time. Ante Valdemar Roos had only ever smoked for about six months of his life, in the early days with Lisen, and he'd never tried a pipe. Just the occasional filter cigarette – he realized this was an activity of an entirely different order.

He sat there for a while after he had finished his pipe and felt the faint, lingering dizziness ebb away. Then he got to his slightly unsteady feet and set off back to Lograna.

He had not gone more than a few hundred metres, down into the hollow through the meadowsweet and bog myrtle round the disintegrating wooden hunting tower. It wasn't much, just a fleeting impression of something appearing and vanishing again, all in fractions of a second; yet somehow he could swear it wasn't an animal.

It was a person. He remembered he'd read somewhere – or heard someone say, in which case it was most likely Tapanen, who tended to claim things about the world and its terms of operation that he sometimes didn't understand himself – that this is precisely how our perception works.

First, that it is the movement itself that we immediately register, even if it is surrounded by a jumble of objects and non-moving stimuli. That's why it is always safer to lie still if you are a hunter's prey. A hunter can perceive the movement of a head or a tail from a hundred metres away, but he could be standing right beside his unmoving quarry and remain oblivious to it.

Second, that we can instantly differentiate between an animal and a human being. Though he did wonder quite how true this was, considering how many people were accidentally shot in the elk-hunting season each year. Maybe it was just an invention. One of those characteristic half-truths so readily accepted as life skills by the common man. Olavi Tapanen, for example.

He stopped walking. Kept still, waiting for the next movement as he engaged in these reflections, but nothing happened. Not even the sound of a bird's wingbeat. The forest stood motionless all around him, brooding secretively.

But he knew. He knew the whole way back to Lograna that there had been another person near him, who had revealed their presence by mistake and who absolutely did not want to be discovered.

Some things you just know, thought Ante Valdemar Roos. You don't understand how, but you know them.

The rest of the day passed without incident. He had a pork chop with lots of onions and three boiled potatoes for lunch, made some coffee, had a cautious pipe of tobacco in his chair in front of the outbuilding, did some crosswords and slept for three quarters of an hour.

But there was still something there. Not the same strong feeling as yesterday, but its content, the nub of the feeling, was the same.

The perception of a presence.

She hasn't gone, he thought. It was her I glimpsed, over at Rödmossen.

And the twin neighbours in his chastened soul, expectation and disappointment, knocked on each other's doors and reached an agreement.

Before he got in the car to return to Kymlinge, he tore a page out of *his* notebook and wrote a simple message.

He left it on the table and as he slid the key into position under the eaves he realized his heart was racing.

14

She counted to 200, just like the day before. It was five o'clock again today and she wondered if that was his regular routine. He would come at about half past nine in the morning, stay all day and leave about five.

But if so, why? Why didn't he stay overnight?

She didn't take the rucksack and guitar straight back inside with her. Retrieving the key from its usual place above the door, she went in to see whether anything had changed. Whether he had read her note and reacted to it in any way. Or simply thrown it away.

He had all but spotted her out in the forest, she realized. She'd spent the morning wandering round a bit aimlessly, mainly to keep from losing too much heat. She'd sat down to read a couple of times in sunny clearings, but only for ten or fifteen minutes on each occasion. Even though she was better dressed than the day before, it was cooler today. As she walked she made sure to remember some landmarks, so she didn't get lost. The huge glacial boulder. The anthill. The road, of course, the rise up to the three tall spruces, the marshy area clogged with tree shoots and thickets down on the other side – and suddenly she saw him coming, making almost straight for her. He was still quite a long way off, and she dived for cover behind a curtain of young spruces. He passed her at a distance of only ten or fifteen metres, and to be on the safe side she stayed there flattened to the mossy ground, her eyes shut, long after he had gone.

What I can't see, can't see me either, that was a good old rule and not to be laughed at.

There was a sheet of paper on the table. She held her breath as she picked it up and read:

> My name's Valdemar. If you stay until tomorrow, we can talk
> to each other, all right? I'll be there about nine thirty as usual.
> Warm wishes
> V.

Valdemar? she thought. What a strange name, she'd never met anyone called that in her entire life. She didn't think she'd even heard of the name.

She went out to get her rucksack and guitar. She lit a fire in the hearth; it was easier now, but the first time she'd used up half a box of matches before it got going. He had fetched in more wood, stacked it in a pile under the window, as if he wanted to make sure she'd be nice and warm overnight.

She made coffee on the stove and put a big saucepan of water to boil on the bigger hotplate; it was a new pan, so he must have brought it with him today. She found a plastic bowl and a packet of washing powder under the sink and spent half an hour washing and rinsing dirty clothes. Socks and underwear. She looked for a line to hang them out on, but couldn't find one. They wouldn't dry outside in any case, she thought; it would be better to hang them over the backs of chairs in front of the fire.

There was a solitary pork chop in the fridge, but she didn't like pork chops. She made herself a packet soup instead, and put liver paté and gherkin on two slices of bread.

Four days, she thought as she sat at the kitchen table working her way through the bread. I've only been here four days, but I feel as though I actually live here. Some of the time I do, anyway.

Right now I do, at any rate.

It was strange, but maybe that was the way of things: there were certain places where you felt at home, while in others you never had that sense of contentment, no matter how long you stayed there.

Yes, but then I'm just a fucking loner, she thought. Sonja at Elvafors was dead right about that. My type doesn't fit in with people, and that's my big problem.

That was true, wasn't it? She'd been in the forest two whole days now, seven or eight hours each day, and in a way it didn't bother her. As long as she had the right clothes on and something to eat, she liked wandering around amongst the trees, the moss-covered rocks, the tussocks of twiggy lingonberry, with no plan beyond doing just that. She felt safe. Calm and contented.

And that was even stranger, really. She was born and raised in an urban setting, and had never spent much time in the country. Those summers at Julek's house in Poland, of course, and at Grandmother's. A few school trips, but that was about it.

Well there'd been a couple of nights camping with Jossan and Emily too, she remembered. They'd hitchhiked their way south for a week one summer a few years back; the idea had been to get to Denmark but they'd ended up by a lake in the forest in Småland instead. It had been so totally different to here and now, she thought. It felt like a hundred years ago and she couldn't help smiling about it. They'd drunk beer and smoked hash the whole time and Jossan had been so scared of the dark and freaked out that they'd had to stay awake and hold her and talk to her all the time.

She wondered how things had turned out for Jossan. She got pregnant and had a baby before she was nineteen. Then she moved to Stockholm with the father and their baby daughter. Hallonbergen, wasn't it? The father was from Eritrea and his family was still there. Maybe Jossan had found her feet thanks to the baby, thought Anna, but things could just as well have gone in the other direction.

At any event, she wouldn't have fitted in here. Living alone, in a little cottage out in the forest, no, that was an existence most people wouldn't leap at the chance of. Or at least, not if they happened to be a girl and only twenty-one.

Though I don't actually live here, was her next thought. This is just temporary. If I had somewhere else to head for, of course I wouldn't stay in a place like this. She went outside and smoked her last cigarette. As she stubbed it out, a great sense of desolation descended on her. She was on the verge of tears, but managed to pull herself together. This is also the way of things, she observed to herself. The needs of body and soul. I shall have to leave here simply because I need to get hold of some cigarettes.

Five minutes later she found his pipe and tobacco where he'd left it, on the shelf above the bed.

That night she dreamt about Marek, her little brother. It was more of a memory than a dream, really, but in the dream, things went far worse than they had done in reality.

The dream was about that time he was in hospital. He was

only four, Anna sixteen. Marek had been getting peculiar pains in his stomach for a while, not every day, but they recurred at irregular intervals. No one was sure if they were real or he was just pretending, and that was almost the hardest thing about it, Anna thought.

Why should a four-year-old boy invent pains in his stomach?

It always happened when he was feeling upset, too. Anna's mother had to fetch him from nursery several times, Anna also had to help out, and in the end they took him to hospital for a proper examination. Anna didn't know why they had kept Marek in overnight, but they did. And Anna was the one who had to stay with him, sleeping in the other bed in the brilliant-white room up on the tenth floor. Her mother wasn't able to stay, for some reason Anna couldn't remember either.

He was so scared, her little brother, and in the end she climbed into his bed; it simply wasn't enough for her to be half a metre away, holding his hand.

And he asked her such strange questions.

Why am I so stupid and unkind?

Are you going to give me away when I'm a bit bigger?

Why does Daddy say such horrible things?

I'm never going to be a white angel, am I?

Was it normal for four-year-olds to ask questions like that? She didn't know, but she found it hard to believe. And what were the horrible things that his dad, who wasn't Anna's dad, had been saying? Well, Marek didn't want to talk about it.

Don't tell Mum what I said, he begged. And not just once, but twice.

She did her best to console and pacify him, of course. Just before he finally went off to sleep, he asked her if he was going to die during the night, if that was why he was here, and she had assured him he would wake up the next morning as hale and hearty as a little foal.

A foal? Marek asked.

As lively and happy as a little horse, she promised. He thought about this for a long time.

I'd really like to be a little horse, he declared in his most earnest voice. Horses don't have hands that can do awful things.

That was how it had been in real life. She had stayed awake for a long time, close beside him, listening to his snuffling breaths and wondering about his questions, and in the morning a doctor and a whole flock of nurses had come round and told her there wasn't anything in the least wrong with Marek, and then the two of them had gone home. She never told her mother about her conversation with Marek in the hospital bed and Marek never returned to the subject either. His stomach problem recurred a few times in the weeks that followed, but then it stopped.

In the dream, things developed differently. When she woke up in the hospital bed the next morning, Marek wasn't there. She tried to find out – from all these people in white – where her little brother had gone, but no one could give her a sensible answer. She ran round the big hospital, asking everywhere, but most people didn't have time even to listen to her. She made her way through long corridors and dark tunnels, but nowhere was there a four-year-old boy who had come in the day before with stomach pains. And nobody knew anything.

In the end she found him in a big room down in the basement, a kind of storeroom, in fact; it was full of little white coffins and in every coffin lay a dead child. There really was an immense number of coffins, and it wasn't until she opened the very last one that she came across her little brother.

He wasn't just dead, he also had a noose round his neck, and on his chest was his favourite teddy, its head cut off.

She was woken by her own tears. When she realized it was only a dream, she felt a surge of relief of course, but her tears continued flowing for a long time.

Why do I have dreams like that? she thought. How is life going to turn out for Marek and why do things always get so horrible when we aren't on our guard?

She checked the time. It was twenty to eight.

High time to get up. Have some breakfast and decide whether she was going to leave or stay.

When she came out of the house – to go for a pee, over by the earth cellar – she found it was raining.

15

Excellent, thought Ante Valdemar Roos. She won't feel like leaving in this weather.

But no sooner had Wilma left him alone at the breakfast table than the rain stopped, and ten minutes later the sun came out. He took this as a salutary reminder of the transience of all things; nothing was what it appeared to be, not even from one minute to the next. As he sat in the hall tying his shoelaces, Signe poked her head out of her room. She looked as if she had just that instant woken up.

'Can you give me a lift?'

'Where to?' asked Valdemar.

'Only as far as Billundsberg,' said Signe. 'I've got a job interview at Mix, and you go right past there anyway, don't you?'

'No,' said Valdemar. 'That is . . . not today. I've got a few things to sort out in . . . in town first.'

'Why's that?' said Signe.

'It's just the way things have turned out,' said Valdemar.

'Fuck,' said Signe. 'I'm running late.'

'You ought to get up a bit earlier, then,' said Valdemar. 'And go to bed before midnight.'

But by then she had already closed the door.

But that little slip of the tongue annoyed him. I must

concentrate better from now on, he thought. Not get careless with the details. These little lives have got ears and brains too, I mustn't forget.

There had been a traffic accident just before Rimmersdal. No fatalities, but there was a red car upside down in the ditch and two police cars were at the scene. Come to think of it, he'd passed an ambulance a few minutes before, going the other way, near Åkerby church.

It took a while to get past, and only a couple of hundred metres further on he saw something else in the ditch. At first he couldn't make out what it was, but as he passed it he saw it was an elk. A big elk, lying on its side and tossing its head to and fro; steam seemed to be rising from the body and one front leg was sticking up at an odd angle.

That was what had happened of course, thought Valdemar. The red car had collided with an elk; presumably the creature had carried on running for a short distance, badly injured, and then collapsed in the ditch. He had read that this could happen.

He weighed things up in his mind for a few seconds, then took out his mobile and rang 112. It was the first time he'd ever done that. He'd once rung the old emergency number 90000, one summer's evening when he and Espen Lund were sitting on Espen's balcony drinking beer and suddenly noticed a fire in the building next door.

That time it turned out the fire brigade was already on its way – but today's dying elk clearly had not been reported by anyone else.

'Could I have your name please?' asked the woman on the police switchboard to which he had been connected.

'I'd prefer to remain anonymous,' explained Ante Valdemar Roos.

'I need your name,' said the woman.

'Why?' asked Valdemar. 'All I want is for someone to see to it that the elk doesn't suffer any longer than necessary. It makes no difference what my name is, does it?'

'You might think that,' said the woman. 'But we have a set procedure for this sort of thing.'

Valdemar took a deep breath. 'With all due respect, I don't give a damn about your procedure,' he said. 'I'm just an honest taxpayer who's done my duty and reported a wounded animal near the scene of the accident in Rimmersdal. The police are already there, so all you've got to do is ring and tell them. I've no intention of giving you my name.'

The line went quiet for a few seconds and he thought she might have hung up.

'Valdemar Roos?' she said. 'That's right, isn't it? If you're calling from your own phone, that is.'

Before he had time to answer she had thanked him for calling and disconnected him.

Badly handled, he thought. Why did I get her back up like that? Now the police have my name on file.

Though what the hell does it matter? he asked himself. My reporting a wounded elk in Rimmersdal is neither here nor there, when I haven't set foot in Wrigman's for over a fortnight. I'm skating on thin ice in any case, no point pretending otherwise.

In the course of the short phone conversation he had gone past the ICA store and most of the village; he had been intending to go in and buy some fruit and a new crossword magazine, though once he had missed the turning he decided they could wait until the next day.

But the image of the wounded elk remained on his retina all the way to the turning into Rödmossevägen. The steam rising from the great body and the head moving so pointlessly from side to side, as if the dying creature had been trying to tell him something. To impart some sort of information. About . . . well, what? he wondered.

The key in which the day was set?

The inherent fragility of life? The path we all must tread?

Strange thoughts again, he registered, and firmly dismissed them from his mind. Not fruitful ones, either. If she's there she's there, and there's nothing I can do to influence that state of affairs.

Beyond hoping a little, he added as the cottage came into sight.

She saw him coming from her usual vantage point on the forest edge above the earth cellar. She had decided she didn't want to be in the house when he arrived; it was a late decision and she grabbed up her belongings in a rush, including her washing which was still slightly damp, and stuffed everything into her rucksack any old how. She shoved her guitar into its cover – she had played a bit the previous day – and took everything to the outbuilding. It was wet in the tall grass after the rain, so she decided to put her stuff in the store shed, rather than leaving it outside. Right inside the door, so he would see as soon as he opened it that she was still there.

If he hadn't already worked it out, that was. She'd been torn. Should she spend another day in the forest? She didn't think so, and she didn't feel like getting a packed lunch ready. She would let him be the one to decide; once she had stowed away her things she went back indoors, thought for thirty seconds and then wrote another note.

She left it on the table, as they usually did. It certainly was a strange means of communication they had, she thought, and in a way it already felt like an old habit.

He stopped in exactly the same spot as on the Monday and the Tuesday. By the apple tree, just a few metres from the road. He switched off the engine, climbed out and stretched a little. He hadn't brought anything with him today, no carrier bags, not even his brown bag. Before he went into the house he stood still, looking about him. Rather uncertainly, it seemed to her, as if he were tying to work something out in his mind. He's trying to guess if I'm still here, she thought. And that's hardly surprising of course. Whoever he is, he must think this is completely nuts.

He was dressed as he had been on the other days. Light-coloured trousers, a shirt and a thin blue jacket. He looked fairly . . . what was the word she was looking for? Innocuous? Yes, exactly, that was precisely the impression he gave. Innocuous. Someone you would be very unlikely to notice in a crowd. Not a person to be afraid of, nor a person who would wish you any harm.

He reminds me of Reinhold, she thought, and as the thought hit her it made her happy but also a little sad. Reinhold was a teacher of hers in Year 5 – their usual teacher was on maternity leave and Reinhold had turned up in January, after the Christmas break.

He was so nice. Everybody liked him, and some of the girls – maybe she had been one of them – were a bit in love with him. And yet they were so rotten to him, especially the boys of course, the girls just sat there as usual and let it happen. Secretly enjoying it, as if being nice wasn't enough. Reinhold did everything for them: gave a party at his place for the whole class, with cake, went to the cinema with them, organized discos, and they thanked him for all this by slowly and methodically breaking him down.

It was just horrible, thought Anna, and when Reinhold went off sick three weeks before the summer holidays, it was too late to do anything about it.

And now there was another Reinhold, a Valdemar, outside his little house in the forest, waiting to meet her. Many years older, admittedly, maybe twice the age Reinhold had been, but there was something about the way he stood and his way of looking around him that revealed he wasn't one to make any fuss.

What a psychologist I am, she thought, and gave a giggle. I don't even need to say hi to people before I know their character.

He was taking down the key. Putting it in the lock, opening the door and going into his cottage.

Wait and see, she thought, aware that her knees were getting damp.

The place looked neat and clean. As if she really had left Lograna, and tidied up after herself by way of thanks.

But then he saw the note on the table.

Aren't you angry with me?
I'm a bit scared of meeting you, but if you come outside and shout 'Come on in, you're welcome', I might just dare.
Yours sincerely,
Anna

He read it twice and found himself smiling. He went into the kitchen and put a saucepan of water on the stove. He waited for it to boil, turned off the hotplate and moved the pan to one side.

Then he went outside. He scanned the scene again but couldn't see anything in particular. He suddenly felt foolish, not knowing which way to look. He assumed she was somewhere in the forest, presumably very close to the house, otherwise she wouldn't be able to hear him.

Where should he stand? Which way should he face? He stuck his hands in his pockets and tried to look nonchalant. As if this was something that happened to him on a daily, even hourly, basis. As if a situation like this wasn't remarkable in the least.

He cleared his throat a few times, looked over towards the car and then announced in a loud voice:

'Hello Anna, you're welcome to come in. I've made coffee!'

He gave it ten seconds, then shrugged his shoulders and went back indoors.

16

'Hi.'

'Hi.'

He sat at the kitchen table, she was in the doorway.

'I'm Anna.'

'And my name's Valdemar.'

He got up and they shook hands. He nodded to her to sit down and they took a chair each. There were two cups on the table, his already filled with coffee. A plate of ginger cake and some cardamom biscuits.

'I expect you'd like coffee?'

'Yes please.'

He poured her some from the pot. They sat for a few seconds in silence, not really looking at each other.

'I want to say sorry,' she said. 'Sorry for getting in here.'

He adjusted his glasses and looked at her.

'It doesn't matter.'

'Aren't you angry with me?'

He shook his head. 'No.'

'Why not?'

'Perhaps you have your reasons?'

She considered this for a moment. 'Yes,' she said. 'That's right. I have my reasons.'

He sat quietly as she put sugar and milk in her coffee and stirred it. 'You can't be very old?' he said.

'Twenty-one.'

'Twenty-one?'

'Yes, my birthday was about a month ago.'

'I would have guessed eighteen or nineteen.'

'I'm quite childish. Maybe that shows on the outside too.'

A loitering fly landed on the edge of his cup and he waved it away. It circled and then settled on her hand; he watched it and cleared his throat.

'I've got a daughter about your age.'

'Oh yes?'

'Not my actual daughter. I'm just her stepdad.'

'Ah, I see.'

'Yes, that's how it is.'

He helped himself to a biscuit, dunked it briefly in his coffee and took a bite. She opted for a slice of ginger cake and ate it without dunking. Half a minute went by.

'Maybe you want to know why I came here?'

'Yes, I'd like you to tell me about that.'

'I'm on the run.'

That made him lean forwards and look at her over the top of his glasses. He looked like some children's TV presenter about to tell a story, she thought. But they'd forgotten the make-up.

'On the run?'

'Yes. Well, sort of. I was in this home, this treatment centre, but I couldn't stay there.'

'Not on the run from prison, then?' he asked, and gave a nervous little laugh.

'No,' she said. 'I'm not a criminal.'

'Good,' he said. 'I'm glad you're not a criminal.'

She gave a cautious smile. 'And I'm glad you're not angry with me. It's just that I had nowhere to go, so that was why I ended up here.'

'When did you come?'

'I came on Saturday. Saturday morning. I really only meant to come in for a few hours' sleep; I was worn out.'

'And then you stayed?'

'Yes. I kind of . . .'

'Yes?'

'Kind of didn't get round to moving on.'

He pondered this.

'Where? Where are you moving on to?'

'I don't know.'

'You don't know?'

'No.'

'Haven't you got a home? I mean . . . ?'

She shook her head. 'Not at the moment. I had a flat before I went into that place, but I haven't now.'

'Your parents then? Your mum and dad?'

More head shaking. He slowly stirred his coffee for a while. Keeping his eyes fixed on the inside of the cup.

'That residential home. What sort of thing was it for?'

'For addicts. I'm an addict.'

He looked at her in surprise. 'But I mean, you can't be? You're only . . . that is, you're so young.'

'Well, true, I'm not very old.' She drank a mouthful of coffee and tucked a strand of hair behind one ear. 'I started too early, that was the thing.'

'What did you start with?'

'Beer and hash.'

'Beer and hash.' It wasn't a question, just a restatement. 'Well I never.'

'Yes, those have been my drugs the whole way through, you might say. Things have been pretty haywire in my life these past few years.'

He leant back in his chair and peered at her through slightly narrowed eyes. Over the top of his glasses again.

'You know what, I don't think I really understand what you're telling me.'

She turned her head and looked out of the window. A bird came and perched on the windowsill outside. Suddenly she didn't know what to say.

'I'm sorry . . .'

'You needn't be. There are lots of things I don't understand. But I don't believe you're a bad person.'

'Thank you. And what . . . what sort of person are you?'

He gave a laugh. 'Me? I'm just an old man. I'm dull as ditchwater and I don't gladden anybody's heart.'

'Well you seem kind, anyway.'

'Kind?'

'Yes.'

'The hell I am. What gave you that idea?'

'You let me stay here. Other people would have thrown me out or called the police.'

'But I *did* call the police.'

She went very quiet and stared at him in consternation. The corner of his mouth twitched but then he was serious again.

'Not about this business. Though I did call the police this morning, as a matter of fact, about an injured elk I saw lying by the side of the road.'

'An elk?'

'Yes, a car ran into it. It's nothing to do with you, I was only joking.'

'Oh, I see. Was it badly hurt?'

'I'm afraid so. Things looked pretty grim.'

'What will they do with it?'

'The elk?'

'Yes.'

'I don't know. I should think they'll have to put it down. If they haven't already.'

'I feel sorry for it.'

'Yes, I did too.' He scratched the back of his neck and thought. 'It was moving its head and looking so confused. As if it didn't understand what had happened to it . . . and it didn't, of course. They're just not built for colliding with cars.'

'No, I suppose not.'

'Elk and cars shouldn't exist on the same planet.'

'You're right, I'd never thought about that.'

They carried on drinking their coffee. Then he got up and went into the living room. He returned with pipe and tobacco. She put her hand to her mouth for a moment.

'I borrowed that, too.'

'This? The tobacco and pipe?'

'Yes. Sorry, but I was dying for a smoke and I'd run out of fags.'

'It doesn't matter. Lucky for you that I started smoking yesterday, then.'

'What? You only started yesterday?'

'Yes.'

'Why? I started when I was fourteen. You must be . . . well, a bit older than that, anyway.'

He laughed. 'Fifty-nine. Well, it's never too late to try something new, is it?'

She laughed too. 'You know what, I like talking to you. You seem so . . . well, so kind, in a way.'

'Hrmm, I suppose I'm not the worst.'

He busied himself with the pipe and tobacco.

'Would you like me to light it for you?'

'Well yes, maybe. I'm not much of a pro yet.'

He passed the smoking kit over to her. She filled the pipe with tobacco and pressed it down with her index finger. He watched her moves and nodded as if in the process of learning something. She lit the pipe, puffed at it a couple of times and then passed it over.

'Peace pipe,' she said. 'But maybe we should go outside so we don't make it smell of smoke in here?'

They went outside together and smoked beside the pump for a while, passing the pipe back and forth between them. The sun had disappeared and ominous dark clouds indicated rain was on the way. A couple of magpies were bouncing around by the earth cellar.

'I think it's a great house you've got here,' she said. 'Do you come every day?'

He nodded. 'More or less.'

'But you never stay the night?'

'No.'

She thought for a while.

'Why not? That is, it's none of my business, but . . .'

'I haven't had it very long,' he explained. 'Only a couple of weeks, actually. So I just come for the day.'

'Oh yes?'

'That's the way it is.'

'What . . . do you have a job or anything?'

He considered for a moment before answering.

'No, I've given up work.'

She inhaled a bit too deeply and started coughing. 'Ooh, this is strong tobacco.'

'I thought you were used to it?'

'Only to cigarettes. And the hash, of course, but I've stopped that now.'

'That was why you were in that home?'

'Yes. But just because I ran away, it doesn't mean I'm going to start again. It was only that . . . that I couldn't stay there any more.'

He cranked the handle of the pump a few times, cupped his hand and drank a little of the water.

'Your parents, though . . . do your mum and dad know where you are?'

She shook her head. 'No, nobody knows where I am.'

He wiped his mouth dry and looked at her, nonplussed. 'Nobody?' he asked.

She shrugged. 'No, I pushed off on Saturday. I've been here ever since and I haven't got a mobile phone.'

'Don't you think they're out looking for you?'

She thought about it. 'I honestly don't know. But no, I don't think so.'

He thrust his hands into his trouser pockets and looked up at the sky. 'There'll be more rain soon. Shall we have another cup?'

They both went into the kitchen and sat down at the table. He poured the coffee. 'Shall I tell you something?' he said.

'Go on then.'

'Nobody knows where I am, either.'

'You're kidding?'

'No. I'm quite sure of it.'

She bit her finger and looked at him with a sudden anxiety in her eyes.

'Don't worry,' he said. 'It probably sounds odd, but Lograna is my secret, you might say.'

'Lograna.'

He made an encompassing sweep of the arm. 'That's what this place is called. Lograna. I bought it three weeks ago, and I haven't told a soul.'

'Three weeks ago?'

'Yes.

'You're married though, aren't you?'

'Yup. Wife and two children. And a son from further back, too . . . he's almost forty, we aren't really in touch.'

'And your wife doesn't know about this house?'

'No.'

'I . . . I don't get it.'

He leant back and clasped his hands on his stomach. 'No, I daresay it does sound a bit weird, but that's how it is, anyway.'

'Yes, that's how it is,' he repeated a few moments later.

She frowned, clearly thinking hard. Neither of them said anything. Half a minute passed.

'Why don't you want to tell anybody?' she eventually asked. 'What I mean is, I might do the same, but I'm wondering . . . no, it's none of my business.'

He appeared to be searching for an answer. The fly returned and landed in the middle of the table, and they both contemplated it for a while, avoiding each other's eyes. As if they had reached a crossroads and were suddenly faced with deciding which way to go on.

'You know what,' he said once he had batted the fly away. 'I think it's nice that you found your way in here and gave the old place a bit of a lived-in feel. Really nice.'

She felt tears well up all of a sudden. 'Thank you. But you must be crazy. I stole your food and all sorts of other stuff. I'll pay you as soon as I—'

He shook his head. 'I won't hear of it,' he said. 'Someone in need is someone in need, and you haven't done any harm.'

'Thank you.'

'What have you done with your things?'

'I put them in the outhouse.'

'Why?'

'I thought . . . um, I don't know.'

Again there was silence between them, and they suddenly heard torrential rain. Beating on the roof, the metal window-sills, the leaves of the apple trees, like three different voices coming from the sky, but what they were saying wasn't easy to interpret.

He got to his feet. 'I think we should light a fire,' he said. 'What do you say?'

'Yes,' she said. 'We might as well.'

17

The rain continued for the rest of the morning. Heavy down-
pours gradually gave way to sweeping veils of finer rain, but
it never stopped completely. She went and fetched her rucksack
and guitar. She draped her damp washing over the backs of
the chairs again, checking first that it was all right to do so,
and he said it was.

Then he lay in bed doing crosswords while she sat reading
at the table. They talked to each other, but sparingly. The
occasional comment, with long intervals in between. It felt to
her like the most natural thing in the world.

'Where are you from?'

'Örebro. My mother is from Poland.'

'Poland? I've never been there.'

'I was born in Sweden, but I speak Polish as well.'

'Mhmm.'

A while later:

'A lot of people get caught up in drugs these days.'

'Yes.'

'It isn't easy.'

'No.'

'No reason to look behind you? Six letters, ends in a t. What
do you reckon?'

'Could be regret?'

'Yes, that fits.'

'Or fright.'

A random mix of questions and answers. Fairly evenly distributed, too; it wasn't just him wanting to know about her.

'What was your job when you were still at work?'

'Finance. I was the finance manager at a small business not far from Kymlinge.'

'Did you like your job?'

'No.'

'Was that why you left?'

'Yes. Isn't your mum worried about you?'

She told him about her mother. That she was in Warsaw for the time being, looking after her sick mother.

'Your grandmother?'

'Yes.'

'So she isn't likely to know you've run away?'

'No.'

'And your dad, do you ever see him?'

'Hardly ever.'

'That's the way it is sometimes.'

'Yes.'

At twelve thirty they had lunch. Packet soup and some bread and cheese and liver paté plus a carrot each.

'I've never been that keen on cooking,' he said. 'It's just the way things turned out.'

'Nor me,' she said. 'I often make do with bread and stuff, I'm afraid.'

'Same here,' he said. 'But there are worse things.'

'Yes,' she said. 'There are worse things than bread.'

She did the washing-up and he went back to bed and his

crossword magazine; when she came in from the kitchen she saw he had dozed off. A sudden feeling of doubt came over her as she resumed her seat at the table. What am I doing? Here I sit in a room in a house out in the middle of the forest. Lying in bed in the same room there's a man older than my father. His name is Valdemar, and I only met him today. He's snoring a bit.

She got out her pad of paper and wrote it down. Just as she had thought it, sentence for sentence, exactly as it was. *Here I sit in a room . . .* She didn't really know why she was doing it; perhaps she thought she could make song lyrics out of it sometime, or perhaps there were other reasons. After a while she remembered something Uncle Julek had once told her.

There are a lot of questions in life, Anna, he had said; it must have been one Christmas or Easter, all the family was there. Pirogi, bigos and the breaking of bread, the whole rigmarole, but he and she had found somewhere quieter, which was what he liked to do when he grew tired of the other grown-ups and their political chatter.

A lot of questions, but only three important ones.

Where have you been?

Where are you?

Where are you going?

If you can answer those three, you have your life in your hands, Anna, he said. And he laughed his loud laugh and tapped his index finger on her forehead to make sure his advice stuck.

There was more to it than your location itself, she realized. You had to know why, as well. That above all else.

Why did you live the life of an addict, Anna?

Why are you here in this house right now?

Why are you going wherever you choose to go next?

I can't answer the first two, she thought. And the third – even harder.

Maybe she wasn't on her way anywhere at all? And in that case, could there be some point in her staying here for now? Possibly?

If you don't know where you're going, the best thing is to stand still. It sounded pretty obvious.

For a few moments she watched Valdemar over in the corner in his bed. He had taken off his shoes and she noticed he had a hole in one of his socks. His hands were clasped together on his stomach and his faint snores sounded safe and reassuring somehow. They fitted well with the gentle whisper of the rain on the windowsills and roof tiles. She wondered whether he was expecting her to leave, now they had finally met. She didn't know, and he hadn't said anything about it. She decided she would ask him when he woke up, and perhaps she could ask to stay another night if it was still raining. Or perhaps he could drive her to Kymlinge, and then she could hitchhike from there.

Gothenburg? That had been the vague idea on Saturday morning. Now, five days later, it wasn't tempting at all. What was there for her in Gothenburg?

If I at least felt some kind of urge to get away from here, she thought. If I at least had some sort of willpower in me.

But all she really felt like doing – truth to tell – was curling up under a blanket and having a sleep, like him.

They were both in use though, the bed and the blanket. Yes, I shall ask to stay until tomorrow, she resolved again. Ask, at any rate, and the worst that can happen is that he says no.

Ask if he feels like smoking a peace pipe with me, as well.

*

He woke without really realizing he was doing so. He had dreamt that he was sitting behind his usual desk at Wrigman's, and when he opened his eyes he couldn't identify the room he was in. There was a girl sitting at a table, reading a book; she was small and slender, with thick auburn hair, and she was chewing on her knuckle with a look of fierce concentration.

Where am I? thought Ante Valdemar Roos. What's happened? Am I dead, or could I be in hospital?

Or am I still dreaming, like I was just now?

It didn't take more than a few seconds for him to bring the situation under control, but it felt longer. He lay still, looking at her for a while.

So she was the same age as Signe. It was strange; they seemed so unalike that you could almost believe they were from different planets. Why was that? This girl seemed much older to him. Older than she actually was. But at the same time, if you just caught a glance, she somehow looked younger.

There's a special kind of experience in her, he thought. For better or worse, because she's clearly been through a lot.

And she read, and wrote. Signe never did. Wilma was slightly better in that respect – at least she'd got through the whole of Harry Potter.

I don't know what to say to her, he thought suddenly. I wonder if she's thinking of leaving today, in which case I'd like to tell her she's welcome to stay a few days.

Will she misinterpret that? Does she think I shall want something from her for letting her live here for a while? And, what is it . . . what is it I actually want?

The thought made him melancholy.

But to make off from a residential centre just like that? What had brought her to it? And were they really not trying to apprehend her? Was he perhaps committing a criminal act by providing her with a roof over her head?

'Anna,' he said.

It made her jump, and she looked at him. 'You're awake?'

'Yes.'

'Sleep well?'

'Oh yes. I expect I snored as well.'

'Only a little.'

'Ha. Anna, can I ask you something?'

'Of course.'

'Why did you run away from that place?'

She hesitated, sucking the pen she had in her hand.

'I'd never really have got well there.'

'Oh?'

'No.'

'And why was that?'

'They never let you be yourself, everyone had to be the same, and the woman in charge didn't like me.'

'You haven't done anything criminal, have you, Anna?'

She shook her head. 'Only using the drugs. And selling some a few times, but that's all over now. The police aren't after me, if that's what you're wondering about.'

He sat up and swung his feet over the side of the bed. He retrieved his glasses, which he had set aside on the window ledge, and put them on.

'I'm glad,' he said. 'Sorry for asking.'

'Thanks for saying sorry,' she said.

He stretched his arms above his head, yawned and straightened his back. 'It feels a bit odd,' he said.

'What, you and me sitting here?'

'Yes. Don't you think so?'

'Oh yes, of course I do.'

'What on earth would we have to talk about, two people like you and me?'

'I don't really know,' she said. 'Have you got any hobbies?'

He mulled this over. 'I watch sport on TV,' he said. 'But nothing much else. What do you like doing?'

She ran her fingers through her hair and thought about it.

'Reading,' she said.

He nodded. 'I like reading too.'

'Playing the guitar,' she said. 'Singing.'

'Can you play a bit of something for me?'

'Do you want me to?'

'Of course I do.'

'I'm not very good.'

'That doesn't matter. Do you write your own songs as well?'

'I try to. But I know some real ones as well.'

'Real ones?'

'That I didn't write myself.'

He got up and put a couple of logs on the fire. 'Why don't you sing a song, and then we'll have our afternoon coffee?'

'And a peace pipe?'

'Yes, a peace pipe too.'

She got out her guitar and started tuning it. 'I think I'll do a real one first. How old did you say you were?'

'What's that got to do with it?'

She gave a little laugh. 'Just thought you might recognize this one. It's from the sixties. "As Tears Go By".'

'"As Tears Go By"? Yes, I remember that. Is it an old Stones song?'

'I think so. OK, I'll give it a go.'

And she sang 'As Tears Go By'. He realized right away that

he knew the words, or the beginning, at any rate. The bit about the children playing in the evening, and the smiling faces and the the singer's sense of exclusion.

She had a lovely voice. Husky and deep – deeper when she sang than when she spoke. If he had just been hearing it, not seeing her at the same time, he would have guessed it was the voice of a woman at least twice the age of the one sitting in front of him, concentrating as she moved her fingers on the neck of the guitar to pick out the chords – and before he knew it, tears were welling in his eyes. She noticed, but did not stop singing. She just smiled at him, and he thought that if he died now, at this precise moment, it wouldn't matter terribly much.

Yes, this was the exact thought that came into Ante Valdemar Roos's head, and he did nothing to detract from it. He didn't laugh at it or dismiss it by blowing his nose on the self-important handkerchief of reason. As one usually did when that kind of thing intruded, he thought.

When she finished her song, they both sat there in silence for a while, looking into the fire.

'Thank you, Anna,' he said at last. 'That was the most beautiful thing I've heard for a very, very long time.'

'It suits my voice,' she said. 'I'm an alto, a low alto even.'

He nodded. 'How about that coffee, then?'

'And the peace pipe?'

'And the peace pipe.'

Passing through Rimmersdal on his way home, he saw they had taken the elk away. There was always a slim chance, of course, that it had recovered and got out of the ditch by itself, but he found that hard to believe.

What an extraordinary day it had been. As he parked the

car in its usual spot in the yard of Lily's Bakery, he realized how hard he would find seeing Alice and the girls. He felt as if they didn't really belong in his world at the moment – or he in theirs, was probably a better way of putting it – and he hoped the flat would be empty. If it was, he would lock himself in the bathroom, turn the light off, sink into some very hot water and think about life. That seemed the only even vaguely meaningful activity he could engage in for the next few hours.

But the flat was not empty. Sitting in the kitchen were Alice and Signe – and an unfamiliar young man with long dark hair and a yellow shirt unbuttoned low at the neck.

'Valdemar, this is Birger,' said Alice. 'Signe's fiancé.'

Valdemar didn't think Birger Butt – that was his name, wasn't it? – looked like a fiancé. More like someone trying not to let the mask slip after coming last in the Eurovision Song Contest. Or whatever they called it these days. Signe had put one hand high up on his thigh, presumably so he would realize he didn't have to get up when Valdemar held out his hand. His trousers were as vividly red as his shirt was bright yellow.

'Nice to meet you,' said Valdemar.

'Er, hi,' said Birger Butt.

'He's staying to dinner,' said Alice.

He can have my place, thought Valdemar. 'I see,' he said. 'So you two are engaged, eh?'

'Valdemar,' said Alice.

'Come on Birger, let's go to my room,' said Signe.

They left the kitchen.

'Idiot,' said Alice to Valdemar.

'I thought fiancé meant you were engaged,' said Valdemar.

'I just don't get you,' said Alice. 'Don't you think he's cute?'

'No,' said Valdemar. 'But he and Signe might be well suited.'

'What's that meant to mean?' demanded Alice.

'It means they might be well suited,' clarified Valdemar.

'We'll have to talk about this later,' said Alice. 'I need you to help me with the dinner now. I want us to make a good impression – his dad owns a successful business.'

'Excellent,' said Valdemar. 'What sort of business?'

'I think they distribute supplies to hot-dog stalls,' said Alice. 'Gherkin mayonnaise and prawn salad and that sort of thing. They go all over the country.'

'Interesting,' said Valdemar.

'And it's great that she's found someone at last.'

'About time too,' said Valdemar.

18

Thursday was pretty much like Wednesday. Admittedly when she went out to pee at half past seven it wasn't raining, but the grass was soaking wet and a little while later the rain started again.

And it went on all day, more or less. Valdemar arrived at his usual time, she helped him unload the bags from the car and they dashed into the kitchen with them. He had really stocked up on provisions: as well as three ICA carrier bags of food he'd also bought a saw, an axe, a sack of peat litter for the compost toilet, a pair of wellies, some thick socks and various other bits and pieces.

A big tin of white paint, for example. Brushes and a roller and tray.

'I thought we could paint the inside walls,' he said. 'Make it look a bit less drab.'

'Let me do it,' came her instant suggestion. 'As a . . . well, as a thank-you gesture for letting me stay here.'

'But I wouldn't expect you to—' he began, but she interrupted him.

'Why not? I'm good at painting walls. I've done it before, at home at my mum's, and then in the flat I lived in.'

'Hm,' he said, looking at her over the top of his glasses.

'And I think you're right, by the way,' she said. 'It'll really brighten things up in here if it's painted white.'

'Humph,' he said. 'I don't know that I should—'

'Oh yes you should. I want to do something for you. Please?'

He gave a shrug. 'Well I'm not so goddamn keen on painting that I'll beg to be allowed to do it. In fact, you might be able to get it done over the weekend, I suppose.'

'You won't be coming at the weekend?'

'No.'

'Why not?'

'I've got a few other things to do.'

'I see.'

'This and that. Like I said.'

'Oh? Well, I can paint on Saturday and Sunday. If you'll let me stay that long, that is?'

'Suppose I'll have to, then,' he said.

One corner of his mouth gave a humorous twitch as he said it, and she found herself thinking it was a shame he wasn't her dad. It was a notion that came into her mind without warning, and she was obliged to chuckle herself.

Then they stowed away the shopping in the fridge and cupboards, and had their morning coffee.

'Mind if I ask you a question?'

'No, ask away.'

'It's something I started wondering about yesterday evening after you'd gone. You needn't answer if you don't want to.'

'That's a right a person always has.'

'Eh?'

'Only to answer if they want to.'

She thought about this. 'Yes, you're right of course. Well, what I'm wondering is whether you drive out here to Lograna every day?'

'Yes I do. In the week, that is.'

'And your wife doesn't know about it?'

'No.'

'What's her name, by the way?'

'Alice, her name's Alice.'

'But where does Alice think you go every morning, then?'

He clasped his hands, propped his elbows on the table and rested his chin on his knuckles. He seemed to be searching for the right words. A few seconds went by and then he sighed, as if he just couldn't be bothered to search any more.

'To work, of course.'

'To work?'

'Yes.'

'But you've stopped work.'

'I haven't told her that.'

She looked at him in bewilderment. 'You've lost me now.'

'Well,' he said, 'I can understand that. But of course it wasn't part of the plan for me to meet you and have to explain all sorts of things.'

'No, I get that.'

He took off his glasses and sighed again. 'Life isn't always a bundle of bloody laughs, you should know that.'

'Yes,' she said. 'Of course I know.'

'Sometimes it feels pretty unbearable.'

'Mhmm?'

'Yes, that was the long and short of it. I couldn't bear it any longer, so I stopped work and bought myself this place.'

'Why couldn't you bear it?'

He pondered this. Clasped his hands behind the back of his neck for variety and looked up at the ceiling.

'I don't know. It just happened that way.'

'Happened that way?'

'Yes. I haven't really got to the bottom of why.'

'Mhmm.'

'And I couldn't care less, actually,' he went on. 'When you get as old as I am, you have to accept some things without digging around in them. The fact that you are who you are, for example.'

She raised her eyebrows in surprise. Then she laughed.

'You know what, Valdemar, I'm glad I met you. Awfully glad, because you're so . . .'

'Yes?'

'Refreshing, I suppose.'

'Refreshing?'

'Yes.'

'You must be out of your mind, Anna.' But he was finding it hard not to laugh, too. 'If you think I'm refreshing, I feel sorry for you. I'm about as refreshing as a rubbish tip. Now I'm going to lie down and do crosswords for a while. It's too wet for a walk in the forest today, don't you think?'

She looked out of the window. 'Yes,' she said. 'You're right. But there was one more thing I wanted to ask . . . if it won't make you cross?'

'Cross? Why should I be cross? Well?'

'You've got a mobile phone, haven't you?'

Valdemar patted the outside of his breast pocket. 'Yes, it's sleeping here today as well.'

'I wonder if I could borrow it and call my mum? I'll just ring quickly and then she'll ring me back. It'll cost you hardly anything.'

Valdemar nodded and handed her his phone. 'You can sit here in the kitchen and ring. The signal can be a bit patchy, mind. I'm going to have a little lie-down in there, like I said.'

He went into the living room and shut the door after him.

'Ania, is anything the matter?'

'Can you call me on this number?'

She ended the call and waited. It took almost five minutes for the phone to ring.

Why? thought Anna. Why can't she ever call me straight away? There's always something more important.

'Ania, is anything the matter?'

The same opening gambit, word for word.

'Yes,' said Anna. 'You could say that.'

'I'm still at Mum's in Warsaw, you know. It costs a lot to ring you.'

'I know. I just wanted to tell you I'm not at the Elvafors centre any more.'

'You're not? Oh God, Anna, why not?'

'So they didn't call and tell you?'

'No. But why are you—?

'I ran away. It was such a shithole, but you needn't worry about me. I'm fine.'

'So where are you now?'

It took her a few moments to bring the name to mind. 'I'm at a place called Lograna.'

'Lograna? What's that.'

'It's a house in the middle of the forest. I'm staying here for a while, then we'll have to see. How long will you be in Poland?'

Anna's mother sighed and Anna heard someone switch on a TV set in the background. Her mother told someone called Mariusz to turn the volume down.

'I don't know how long I shall have to stay, Anna. Mum's not at all well. She's in hospital, and I don't know if she'll pull through this time.'

Anna felt a hot prickling in her throat and at the backs of her eyes. 'And Marek?'

'He's at Majka and Tomek's. He's fine. But he might be coming down here too, I'm not sure.'

'Right,' said Anna.

'But this . . . Lograna?' said her mother. 'Where is it? And who are you staying with?'

'I'm just fine,' said Anna. 'You don't need to worry. I only rang to let you know I'd left Elvafors.'

'Anna, you haven't . . . please tell me you haven't started . . . ?'

'No,' said Anna. 'I haven't started again. Bye then, Mum.'

'Bye,' said her mother. 'Look after yourself, Anna.'

She quickly rang off before tears got the better of her.

Fuck, she thought. Why does it always have to be like this?

He set off for home at five o'clock as usual, promising to bring sandpaper and a roll of masking tape the next day.

They hadn't talked a great deal that afternoon. It had rained almost non-stop and they'd kept the fire well fed with wood. Spent the time reading and doing crosswords, and she'd sung him another song. *Are you going to Scarborough Fair?*

'You sing so beautifully it makes me feel as though I'm in Heaven, Anna,' he'd said.

'Maybe this is what Heaven looks like,' she'd quipped with a laugh.

'Why not?' he'd agreed. He'd looked around the modest

room and given a laugh of his own. 'Anna and Valdemar in the heavenly kingdom of Lograna.'

She'd felt a bit bereft after he had gone. Heaven? she thought. Well, maybe they were right. Maybe it was as simple as that.

'Never better than this,' he had said as well. It was just before he got into the car and drove away. 'But you're too young to know it.'

She hadn't understood what he meant – or perhaps she had. In any case, it was such a melancholy piece of knowledge that she hadn't really wanted to accept it.

Just as he had said. She was too young. She thought that she ought to be feeling happy. She would be allowed to stay here for at least three more days. Paint walls and make herself a bit useful; she liked painting and if she happened to want to stay on, he presumably wouldn't deny her that, either. For a few more days, anyway. A week, give or take. So what was wrong? Where had this sudden gloom come from?

She hadn't tired of the heavenly kingdom of Lograna, that wasn't what was putting her in low spirits – though she knew the euphoria of the first few days couldn't last for ever. *Euphoria*, she liked that word. Because if the word existed, so must the feeling. She remembered that poem by Gunnar Ekelöf they'd read in upper secondary; it was a shame that Swedish lessons hadn't been devoted just to poetry, then she wouldn't have disliked them as much as she had.

But this was a different feeling. A sort of mournfulness, yes, and she realized it was her conversation with her mother that was lingering inside her and making her sad. And this above all: when life got fragile, her mother had always been the most important lifeline, and if she noticed that the line was stretched too thin, that it couldn't really take her weight, well, that was when the darkness and the abyss suddenly loomed dangerously close.

Young girl, dumb girl, try to be a brave girl, she tried telling herself. She sat with her pen and pad for a while, writing and crossing out one stupid line after another. It just wasn't working, the words on the paper looked banal and meaningless as soon as she looked back at them, and she gave up after twenty minutes. She went out and stood under the little overhanging roof of the front door; she smoked a full pipe, making herself feel dizzy and slightly queasy. The rain was persistent and surrounded her with a thin but hostile wall, and she was very aware that if she had had access to a drug stronger than tobacco, she would have taken it without a moment's hesitation.

That's the thing, she thought once she had lit a fresh fire and curled up under the blanket. It's not enough to be strong ninety-nine times, you have to hang on through the hundredth, too.

Although it was only seven o'clock, she fell asleep, and when she woke up two hours later the room was dark and the fire had gone out. She was really cold; without putting the light on, she grabbed her thicker top off the back of the chair and put it on, and it was then, glancing out of the window, that she saw a man standing out on the road, looking at the house.

19

Valdemar woke up with a tangible feeling of anxiety in his chest.

Almost like shortness of breath. He clenched his fists and took several deep breaths before turning his head to look at the clock. Quarter past five. He wondered if he had been having a dream, and if that could be the source of the trouble.

Hard to say; no dream images presented themselves, and he pinched his nostril and confirmed that he really was awake. Then he lay there thinking for a few minutes, and as it became clear that sleep had no intention of returning, he got up and went to the bathroom.

Fifteen minutes later he was sitting fully dressed at the breakfast table, feeling poised for flight. That was a strong phrase, but even once he had given it some conscious thought, he realized it was the right one. Poised for flight? God almighty.

But that was how things stood; with every passing day in the past few weeks – ever since he struck lucky with his pools coupon and became the owner of Lograna – the company of Alice and their daughters had grown harder to bear. It was like a growing itch, he thought, albeit accompanied by a powerful and well-founded sense of shame; but the prospect of having to get through the whole morning in the company of his nearest and dearest suddenly seemed almost intolerable.

He thought about something his father had once said. It's not the weeks and years that are hard, my boy, it's the minutes and hours.

And the anxiety he had woken up with was still there. In some strange way it all seemed to be getting mixed up with other images of his father. Later images, above all from that final period, when Eugen Roos was so dejected that he couldn't bring himself to talk any more. Valdemar recalled those months very well. His father would spend virtually the whole day sitting by the kitchen window, staring out at the dismal rows of factory buildings on the other side of the railway tracks and not seeming to take any interest in anything going on around him.

Like his wife and son trying to talk to him.

Like visitors arriving. Like spring being on the way in the birches outside. Like the lilacs coming into bloom.

As if he was drowning in his own inner darkness.

And now here was his son, sitting staring out of a different kitchen window forty-seven years later – no railway and no factory buildings, a red-brick roof and some pollarded limes instead – as he asked himself whether he really had to wait two painful hours before he could set off for the place where everything even remotely essential to his life now happened.

By the time it was twenty to seven and the risk of Alice starting to get up and make her presence felt had become imminent, he made up his mind. He fetched a piece of paper from the study and scribbled a note to say he had lots on at work and had therefore left a bit earlier than usual.

He signed it with his customary 'V.' and hurried out to the hall. He noted that Birger Butt's pale-blue sandals were in residence, put on his jacket and left home.

Lily's Bakery had just opened, the smell of newly baked bread came wafting out of the open door like a vague promise, and in an instant Ante Valdemar Roos's anxiety evaporated. Fresh rolls for breakfast at Lograna, he thought as he went into the shop.

He didn't just get the rolls, he also bought a loaf of rye bread and a bag of biscuits. He had a distinct feeling he recognized the woman behind the counter, but as he drove out of town on the virtually empty roads – there really was a difference between five past seven and quarter past eight – he wondered where he had seen her before. He hadn't been in Lily's Bakery for quite a while, but he was sure he knew her from somewhere else.

As he was going round the Rocksta roundabout it came to him that she was Nilsson's wife. The free-church member and mother of six children – she'd paid a visit to Wrigman's once, a couple of years back, and something about her red hair and her blazing eyes had etched itself in his memory.

Particularly the latter; they were the sort of eyes you were expected to have if you had beheld Christ, Valdemar supposed, and wondered if he was allowed to laugh at the thought or not. There was something particular about Nilsson's eyes, too, when he came to think about it; presumably it was the same for male believers as for the female ones.

That positive prospect of the hereafter.

For his own part, Valdemar Roos didn't believe in God. Not your standard, white-bearded Heavenly Father, anyway. Perhaps there was something else, he would think. Something higher, which we couldn't comprehend and weren't intended to, either. In the months after his father took his own life, he had occasionally put his hands together and sent up a doubtful prayer –

but he had never detected any response and he had not tried again since. Life was one thing, what potentially came after it was another matter. Why should I think about something I can't even conceive of? he would ask himself from time to time. When I find it so hard to comprehend what's right beside me.

In any case, this was no morning for speculative theology; that was plain to see once he had joined the 172, when he started to catch glimpses of the dark waters of Kymmen between the trees and his rear-view mirror showed him the sun starting to break through the clouds.

No, it was a morning for drinking coffee and eating fresh rolls. With his young guest out at Lograna. Two chairs and a stool set against the wall of the outbuilding, a pipe of tobacco with their second cup . . . Jesus, he thought, putting his foot down, sometimes life's so simple it's almost laughable.

And as for that anxiety with which he'd woken a couple of hours before, where it came from and where it had gone, well, there really was no point speculating.

He parked beside the apple tree and got out of the car. No sign of life, apart from a few late bumblebees buzzing in the mignonette by the stone base of the cottage. Maybe she was still asleep; it wasn't even eight. Young people tended to sleep later in the mornings, he knew that – Wilma and Signe were world champions in the art – and she wouldn't be expecting him until half past nine.

He tried the door. Locked.

He felt for the key, but it was not in the lock. Of course not, he thought. She's bound to lock the door from the inside at night. I'd do the same.

He tapped lightly at the door, but there was no reaction from inside. He banged on it with his fist, and then went over to one of the living room windows and rapped on it a couple of times with the dangling hook of the window catch. Strange that it was on the outside, he hadn't thought about that until now.

Five seconds went by, then she opened the window and stuck her head out.

'Sorry, I didn't mean to lock you out. I had such trouble getting off to sleep last night.'

'It doesn't matter,' said Valdemar. 'It's only eight o'clock, I'm a touch early today.'

'Only eight? Hang on a minute and I'll open the door.'

'It's a fine morning,' he declared, putting the paper bag from the baker's on the kitchen table. 'I bought us a few fresh rolls. Why did you have trouble sleeping?'

She bit her lip and hesitated.

'I was a bit scared,' she said.

'Scared? Why?'

'Just as I was on my way to bed I noticed a man out there, looking at the house.'

'What?' said Valdemar.

She gave an earnest nod.

'But what in heaven's name are you saying?' asked Valdemar.

'Yes, he was standing out on the road, just staring in. I was scared shitless.'

'What happened?'

She shrugged her shoulders. 'Nothing. I hadn't put the light on, so I don't know if he saw me. I kind of hid and when I looked again a bit later he'd gone.'

Valdemar pondered this information. 'Nothing to worry

about, I'm sure. It might just have been the farmer from Rödmossen, out for a walk. Or someone picking mushrooms.'

'I know. I thought the same. But it was nearly nine, and getting quite dark. It scared me a bit, anyway, and that was why I couldn't get to sleep.'

Valdemar laughed and patted her on the shoulder. 'You know what I'm going to do? I'm going to get hold of a gun, a proper shotgun, and bring it out here so you can defend yourself if any uninvited guests turn up.'

Anna laughed too. 'You do that,' she said. 'By the way, weren't you meant to be bringing some sandpaper and stuff today?'

Valdemar cleared his throat. 'Well this is what I thought,' he said. 'We'll have breakfast and smoke a pipe, then we'll go into town and do the shopping together.'

She couldn't contain her delight. She threw her arms round his neck and gave him a big hug. Like a ten-year-old at Christmas, he thought. Where is all this leading, I wonder?

But there was no time to dwell on the question.

'Thank you Valdemar,' she said. 'You know what, I was so lucky to meet you. I just can't get over it.'

He felt himself blush – something he thought he had given up about forty years ago – and self-consciously scratched the back of his neck. 'Steady on,' he said. 'Time for some coffee, I think.'

'What do you say to having lunch while we're in town?'

It was eleven thirty. They had bought not only sandpaper and masking tape but also a few other things Valdemar thought might come in handy: two rag rugs, a red and white checked cloth, some pot-holders, a wooden bowl, a couple of candlesticks, a doormat, some hooks to put up on the wall, towels, coffee mugs, an electric kettle, two folding garden chairs and a matching table. The car was chock-a-block with purchases. Anna had not been in a town for a month and a half, nor in a shop for almost as long – except for chocolate and cigarettes when the Elvafors girls were taken on their trips to Dalby – and was feeling exhilarated and a little dizzy after two hours of rushing around the shops and to and from the square at Norra torg where they'd parked.

Almost happy. I'm like a kid at the funfair, she thought, and the notion that he ought to have been her dad kept stubbornly coming back.

'Lunch?' she said. 'But surely we can't . . . ?'

'Of course we can,' he said. 'We'll go to Ljungman's for herring and creamed potatoes. You like herring, don't you?'

'I don't know,' said Anna. 'I don't think I've ever had it.'

Valdemar stared at her.

'You're twenty-one years old and you've never had herring? Well you ought to thank your lucky stars you met me.'

'That's what I told you,' she said, tucking her hand under his arm as they cut across the square to Ljungman's restaurant.

'Like it?'

'Very much.'

'Well there you are. But you have to have lingonberry jam with it. Ideally the one made with the uncooked berries.'

'I thought you didn't care about food?'

'Sometimes,' said Valdemar. 'When it comes to herring and creamed potatoes I'm very choosy.'

Anna finished her cola and looked around the busy dining room. 'What do you suppose they're thinking?' she asked.

'About what?' said Valdemar.

'About us,' said Anna. 'Do you reckon they think we're a dad eating lunch with his daughter? Or . . . ?'

Valdemar thought about it. 'Why not? Or we could be work colleagues.'

'Yes, though you don't go to work any more. Not that they would realize that, of course. Is . . . is there anybody you know in here?'

'I hope not,' said Valdemar, looking around him with slight concern. 'And I shouldn't think so. I don't know many people. I'm an antisocial loner, like I told you.'

'I don't think you're an antisocial loner at all,' said Anna, putting her hand on his arm and giving him a broad smile.

I like the way she dares to smile at me so openly, thought Valdemar. I really do.

'It's only because I'm in such charming company,' he said. 'But perhaps we ought to be making tracks for Lograna now, eh? So I have time for my afternoon nap, at least.'

'Yes, let's,' said Anna. 'And I'll start on the painting after you go. It's a bit of a shame that . . .'

'Yes?'

'That you won't be coming to see how I'm getting on until Monday.'

'We'll have to see,' said Valdemar. 'If I get a chance, I might drop by on Sunday.'

'Hope you will,' said Anna.

They left their table and moved towards the exit; at the door they came face to face with a couple on their way in, a man and woman in their fifties.

'Hello Valdemar,' said the woman, looking surprised.

'Hello,' said Valdemar.

'Everything all right?'

'Yes, fine,' said Valdemar, elbowing his way past with Anna in tow.

'Who were they?' she asked once they were out in the square.

'I don't know who the man was,' said Valdemar, 'but I'm afraid the woman was one of my wife's best friends.'

'Oh dear,' said Anna. 'Do you think . . . I mean . . . ?'

'To hell with it for now,' said Valdemar. 'Sufficient unto the day and all that. Let's talk about something nicer.'

He left Lograna just after five and a sudden feeling of abandonment descended on her. Like a wet blanket, or whatever the saying was.

I'm ridiculous, she thought. I've only been in his company for three days and I'm already like a puppy missing its mother. How did I ever think I would cope on my own in the world? *Young girl, dumb girl.*

She sat in one of the new chairs outside and lit the pipe. The sun had still not gone down behind the fringe of trees and it was pleasantly warm. I wish I really did live here, she thought. And that Valdemar, my extra dad, did too. And that . . . that I had a job I could get to by bike or moped every morning, and that I didn't need to worry one bit about the future.

She knew these were childish thoughts, and that the childishness, the finding it so hard to grow up, was linked to the drugs.

All her addict friends had been the same, wanting to stay in some kind of childhood state, maybe because they had never properly experienced such a thing when they were little.

Yes, it probably was as simple as that. That they had, for

whatever reason, been robbed of all those things that are so important in the early years – play, laughter, freedom, a carefree heart – and that this was what they were now attempting to compensate for by using one drug after another. It was so bloody tragic, thought Anna, and so utterly doomed to failure.

At any rate, that was the analysis all the so-called experts liked to present, she thought. She didn't normally have much time for experts, but in this case she did. If there was one common denominator for all the losers in the world, it was surely that they had a lost childhood which they now carried with them.

She set down the pipe and put her hands together. Dear God in your goodness, she prayed, please can you see your way to keeping a watchful eye on me. I really don't want to fall into that again, I want to live life with dignity. I'm not fussy about the details, but I think what I need is a generous dose of security, at least for the next little while. Thank you for putting Valdemar in my path. He is very welcome to stay in my life for a long, long time, and I actually think I do him a bit of good as well. Thank you in advance, very best wishes from Anna. Amen.

She sat there for a while longer, until the sun had vanished behind the forest to the west and the evening chill had come creeping in. Then she went into the house to make a start on the decorating.

20

'The Faringers are coming this evening. That's all right with you, isn't it?'

'What?'

'So then you won't need to go to his surgery on Monday.'

It was Saturday morning. Valdemar was lying in bed with his newspaper, coffee and a fair sprinkling of crumbs. Alice had just come out of the shower.

'Well, we were going out to meet up with Mats and Rigmor,' she went on, 'but they had some problem with their dogs, so I rang the Faringers instead.'

'You rang them while you were in the shower?'

'No, I rang them last night.'

'You didn't mention it last night.'

'No, I didn't.'

Valdemar waited for an explanation, but none was forthcoming. Alice stepped onto the scales instead and checked the result with a worried expression. 'Useless bloody scales,' she muttered out of the corner of her mouth. Then she stepped off and repeated the procedure. As far as Valdemar could tell, the result was just as depressing second time around.

'Aha,' he said. 'We'll be spending six hours shopping and cooking then, I presume?'

'No,' said Alice. 'What we thought was that we'd just have

mussels and garlic bread. Ingegerd and I will get it ready while you talk to Gordon. I asked him if that would be all right.'

Valdemar drained his coffee and closed his eyes.

'I see,' he said. 'So while you and Mrs Faringer deal with the mussels and sample the wine in the kitchen, Mr Faringer and I are going to sit in the study analysing my depression.'

'Exactly,' said Alice. 'What's wrong with that?'

Valdemar paused for thought.

'Nothing, Alice dear. It sounds a brilliant idea. Where do you get them all from?'

'Eh?' said Alice.

'I hope Wilma and Signe and Birger Butt will be joining us too,' continued Valdemar, inspired. 'Gordon could grab the chance of examining Birger Butt while he's at it, I think he could do with it. But maybe he hasn't got a psyche?'

Alice, arms akimbo, dug her clenched hands into what had once been her waist and glared at him.

'Now you're being unfair again, Valdemar! Of course he has. But none of them are going to be in tonight. Wilma and Signe are going to Stockholm to the dinner show at Wallmans salonger with their father, I've told you that ten times already.'

'Oh, is it today?' said Valdemar.

'Yes,' said Alice. 'It's today.'

'I thought it was next weekend.'

'It's all part of your depression,' said Alice. 'Not concentrating, forgetting things.'

'I have been feeling a bit forgetful lately, it's true,' admitted Valdemar, heading for the bathroom.

★

'So how are you?' Gordon Faringer asked him, ten hours later. 'No need to see this as an official consultation, by the way. But we can have a little chat now we're here, seeing as Alice is so keen.'

'At least we get out of scrubbing the mussels,' said Valdemar.

'Jolly good,' said Faringer. 'And this will be as confidential as any formal session, of course. So if you want to unload, be my guest.'

'There isn't much to unload, I'm afraid,' said Valdemar. 'It's Alice who claims I'm depressed, not me.'

'Yes, I know that,' said Faringer. 'But mild depressions are actually easier for other people to pick up on than for the person affected. Even the mild kind aren't much fun, you know, they can be a real drag.'

'I agree depression isn't a fun subject,' said Valdemar.

'Now now, no need for sarcasm,' said Gordon Faringer, winking as he raised his glass. 'Cheers, by the way.'

'Cheers,' said Valdemar.

They drank, and sat in silence for a while.

'Would you like me to ask a few questions?' Faringer said after a while.

'Yes, go on,' said Valdemar.

'You know that psychiatry isn't an exact science, not like you with your financial figures. But it is based in observable phenomena, nonetheless.'

'Naturally,' said Valdemar. 'There's no need to apologize.'

'Thank you,' said Faringer. 'Well, let's start with your mood. Would you say you were feeling in low spirits?'

Valdemar mulled this over. 'Sometimes,' he said. 'But it's been like that for forty years.'

'Nothing special to exacerbate it recently?'

'Nothing I can think of.'

'How are you sleeping?'

'I feel pretty tired.'

'But when you sleep, you sleep properly?'

'Yes.'

'Any recent change you've noticed?'

'I don't think so. Though one doesn't feel any perkier as the years go by.'

'Don't I know it,' said Gordon Faringer, plucking out one of his nose hairs. 'Your concentration, then? How's that? Any problems with that at work?'

Valdemar sipped his wine. 'Um, it's pretty much as usual there, too. But then concentration's never exactly been my strong suit. Alice says I forget things and I expect she's right.'

'Mhmm?' said Faringer. 'But you can still look forward to things?'

'Er,' said Valdemar, 'Christ knows. Can you?'

'Thanks for asking,' said Faringer. 'Well I've got my boat and the sea, you know. And the grandchildren, I get a lot out of all that, actually. But if I can press you a little on this one, how about your spark, your zest for life?'

'Spark? Zest for life?'

'Yes. It's only natural for things to get us down sometimes, but are there still things you can find fun in?'

Valdemar took off his glasses and started polishing them on his shirt. 'Listen, Gordon,' he said, 'if I really am depressed, what could be done about it anyway? I don't want to start taking a load of stuff. Happy pills and that kind of crap.'

Gordon Faringer nodded and put on a professionally grave expression. 'I can well understand that you don't, Valdemar. But they can give you a little lift, and that means quite a lot.

Give you back some pleasure in life and sense of purpose; you'd be surprised how many people are on a mild dose. Zest for life is damned important, anybody can see that. Going round feeling everything's at rock bottom really wears us down, to put it simply. Do you often think about death?'

'Off and on,' said Valdemar. 'But it's the same as the rest, I always have done.'

'Your father committed suicide, didn't he?'

'Yes he did,' said Valdemar. 'Thanks for reminding me.'

Faringer quietly studied his nails for a few seconds.

'Why do you say that?' he asked.

'Eh?' said Valdemar. 'What did I say?'

'You said: "Thanks for reminding me." About your father's death, that is.'

'Sorry,' said Valdemar. 'I don't know why I said that.'

'But you're not thinking of doing the same thing?'

'Not at all,' said Valdemar. 'Once you've managed to keep it at arm's length for so long, you can do it for the years you've got left as well.'

'Is that how you see it?'

'I don't really know how I see it. Life's bloody complicated . . . yes, that's more the problem as I see it. And it seems easier to lie to yourself, the older you get.'

'I don't quite follow,' said Faringer. 'You're sure nothing's happened recently to drag you down?'

'No,' said Valdemar.

'Absolutely certain?' said Faringer.

'I've no idea what it could possibly be, if so. Shall we go and see how they're getting on in the kitchen?'

'By all means. I'm glad to see you've got an appetite, anyway; that's a good sign. But, you know, I wouldn't mind seeing you again to do this a bit more formally, a proper appointment. How does next week look for you?'

'I've got a lot on next week,' said Valdemar.

'The week after?'

'All right,' said Valdemar. 'If you really think there's any point.'

'I most certainly do,' said Gordon Faringer, raising his glass. 'Here's to you, and now let's rejoin the womenfolk and get to work on those mussels.'

She finished the painting job late on Saturday night.

She judged it to be finished, at any rate, but it was tricky to be sure without seeing it in daylight. She would check in the morning, and there was plenty of paint left if she needed to do any touching up.

She knew he wouldn't be fussy, though, because he had said so and it was only the cheapest kind of topcoat. No need for it to be tip-top, Valdemar had stressed; she liked the word *tip-top*. It sounded so old-fashioned and safe, somehow. Especially the fact that there was no need to strive to be it.

Like with life, she thought, that didn't need to be tip-top either, but it could still have a touch of style. More or less like these walls, clean and neat, but not excessively smooth or special.

She'd enjoyed the work, too. The taping, the brushwork for corners and fiddly bits, then the tray and the roller, from the top down in long, even strokes; you could see the result straight away, and the whole thing looking smarter and smarter, stripe by stripe, metre by metre. There certainly weren't many jobs where you could see such instantly rewarding results as you could when you were painting, she thought. And it was easy to have a few general thoughts about life while you were doing it; nothing too deep, half your concentration on what you were doing, half on whatever happened to come into your head. It was a good combination. And then of course there was the symbolism of it: painting over all the old dirt and starting something new. Looking forward.

But now it was Saturday evening and the job was finished, both the kitchen and the living room. She couldn't do any more to it for now, at any rate. She put on her thick jumper and her jacket, went outside and sat in one of the new garden chairs. She lit the pipe and thought that the house really ought to have a lamp at the corner, or some other sort of outdoor lighting; maybe she could take it up with him on Monday. Suggest straight out that they fix up a lamp, why not?

Or even tomorrow. She hoped he might get time to come for a while on Sunday, as he had hinted. She shivered, in spite of her layers of clothes; there was a distinct feel of encroaching autumn, it couldn't be many degrees above zero this late in the evening and the darkness felt denser somehow. As if the cold was packing it more closely together and making it harder to forge your way through.

When there's no light, it's more important to be able to listen than to see, she thought. At night it's the sounds that matter, not the pictures; she tried to focus on her hearing but could only hear the usual muffled murmur of the forest. She wondered what kind of wildlife there was out there. Elk and foxes, that was for sure. Badgers too, and lots of smaller species: mice and voles and all those other names she couldn't bring to mind. And birds, of course; she wasn't very good at species of anything except snakes, because she had gone to a Montessori school for a term and a half, and they had spent almost all their time on snake-related projects, for some reason. But there weren't many kinds in Sweden. Adders, grass snakes and slow-worms, if she remembered rightly. And wasn't the slow-worm actually a lizard, if you wanted to split hairs?

Wolves? The thought suddenly occurred to her: what if there are wolves in the forest? Maybe there's a big male with yellow eyes and slavering jaws out there staring at me, over by the earth cellar.

But the idea didn't scare her, even if it was the case. Wolves didn't attack people, she knew that. Hardly any other animals did either, come to that, according to her biology teacher at upper secondary. No, it was humans who were humans' worst enemy, he told them in his distinctively mournful tone – he had just got divorced and moved to the area from some other town. She could sense that his wife was one of the enemies he had in mind.

And they were the only species on earth to behave like that, he added, more mournfully still. Svante Mossberg – his name suddenly came into her mind. The boys had called him Mossy, of course.

She moved a few metres, across to the currant bushes, pulled down her trousers and squatted to pee.

Humans are humans' worst enemy? That was undoubtedly correct. Why are we so bloody brilliant at being horrible to each other and hurting each other? As she pondered this conundrum, a penguin film she had seen a few years ago came into her head. It was about emperor penguins, those comical creatures that lived down in Antarctica in the harshest of conditions. Keeping their eggs safe, the male and female taking the responsibility in turns, walking long distances across the ice to get food and being entirely dependent on one another for their survival. Even though they barely met.

She pulled up her trousers and went indoors. She locked

the door and thought that was exactly what he was. Valdemar, her penguin.

Emperor penguin, no less.

She had a wash, cleaned her teeth and got into bed. I must remember to tell him, she thought.

Valdemar the Penguin. Perhaps she would have a go at writing a song about him. Why not?

She fell asleep with butterflies of expectation in her stomach.

Waking several hours later, she had an entirely different feeling. She stayed still, lying on one side with her hands between her knees, and tried to work out what it was. What had woken her. Whether it was something external or something internal; a sound from the house or the forest, or something she had dreamt. It was pitch black all around her, without a single streak of dawn light; she realized it couldn't be more than three or four o'clock, but stupidly enough she had left her watch over on the table, which she could not even see in the dense, inky blackness, however hard she strained her eyes. It made no difference whether her eyes were open or closed. Darkness, nothing but darkness.

But the sense of unease quivered within her. Maybe it didn't even need an excuse, she thought. Maybe you could be scared and distressed without particular cause? As if it was a sort of underlying state, at least at this time of night.

Could it be as simple as that? When you let your guard down and weren't ready for action, all the horrible, frightening things could worm their way inside your shell. Even though they had no name. Perhaps this was how small creatures felt, lying low in the primitive shelter of their holes while birds of prey circled beneath the sky with their sharp beaks and talons, trying to spot them.

The permanently ticking clock of fear. The undefined anxiety. The fragility of life. It could break at any moment; when you were least expecting it, death came knocking at the door.

Fuck, she thought. Why am I lying here worrying like this? It doesn't help to imagine myself as some cowering little creature, waiting for the hawk. What's the matter with me? What was it that woke me up?

She hadn't felt like this at Lograna before. Not even when that man was outside, staring at the house; that time she had known what it was that had scared her, but now it was kind of shapeless and inexplicable. And she'd always been afraid of the dark.

So I suppose it's the solitude, she thought. Sooner or later it'll drive you mad; her mother had said that once, and she couldn't remember if it was directed specifically at her or if it was a more general statement. You need other people in your life, she'd said anyway, no one can manage on their own in the long run.

Just like the penguins then, thought Anna. A solitary penguin is a dead penguin. And wasn't that precisely the warning Sonja at Elvafors had been trying to give her? Not to withdraw, because it was the contact with the others that offered the route to healing.

The others who were in the same boat. Yet you were supposed to cut all ties with the fellow addicts you'd hung around with. That was necessary in a way, she knew that, but it certainly encouraged you to seek solitude. Especially if you were already the kind of person who thrived on it.

But of course there were different kinds of people. The only thing you really had to fear was certain other people, she thought. And the only thing you absolutely couldn't do without was . . . certain other people.

Sensational conclusions I'm coming to here, she observed. There are people called Valdemar and there are people called Steffo. What a scoop.

She sighed and got up. Fumbled her way to her jumper and jacket without putting on the light. Pipe, tobacco and matches; then she put on Valdemar's boots and went out into the pitch black autumn night.

21

THE SECRET LIFE OF MR ROOS

The ICA store in Rimmersdal was open on Sundays, just as he had hoped. Only for a few hours, but it was eight minutes to closing time as he pulled up on the gravelled area outside, so they wouldn't have to stay late on his account. He was only buying a few bits today.

Yolanda wouldn't have to stay. It was funny: he hadn't been in her shop for several days now, and in that time he had barely spared her a thought. That's the way it is, he thought. When you get a grip on your life, it fills up with substance and meaning.

Never better than this.

He hadn't told Alice he was going out for a couple of hours, but he didn't need to, either. The opportunity simply presented itself: Alice had a meeting of her women's network Nymphs Unbound that afternoon, and Wilma and Signe still weren't back from their Stockholm jaunt.

A couple of buns and a litre of milk for their coffee, a bit of fruit and an evening paper, that was all, but when he got to the till he saw it was a different checkout operator. A rather pale young woman, who couldn't be much older than Anna or Signe. But of course, he thought, of course Yolanda has to have her days off, too.

Like everyone else.

He paid, packed his purchases in a plastic bag and left the shop. He got into the car and was just closing the door when his mobile phone bleeped. A text message had come in, something that seldom happened to Valdemar, and it was even more of a rarity for him to send one.

He thought he could still remember how to do it, though. He put the key in the ignition but didn't start the engine, fished the phone out of his breast pocket and brought up the message.

Why are you hiding from me? You're mine and I shall be with you very soon. S

He stared at it, not understanding a word. Who was S? Who was he supposed to have been hiding from?

You're mine? It sounded like . . . like a message of love. A woman writing to him and saying she would be with him. Good grief, thought Ante Valdemar Roos, surely it's not possible that . . . ?

No, he decided. Absolutely not. However much you had taken your life in your own hands, there were limits to what could happen. He was still in so-called reality; the notion that a woman with a name beginning with S was secretly in love with him – had been yearning for him for a long time, and was now going to be with him in some way or other – no, that was simply too much.

Or any woman beginning with any other letter, for that matter.

One has to understand life's possibilities, thought Ante Valdemar Roos, but also appreciate its limitations. Draw a clear boundary line between them, that was the trick.

So it had reached the wrong recipient. As simple as that. The sender had put in the wrong number, which he had quite often done himself, mainly because the pads of his fingers covered three or four keys simultaneously.

He reset his phone to its home screen, started the car and pulled out of the parking area. He was aware of a faint thrum in his temples; perhaps he'd had a few glasses too many last night with the Faringers, but if so, he was in good company. They hadn't gone home until after one, and even though the menu was only mussels, with fruit and ice cream for dessert, it was still quarter past two before he and Alice finished the washing-up and got to bed.

All these blessed glasses, Valdemar had found himself thinking. Why couldn't people just carry on drinking out of the same glass, maybe rinsing it out between times if they felt the need?

But he had downed at least a litre of water in the course of the morning, so hopefully his temples would stop throbbing once he was out in the fresh air at Lograna.

Imagine if I could simply stay over, he suddenly thought. Say to hell with going back tonight. We could both squeeze into that bed, the girl and me, couldn't we?

He cast a glance at his reflection in the rear-view mirror and reminded himself what he had just been thinking about boundary lines. Between possibilities and limitations.

I'll have to make do with coffee and a pipe of tobacco, he decided.

And an inspection of the paint job, of course.

'You've finished already?'

'Yes, I think I have.'

'What a difference it makes. You ought . . .'

'What?'

'You ought to be an interior designer or something.'

She laughed. 'Interior designer? Oh Valdemar, I only painted the walls. It takes a bit more than that to be a designer.'

'Maybe so,' nodded Valdemar. 'You made a bloody fine job of it, all the same. But what sort of career were you thinking of? Even if things have veered a bit off course for you lately, you must have plans?'

Anna stuck her hands in the pockets of her jeans and thought. 'Um, well, I don't really know,' she said. 'Maybe I ought to carry on studying. Finish upper secondary, at least. I'm not very good at deciding, it's difficult.'

'It isn't easy,' said Valdemar. 'It was simpler in my day.'

'Oh?' said Anna. 'In what way?'

He sighed. 'You ended up in some line of work. However you approached it. I happened to study economics, but was I interested in it? Like hell I was. Money's nice to have, but sitting there counting it day in and day out? No, stuff that.'

'So what would you have liked to do instead?'

He shrugged. 'I don't know. I'm just like so many people, getting grumpy and less satisfied as the years go by.'

'How do you mean?'

He did not reply, and after a while she prompted him. 'What are you actually trying to say, Valdemar?'

He gave another sigh. 'Well I expect you've noticed. I find it hard to make contact with people, hard to make contact with life, you could say. I suppose that's the big question, really . . .'

'What is?'

'What the hell the meaning of my life is.'

She sat down at the kitchen table and he joined her. She was watching him, her eyes looking restless and a bit uneasy, and he wondered why on earth he had said that to her. She was at least fifteen years younger than his son.

'Are you unhappy, Valdemar?'

'Oh no.'

'Are you sure about that?'

'Hmm, I suppose there are plenty who feel better. I hope so, anyway. It doesn't bloody well bear thinking about, otherwise.'

'So what would you like to do?'

'To do?'

'Yes.'

There was a long silence. He looked round the freshly painted walls, scratched the back of his neck and eventually his face broke into a cautious smile.

'It's really nice, Anna.'

'Yes,' said Anna. 'But you haven't answered my question.'

'About what I'd like to do?'

'Mm.'

He cleared his throat. 'Maybe that's the problem,' he said, and looked out of the window. 'If I really felt some real urge, it probably wouldn't be all that hard to set about it. But when you don't know, when you just feel out of place but haven't got a clue where you really want to be . . . well, then it seems a bit gloomier, somehow.'

'But you've got this.' She threw her arms wide. 'You bought this, didn't you? Wasn't this what you were longing for?'

Valdemar leant back. 'Well, yes,' he said. 'Yes, damn it, it is. But you get greedy, don't you? You want more.'

'I don't follow.'

He thought some more. 'I don't want to leave here, Anna. That's the trouble. Only being here on weekdays just doesn't feel enough.'

A few seconds passed in silence.

'How are things with you and your family?'

'Not good,' said Valdemar with a shake of the head. 'I expect you'd already worked that out. The girls couldn't care less about me. Alice is tired of me and I can completely understand that, but . . .'

'But?'

He gave a laugh. 'Little Anna, I really have no idea why I'm sitting here complaining to you. I'm almost forty years older than you, but you're the one who started it. It's as if . . . well, as if you're the one drawing it out of me.'

She gave a smile. 'Maybe I ought to be a psychologist or something.'

'Why not? You seem to have the knack.'

She considered this. 'Well, it does tend to be other people coming to me with their problems. Not the other way round, though it probably oughtn't to be that way.'

'Oh?'

'I feel as if I've spent so much time listening to friends who were unhappy.'

'Is that so?' said Valdemar. 'Well it's important not to mislay your instruction manual to life, that's what my grandad always used to say. Do you know what happened to me on the way here?' He brought out his mobile and glared at it. 'What do you think of this?'

It took him a while to locate the message but once he had, he passed it over. She took it and read the words on the screen. First with expectant curiosity on her face, but then her smile evaporated. She clapped her hand to her mouth and stared at him.

'What is it?' said Valdemar.

She shook her head and looked at the display again. 'This . . .'

'Yes?'

'This isn't to you, Valdemar. I think . . .'

'Isn't to me?'

'No, but I don't understand, how . . . ?' She stood up and began pacing the floor. 'I don't see how he can have got . . . ? Wait a minute, there must be a sender number.'

She grabbed the mobile phone and pressed a few keys, staring at the screen. 'Yes, there it is! Fuck, it's him. How the hell . . . ?'

She trailed off and stood there, mouth half open, a mixture of bewilderment and concentration in her eyes. Tiny pupils trying to bore their way to some kind of coherent whole. Valdemar, watching her, saw that she was holding her breath.

'That must be it,' she said in the end.

'Would you mind telling me what the heck is going on?' said Valdemar.

'Soon,' said Anna. 'Soon, I promise. Is it all right if I just ring my mother first?'

'Yes of course, give it a try. But remember how patchy it is. I'm not sure how you got through last time.'

She started tapping in the number and Valdemar got to his feet. 'I'll go in the other room while you ring.'

She nodded and put the phone to her ear. 'Shit! No reception.'

Valdemar turned in the doorway. 'Damn.'

She bit her lip and he suddenly realized she was close to tears – for some reason which he didn't understand, but which he hoped she would explain to him in due course. What he would have liked most of all was to give her a hug, to simply hold her for a little while – that was his first impulse, but he realized it didn't lie in the realm of possibility.

That boundary line again.

'You can try going a little way up the hill,' he said. 'You know, back along the road a hundred metres or so, and then left at the timber piles. I've rung from up there a few times.'

She nodded again. 'I'll just call her, and then she'll call me back.'

'No need to do that,' said Valdemar, and then she was out of the door and gone.

It was almost half an hour before she got back. He spent the time stretched out on the bed, looking at the walls and trying to enjoy the fact that they were newly painted. With scant success, but it was nothing to do with the paint colour or the workmanship. Of course not.

What's happened? he wondered. What in God's name did that message mean?

She'd said it was sent to her. It was Anna who had been hiding from someone called S, and she was the one who could expect a visit. She had known it instantly.

But it wasn't a source of pleasure to her. Quite the opposite; her reaction had made that abundantly clear. The text message had scared her, there was no doubt about it. She had no wish to see this S.

The good days are over now, thought Valdemar Roos, and he wondered why that particular phrase had decided to lodge in his brain. *The good days are over now.*

Not even a week had gone by.

But that was typical, of course. One hadn't the right to expect much.

*

'His name's Steffo,' she said as she came into the living room.

He sat up and swivelled his legs over the edge of the bed. 'Steffo?'

'Yes. He was my boyfriend.'

'I see.'

'He got the number from my dopey mum.'

'My mobile number? How did that happen?'

She sank down at the table and put her head in her hands. 'I called her from your mobile before, didn't I? Then he called her and asked where he could get hold of me. And my idiot mother gave him the number.'

'And you didn't want—'

'No way!' said Anna. 'He's crazy. I'm scared stiff of him. He thinks . . . no.'

'Go on.'

'He thinks he owns me, just cos we were together for a few months.'

'But you broke it off with him.'

She sighed and bit her lip. 'Sort of,' she said. 'Yes, I did, of course. When I went into that residential centre I broke off all contact with him, he must realize it's over. But . . .'

'But what?'

'But he's so fucking evil. I've made a lot of mistakes in my life. But getting together with Steffo was the worst one ever.'

She clasped her hands on her lap and for a moment he thought she was praying.

'Well, you'll just have to tell him.'

'Tell him what?'

'Tell him you don't want anything more to do with him.'

She shook her head. 'You don't understand,' she said.

'Oh?' said Valdemar.

'Steffo thinks you can own people the way you own things. And his message said he's coming here.'

Valdemar gave a laugh. 'Here? But how on earth would he find his way here?'

Anna looked at him doubtfully, chewing her knuckle. 'I don't know if he'd really be able to,' she said, 'but my mother gave him the name, too.'

'What name?'

'The name of this place. Lograna. I'd told her I was some-where called Lograna – I don't know why I did that. Because she asked and I wanted to reassure her, I suppose. She was really shaken when I told her I'd run away. But basically it means Steffo knows I'm at a place called Lograna.'

Valdemar pondered this for a moment. 'Hang on though,' he said. 'I don't think the name Lograna would be on any maps, would it?'

'That's what I'm not sure about,' said Anna. 'Have you ever tried doing an internet search for it?'

'No,' said Valdemar.

'It might come up,' said Anna. 'And then he'd be able to find his way here. I've got to get away, Valdemar.'

'Now just you wait a minute,' said Valdemar. 'Let's put the coffee on and talk this over.'

'What is there to talk about?'

'Plenty. You can't carry on running away from this Steffo, surely you can see that?' He paused and reflected. 'I mean, what sort of life is that for you? He's just got to get it into his head that you don't want any more to do with him.'

'I wish it was as simple as that,' said Anna. 'If all I had to do was tell him.'

'Have you tried?'

She shrugged her shoulders. 'Not in so many words. Do you think we should answer his text?'

Valdemar suddenly felt a sort of warm glow inside him, and he realized what had prompted it. She had used that little word *we*. Shall *we* answer his text?

'We'll put the coffee on and talk it over,' he said again. 'And I don't really think he could find his way here. This place has been hidden from the world for a good few years. And I've no intention of letting you run off in a panic.'

Anna nodded and they both went into the kitchen. 'I'm so grateful that you exist,' she said.

Her eyes were glistening as she said it. He looked at the clock. It was already half past five; he wondered how long that women's network meeting could be expected to last.

22

They decided against replying to the text.

But if she asks me to stay, I will, he thought several times as they had their coffee, talked and shared a pipe. I don't give a toss about the repercussions; I've got to behave like a moral human being. I can't damn well leave a frightened kid out in the middle of the forest.

If she asks me, that is.

Expressly asks me.

But she didn't. Maybe she came close to it, he couldn't really judge. Several times he thought he detected the question in her eyes, but it was never put into words. He made her promise to stay a couple more days, at least. She took some persuading, but in the end she agreed. Once he had said goodbye and climbed into the car, it struck him that she had only done it to avoid discussing the matter. Perhaps she would be gone when he returned the next morning?

It was an almost unbearable thought. That was how it suddenly felt. Unbearable. What the devil is happening to me? thought Ante Valdemar Roos as he turned out onto the Rödmossen road. What's become of my old life?

He could see in his mind's eye how it would be the next morning.

He saw himself feel for the key in its hiding place, unlock

the door, come into the newly painted and utterly empty house. Just a note on the table: *I decided to go after all. Thank you Valdemar. Good luck with Lograna and everything else. Hugs from Anna.*

Christ almighty, he thought. It can't turn out that way. Life can't be that fucking awful. Not even mine.

And the painted walls, which would forever remind him of those strange days they'd spent together.

A week – it was the previous Monday he had discovered there was somebody living in the house, but it was only on the Wednesday she'd plucked up the courage to show herself.

She had played the guitar and sung for him. No one else had ever done that for him, especially not a woman. He had cried and she had let him cry without asking questions.

As tears go by.

He shook his head and clenched his teeth until his jaw ached. He didn't know why, but he found himself grasping the steering wheel more tightly too, and saw that his knuckles were turning white – and then his father popped up again.

That walk in the forest. The tall, straight pines. The rocks and the clumps of lingonberry bushes. This is where we see the elk.

Never better than this.

I'm falling apart, thought Ante Valdemar Roos. I'm close to breaking down.

She stayed at the window for a good while after he drove away. She was trying to find some approximation of a stable feeling amongst all those that were swirling round inside her. A centre of gravity.

But nothing seemed in the mood to stabilize, everything

just went on spinning and dancing like specks of dust in a ray of sunlight. It was only once she had sat down at the table again and poured herself another cup of coffee that she was able to hold on to anything concrete. It wasn't much, but at least it could be put into words.

The first thing was a question: What the hell shall I do?

The second was an exhortation: Make up your mind, Anna Gambowska!

The third was an old song: *Should I stay or should I go?*

She couldn't remember the name of the group, but it didn't matter. That was just the way of things: whatever agonies you were suffering, whatever acts of folly or states of wretchedness you had got tangled up in, there was always some hackneyed pop song to match the occasion.

But no wonder, really. Everything in music was about life and death and love, and when it came to the crunch in real life, it was as serious there, too. Just as serious and just as hackneyed.

Should I stay or should I go?

And go where, if she opted for the latter?

It was the same old question. Though now it was suddenly so much worse, if Steffo really was on his way. Anything at all, she thought, I can bear anything at all except seeing Steffo right now.

That, at any rate, was a feeling that felt pretty stable.

The worst thing was that she could so easily imagine him tracking her down. He was that sort of person. He would relish it in his own perverse way. Go online, search for *Lograna*. Find it on the map, pack his rucksack with some beer and hash, hop on his scooter and set off.

Stay or go?

How far could it be from Örebro to Lograna? Two hundred

kilometres? Three hundred, maybe? One thing was for sure, it wouldn't be too far for Steffo once he'd set his pig-headed mind on it.

If Steffo comes here then that's the end for me, she thought. There are no two ways about it. I shall give up.

She went outside and lit the pipe. It was already starting to get dark and the sky was covered in thick cloud, which helped the darkness come all the quicker, of course. Once she had taken a few puffs her conversation with Marja-Liisa came into her mind.

It helped the darkness come all the quicker.

Go, she thought. I daren't stay another night.

And if Valdemar had genuinely wanted her to stay, she asked herself, why had he left her? He must have realized she was scared. She didn't want to admit it to herself, but she knew this was what tipped the scale for her.

He didn't really want her to stay.

And why should he? What was she imagining? She had painted the walls and done her share. Paid her debt of gratitude and now they were quits.

So go it was.

She swallowed down the lump in her throat and went indoors.

And it was only a short while later, as she was in the living room packing her rucksack, that she looked out of the window and noticed two things.

One was that it had started to rain.

The other was that there was a scooter parked on the road, a short distance away.

She hadn't heard it. He must have freewheeled the last bit, she thought. That was typical of him, too.

23

He had just come through Rimmersdal when his mobile rang.

He saw it was Alice and afterwards he really didn't know what had made him answer at all.

'Where are you?'

'I went out for a drive.'

'Went out for a drive?'

'Yes.'

'You've never done that before, have you?'

'I drive my car every day, Alice dear.'

'But today's Sunday. I want to talk to you, Valdemar.'

'Oh yes? How was the Nymphs' meeting?'

'Interesting. To put it mildly.'

'Oh yes?'

'Where are you? Are you alone in the car?'

'I beg your pardon?'

'Are you alone in the car?'

'Of course I'm alone. I'll be back in quarter of an hour. I just went for a drive . . . well, out towards Kymmen, that's all. What did you want to talk about?'

She paused for a moment. He could hear her drinking something.

'What were you doing on Friday, Valdemar?'

'On Friday?'

'Yes.'

'Nothing special, I don't think.'

'You didn't go into town or anything?'

'During the day?'

'Yes, during the day.'

'No. Why would I have done that?'

'You didn't go to Ljungman's for lunch?'

'Ljungman's? No, of course not.'

'That's very odd. Because it so happens Karin Wissman saw you there. Can you explain that to me, Valdemar?'

He thought for a moment.

'I really don't know what you're talking about, Alice.'

'Don't you? And you had a young woman with you, Karin says. A *very* young woman.'

'What?'

'You heard.'

'This makes no sense, Alice. I simply don't understand how she could have made that mis—'

'She saw you from just a few metres away, Valdemar. You said hello to her. What the hell are you up to?'

He removed the phone from his ear and contemplated the little gadget with distaste. Then he pressed the Dismiss key as hard as he could, tossed the phone into the glove compartment and pulled in at the side of the road.

He switched off the engine and leant his head back on the headrest.

So there we are, he thought, taking off his glasses. It's come to this. Time to decide.

And the first heavy raindrops landed on the bonnet.

TWO

24

Detective Inspector Barbarotti was sitting at a poker table.

A low-hanging lamp cast a sallow light over a green baize surface. A considerable pot made up of coins, counters and banknotes took pride of place in the middle of the table while cigar and cigarette smoke spiralled slowly up towards the ceiling, dissolving in the gloom above the lampshade. Quiet music, a silky female voice singing jazz, was issuing from invisible loudspeakers as he slowly, slowly slipped a third ace behind a ten and transformed two pairs into a full house.

There were three of them playing. Apart from Barbarotti himself there were two other gentlemen, whose faces he could not really see because the confounded lamp was so low, but he was sure they were worthy, not to say superior, opponents.

On the other hand: a full house with aces was not to be sniffed at. He scrabbled in his jacket pockets for extra money to add to the pot, but soon discovered that the only funds he had left were a few superannuated and worthless Polish złoty notes and a postage stamp of very dubious value. He could see that his opponents were aware of his awkward situation and before he could reach any kind of decision, one of them bowed his head into the circle of light and smiled a very sardonic smile, his cigar still in his mouth.

'It is your soul you are expected to stake, Monsieur Barbarotti,' he said with studied oiliness. 'Nothing less than your soul.'

The other gentleman did not lean his face forward for inspection but contented himself with a curt 'Correct', and Gunnar Barbarotti realized all at once who he was playing against. They were the Devil and God, not just any old players, in other words, and the instant this came home to him, he was no longer in his seat but floundering on his back amongst the coins, counters and notes in the big pot beneath the lamp, a poor, pathetic, Lilliputian figure dressed in nothing but his pride, his watch and his underpants and without the slightest chance of influencing the course of events.

'That's right, my little friend,' mumbled Our Lord distractedly. 'You're nothing more than a pawn in the game, had you forgotten that simple precondition?'

'No talking to the pot, dear brother,' the Devil chided him. 'Is that puny little thing all you want to stake? It certainly points to the direction this game is heading.'

'He is as he is,' commented Our Lord in a slightly mournful tone. 'You have to take the rough with the smooth.'

'Sometimes you really hit the nail on the head, I have to give you that,' chuckled the Devil.

Gunnar Barbarotti tried to get to his feet but slipped on a five kronor coin that had missed its mark, came down hard on his backside and woke up.

White walls, white ceiling. Bright light, some kind of disinfectant smell and a taste of metal on his tongue. He was lying on his back, feeling sick; one of his legs was as heavy as lead, and there was a distant echo of voices and footsteps out in a corridor.

I'm in hospital, was his first thought after God and the Devil had deserted him. I've just come round, something must have happened, but there's nothing wrong with my head. It must be that leg, of course.

Satisfied with these conclusions, he fell asleep and woke again after a period of time that was probably only a minute or a few seconds, because he had no difficulty taking up the thread of his thoughts where he had left it.

That leg. It was in plaster. His left leg, the whole foot and the entire lower leg, up to the knee. But he could move his arms, he could clench his fists and when he gave the order to his packaged foot to wiggle its toes, they wiggled.

So, thought Gunnar Barbarotti, closing his eyes, I've broken my left leg. It happens in the best families. Everything else is in order. They've operated on it and they had to put me to sleep, of course.

Then he went back to sleep again.

Waking for the third time, he remembered the whole story. The poker game in the dream came back to him as well, and in some way it felt as if the one was interconnected with the other.

His falling off a roof, and God and the Devil playing poker for his soul.

Rubbish, he thought irritably. I can't have been that close to death, and Our Lord would doubtless have given me a heads up if that much danger were imminent.

Our Lord was currently thirteen points above the existence line – Barbarotti was taken aback for a moment that he could remember the exact figure so clearly – and had every reason to keep on good terms with the inspector. So that was that.

He was aware that this line of argument wasn't exactly

unimpeachable, logically speaking, but the sharp, metallic taste in his mouth was no doubt affecting his concentration. But there had been no anaesthetic, after all. He found he could remember the whole operation, one excruciating detail after another, so perhaps they had given him some kind of sedative afterwards. That must be it. If it were left to him he would always prefer to sleep through the whole thing; that sort of decision, however, was entrusted not to the patient but to the orthopaedic specialist. For good reason, he supposed.

One thing was indisputable, anyway, and that was the fact that he had tumbled off the roof. He had landed left foot first in a wheelbarrow some idiot had left out on the soft lawn – presumably that idiot was himself – and it had hurt so bloody much that he had fainted.

Marianne had rushed to the rescue with that prize pest Brother-in-law Roger hot on her heels, and eventually they were joined by a neighbour called Peterzén, a retired pilot and fanatical supporter of the Stockholm football team AIK, and then the ambulance and its crew, who set to work twisting his foot straight, and he fainted again, because it hurt more than anything conceivably could.

Then something for the pain and the trip to the hospital, and a host of nurses and doctors pushing and pulling, breaking and observing and conferring, and finally making sure he didn't pass out for a third time, because it would be a shame for him to miss something as interesting as his own operation.

And now the operation was over. Now he would be fine. Now all he had to do was lie in a bed and be looked after for days and weeks, he would never . . . Well, at any rate, he would never go up on the roof and hammer nails into laths and try to prove to Brother-in-law Roger what a handy devil he was. Or to Marianne or her children or anybody else.

You had to be aware of the possibilities open to you, but above all of your limitations, thought Gunnar Barbarotti. Admittedly he was a detective inspector and had had a degree in law hanging around unexploited ever since his student days in Lund, but he was born all fingers and thumbs and had always been slightly afraid of heights.

And even though the pain had sent him to the very edge of consciousness, he had not managed to avoid hearing what one of the paramedics said to the other.

'Here he is with five hundred square metres of soft grass, and he goes for a wheelbarrow. Smart guy.'

The door opened and a nurse came into the room.

'So you're awake?' He'd thought people only talked like that in old movies and books, but evidently not.

He tried to agree with what she had said but his metallic mouth had stopped working. Nothing came out but a sort of wheeze, followed by a coughing fit.

'Try to drink something,' she said, passing over a cup with a straw in it.

He did. He cast a meaningful glance at the lump of plaster and then an enquiring one into her blue eyes.

'Yes,' she said. 'It went well. Dr Parvus will be coming in to talk to you. You're not in any pain?'

He shook his head.

'Press the button if you need anything. Dr Parvus will be in to see you soon.'

She studied a chart hanging at the foot of the bed, then gave him an encouraging look and left the room.

★

Before he nodded off again he lay very still in the bed and looked out of the big window, where he could observe a yellow building-site crane moving with slow gravity against the bright-blue autumn sky. It had a beauty to it, thought Gunnar Barbarotti, a kind of majesty. And dignity. I want to be a crane in my next life, he decided, and then the women will come flocking round me.

As he watched its beautiful, dignified motion, he also took the opportunity of reflecting a little on the situation; even if the fall from the roof hadn't been a near-death experience, it somehow seemed natural to do so.

His own personal situation, that was to say – his place in the system of coordinates known as life in his forty-ninth year – and whatever attitude one took to cause and effect and consequence, one could only endorse the view that quite a lot had happened recently.

In the past year, in fact. This time last autumn – September, or the end of August anyway, if you wanted to be particular – he had been living all alone in his three-room flat in Baldersgatan. Hard to believe, but it was true, and he remembered his habit of sitting on the balcony in the evenings, watching the swarms of jackdaws circle over the steep roofs of the Cathedral School as he brooded on strange events in Finistère in France and wondered what would become of him in life. Whether he would spend his remaining ten or twenty or thirty years in the same solitary, increasingly depressing and tucked-away life – or whether Marianne would say yes and a new spring would lie ahead for him.

Yes, they had been pretty much the options, thought Barbarotti, taking his eyes off the stately crane for a second to behold his gigantic – and, like the crane, not unimpressive –

plastered lump of a leg. There was something itching in there, but he assumed he would just have to grin and bear it. He didn't think they would be prepared to crack open their splendid handiwork just so a simple DI could scratch an itch.

He went back to the crane and his life. Mused on how immensely remote Baldersgatan now felt, like something he had left behind him long, long ago – in a life that had actually been nothing but a waiting room. A pause for breath after his divorce from Helena. Waiting for something new and real, you might say.

He had hibernated there for five years, sharing the place with his beloved daughter Sarah, who had most certainly provided a bit of light in his darkness; then . . . well, then it had happened, a new life had started. All of a sudden, just like that. Or so it might appear in retrospect. Now he had 350 square metres to play with, in a big old wooden house by the shore out at Kymmen Point. Neighbours pleasantly far removed, a garden that had run rather wild, a loan of one and a half million from Swedbank, and a woman he loved.

And that amount of floor space really was needed, seeing as there were currently – he paused and tallied them up – nine people living there.

Good grief, he thought. From a one-person household to a family of nine within a year. Talk about consequences. He stared at the crane and found he was smiling. There was a quietly purring sense of satisfaction deep inside him, no point trying to hide it, and it was all about . . . well in actual fact, it was only about him and Marianne, when it came down to it.

But a lot of other baggage had come as part of that deal, and as Inspector Barbarotti had always liked making lists –

since right back when he was in short trousers – he made one in his head now.

A list of the residents of Villa Pickford, as Mr Hugger, the factory owner whose house it originally was, had named his creation. He was an early film fan and when he built the house in the mid-1930s he named it after his favourite actress.

So there were *Gunnar* and *Marianne* for a start. They were the ones who had decided to get hitched and now lived together as man and wife – though she had decided to stick to her maiden name of Grimberg. He had never criticized her for it, and if she felt like changing her name to Barbarotti at some future date, it could no doubt be organized. Who else then?

His kids, of course: *Sara*, 20; *Lars* and *Martin*, 14 and 12.

Marianne's children: *Johan*, 16; and *Jenny*, 14.

Sara's boyfriend *Jorge*, 20, but they would both be moving out soon because they had a flat – a shabby but cheap bedsit in Kavaljersgatan in the Väster district that they were doing up, a project that was now into its third month, but by all reasonable estimates it ought to be finished before Christmas. The problem was that both of them had their studies and their jobs and all sorts of other things to take into consideration, and they evidently felt very much at home at Villa Pickford.

They had known each other for six months and Papa Barbarotti thought they could very well wait a while before moving in together, but in this – as in much else – he had no say.

Anyway, for now they were still living at Villa Pickford, and as there were at least ten rooms in the big old place, it didn't present any problems.

Problems abounded, on the other hand, in the person of

the extended family's ninth member, *Brother-in-law Roger*. The prize pest.

Roger Grimberg was Marianne's brother, ten years older than she was, and of course the intention was not for him to stay indefinitely.

But he was as handy as a MacGyver; if you gave him an egg, two pencils and a rubber band, he could make a helicopter in eight minutes. It was practical having him in the house while renovations were still in progress, there was no denying that. And renovations had been in progress ever since they moved in on the first of November. Ten and a half months now. Brother-in-law Roger had been with them full-time for the last five of those, which was the period for which he had been unemployed.

Normally – when he wasn't banging in nails or sawing or painting or replacing window frames or laying floors or rewiring or installing stoves at Villa Pickford – he lived in Lycksele and worked as a traffic warden.

I can't imagine there's much call for traffic wardens up there in a little place like Lycksele, Barbarotti would often think. So of course he's bloody unemployed.

The thing about Roger Grimberg, apart from the fact that he was so horribly handy that he brought the backs of Barbarotti's knees out in a rash, was that he liked his drink, and was very fond of airing his views on the state of the world.

The alcohol was relatively under control; he limited himself to a six-pack of beer a day, weekdays and weekends alike. His analysis of the world about him, on the other hand, was harder to put up with.

When you were crawling about with him on a hot roof, for example, knocking nails into things called laths. Was that what made me fall off? thought Barbarotti. Was it one of Brother-in-law Roger's pronouncements? He couldn't remember exactly what had preceded his plunge into the wheelbarrow, but he did recall Roger going on at some length about Swedish companies that moved their production abroad – to Eastern Europe and South East Asia – but that was while they were still down on the ground, packing nails into their hernia belts. He and Roger, that was, not the companies. Presumably they weren't really called hernia belts, but Gunnar Barbarotti liked giving his own names to all those workmen's accoutrements. It was a matter of integrity and the right to defend your own philosophy of life, and if it got on the prize pest's nerves into the bargain, then that was a bit of a bonus. If he could annoy him so much that he decided to move back home to his little flat in Lycksele, then that was a hell of a bonus.

Marianne had hinted at it, just the other day. She said her brother was homesick.

It would undeniably be ideal, thought Inspector Barbarotti, adjusting the pillows under his head, if that numbskull could finish banging in the nails on his own while I'm in hospital recovering. Then shove off back up north to his parking meters and stay there.

With this optimistic thought in his head, and the image of the stately crane before his eyes, he fell asleep again, and neither God nor the Devil saw fit to trouble him any further that day.

Not with poker games nor with anything else.

A woman turned up instead, and it took him a few seconds to realize he was actually awake.

She was standing at his bedside, a woman of about fifty. She was sturdily built, though you couldn't exactly call her fat, and her hair colour, reminiscent of a glass of burgundy, really did not go with her restless, pale-blue eyes.

She was dressed in white, and he realized she must be on the staff in some capacity.

'Excuse me,' she said. 'My name is Alice Ekman-Roos. I'm a nurse on this ward. You aren't one of my patients though, and perhaps you don't remember me?'

He read the name badge on one side of her chest. Her name was indeed Ekman-Roos, and it was also very true that he did not remember her. He shook his head and tried to look apologetic.

'No, I'm sorry.'

'We were in the same class at upper secondary,' she said. 'Only for one year, but anyway.'

Alice Ekman? he thought. Yes, maybe. Maybe there had been someone of that name, though not that hair colour, he was sure of that . . . in the first year, he assumed, because he'd changed to a different course at the start of the second year. Yes, it could be her.

'I know you're a police officer and all that, and if you're too tired you must just say. I was wondering if I could ask you something.'

He could see that she was uncomfortable. That she felt some sense of shame about approaching him in this way. Perhaps she'd been there for a while, waiting for him to wake up?

'Alice Ekman?'

'Yes.'

'Yes, I think I remember you. You had a friend called Inger, didn't you?'

Her face relaxed and looked a little less worried for a moment.

'That's right. Inger Mattsson. We always went around together.'

'What can I do for you?' he asked. 'I've just had an operation, but I'm sure you know that.'

'Yes, I know,' she said. 'That was why I thought I should grab the chance . . . while you're on my ward, that is. You'll be going back to orthopaedic soon.'

'Where am I now?'

'This is post-op. You'll only be here a few hours.'

'Ah, I see,' said Barbarotti.

She ran a hand over her hair and glanced uneasily towards the door.

'The thing is . . . the thing is that I've got a problem and I don't know whether to tell the police or not. I don't know anyone I can ask, either.'

Barbarotti let his eyes rest on the crane while he waited.

'It's a bit embarrassing and I don't really want it to get out. But on the other hand . . .'

'Yes?'

'On the other hand, it could be serious. I've been thinking about it for two days now and I simply don't know what to do. So when I saw your name here, well . . . I thought maybe I could ask your advice, at least.'

She paused and cleared her throat, clearly nervous. 'I'm sorry for barging in like this, it's not something I'd do in normal circumstances, of course, but . . . well, I'm a bit desperate, basically.'

'Desperate?'

'Yes.'

Gunnar Barbarotti clutched the mattress with both hands and tried to pull himself more upright in the bed.

'What's happened, then?' he asked.

She looked at his plastered leg for a while before she answered. She bit her lower lip as her index fingers restlessly massaged the insides of her thumbs.

'It's my husband,' she said. 'He seems to have gone and disappeared.'

25

'And why don't you want to report it?'

Four hours later.

A different ward and no yellow crane. Instead, a green folding screen round two sides of the bed, a laudable attempt at creating an illusion of privacy.

But only an illusion. There were two other patients in the same room, sporting plaster casts on various parts of their anatomy, and clearly within hearing distance unless you whispered. One of them, a gentleman in his eighties, was speaking loudly to his wife on the phone and leaving no one in any doubt that this was the case.

Marianne had been to visit. Sara and Jorge, too. A number of doctors and nurses had taken a look at Barbarotti and assured him everything had gone to plan and he was doing fine. He would be discharged tomorrow or the day after, and he could reckon on being in plaster for four to six weeks. They would probably need to redo it once or twice in that time.

But now Alice Ekman-Roos was back again, even though he wasn't on her ward any longer. It was half past seven in the evening and the sky outside the window had started to deepen towards violet.

She filled her lungs and looked at him earnestly.

'Because it might only be one of those embarrassing everyday stories, the whole thing.'

He gave himself a moment before responding.

'The police are used to embarrassing everyday stories.'

She sighed and her gaze drifted away from him. She stared out of the window instead. 'I know that,' she said. 'I just don't want word getting out, if it turns out to be that way . . . but it could be something really serious. Like I said.'

'Serious?'

'Yes, something could have happened to him. Something awful.'

'I don't quite understand what it is you want me to do,' said Barbarotti. 'I'm somewhat indisposed, as you can see.'

He gestured towards his plastered leg and tried to produce an ironic grimace.

'Of course. I'll leave you in peace right away if you'd rather. I just wanted a bit of advice. Seeing as we were both in the same school class once, and you're a policeman and so on.'

Gunnar Barbarotti nodded. She had got that far already, before they were interrupted in post-op.

And there wasn't much more to it, either. Except that the missing husband was called Valdemar and she hadn't seen him since Sunday. Today was Tuesday. He took a drink of water from the paper cup on his bedside table and made up his mind.

'All right,' he said. 'You're welcome to tell me the whole story. It's not as though I've anything else on at present.'

'Thank you,' she said, pulling up her chair. 'Thank you so much. Yes, I remember you always seemed a decent type . . . back then, I mean, when we were at school. Not that we ever really got to know each other.'

'Sunday,' said Barbarotti, to divert her from any more school chat. 'You say your husband has been gone since Sunday.'

She gave a little cough and folded her hands. 'That's right. I spoke to him on the phone around six. Since then I haven't heard a word from him.'

'On the phone? He wasn't at home, then? Do you live here in Kymlinge?'

She nodded. 'Yes, in Fanjunkargatan. We've lived there ever since we got married. About . . . ten years ago. We've each got a first marriage behind us. That's the way it goes these days.'

'I'm in the same position myself,' admitted Barbarotti.

'Oh? Well, nothing like this has ever happened with Valdemar before. He's quite a safe – a lot of people would probably say boring – sort of man. Rather reserved, if you know what I mean? He really isn't the kind of person you'd expect to disappear. It's totally unlike him, and besides, he's ten years older than me.'

Barbarotti was slightly at a loss to understand what the age difference had to do with any tendency to disappear, but he didn't bother to query that detail.

'What you can't decide,' he said instead, 'is whether he did it of his own volition?'

She looked startled. 'How can you know that?'

He spread his hands. 'Unless you had some suspicions of that sort, I don't get what's embarrassing about it.'

She let this sink in and he could see that she was buying his line of argument. 'Of course,' she said. 'Of course it can hardly be the first time you've come across something like this. Well, yes, it is possible that he's staying away because he wants to, just as you say.'

'How much have you tried to find out?' asked Barbarotti. 'Off your own bat, so to speak.'

A blush spread across her large, smooth face.

'Nothing,' she said.

'Nothing?' said Barbarotti.

'No. It would be . . .'

'Yes?'

'It would be dreadfully embarrassing if that turned out to be true. If he'd simply left me. I've been telling myself he'll probably be in touch before long . . .'

'His place of work? He has a job, I assume?'

She nodded and shook her head in a single, confused movement. 'Yes, but I haven't called them.'

'Why not? Where does he work?'

'Wrigman's Electrical. I don't know if you know them. They make thermos flasks and suchlike. Out in Svartö.'

'I know where it is,' said Barbarotti. 'Well, that's one thing I would advise. Ring them and see what you can find out before you contact the police.'

'Yes,' she said, and looked down. 'I ought to do that, of course. And I know I'm being a bit silly about all this.'

He felt a vague sense of sympathy for the woman starting to stir inside him. If her husband really had left her without a word of explanation, there was no need to be condescending. And he had the time, as he'd said.

'So there are particular reasons making you think this might be his own choice?' he asked. 'Am I reading you right on that point?'

She studied her clasped hands for a moment before she answered. 'Yes,' she said. 'There are particular reasons. Valdemar hasn't been behaving quite as normal recently. The girls and I all noticed it.'

'The girls?'

'We've got two daughters. Well, they're both mine, from my previous marriage. But they live with us. Signe and Wilma. They're twenty and sixteen.

'And you . . . you've all felt your husband hasn't been behaving normally lately?'

'Yes.'

'In what way?'

She tried to frown, but there was far too little skin and far too much brow bone for this to succeed. 'I . . . don't really know,' she faltered. 'It isn't anything I can put my finger on, but it's definitely been noticeable. Things he's said and so on . . . you pick up on little changes like that when you've been living together a long time. I think . . .'

'Yes?'

'I don't know, but I thought maybe he was suffering from some kind of depression. He wondered the same thing himself, and we even had a chat with a psychiatrist we know . . . but there's something else as well, which I heard about on Sunday. It may have nothing to do with this, but I still couldn't help worrying.'

'I see,' said Barbarotti. 'And what was it you heard about on Sunday?'

She swallowed and her blush reappeared, accompanied by the sun, which took the opportunity of sending its final rays of the day through the window.

'One of my friends reported a sighting,' she said.

'A sighting of what?'

'I don't really know how to describe it. But basically she saw Valdemar with . . . with a young woman.'

Aha, thought Barbarotti. There we have it. I thought so.

'It's possible, of course, that it was something entirely innocent,' Alice Ekman-Roos continued. 'I mean to say, she could have been a colleague or whatever, but the thing is that . . . well, that he denies it. My friend saw them from about a metre away and she and Valdemar said hello to each other. Valdemar and this woman were coming out of a restaurant. Why should he deny it, if it was so innocent?'

'That's a good question,' said Barbarotti. 'And when did this . . . sighting occur?'

'On Friday. They were coming out of Ljungman's on Norra torg. You know where . . . ?'

'Oh yes,' confirmed Barbarotti. 'But how did your husband react when you confronted him, so to speak, with this? That was on Sunday wasn't it, if I've got this right?'

'Yes, quite right,' said Alice Ekman-Roos. 'But all I can say is that he denied it. And that's the last thing I heard from him.'

'The last thing?'

'Yes.'

'Hang on, was this in the phone conversation you had that afternoon? You telling him the story and him denying it?'

She nodded, and for the first time her eyes looked unnaturally bright, as if she was on the verge of tears. 'I'd just heard it from my friend. I came home and he wasn't in. I called his mobile and told him what I'd just heard, and he . . . well, he said she must have made a mistake. He wasn't at Ljungman's on Friday at all. Then he cut me off mid-call. Or there was a problem on the line, I don't know which.'

'When was this encounter on Friday supposed to have taken place?'

'At lunchtime. That's another odd thing. Why would he have been in town at that time of day?'

'He should have been out in Svartö, at work.'

'Yes.'

'But perhaps he did come into town occasionally?'

'Not that I'm aware.'

Barbarotti pondered and the sun disappeared.

'Where was he?' he asked. 'When you called him, I mean.'

She sighed. 'He said he'd taken the car out for a drive round by Kymmen, but I don't know. He never does that sort of thing. He said he'd soon be home.'

'But he never came home?'

'No. I called him again that evening, of course, but I got no answer. Nor yesterday, nor today.'

'Have you called him a number of times?'

'Yes.'

'Tried texting?'

'Yes.'

'I see,' said Barbarotti. 'Well, I think the situation's clear to me now.'

'Is that the expression you use?'

'What?'

'In the police. Do you say the situation's clear to you?'

He gave no answer. She pulled back her shoulders and took a deep breath, and he waited for whatever was coming next.

But nothing came. She just sat there, looking out of the window, out onto the forest and the river, not caring that tears were running down her cheeks. On the other side of the protective screen, someone entered the room with a clattering trolley and he realized their conversation would soon be at an end.

'One more thing,' he said. 'Who knows he's missing?'

'Only me.'

'Not your daughters?'

'I told them he was away on a business trip.'

'Is that something he does, go away on business trips?'

'Never. But they're very wrapped up in themselves. It's their age.'

Barbarotti nodded and thought for a moment. 'All right,' he said. 'Well, it sounds like rather an unfortunate matter, regardless of what's actually happened. I can understand you feeling worried, but I still think the best thing you can do is ring his place of work and make some enquiries.'

And this was the point at which she surprised him even more than she had done already.

'Couldn't you do it?' she said. ' I'd consider it a real favour.'

His own answer was no less surprising.

'OK then. If you give me the number, I'll do it in the morning.'

Half an hour after Alice Ekman-Roos left him, Marianne rang.

'How are you, my darling?' she wanted to know.

'Better than I deserve,' admitted Gunnar Barbarotti. 'And they say I won't have to go do any work for a while.'

'All kinds of work?' asked Marianne.

'Especially all kinds of DIY,' said Barbarotti.

'And is there any pain?'

'None at all.'

'You really are lucky, then,' said Marianne with a laugh. 'You know what, I'm so awfully glad you're alive. You're so clumsy and things could have turned out a great deal worse.'

'Thanks,' said Barbarotti. 'Well anyway, I'm looking forward to making love with one leg in plaster. It's something I've always wondered about . . . how it would work, that is.'

'Would you like me to come over tonight?' asked Marianne.

'I don't think it's entirely set yet,' said Barbarotti. 'Don't take this the wrong way, but I think we might have to wait until I get home.'

'I didn't mean it like that,' said Marianne. 'Just thought I could look in and kiss you goodnight.'

'You'd be better off kissing the rest of the family goodnight,' said Barbarotti, 'wouldn't you?'

'I suppose so,' sighed Marianne, and he could virtually hear her rolling her eyes. 'Six kids and a boozing brother – sounds like a film, doesn't it? Yes, I guess it would be best for me to stay here.'

'Sara and Jorge aren't kids,' Barbarotti reminded her. 'Not all the time, at any rate.'

'I grant you that. But Jenny's got a maths test tomorrow and Martin needs help with his fish tank. And there are two tons of dirty washing, so I won't be twiddling my thumbs, that's for sure.'

'I'll be home to get stuck into the thumb twiddling tomorrow,' promised Barbarotti. 'Or the day after. Tell Brother-in-law Roger to get a move on with that roof.'

'He's almost finished it. He says he gets on quicker when you're not there.'

'Fuck that,' said Barbarotti.

'He might have been joking,' said Marianne.

'He clearly was,' said Barbarotti. 'Right, I must try to get some sleep now. Sleep well, fair nymph. Enfold me in your dreams.'

'I thought you'd come round from the anaesthetic,' said Marianne.

A few minutes later it was Inspector Backman's turn.

'Smart move,' she said.

'What is?'

'Take a day off to rebuild your palace. Fake a broken foot and get out of work for a month.'

'Spot on,' said Barbarotti. 'I calculated it all pretty well, if I do say so myself.'

'Though Asunander says he's putting you on desk duties once your cast has set properly. I think he means tomorrow.'

Barbarotti considered this. 'You can tell our eunuch-in-chief I'm longing to be back,' he said. 'But unfortunately I feel I can't go against doctor's orders.'

'I'll pass that on,' promised Eva Backman. 'But I don't think he's very fond of doctors.'

'Well what is he fond of, then?' asked Barbarotti. 'When it comes down to it. I've thought about that a fair bit.'

'Me too,' said Inspector Backman. 'I think he has some fondness for a particular kind of eccentric and slightly ill-tempered dog.'

'He did have one like that,' said Barbarotti.

'Yes, but it died,' Backman reminded him. 'You remember that, surely?'

'Of course I do,' said Barbarotti. 'So these days he isn't fond of anything?'

'That's what I was coming to,' said Backman. 'Especially not of lazy cops who fall off roofs and call in sick.'

'Thank you, I think the situation's clear to me,' said Barbarotti. 'Why are we rabbiting on about Asunander, by the way?'

'No idea. Is it true you landed in a wheelbarrow?'

'Yes,' said Barbarotti, realizing that this was another topic he didn't feel like discussing. 'How are things with you?' he asked.

'There are a few things I'd like to talk over with you,' said

Eva Backman. 'Not least the Sigurdsson case. The interviews you did with Lindman and the vicar.'

'I can see that you might,' said Barbarotti. 'Is it urgent?'

'How long will you be staying in hospital?'

'I assume they'll send me home tomorrow . . . or the day after. But I'm perfectly capable of having a conversation right here and now, as I expect you can hear?'

'I don't like hospitals,' said Backman. 'But if I could drop round and see you at home the day after tomorrow, I'd be more than happy. Then the prosecutor can put away that creep Sigurdsson next week.'

'Fine by me,' said Barbarotti, suddenly not feeling up to any more talking. He'd just had an operation, hadn't he?

'Call me tomorrow,' he said. 'We'll see what the situation is then.'

'Make sure you don't fall out of bed and hurt yourself,' said Eva Backman, and then they wished one another good night.

Before he fell sleep he lay there for a while, letting his thoughts wander. In actual fact he was trying to steer them – away from his conversation with the anxious anaesthetic nurse, towards his own life and circumstances.

The implications of having to drag a broken foot around with him, for instance. It was the second time in his life that one of the bones in his body had suffered a fracture; the last time he had ridden his bike straight into a carpet-beating rack and broken his collarbone. That was forty years ago and it had healed without the help of any kind of plaster cast within a fortnight or so. Gunnar Barbarotti assumed there was quite a difference between how readily tissue heals at the ages of eight and forty-eight respectively.

But it didn't work. It wasn't these reflections that took control of his thoughts, it was Alice Ekman-Roos. Whether he wanted her to or not, and however hard he tried to steer away from her.

Maybe it was because he felt sorry for her – and he did. There couldn't be much doubt about what had happened, could there? Her husband had grown tired of her and found another woman. It was bloody awful of him just to leave her without a word of explanation, of course, but a lot of men functioned that way. Not daring to look their own actions in the eye, or not too soon, at any rate. Valdemar Roos would probably be in touch in a few days' time, but for now he was far too absorbed in his new life and his new woman.

Bastard, thought Gunnar Barbarotti. That simply isn't the way to behave. You have to exert yourself to . . . to keep such spineless actions at bay.

Although inside him he had a feeling – in some dark and twisting male recess – that if he had happened to be the one married to a woman like Alice Ekman-Roos, he might very well have acted exactly the same way as Valdemar Roos. Left her without a word. That was the way it was, no point being dishonest about your motives.

But he wasn't married to Alice Ekman-Roos; he was married to Marianne Grimberg. There was a world of difference.

Some bastards have more luck than other bastards, thought Inspector Barbarotti. That's the injustice of life's lottery, and thank you, dear Lord, for sending her my way.

Coming to the end of these modest ideas and analyses, he fell asleep.

26

'Wrigman's. Hold the line, please.'

It was Wednesday afternoon. Admittedly he had promised to ring Wrigman's that morning, but events had intervened. Conversations with doctors. Advice and instructions for his coming convalescence. Testing out crutches and learning to negotiate visits to the toilet, the latter a lot more tricky than he had anticipated.

Marianne had been to see him twice, as well. She worked in maternity so it only took her three minutes to pop over to the orthopaedic ward.

They would keep him in until the next day, he had been told. They wanted to do an X-ray before sending him home. Or was it something else? He had a tendency to switch off when faced with medical science. For some reason.

'Can you really manage without me for another night?' he had asked Marianne.

'I'll just have to grin and bear it,' she had replied.

He'd been having some pain, too, on and off. The leg inside the lump of plaster felt like something that belonged to him and yet did not. Sometimes it itched, and the itchiness definitely belonged to him.

So it was half past two by the time he decided to make his enquiry about the missing bastard.

'Yes, Wrigman's Electrical. I'm sorry for the wait.'

'I'd like to speak to Valdemar Roos.'

'Valdemar?'

'Yes please, Valdemar Roos.'

The woman at the other end gave a laugh. A slightly throaty, vaguely waspish laugh.

'But he's not with us any more.'

'Not with you any more?' said Gunnar Barbarotti.

'That's right.'

'I don't quite understand,' said Barbarotti. 'You're saying Valdemar Roos doesn't work there any longer?'

'That's what I'm saying,' said the woman. 'Who am I speaking to?'

'My name's Barbarotti,' explained Gunnar Barbarotti. 'But in fact I'm ringing on behalf of a good friend of mine. Tell, me, when did Valdemar Roos leave the firm?'

The woman coughed and considered the matter.

'Well it must have been about a month ago,' she said. 'He handed in his notice, just like that. No warning at all. And Wrigman let him go.'

'I see,' said Barbarotti, feeling at the same time that he didn't see at all. 'Do you know if he got a job somewhere else?' he asked.

'Haven't a clue,' said the woman. 'He worked here for twenty years, then he left. That's all.'

Gunnar Barbarotti thought quickly.

'Do you know where I can get hold of him?'

'No.'

'You don't happen to have his mobile number?'

'Er, yes, I think it's here somewhere. Hang on.'

He waited, listening to the click of her fingers on a computer keyboard. Then she gave him Valdemar Roos's mobile number and they ended the call. It was evident to him that Wrigman's Electrical wasn't the sort of company that sends its employees to charm school.

He adjusted the pillows behind his back and stared at his leg for a while.

He'd given up work?

A month ago?

His wife hadn't said a word about it. Why not?

On impulse he rang the number he'd been given by the woman at Wrigman's. After all, it might only be his wife the man was refusing to talk to.

No answer.

Gunnar Barbarotti shook his head and brought Alice Ekman-Roos's number up on his screen instead.

Twenty minutes later she was sitting at his bedside again.

'What on earth are you saying? He doesn't work there any more?'

He could see that she had been crying. Her large, smooth face was slightly swollen and a little flushed. If she had felt embarrassed the day before, it was presumably seven times worse now, thought Barbarotti, deciding his conclusion that Valdemar Roos was a bastard had probably been entirely correct. Not only had he found himself another woman, he had pulled the wool over his wife's eyes in the most appalling way by leaving his job without a word to her.

'I don't understand,' she said. 'He went off there every single morning as usual . . . and came home in the evening.'

'They claim he left a month ago,' said Barbarotti.

'But that's . . . that's not possible. If he didn't go to Wrigman's, where did he go?'

'He takes his own car there and back?' asked Barbarotti.

'Oh yes. He always has done . . . even before we met. He's worked there for . . . well, I don't know, at least twenty years.'

'And he didn't car share with anybody?'

She shook her head. 'I don't think anybody wanted to get a lift with Valdemar.'

Barbarotti pondered this as he scratched his plaster cast.

'He never mentioned any plans to give up his job?'

'Never,' said Alice Ekman-Roos, staring at him with big, helpless eyes. As if she had encountered some hair-raising supernatural phenomenon and didn't know how to react. 'He never said a word about anything like that. Oh my God, what can have happened?'

'I don't know,' admitted Gunnar Barbarotti. 'Do the two of you – or did he – have any close friends who might possibly know something?'

She thought for a moment but then shook her head.

'Anyone who he knows and might have confided in?' he added.

'No, I don't think so,' she said eventually. 'Valdemar's got hardly any friends. He's the uncommunicative type. So you think, then, that he . . . that he . . .'

'Yes?' Gunnar Barbarotti prompted her cautiously and ventured an encouraging smile, which unfortunately came out as more of a grimace. Alice Ekman-Roos took a deep breath and pulled herself together. Five seconds passed.

'So you're saying,' she went on, 'that he pretended to go off to work every morning for a whole month? Why . . . I mean, what would make a grown man behave like that?'

You're the one married to him, not me, thought Barbarotti as he tried to unobtrusively pick out some of the plaster that had got stuck under his nails, and wondered what to say to her.

'Maybe it would be best for you to contact the police after all,' he suggested finally. 'Unless you happen to think of anybody who might know where he is.'

She said nothing and looked down at her clasped hands for a while. Then she gave a deep sigh and straightened her back. 'No,' she said. 'He's with that woman, of course. That's where he's been going every day.'

'It's possible.' Barbarotti agreed.

'I knew there was something,' she went on. 'He hasn't been himself this past month . . . I could tell things weren't right. He's found someone else and now he's gone.'

Yes, thought Inspector Barbarotti. That's the most likely explanation of the situation when it comes down to it. He expected her to get up from her seat and leave him – her bearing and her last remark both indicated it – but instead she crumpled a little, shifted her eyes to the view through the window and chewed her lower lip. She sat there in silence.

'But such a young woman?' she said at last, her voice filled with doubt. 'What in heaven's name could a young woman see in someone like Valdemar?'

Barbarotti shrugged his shoulders but said nothing.

'And why did he resign from his job? No, there's something else that doesn't fit here. There must be more to it.'

'I don't think there's a great deal of point in—' began Barbarotti, but she interrupted him.

'That woman can't have been more than twenty-five

according to Karin, my friend who saw them. Valdemar's nearly sixty. He's got a son of thirty-seven or thirty-eight.'

'A son?' said Barbarotti. 'Maybe *he* knows something?'

'I don't think so,' Alice Ekman-Roos said firmly. 'They have scarcely any contact with each other. He lives in Maardam.'

'Ah, I see,' said Barbarotti. 'But even so, my recommendation is that you get in touch with the police. If you don't hear from him in the next few days, at any rate. It could still be that something's happened to him, we mustn't forget that.'

She shook her head. 'I doubt it,' she said, getting to her feet in a rather ungainly fashion. 'Valdemar isn't the type things happen to. He's more . . . well, more like a piece of furniture, you might say.'

'Piece of furniture?' said Barbarotti.

'Yes, a sofa or something. He falls asleep in front of the TV every evening and he never says a word unless you speak to him first.'

Having offered him these insights, she thanked him for his help and left the room.

Good, thought Inspector Barbarotti. That's the last I have to hear about Valdemar Roos. The man with the charisma of a sofa.

His surmise, however, was not to prove entirely correct.

Eva Backman extracted her bicycle from the rack by the police station entrance and thought how lovely it would be to get home. How absolutely lovely. She'd been working solidly at her desk for two days, as the bright autumn sun progressed scornfully across her window from east to west, going completely to waste.

She hadn't even had access to Barbarotti, the blockhead having fallen into a wheelbarrow and broken his leg.

This wasn't my purpose in life, she thought as she turned into Kvarngatan. I should have been a forester or an architect or a fashion model instead.

Or any other damn job. At least a police officer with the sense to opt for outdoor duties when the most beautiful month of the year was in full swing.

These weren't new thoughts; in fact they barely qualified as thoughts at all. Hackneyed old phrases, rather, which woke up and buzzed around in her head as soon as she turned off her brain.

Things didn't go as they should have done, they turned out this way instead, these pseudo-thoughts nagged on. At twenty, Eva Backman – attractive, ambitious, well-read, long-legged and as smart as a whip – had had every opportunity to do what she wanted with her life; twelve years later she was married with three children, police training and a house in the Haga district of town, which she secretly loathed. The district, that is. The house was tolerable.

Shit happens, but it could have been worse.

Twelve years after that she was forty-four, still in the same house with the same family, and with a bit of luck she still had half her life left to live. Almost half, anyway; only bitter bitches complained.

And on this day in particular, she was really looking forward to getting home. Her husband Wilhelm, commonly known as Ville, and their three unihockey-playing sons had gone off to a training camp somewhere near Jönköping. It was new-season preparation time for the Kymlinge Unihockey Tigers, and she would have the house to herself until Sunday evening.

Today was Wednesday, so there wouldn't be a single hockey stick to trip over for four whole days.

Yes, it could be worse. She pedalled faster, weighing up the likelihood of Ville really having fixed the whirlpool bath as he'd promised.

She had been home for ten minutes when her father rang. She saw his number on the display and after a brief inner struggle she decided to answer.

'Eva, I've had the most dreadful experience,' he began. 'You're not going to believe this.'

I don't suppose I am, she thought grimly.

'Eva, I think I've seen a murder.'

'Oh Dad, I'm sure—'

'I know I sometimes imagine things. My head's just like that these days, it's getting old that does it, Eva. You'll be the same one day.'

He lapsed into silence. Was he already losing the thread, she wondered. But then he cleared his throat and continued from where he had left off.

'It wasn't today. It was a day or two ago, but it's been on my mind and then it came to me that you're in the police, Eva. It was silly of me, I should have thought straight away, I know, but I sometimes get a bit confused, like I've told you. And I was in a terrible state, of course, which didn't make things any easier, but I had a little sleep this afternoon . . . and when I woke up I felt completely clear in the head, and that was when I realized I'd got to ring you, Eva.'

She checked her watch. It was quarter to six. All right, she thought, I'll give him ten minutes, that's the least anyone can expect. If nothing else, it'll help to assuage my guilty conscience.

It ebbed and flowed, her sense of guilt about her father. Or her brother, to be exact; he was the one to whom she owed a debt of gratitude. Erik and his wife Ellen made sure Sture Backman could live a life of some dignity even though his mental faculties were starting to desert him. Even though he was slowly but inexorably journeying towards the final darkness.

For the past two and a half years, he had been living with Erik and his wife. That had been the only alternative to some form of institution, and Eva knew it hadn't been an easy decision for them. Erik was five years older than her; he and Ellen hadn't had any children of their own but they had adopted a boy and a girl from Vietnam. They were now twelve and ten, and the family lived out in the country. Erik and Ellen were part-time farmers, you might say, both doing other jobs on the side and somehow making ends meet.

In fact much more than that, when she came to think about it. They had just bought two new horses and the big SUV had looked conspicuously well-polished last time Eva had seen it. Their farm, Rödmossen, was about forty kilometres west of Kymlinge and every time she went to visit she told herself this was the way to live. Exactly this way. In harmony with one's family, one's surroundings and oneself. Neither Erik nor Ellen had ever dropped even the slightest hint that Sture was any kind of burden to them.

And perhaps he wasn't, Eva would think. The house was big enough to accommodate him, he still coped with showering and so on, and as far as she knew he kept himself to himself most of the time. He would lie in his room, thinking, or go out for strolls through the forest around Rödmossen. Twice he hadn't been able to find his way back home, but now he was equipped with a small transmitter, which meant they could locate him even if he got lost on his walks.

These days, Sture Backman's thoughts came and went. Old

and new blended seamlessly, and meaningful conversation with him was only ever piecemeal and sporadic.

But who decides what's meaningful or not? she thought. Something that's meaningful for Andersson and Pettersson naturally needn't necessarily be so for Lundström.

Or Backman. Who was now clearing his throat at length before launching himself back into his account.

'It was over by that crofter's cottage. The first one, not the other one. I go past there sometimes and they sort of came running out, her and then him. It was evening time, it felt so unreal, Eva, as if . . . well, it felt as if I was watching a film or the television, but I wasn't. I swear it wasn't a film, Eva, are you listening to me?'

'Yes, Dad,' she said. 'I'm listening. So what happened then?'

'I was so scared, Eva. Can you understand how scared I was? And how red the blood was . . . I mean bright red, I've always thought it would be darker. A lot darker, but maybe that's because we always see it when it's started to congeal. When it's not so fresh. Though I'll never forget when you cut yourself on that dreadful carving knife when you were little, do you remember that? My God, you bled so much. We'd borrowed it from the Lundins for some reason, and that . . . well, that was bright red, too. And your mother fainted, she was so frightened, thought you were going to bleed to death I suppose, well of course she fainted, she was always prone to . . .'

He started chuckling and she realized he was a long way back in the past.

'How are Erik and Ellen?' she asked in an effort to bring him back into the present. 'And the children?'

But he ignored her. 'There was that time we went to visit

269

Margit and Olle,' he went on with sudden enthusiasm, 'and one of their kids, I think it was that Staffan, he was always a proper little monkey, though they made him headmaster of a folk high school later on, isn't it odd the way things can turn out? He'd climbed down into a well, no idea what he thought he was doing there . . . but perhaps he was hiding in it to give us a scare, what a prank, eh? You agree with me on that, don't you . . . Eva?'

She detected the tone in his voice that meant he couldn't quite remember who he was talking to.

'Yes,' she said. 'I remember Staffan.'

'Staffan?' said her father. 'Who the heck is Staffan? I can't say I really . . . he's not some new man you've found, is he? Aren't you married to that Viktor any longer?'

'Dad,' said Eva Backman. 'I think we've been chatting for long enough. It was nice of you to call.'

'Yes . . . ?' he said. 'Thank you, there's always so much happening all the time, I think I need to go for a little lie-down.'

'You do that,' she said. 'And give my love to Erik and Ellen and the children.'

'Of course I will,' he said. 'They live here too, you know, so I'll be able to do that in a jiffy.'

'Bye bye Dad,' she said, and they hung up.

She devoted the rest of the evening entirely to herself.

She did her usual five kilometres on the forest jogging trail and along by the river. Heated a risotto in the microwave and had it with a bit of cheese and a glass of red wine. Luxuriated in the whirlpool bath for forty-five minutes – contrary to her expectations, Ville had got it working – and then climbed into bed to watch an old Hitchcock film she found in their DVD collection.

The Man Who Knew Too Much.

My father, she thought. He was young when they made this. Maybe only half the age I am now.

Why do people have to age so much quicker than the imprints they leave behind them?

It was a good question, she decided. Time rushing away from us. Could be a suitable topic for a chat with Barbarotti? Over a beer at the Elk, why not?

As soon as he could manage to drag his damned leg back.

27

'I don't think much of the medical treatment in this country,' said Brother-in-law Roger, opening a can of beer.

'Oh?' said Barbarotti.

'You'll be walking with a limp for the rest of your life. Give me French or German healthcare any day.'

'Is that a fact?' said Barbarotti.

Brother-in-law Roger poked the ring pull through the opening in the top of his beer can and took a deep swig. It was Friday morning. Barbarotti was lying on the living-room sofa with his leg well propped up on a couple of cushions. The leg hurt a bit and was rather itchy. Brother-in-law Roger was sitting in an armchair in underpants and an unbuttoned shirt and was evidently not planning much in the way of DIY that day. Perhaps he was waiting for some particular putty to dry. It had happened before.

They were on their own in the house. All the other residents had gone to their various jobs and places of learning, and it suddenly hit Gunnar Barbarotti that he could well be sitting – or lying – here with the unemployed traffic warden from Lycksele for . . . well, three to four hours wasn't beyond the realms of possibility.

'Jesus Christ, they let anybody train as a doctor here these days,' the man was saying now. 'Not to mention all the quacks who come pouring over the border. Poles and Arabs and God knows what. They can't speak a word of Swedish and they can't tell the bloody difference between a kidney and a knee. You fancy a beer?'

'No thanks,' said Gunnar Barbarotti.

Good job I haven't got a pistol to hand, he thought. I'd shoot that tosser if I had. In the leg, say, then the hospital transport people could cart him off to Germany to have it operated on.

'I've got to make a phone call,' Barbarotti said. 'Do you think you could pass me the cordless phone and give me a few minutes?'

Brother-in-law Roger took another swig and scratched his belly. 'I've only just sat down. You're not as immobile as you damn well make out, constable. I heard there was a bloke back home they put in plaster for a pulled muscle. Doctor from Iran or somewhere like that.'

Barbarotti made no comment. After a while, Brother-in-law Roger heaved himself out of his chair and went to get the phone.

'I'll sit out on the terrace for now,' he announced. 'You can give me a shout when you're done, OK?'

You can bet your life I won't, thought Gunnar Barbarotti.

He got straight through to Eva Backman.

'Thanks for yesterday,' she said.

She had been round at Villa Pickford for an hour on Thursday evening to talk over the Sigurdsson case. They'd had a glass of wine, he, Marianne and Inspector Backman – the prize pest had stuck to the TV and a can of beer – and he had found himself thinking that in fact there were only two people in the world in whom he had blind faith: this very pair of women. His wife for the last year, his colleague for the past twelve.

He also contemplated whether he would ever have dared to ask Eva Backman to marry him. If things had been different, that is; if she hadn't been occupied with her Ville and her trio of other unihockey players, and if he hadn't found Marianne on that Greek island.

It was an old and increasingly hypothetical question, with a tendency to sail swiftly through his head now and then, sort of in through his left ear and out through his right one, requiring no answer. It's a relief that there are questions in that category, too, Inspector Barbarotti would think to himself.

Alternative paths through life that one would never have to take.

'It was good to see you,' he said. 'And, er, there was something I wanted to tell you.'

'Oh yes?'

'I've made up my mind. I shall be coming into work on Monday. You can pass that on to Asunander.'

'No way,' said Eva Backman. 'I mean, why on earth?'

'I feel it's my duty to pull my weight,' said Gunnar Barbarotti.

Eva Backman was momentarily reduced to silence. 'Are you sure it wasn't your head you landed on in that wheelbarrow?' she asked eventually. 'Why come to this madhouse when you can lie at home on the settee, picking your navel?'

'I have my reasons,' said Barbarotti.

'I hope so,' said Eva Backman.

'But I'll be tied to my desk, of course, and if my leg gets too painful I shall go home. You can pass that on to Asunander as well.'

'OK then,' said Inspector Backman. 'You must do as you see

fit, but legs aren't first and foremost in our line of work, are they?'

'You're right there,' said Barbarotti. 'It's almost impossible to work with both legs stretched out in front of you.'

'That's quite enough from you,' said Backman and hung up.

'I had a word with him.'

'That wasn't what I meant.'

'He's my brother, Gunnar. I don't like being made to feel ashamed of my own brother.'

'He's a prize pest.'

'I know. But you've just got to accept him as an imperfect human being.'

'Unlike you.'

She shot him a look, presumably trying to detect some kind of sarcasm.

'I genuinely meant that,' he clarified to be on the safe side. 'I think you're perfect.'

'And you are as you are,' was all she offered. 'Does it hurt?'

'No. Not much, anyway. But I'm more aware of it when I'm not concentrating on something else. I need distractions, you might say.'

'That makes sense.'

It was five to midnight and they had finally got to bed. The offending leg was propped up on pillows and was aching slightly; he assumed he had stumped about too much in the course of the evening and over-stimulated the circulation. Could they make love, he wondered. It seemed a daunting undertaking and would probably just have to wait a few days. Or weeks.

'I'm sorry,' he said. 'The prize pest is as he is, too, but I ought to have learnt how to deal with him. He's helped us more than anyone could expect. Can't we talk about something else?'

She switched off the bedside light. 'Sure. But I did just want to tell you he'll be staying one more week. We agreed on that. If those materials for the jetty come on Monday like they're meant to, he'll need three or four days, then he'll head home next Saturday or Sunday. You'll just have to put up with him, and preferably try to be nice as well.'

'I know,' said Gunnar Barbarotti. 'I'm ashamed of the way I've treated him. And I'll be back at work on Monday, anyway.'

'Is that wise?' said Marianne. 'You've got a broken foot to lug around with you, you know.'

'Only desk duties,' he assured her. 'I'm as well off at work digging around in paperwork as I am at home being irritable with your brother, aren't I?'

'I suppose so,' said Marianne.

She sounded a bit fed up. Or perhaps just tired. Both would no doubt be justified. They lay there quietly for a while before she switched the light on again, extended a hand and pulled out the drawer of the bedside table.

She took out the Bible and held it in both hands for a few moments, closing her eyes and taking deep, calming breaths. Then she put in one finger and opened the book about halfway through.

He nodded. 'A bit of guidance?'

'A bit of guidance.'

She ran her finger down the page, stopped at random, looked at the text and gave a little smile.

'Let's hear it,' said Gunnar Barbarotti.

Marianne cleared her throat and read aloud.

'*The fool folds his hands together and ruins himself. Better is a handful, with quietness, than two handfuls with labour and chasing after wind.*'

Gunnar Barbarotti considered this for a few seconds.

'Chasing after wind,' he said. 'I like that expression. Though I don't see what it's got to do with the prize pest.'

'It could be he's not the one needing the guidance,' said Marianne.

'A handful, with quietness?' said Barbarotti. 'Well yes, that's about all the quietness I really want. I assume that's why I'm going into work on Monday. What's this text?'

'Ecclesiastes, also known as the Preacher,' said Marianne. 'He's not exactly cheery, but I agree with you. The bit about chasing the wind is good. That's not what we're doing, are we?'

'Most definitely not,' said Barbarotti. 'And I'm going to be nice to your brother, I promise. Just one more week, you say? Seven days?'

'Ten at most,' Marianne assured him.

Then he told her about Alice Ekman-Roos and her missing husband. He wasn't sure why he was doing so, but Marianne was instantly interested.

'So he's been gone since Sunday?'

'Yes. That's to say, I don't know, he could have turned up by now.'

'When did you last speak to her?'

'Yesterday afternoon. Before I came out of hospital.'

'And at that point she still didn't know anything?'

'No.'

'And she hadn't informed the police?'

'No.'

'I don't understand her. He could have been killed or anything.'

'Seems unlikely. And she's got this sense of shame because he's been pulling the wool over her eyes for quite a while.'

'You said he gave up his job about a month ago?'

'At least a month.'

She thought for a while.

'There's only one theory then,' she said. 'Isn't there? That he's run off with the other woman.'

'Well, yes,' said Gunnar Barbarotti. 'That seems the most plausible explanation.'

Marianne lay there, thinking in silence.

'But say that's wrong?' she went on. 'Then it would be very much a police matter. It would mean some kind of crime must lie behind it. Correct me if I'm wrong.'

'You're not wrong,' said Barbarotti. 'I think I'd better check it out on Monday after all.'

'Promise,' said Marianne. 'In fact, I think you should call her tomorrow. Poor woman, she must be going through hell.'

He adjusted the pillows under his leg and pondered.

'Maybe,' he said. 'But bearing in mind the way she described him, she might well be thinking how nice it is to be rid of him. She compared him to a piece of furniture.'

'Furniture?'

'Yes. A sofa, to be precise.'

'Hmm,' said Marianne. 'I'm sure it's a bit more complicated than that. Women whose husbands have been unfaithful have a particular psychological take on things.'

'Now we're getting into areas I've no chance of understanding,' observed Gunnar Barbarotti. 'But I can call her tomorrow by all means and check how things are.'

Five seconds passed. She switched off the light.

'I've got an idea Johan might have started smoking on the sly.'

'I'll check that out as well.'

'Thank you,' said Marianne. 'I love you. In fact I love this whole horde we've surrounded ourselves with, but right now I can't keep my eyes open a moment longer.'

She yawned and rolled over onto her side.

'I love you too,' said Barbarotti. 'The whole show, just as you say. And I feel in my bones that we're not chasing the wind.'

'Mhm?' said Marianne.

28

Chief Inspector Asunander looked sceptical.

He generally did, but today it was even more obvious than usual.

'A man who's run off with some woman he loves?' he said. 'And you're telling me it's something worth spending our valuable time on?'

'Things may not be as simple as they initially appear,' said Barbarotti. 'I thought it might be worth taking further . . . a bit further, anyway.'

'Has his wife reported it?'

'No.'

'Are there any other theories besides this lover hypothesis?'

'Not really,' said Barbarotti, squirming slightly. It isn't very easy to squirm when you're in plaster, so this one was more the internal variety.

'You suspect some sort of crime?'

'I can't rule it out,' said Barbarotti.

'It isn't by any chance that you think you can do what you like, just because you've shown up here with that club foot?'

'Perish the thought.'

Chief Inspector Asunander gave a snort. He's grown eloquent since he got those false teeth of his to stay in place, thought Barbarotti. Annoyingly eloquent, in fact – things were better before.

'As it happens,' continued Chief Inspector Asunander, 'I have a task that's pretty much tailor-made for an eager inspector with a club foot.'

'Oh really?' said Barbarotti.

'I think we'll do it like this: you solve my little spot of bother first and once that's done you can turn your attention to this runaway. What did you say his name was?'

'Roos,' said Barbarotti. 'Ante Valdemar Roos.'

'Interesting name,' said the chief inspector. 'But presumably that's the only interesting aspect of the whole thing.'

'What spot of bother did you have in mind?' asked Barbarotti, suppressing a sigh.

'The graffiti problem,' said Asunander, and Barbarotti could have sworn he saw a smile tug at the corner of the chief inspector's mouth for a fraction of a second. For his own part, he felt a surge of pain in his leg.

'The graffiti problem?' he said, trying not to sound as though he felt like throwing up. 'I don't think I—?'

'It's time to put an end to the whole saga now,' the chief inspector interrupted as he lifted a corner of his desk blotter and fished out a sheet of paper. 'We've been after this bastard – or these bastards – for nearly two years now, and with Inspector Sturegård going on maternity leave for at least eight months, I need someone to take over.'

This time Barbarotti couldn't hold back the sigh. He was well aware of how things stood with the *Graffiti Master*. Or *Masters*, as the case might be. Or *Those goddamned petty hooligans who deserve to be burnt at the stake*. They (or he, but scarcely a she) had been on the rampage in Kymlinge for at least two and a half years, but not much attention had been paid to the problem until the editor of the local paper, one Lars-Lennart Brahmin, had moved into Olympia, one of the old fin-de-siècle buildings on the east side of the river. He had immediately been elected chairman of the residents' association, and it so happened that the pale-cream-coloured facade of Olympia was one of the Graffiti Master's favourite locations for his offensive tags.

Then each time he had been in action, about once a month for the past year, the subject got an airing in the local paper. A very prominent airing.

'That bloody Brahmin's been ringing me seven times a week,' said Asunander. 'I've cancelled my subscription to the paper – its editor brings me out in a rash.'

'I see,' said Barbarotti.

'I thought Sturegård would get it sorted out in no time, but something's gone awry, apparently.'

'Clearly,' said Barbarotti.

He didn't know Inspector Malin Sturegård very well, but he knew she had been put in sole charge of putting a stop to the vandalism. He also knew she had got nowhere, despite dogged efforts over an extended period of time – and he seemed to remember hearing a rumour that she had got pregnant just to escape the whole mess. She was over forty and already had three or four children, so he felt there could be a grain of truth in such speculations.

These dismal facts ran through Inspector Barbarotti's mind as Chief Inspector Asunander clasped his hands on the desk and regarded his officer with an expression that . . . well, it was hard to say. And that was rare with Asunander. But it was plain in any case that it did not contain any sympathy for a subordinate who had fallen off a roof and broken his foot on a wheelbarrow.

Nor had Gunnar Barbarotti expected any sympathy of that kind. He cleared his throat, fumbled with his crutches and hauled himself to his feet.

'Of course,' he said. 'I'll make sure to get Sturegård's material sent to my office.'

'I've already given the order,' said Asunander. 'I expect the files are there by now. Just get this damn nuisance sorted out once and for all.'

'I'll see what I can do,' said Barbarotti as he hobbled out of the chief inspector's office.

'Then you'll have your hands free to get to grips with that Roos,' Asunander reminded him, just as he was closing the door.

Thanks boss, thought Barbarotti. Very nice of you. I'm not so bloody sure the prize pest wouldn't have been a better bet after all.

'How did it go?' said Eva Backman. 'What are these files?'

'Graffiti,' said Barbarotti. 'Inspector Sturegård's one-woman investigation.'

'What are they doing in your room?'

'I needed something to prop my leg on,' said Barbarotti.

'Don't think I'll fall for that,' said Eva Backman, and her face suddenly broke into a smile. 'You don't mean to say . . . ?'

'Yep,' said Barbarotti, 'and if you laugh I shall clout you with this crutch.'

'Sturegård?' said Backman. 'Oh my God, of course, she went off on maternity leave last week.'

Barbarotti tossed two pieces of chewing gum into his mouth and started to chew.

'So you're going to take over and sort out that scumbag?'

'Did you come in for anything in particular?' said Barbarotti.

'Hm,' said Backman. 'I thought you were going to spend your time on that runaway bloke.'

'Asunander thinks differently,' said Barbarotti.

'Is that so?' said Backman, installing herself on the visitors' chair of tubular steel and hard yellow plastic. She crossed her legs with an expression of worried scepticism.

Or whatever it was she was trying to convey.

'There's something fishy going on there,' said Barbarotti.

'Where?' said Eva Backman. 'With . . . what's his name? Ante Valdemar Roos?'

'Precisely,' said Barbarotti.

'Explain,' said Backman.

'With pleasure. Though there isn't much to explain. He's been missing for over a week now. Of course he might just have run away with his lover, but I don't think so. It doesn't feel plausible, frankly.'

'Oh?' said Eva Backman. 'I thought that was every man's dream. Just leaving everything without explanation. Moaning wife, kids and a lousy job. What's to say this Roos didn't finally take the plunge? Frankly, as you put it.'

Barbarotti scratched his plaster. 'The drive to act,' he said. 'It takes a heck of a lot of drive to take that kind of initiative. His wife says he hasn't had a new thought since 1975.'

'When did you last speak to her?'

'On Saturday.'

'And she'd nothing new to tell you?'

'Nothing at all. But she didn't want to report him missing

formally. And for as long as that remains the case, Asunander thinks we should keep a low profile.'

'But you don't?'

'Correct,' said Barbarotti, cautiously lifting his leg up onto the desk. 'I don't.'

'Do you need any kind of help with that?' asked Backman.

'Not at all,' said Barbarotti.

Backman sat there in silence for a while.

'I've got a bit of slack in my schedule at the moment,' she said eventually. 'What do you say to me having another chat with that place where he worked? You might have missed something. His wife might ring in again, too, and perhaps she'd find it easier to talk to a woman.'

'She decided to open up to me because she trusted me,' Barbarotti reminded her. 'Has done since we were at school together.'

'What exactly are you trying to tell me?' said Backman.

'Nothing,' said Barbarotti. 'But yes, why not, you put out some feelers and we'll see what happens. Perhaps we can catch up over lunch later? How about the King's Grill?'

'Fine by me,' said Backman. 'Right, I can't stand here chatting to you all day. Good luck with your graffiti artist.'

'Thanks, Inspector,' said Barbarotti. 'Close the door properly behind you, if you wouldn't mind.'

It took no fewer than six ring binders to accommodate the paperwork in the Graffiti Master case. Three were yellow and three were red. Gunnar Barbarotti looked at the clock and saw it was twenty-five past nine.

All right then, he thought. Two and a half hours until

lunchtime, so let's see what an alert pair of eyes and a bunch of potent brain cells can achieve.

By quarter to twelve he still had no satisfactory answer to that question. There was absolutely no doubt that Inspector Malin Sturegård had put tremendous effort into identifying the elusive vandal. She had been working on the case for just over eleven months, as the dates on the files confirmed. Along the way a number of spray-can artists had been apprehended and issued with a variety of well-deserved fines, but she had made no progress towards her main target, the worst miscreant of all.

Or could there in fact be two of them at it? There were evidently two so-called tags in use, and in almost all cases the police were aware of, both occurred together, in the same place. When they were discovered the next morning, some ten properties had often been targeted, always in the centre of town – and in nine out of ten cases, over the past year at least, the stately Olympia building on the east bank of the river was one of them.

The tags were also fully legible and pronounceable, which was not always the case with this sort of vandalism, so Barbarotti learnt as he read. According to Inspector Sturegård's conscientious summary, the two had first made their appearance at the same time, about three years before. They were generally sprayed in red or blue paint – often one in each colour on each wall – but black and dark green had also featured a few times.

One was PIZ.

The other was ZIP.

It was unusual for a tag to have a lifespan of three years.

The perpetrators were almost always teenagers, and male, and the few studies that had been done on the subject found that most practitioners soon tired of the activity and moved on to new interests. Artistic or criminal, predominantly the latter.

To a layman, putting away one or two graffiti artists might seem like child's play – and if more serious crimes were being committed, the police would presumably have got to the bottom of the problem in a considerably more effective way. It could, for example, 'be assumed with some certainty that the Olympia apartment block would be defaced at some point (i.e. *some night*) in any given thirty-day period in the coming year' (wrote Inspector Sturegård in two different places, as she vainly requested a slight boost to resources), but putting the place under police surveillance to catch the perpetrator(*s*) red-handed when he (*they*) next struck . . . well, that was as financially unthinkable in Kymlinge as in any other town or city in Sweden. And presumably in any other country, too.

There had been some surveillance, in fact, initiated by Brahmin the newspaper editor, though his fellow members of the residents' association soon grew tired of it. Lurking behind a curtain for two or three hours, two nights a week, staring out at a sluggishly flowing river and a deserted street in the company of a few other slightly tipsy – but otherwise irreproachable – citizens was not something the average residents' association member found particularly rewarding.

So ZIP and PIZ were left in peace to continue their infuriating activities. He (or *they*) presumably had no idea there was a full-time inspector at police HQ devoting all her technical knowledge and investigative zeal to stopping his (*their*) campaign.

And even if he (*they*) did know, it did not appear to bother him (*them*) particularly. Quite the contrary, in fact; he (*they*) would presumably have died laughing.

Inspector Barbarotti sighed, closed file number three and decided to have lunch before he tackled number four, the first of the yellow ones.

I wonder why she changed colour, he thought.

And would she have gone for yet another colour if she had embarked on a seventh file? Was that when she decided pregnancy was the solution? Time for a break, there was no doubt about it. He lifted his leg down from the desk and picked up his crutches.

Inspector Eva Backman was not in her office.

At the front desk they said they didn't know where she was.

She wasn't in the King's Grill. And she wasn't answering her mobile. Gunnar Barbarotti gave another sigh and ordered the dish of the day – beef with fried potatoes and onion sauce – and sat down at one of the tables that looked out on Riddargatan.

So I can see her when she comes, he thought. It was only ten past twelve. They had not arranged a time, and it was possible she would turn up nearer half past, if some task had come up.

He sat there until five to one. He called her mobile again, got no answer, and left a message asking her to get in touch, and telling her he had no beef with the beef, it had been delicious.

Then he limped crookedly over Riddargatan, crookedly over Fredsgatan, crookedly over the level crossing and by eight minutes past one he was back in his office with Sturegård's graffiti files.

THE SECRET LIFE OF MR ROOS

And a big cup of black coffee. Plus an almond tart he ferreted out of a packet in the bottom right-hand drawer of his desk, registering that he must have bought it sometime in Easter week. It was now September.

ZIP and PIZ, he thought. Chasing the wind?

29

On the way back into town from Svartö, Inspector Eva Backman reflected on two things.

Firstly, what actually made a woman like Red Cow tick.

Or to be more accurate, she brooded on how anyone could relate to their own nickname that way. Particularly a nickname like that. The woman's real name was Elisabet Rödko, and she was of Hungarian or possibly Transylvanian stock, it hadn't been altogether clear – and when one of the bright sparks at Wrigman's Electrical had hit on the idea of giving her name an American touch, she had gone along with it. Not just by accepting the name, but also by dyeing her naturally mousy hair a vivid red.

Today, fourteen years later, it was still bright red and she had confided to Backman that even her husband and children called her Red Cow.

A cow, thought Eva Backman. Tarting it up with a bit of English and a touch of colour didn't really help, did it?

But the name was significant in terms of her credibility – and that was the second, and considerably more important question Eva Backman was struggling to answer as she sat at the steering wheel.

Could her word be relied on, or more specifically, her judgement of Valdemar Roos?

Backman hadn't had a chance to talk to anyone else at Wrigman's, so it would be a good thing if she could make up her mind on that point. At least for now; they could always revisit the question later, if it proved necessary.

Though why should it prove necessary? she thought. Why on earth? Her decision to go out to Svartö had been a last-minute one, after she failed to get hold of Alice Ekman-Roos. Perhaps she had done it mainly to surprise Barbarotti, but her own curiosity had been piqued as well, truth be told.

But Red Cow had provided nothing to still her curiosity whatsoever.

'A lover?' she'd snorted derisively. 'Valdemar Roos? You're kidding.'

'He seems to have pulled the wool over his wife's eyes,' Backman pointed out.

That may be true, thought Red Cow. But the very idea of a younger woman choosing Valdemar was as unthinkable as Madonna falling into bed with some pot-bellied neo-Nazi. If you get my drift, Inspector?

Backman thought about it and said she did. Then she asked whether Red Cow had any kind of theory to explain why Roos had decided to leave Wrigman's Electrical so abruptly after more than twenty years, and why he hadn't said a word about it to his family.

Red Cow declared she hadn't the faintest idea about either of those things. There'd been a fair amount of talk about it in the staff room, of course, especially in the past few days, once it came out that Valdemar had been keeping his wife in the dark. And had gone missing, to top it all.

But none of them had come up with any halfway plausible explanation. Neither Red Cow herself nor anybody else.

Perhaps, she concluded with barely concealed relish, Tapanen had come closest to the truth in maintaining that the ape-brain Roos had blown his last fuse and couldn't tell the difference between his arse and a hole in the ground.

This was a quote, admittedly, but it was Red Cow who delivered it, with every appearance of finding it piquant, witty and accurate.

Which was something else to be weighed in the balance when assessing her credibility, thought Eva Backman, braking as she came up behind an articulated lorry. She glanced at the clock.

It was twenty past four. She still had some way to go to the Rocksta roundabout and she decided on the spur of the moment to head straight for home rather than going back to the police station to do her duty for the last ten or fifteen minutes.

I'll have to take it up with Barbarotti tomorrow, she decided. There's something fishy going on here, just as he said. Possibly there's a woman involved as well – in some way or other – but definitely a fish.

Curiosity was like an itch, she thought, not for the first time. Hard to ignore.

Gunnar Barbarotti immediately recognized the man who opened the mahogany-veneered door, but it took him a few seconds to place him.

The man was short and stocky, one of those people with greater specific gravity than his surroundings, and he did not look happy.

Nor had he done the last time Barbarotti encountered him. He tried to work out how many years ago that had been. A parents' meeting to talk about plans for a class trip when Sara was in Year 8 . . . it must have been December 2002, a year after his divorce from Helena. He remembered it had been hard to cope with.

The meeting and life in general.

Kent Blomgren had clearly been finding the parents' meeting hard to cope with, too. He had sat in dogged silence throughout the meeting, voting neither yes or no to all the points that came up in the course of the discussion, and when it was eventually decided that the class would go on a trip to London the coming May, he resolutely pushed back his chair, got to his feet and declared that his Jimmy bloody well wasn't going on any luxury trip to London. The middle-class kids and their parents were welcome to it if they thought it was so important.

Having clarified this he'd left the classroom, slamming the door behind him and making the walls shake.

Barbarotti did not know if it was as a result of Kent Blomgren's demonstrative behaviour or for some other reason, but instead of the proposed week in London, Sara and her class spent three rainy days in Copenhagen. Blomgren junior did not go with them.

And now here was Blomgren senior, scowling at Barbarotti and his crutches. He seemed to be weighing up whether to slam this door as well, but Barbarotti anticipated him.

'Hello,' he said. 'I think we had kids in the same class. I'd forgotten that when I rang you.'

'Oh?' said Kent Blomgren.

'What was his name, your lad? Jimmy?'

'Jimmy and Billy,' said Kent Blomgren. 'I've got two.'

Barbarotti nodded and stepped into the hall, plastered foot

first. Kent Blomgren closed the door behind him, rather than slamming it.

'I had to bring them up myself, too,' he added. 'The wife shoved off with someone else when they were little. Just as well, and all.'

Surprised to find the man confiding in him, Barbarotti cleared his throat and hesitated.

'That's the way things go,' he said. 'I don't live with my children's mother, either. Life doesn't always turn out how we expected.'

Why am I jawing on about life with this human battering ram? he asked himself. Wasn't I meant to be talking about graffiti?

'You'd like coffee, yeah?' said Kent Blomgren, going ahead of him into a cramped kitchen. 'It's all ready, it's no bother.'

They sat down on opposite sides of a blue-painted wooden table. A diminutive potted cactus stood between them. A plate of four cinnamon buns defrosted in the microwave and two mugs bearing the club badge of the football team IFK Gothenburg sat on the table.

'As I told you,' said Barbarotti, 'I'm looking into the graffiti problem.'

'You're working even though you're in plaster,' said Kent Blomgren, nodding in the direction of Barbarotti's foot, which the latter had cautiously raised onto a chair. The chair was yellow. There were only three chairs in the kitchen. One yellow, one red and one green.

'I don't like being stuck at home,' said Barbarotti.

Kent Blomgren pulled a face that was hard to read, poured the coffee and sat down on the green chair.

'You see a good deal of the stuff, I assume?' said Barbarotti. 'Graffiti, I mean.'

Kent Blomgren took a slurp of coffee, wiped his mouth with the back of his hand and seemed to be thinking. Or groping for the right word.

'Too fucking right I do,' he said, slowly and emphatically. 'If I got my hands on a single one of those bastards, I'd wring his neck and throw him to the pigs.'

'Just so,' said Barbarotti. 'No beating about the bush. How long have you had this cleaning company?'

'Ten years,' said Kent Blomgren. 'I worked at Brink's before that, but then I set up on my own.'

'There's one graffiti merchant causing us particular trouble,' said Barbarotti. 'Or possibly two? The PIZ and ZIP tags, I expect you've come across them often enough?'

Kent Blomgren took a bite of cinnamon bun and chewed it at length, staring deep into Barbarotti's eyes.

'I've power-hosed more PIZ and ZIP than you've had hot dinners,' he said at last through gritted teeth, stressing every word. 'It's a fucking nightmare. How hard can it be to stop this hooligan?'

'I'm new to this,' Gunnar Barbarotti told him cautiously. 'Not quite on top of all the details of the case yet. But he's clearly a problem.'

Kent Blomgren was still glaring at him and munching the bun.

'You haven't any theories?'

'Theories?'

'As to who might be behind this wilful damage? One person or several. You've been in this business quite a while, after all.'

'Far too long,' said Kent Blomgren.

But he was unable to come up with any theories. 'I deal with the mess,' he observed laconically. 'I never see the people who make it.'

A door opened, somewhere in the flat, and a long-haired young man came into the kitchen. He was wearing underpants and a T-shirt with Homer Simpson on it.

'Jimmy?' said Barbarotti.

'Billy,' said the young man and held out a hand. Barbarotti took it. Kent Blomgren looked at the clock and muttered something.

'Don't panic,' said Billy Blomgren. 'They said to get there after lunch.'

He opened the fridge door, drank some juice straight from the carton and went out again.

'It's tough,' said Kent Blomgren. 'Tough for them to find jobs these days. This country's going down the drain.'

Gunnar Barbarotti realized he was sitting opposite someone from the same school of thought as Brother-in-law Roger, and decided not to stay much longer. He didn't really know why he had come here, but he had happened on Kent Blomgren's name in the fourth of Sturegård's files and had decided it couldn't do any harm.

'It's never been easy to be young,' he said. 'Anyway, I shall carry on working on this. We'll find some way of stopping PIZ and ZIP. Could I ask you to do something?'

'What?' said Kent Blomgren, after draining his coffee mug. Barbarotti struggled to his feet and took up his crutches.

'Next time you get the order to clean up a ZIP or a PIZ, give me a call so I can take a look first.'

Kent Blomgren raised an eyebrow, but then nodded.

'Sure,' he said. 'Expect they'll go for Olympia again, so it'll be in the paper. That moron Brahmin doesn't seem to have much to write about.'

'We'll just have to wait and see,' said Barbarotti, and made his exit from the Blomgren establishment.

I forgot to ask why on earth he called his company Cerberus, Barbarotti thought once he was out in the street. If he remembered rightly, Cerberus was a dog that guarded the crossing to Hell, and he found it hard to imagine what possible link it could have to cleaning off graffiti.

But he didn't really feel on home ground out here in the sticks of petty criminality.

I'm better at murderers than graffiti merchants, he thought as he inserted himself awkwardly into the car.

Good job it's an automatic, he reflected. And good job it wasn't my right foot I broke. He wasn't entirely sure it was legal to drive with your foot in plaster, but there were things one didn't need to investigate too deeply.

Perhaps the Cerberus Cleaning Company Ltd was another of them.

'I think I'm starting to get somewhere,' said Eva Backman.

'With what?' asked Barbarotti.

'With Alice Ekman-Roos,' said Backman.

It was quarter to one. It was Tuesday, they were sitting in King's Grill and their order had just arrived. Two portions of the dish of the day: beef stew with beetroot and charcoal dumplings.

'I'm delighted to hear it,' said Barbarotti. 'Would you care to elaborate?'

'I think she's willing to come in and report him missing,' said Backman. 'I talked to her this morning.'

'About time too,' said Barbarotti. 'He's been missing for ten days now. It's a scandal that we haven't started looking into it seriously.'

'I wouldn't exactly call it a scandal,' said Backman. 'But I agree it's a strange business. Do you think he had it all planned, vanishing into thin air like that?'

Barbarotti pondered. 'It could seem like a tempting option to a lot of people, but in that case, I can't see why he didn't do it straight away. Why bother pretending he was going off to work for a month first, and then vanish? It seems crazy.'

'Maybe he needed that month in some way,' suggested Backman.

'What for?' said Barbarotti, scratching his plaster.

'What's the point of scratching your plaster?' said Eva Backman. 'I've noticed you do it quite a lot.'

'It's a symbolic act,' said Barbarotti. 'When you can't take some action you really want to take for some reason, then you resort to a symbolic act.'

'Like burning flags?' said Backman.

'Burning flags?' said Barbarotti. 'No, I don't think that counts as a symbolic act – but never mind that. Why would Valdemar Roos need a month before he could bring things to a head and escape once and for all?'

'I haven't worked that out yet,' said Backman. 'But maybe he needed a bit of time for planning. Or getting money. Robbing a bank, say?'

'I don't think we've had any bank robberies since January,' said Barbarotti.

'Maybe he went somewhere else.'

'Crafty devil,' said Barbarotti.

'A criminal genius,' said Backman. 'Do you believe any of this?'

'No,' said Barbarotti.

'So what *do* you think?'

Gunnar Barbarotti set down his knife and fork and leant back. 'I don't really know,' he said. 'But if we can now consider this a police matter, I presume we're also allowed to start talking to people. Who do you want to take first?'

'That friend,' said Eva Backman. 'The one who claims she saw him coming out of Ljungman's with a young woman.'

'Bingo,' said Barbarotti. 'The lover theory hinges entirely on her.'

'It would be useful to have a proper description sent out, too,' said Eva Backman. 'It could well be that he's popped up here and there. It's only his wife who's missed him so far . . . so to speak.'

'So to speak,' agreed Gunnar Barbarotti. 'I'm with you on issuing the description. You get that sorted, will you? I think it's best if I steer clear of Asunander. Oh, and by the way, don't you want to hear how my hunt for the elusive graffiti master's going?'

'Not at the moment,' said Eva Backman. 'If you don't mind. Let's pay and get back to our desks. But I'll keep you updated on Roos.'

'Thanks,' said Barbarotti. 'Could you pass me my crutches, please?'

30

The picture of the missing man, Ante Valdemar Roos, was published in the Thursday edition of the local paper, and at ten thirty that morning they received their first call from that doughty detective, the Swedish public.

It came from a woman called Yolanda Wessén; she worked in an ICA supermarket in Rimmersdal and claimed that the man in the photo in the paper had made purchases at her checkout a number of times recently. He had also introduced himself as Valdemar.

But he hadn't been in the shop for a while. If she remembered correctly, it was a week since she last saw him. Maybe even ten days.

'Rimmersdal?' said Eva Backman when she got a chance to speak to the woman on the phone. 'Out towards Vreten, isn't it?'

Yolanda Wessén confirmed that Rimmersdal was five kilometres from Vreten and added that she had a good memory for faces. She liked talking to her customers, even though she was always at the checkout and had to confine herself to a few words about the weather.

Backman asked her when she had seen Valdemar Roos for the first time. Yolanda Wessén said it must have been about a month ago, and that was when Backman decided to go out to Rimmersdal to ask some more detailed questions.

Meanwhile – that is to say, between eleven and half past on that Thursday morning – Inspector Barbarotti tackled Gordon Faringer, the psychiatrist acquaintance of the Ekman-Roos family, who had had a chat with Valdemar a couple of weeks before about his general mental well-being and possible depression.

Gordon Faringer was a rangy man of fifty-five. Barbarotti registered that he looked tanned and healthy and was confidently sporting a violet-coloured handkerchief in his breast pocket, but his greatest asset in patient consultations must surely be his voice.

It was deep and melodious, rather like the tone of a cello, and made every word he uttered sound reasoned and wise. Barbarotti found it was far from easy to doubt anything he said, however hard one tried. 'Of course I only talked to Valdemar about his emotional state on one occasion,' he explained, for example. 'It wasn't an official consultation, but I nonetheless formed the judgement that he could not be termed depressed in the classic sense.'

'I see,' chimed in Barbarotti.

'He's never been a particularly enthusiastic person; we are all pitched differently in that regard. But no, I don't believe his going missing stems from any sort of mental instability.'

'He quit his job five weeks ago,' Barbarotti pointed out. 'Without telling his wife.'

'Yes, I am aware of that,' said Faringer. 'Alice rang me yesterday and we had a long talk. It's as incomprehensible to me as to everyone else.'

'So his wife didn't say anything about the possibility of another woman in the frame?'

Gordon Faringer nodded with a troubled look and lightly massaged his right temple, an unconscious (or perhaps highly conscious) signal that he was thinking. He coughed and adjusted his glasses.

'Well yes,' he said, 'she told me that, too. Evidently a friend of hers had observed something to indicate it. Remarkable, I must say. I wouldn't go so far as to call Valdemar an asexual person, but the notion of his being unfaithful to Alice with some young woman seems so unlikely that we can hardly imagine it . . . When I say "we", I mean my wife and I.'

'Hmm,' said Barbarotti. 'But his leaving Wrigman's is an indisputable fact. Perhaps it's time for a complete re-evaluation of Valdemar Roos, if you see what I mean?'

'I see very well what you mean,' said Gordon Faringer with the briefest of smiles. 'And every individual definitely has aspects that remain hidden to those around them. Often we are not even aware of them ourselves.'

'Too true,' said Barbarotti. 'So a particular situation could prompt all those unknown aspects to surface and result in . . . unexpected actions?'

Faringer's hand brushed his temple again. 'That's a fair description,' he said. 'One could perhaps add that it normally takes some kind of trigger. A catalyst.'

'And that could be the case with Valdemar?'

'One can't rule it out,' said Gordon Faringer. 'Although I naturally have no idea what the catalyst could have been.'

Barbarotti thought for a moment.

'Would you say you know Valdemar Roos well?'

'Not at all,' Gordon Faringer replied instantly. 'I'm actually better acquainted with his wife. We've known one another for at least twenty years. Valdemar only came into her life about ten years ago, you know. But we don't meet up that often socially; we get together over dinner a couple of times a year, that's all.'

'I see,' said Barbarotti. 'Incidentally, how do you interpret her reaction, keeping quiet about his disappearance for so long before she told anybody?'

Faringer gave a shrug. 'It's a fairly standard human reaction,' he said. 'There's a good deal of shame involved if your husband walks out without a word.'

'If that's the real state of affairs,' said Barbarotti.

For the first time, a hint of surprise crept into the doctor's face. 'What else could it be?' he asked.

'You said yourself that you found it hard to believe there was another woman,' said Barbarotti.

'Yes I did,' said Gordon Faringer, and allowed himself another fleeting smile. 'But I didn't claim it would take another woman to make Valdemar leave Alice.'

Barbarotti pondered this.

'Are you saying it wouldn't surprise you if Valdemar Roos is sitting in Malaga enjoying a sangria at this very moment?'

'Or a Singha beer in Phuket,' suggested Gordon Faringer with a glance at his watch. 'Yes, I reckon I could stake a hundred kronor on that version of events. If you'll excuse me, I have a meeting at the hospital in fifteen minutes. Would you mind if I . . . ?'

'Feel free,' said Barbarotti. 'I may get in touch again, if the need arises.'

'You're most welcome to do so,' said Dr Faringer.

He stood up, shook hands with Barbarotti and left the room.

*

Once he was alone, Barbarotti gingerly lifted his plastered foot onto the desk, leant back in his chair and clasped his hands behind his neck. He sat like that for at least ten minutes, trying to piece together a clear picture of Ante Valdemar Roos in his mind.

He noted first that the descriptions he had received so far – from the man's wife, from Red Cow and from Gordon Faringer – were pretty consistent.

Weren't they? Valdemar Roos was dreary, withdrawn, uncomfortable in social settings and not much liked. A slow, dull and predictable fellow who never raised anyone's spirits and from whom no one expected anything extra or surprising.

Yes, that was roughly the shape of it. But just think, Gunnar Barbarotti challenged himself, just think if Valdemar Roos was in fact a much more complicated individual than those around him gave him credit for. What did Alice Ekman-Roos know, for instance, about the deeper layers of her husband's personality? Dreams and yearnings and motives. What did Red Cow know? Or Gordon Faringer?

Surely no one could have an interior to match the exterior that Ante Valdemar Ross's acquaintances had sketched out? Surely everyone had a right to their own world view and attitude to the big questions in life? Surface was surface, but depth was depth, and many people simply preferred not to admit just anybody to their most private spheres. For varying but maybe wholly legitimate reasons. Who was to say Roos wasn't an interesting and multi-faceted person, just because he didn't make a song and dance of his innermost thoughts?

Barbarotti leant even further back in his chair and looked out of the window.

And what am I trying to achieve with this pseudo-reasoning?

he thought. Why can't I just accept that dull is dull, and that's all there is to it?

Because it's more exciting if they have a secret? Why do I always want life to be constructed that way?

Life has to be a story, otherwise it's meaningless. And consequently unendurable. That's it, isn't it? *Isn't it?*

There was a knock at the door and Asunander stuck his head into the room.

'How are you getting on with the graffiti? Any solution in sight?'

Barbarotti slammed on the brakes of all trains of thought about Valdemar Roos and the essence of life, and attempted to haul himself upright in his chair while still keeping his leg on the desk. It sent a twinge of pain through his back.

'Ouch,' he said. 'Thank you, Chief Inspector, it's going very well. I'm just trying to evaluate a couple of leads.'

'Really?' said Asunander, not bothering to come into the room. 'What sort of leads?'

'It's a bit complicated,' said Barbarotti. 'I was going to come in and give you an update tomorrow . . . or Monday.'

'Good,' said Asunander. 'I'll look forward to it. But I want no more bullshit from you and no more files either, thank you very much. I want that infernal joker stopped and I'm expecting you to get results.'

'Of course,' said Barbarotti. 'I see it as just a matter of time.'

'You're right to do that,' said Asunander, and closed the door.

The problem, thought Inspector Barbarotti, the *real* problem, is that I'm not remotely interested in that graffiti merchant. Now what was I just thinking about Valdemar Roos?

*

'Listen to this,' said Eva Backman. 'It's really interesting.'

Barbarotti nodded and glanced at his watch. It was half past four. He had promised to pick up Marianne at quarter past five for the big weekly shop at the Co-op superstore in Billundsberg. It was their standard Thursday routine. If there was one thing in the world Barbarotti didn't enjoy, apart from graffiti artists, rap music and tabloid journalism, it was the big shop. But he was well aware that with a family of eight to ten people, it had to be part of life. Even if certain family members were on crutches.

'I've got to be home in good time,' he said. 'You couldn't have come in a bit sooner?'

'I tried to get hold of Karin Wissman while I was at it,' Backman explained. 'The witness at the restaurant. But she must still be away at her conference in Helsinki. I thought she was due back today, but apparently she won't be home until Saturday.'

'Is that a fact?' said Barbarotti. 'But what's so interesting?'

'Yolanda Wessén,' said Eva Backman. 'The woman at the ICA store in Rimmersdal who rang in this morning. I went there and we talked for an hour and a half. It was extremely revealing, and not just on the subject of Valdemar Roos.'

'Woman to woman?' asked Barbarotti.

'If you will insist on bringing it down to the level of your own understanding,' retorted Backman.

'Sorry. What did she have to say about Valdemar Roos, then?'

Eva Backman opened her notepad. 'Well, this exceptionally nice woman, Yolanda Wessén – or Yolanda Pavlovic, as she was called before she arrived in our wonderful country and married a bad-tempered baker called Wessén – says Valdemar Roos shopped there on at least five occasions in the past month.

With the exception of the week just gone, when she didn't see him at all.'

'Hang on,' said Barbarotti. 'This shop's in Rimmersdal, right, which is something like thirty or forty kilometres from town?'

'Thirty-five,' said Backman. 'Out towards Vreten. My brother lives around there.'

'And we're talking about a small local supermarket?'

'Correct.'

'What did he buy?'

'All the staples,' said Eva Backman. 'Milk, bread, coffee, eggs. The essentials, basically.'

'And what does that tell us?' said Barbarotti.

'What do you think?' countered Backman.

Barbarotti considered the matter.

'We don't want to go leaping to conclusions,' he said.

'Goodness, no,' said Eva Backman.

'It's easy to get carried away.'

'Goodness, yes.'

'Maybe he took his groceries home to Fanjunkargatan.'

'Every chance of it,' said Eva Backman. 'I'm sure you've hit the nail on the head. He gets in the car every morning, drives thirty-five kilometers west, stops at nice little ICA shop and buys all the essentials. Then he takes them back home. A round trip of seventy kilometres.'

'Exactly,' said Barbarotti. 'Completely normal behaviour for a Swedish man of his calibre.'

'So?' said Backman.

'So he's got another place,' said Barbarotti, 'where he goes.'

'I'd decided that too,' said Backman.

'Good,' said Barbarotti.

'Perhaps to see his mistress?'

'Could be. Though I find it hard to believe in this mistress.'

'Me too,' said Backman. 'But in any case, it must be somewhere thereabouts. The area around Rimmersdal. Mustn't it?'

'Sounds very much like it,' said Barbarotti. 'Did you learn anything else from Yolanda Wessén? He introduced himself to her, didn't you say?'

'That's right,' said Backman.

'Do you generally introduce yourself to the checkout staff when you go shopping?'

'No,' said Backman. 'To be honest, I keep my name to myself.'

'Same here,' said Barbarotti.

'But Yolanda said he was very pleasant and polite, and seemed rather keen to chat. And then . . . well then she seemed to confirm it.'

'Confirm what?' asked Barbarotti.

Backman rubbed at her hair and frowned. 'She thinks he once said something along those lines. That he'd be coming in quite often, because he'd just moved to the area.'

'Moved to the area?' said Barbarotti. 'He said that? Then there's no doubt, is there?'

'Er, well,' said Backman, 'she can't remember if he actually said it in so many words. It was more, um, an impression she got. And when he started showing up a couple of times a week, the impression stuck.'

'But she can't remember if he actually said he'd got a place round there.'

'No, she can't swear to it. Could be she just assumed.'

'Hm,' said Barbarotti. 'Well, this is certainly interesting. Anything else?'

'Not much,' sighed Backman. 'Unfortunately. What do you think we ought to do next?'

Barbarotti scratched his plaster and was silent for about ten seconds.

'Think,' he said. 'Sit ourselves down and think hard about what the hell this means. And interview that witness of course . . . when did you say? Saturday?'

'Saturday evening,' confirmed Backman. 'So we've got two full days for pure unadulterated thinking. Assuming that's what we want. This is just some dry old stick who's gone missing, after all.'

Barbarotti nodded. 'I know,' he said. 'I don't understand why I care so much about this piece of human furniture, either.'

Eva Backman seemed to be searching for an answer, but clearly failed to find one, because she closed her notepad and gazed out of the window.

'Looks like rain,' she said.

'Yeah,' said Barbarotti. 'Anyway, I'm fiendishly good at pure unadulterated thinking. But I don't need to tell you that.'

Eva Backman rolled her eyes and then looked at the clock. 'Weren't you supposed to be off shopping with your beloved?'

'Christ, yes,' said Barbarotti. 'Where are my crutches?'

31

That last thing he and Eva Backman had talked about on Thursday evening stayed with him.

That is to say, what their fascination with Valdemar Roos was. The thought lingered, not only for the rest of Thursday evening but also on Friday, when there were no new developments in the case, on Saturday, when he had the day off and Brother-in-law Roger made good on his promise to go home – or at least as far as Bollnäs, where he reckoned he could stay over with someone he knew – and on Saturday night, when he and Marianne made love for the first time since his dive into the wheelbarrow twelve days previously.

Of course the Valdemar Roos business wasn't in his head the whole time – especially not during the rather complicated act of lovemaking – but it was aggravatingly tenacious.

Disappearance of a dullard?

A good title for a play, perhaps, but what about the actual and current content? What was it about this sad tale of a sixty-year-old man who leaves his job and family that lent it such a shimmer?

Shimmer? thought Barbarotti, watching the display of the clock radio move from 02.59 to 03.00. Wherever did that word come from? If there ever was a word ill-matched to Ante Valdemar's life and times, it was surely *shimmer*. No, there must be some other component.

I feel sorry for him, Barbarotti hit on. It's my most profound humanity that gives me this interest in the dismal destinies of such people. Nobody in the world gives a toss about Valdemar Roos, and that's precisely why I do. I want to get to the bottom of this, regardless of Asunander and his graffiti; it's my duty to one of the least of these my brothers.

But this philanthropic approach didn't really match reality, either; after a bit of self-scrutiny, he was forced to admit it. However much he wished it had been the case. Eva Backman was as curious about what had happened to Roos as he was, and perhaps she had put her finger on the spot on Friday, when she told him the whole thing could be some kind of universally human wet dream.

Maybe a specifically male wet dream, she had added after a few moments' thought. The idea of climbing out of your life as if it's an item of clothing you're bored with. Of changing your entire existence from one day to the next. Discarding everything dull and habitual – work, wife, home and family – and starting something fresh and new in a different place.

Tempting? thought Barbarotti. Well certainly, for some people in some situations in life, but presumably also quite naive. The grass is not greener on the other side of that fence, and wherever you end up, you'll always be bringing some baggage along with you.

And was that really – when all was said and done – what lay behind this strange business?

If so, it must have been a very odd plan Valdemar Roos had drawn up. If he really had wanted to leave his wife and daughters, why hadn't he got on with it right away? A question they had asked themselves before. Why quit his job and then keep up appearances by pretending to go there every day? For a whole month. What was the point of such an arrangement? And why did he drive all the way to somewhere near Vreten? What had he got out there? A mistress?

Good questions, perhaps. Or entirely the wrong questions? At any rate, Barbarotti had not come up with any sensible answers; he had found no answers for several days now, and that was quite possibly why the missing dullard would not leave him in peace.

Because it was so bizarre.

Because Inspector Barbarotti hadn't the foggiest idea what had happened, and it was getting on his nerves.

He talked to Marianne about it on Saturday evening, once the kids left them alone with the washing-up.

'It could be,' he said, 'that this business will only be interesting until we find out the truth. As soon as we know, the minute all the cards are on the table, it's going to seem boring and banal.'

'Yes, but the same applies to life in general, doesn't it?' Marianne replied after a moment. 'It's the questions and the unexplored areas that are the big things, not the answers and what's obvious.'

'And the search for the answers?' he asked. 'Is that chasing the wind, like we were saying?'

'Not always,' she said, but he could see she wasn't happy with the answer.

'God?'

'God, yes? I don't know, but I'm sure anyway that a god without questions and mysteries can never be more than an idol, a false god. We're not meant to understand everything. Especially not Him.'

She then kissed him at slightly greater length than the moment, the washing-up or the hereafter really required.

Wonderful, thought Gunnar Barbarotti. It's wonderful to be married to a woman who understands so much more about life than I do.

But what must it be like for her to be married to me?

On Sunday morning he rang Eva Backman.

'Sorry to disturb you,' he said. 'I know it's Sunday and unihockey and all that, but were you able to get hold of that witness last night?'

'How's the pure unadulterated thinking going?' replied Backman.

'I haven't really got where I want to be yet,' admitted Barbarotti. 'But I will. The witness?'

'Ah yes,' said Eva Backman. 'I spoke to her. But I'm afraid she wasn't able to shed much light on the matter. I would have called you if she had.'

'Thanks, that's good to know,' said Gunnar Barbarotti. 'But she must have had something sensible to contribute?'

'We've got a good description of the girl.'

'Girl?' said Barbarotti.

'Yes,' said Backman. 'She chose the term herself. Barely more than twenty, she thought. Perhaps even younger.'

'A teenager?' said Barbarotti. 'Good grief, Valdemar Roos is almost sixty.'

'I know,' said Backman. 'Yes, the mistress theory is starting to seem more and more absurd. And the witness – her name's Karin Wissman, did I say? – found the idea pretty incredible, too, when I pressed her. But she didn't offer any credible alternatives, either. Valdemar Roos came out of a restaurant with a young girl just over two weeks ago and that's basically all we can say for certain.'

'And he disappears two days later when his wife tells him he's been seen with said young girl.'

'Exactly,' said Backman. 'It's pretty obvious the phone call must have been some kind of trigger. But beyond that . . . well, we're at a loss.'

'Sod it,' said Barbarotti.

'Yep,' said Backman. 'You could say that. But I didn't think there was any point bothering you with it yesterday.'

'Understood,' said Barbarotti.

'Though there is one other little thing.'

'Oh yes?'

'Just an odd trivial detail, I expect, but I talked to another informant yesterday afternoon.'

'And who was that?'

Eva Backman hesitated for a second or two. 'I'm sure it isn't important. A woman who had chatted to Valdemar in a bar.'

'In a bar?'

'Yes. Prince, on Drottninggatan. This was two months ago, mind. Or one and a half, anyway, but she couldn't remember the date. She recognized him from the photo in the paper, which was why she rang in.'

'Oh. And?'

'He was a bit drunk, apparently. He'd bought her a couple of drinks and they sat there talking for about an hour, she maintains.'

'Prince on Drottninggatan?'

'Yes.'

'I didn't have Valdemar Roos down as the sort who chats up ladies in bars.'

'Nor me,' said Eva Backman. 'I told you it was odd. She's coming to the station tomorrow afternoon so we can talk to her properly.'

'Good,' said Barbarotti. 'I think . . . well, I think this sounds pretty damn weird.'

'What he said was evidently pretty weird as well.'

'Pardon? Who said what?'

'Valdemar Roos. This woman claims he went on and on about one thing the whole time. About walking in a forest with his father.'

'You've lost me,' said Barbarotti.

'I'm not surprised,' said Eva Backman. 'But that was what she said. That *he* said, I mean. Something about the sun shining on the spruce trees and it being the most important moment of his life . . .'

'Walking in a forest with his father?'

'Yep,' said Eva Backman.

Barbarotti was reduced to silence for a moment.

'Do you think he's a nut job?' he said eventually. 'Simple as that.'

'I don't know,' said Eva Backman. 'We'll hear a bit more from that witness tomorrow, as I say. But I agree it sounds distinctly peculiar.'

'Peculiar doesn't begin to cover it,' said Barbarotti, and they hung up.

But there was another phone conversation with Backman that cloudy autumn Sunday.

She was the one who made the call, and it was half past ten in the evening.

'Sorry to disturb you,' she said. 'I know it's Sunday and

leaf-raking and pure unadulterated thinking and all that,' she began.

'White woman speak with forked tongue,' said Barbarotti.

'I think we've got a breakthrough.'

'What the hell do you mean?' said Barbarotti.

'It could be, anyway,' said Backman. 'But I'm not sure.'

'Go on.'

'I've just been talking to an Espen Lund.'

'Espen Lund?'

'Yes. He's an estate agent and an old friend of Valdemar Roos's. He's been away, but he got back today and saw the picture in the paper about an hour ago. He says he sold Valdemar a house about a month ago. Out Vreten way. What do you say to that?'

'What do I say to that?' said Gunnar Barbarotti. 'I say we put the estate agent in a car and take him out there right this minute. Fuck, what else would we do?'

'I decided roughly the same thing,' said Eva Backman. 'But I decided to postpone it until tomorrow, seeing as it's half past ten and Espen Lund says he's jetlagged.'

'All right,' said Barbarotti. 'We'll say tomorrow. What time?'

'He's coming to the station at nine,' said Eva Backman.

'Christ Almighty,' said Barbarotti.

'Why do you keep swearing?'

'Because I've got a hospital appointment for this leg tomorrow. I shall have to—'

'That's what happens when you land in the wrong wheelbarrow,' said Eva Backman, and another profanity almost escaped Barbarotti's lips.

'I'll put it off,' he decided. 'My follow-up appointment, that is. Have you spoken to Mrs Roos about this latest development?'

'No,' said Eva Backman. 'I thought it best to wait until we'd been there to make an inspection.'

Gunnar Barbarotti thought for a moment, and then agreed this was the right decision in the circumstances.

THREE

THREE

32

He came down to the beach just after six, and the sun had still not risen.

But it was not far off. The rosy flush of dawn suffused half the sky to the east, birds described their extended ellipses inland over the meadows and the sea lay in expectation, absolutely calm and still.

Expectation? he thought. Was there any better state of being?

He decided to walk south. After a few hundred metres he stopped and took off his shoes. He left them there on the sand in the lee of an upturned wooden boat with peeling paint, abandoned a good way above the shoreline. His socks were stuffed inside, one in each shoe. He didn't think anyone would bother helping themselves to such a tatty old pair of loafers but if they did get taken, it would be no problem going back into the boarding house barefoot.

He had a pair of sandals in reserve. He had bought them in Malmö when he went out to stock up on provisions before they crossed the Sound; she said they suited him but he was on no account to wear them with socks, and he hadn't tried a proper walk in them yet.

The name of the boarding house was Paradise; they had spent four nights there now and last night was the first time he hadn't been able to sleep. He didn't know why; he had dropped off around midnight after doing a few crosswords, but had woken up again at three and found it impossible to get back to sleep. He got up quietly at quarter to five, took a long shower and then dressed and crept out. The boarding house was in the middle of the little town, a two-storey wooden house, painted pink and nestled amongst lilacs and fruit trees, but it only took five minutes to get down to the sea.

And Anna was asleep when he left. She lay there in her usual way, curled up with her hands between her knees and the pillow over her head. He paused in the doorway for a few seconds, watching her. It's so strange, he thought, how fast she's become the centre of my life. I almost can't imagine us ever having been apart.

Her image was still before his eyes as he slowly moved south, along the never-ending beach. As far as he knew, it extended right down to the German border and probably further still. Yes, the world is boundless, he thought all at once. It really is. Our lives and our opportunities are boundless; it's just a matter of discovering that and taking it in.

And every day is a gift.

Fourteen of them had passed. Two weeks and one night since that Sunday evening when life switched onto a completely new and unpremeditated track. Ante Valdemar Roos knew that this time with Anna – regardless of what lay ahead of them, regardless of whether it all ended in a major or a minor key – was the most momentous thing he had ever experienced. Maybe, he had begun to think, maybe this had been the point of it all. His birth, his development to adulthood, his passage through the vale of tears. So he could live for a while with this remarkable girl.

He had carried on writing his aphorisms in the black notebook, one a day. Sometimes they were quotations, sometimes he was able to put the words together for himself. Twice it was something Anna said. Yesterday's source was once again the Romanian:

> He still cherished the illusion that he walked there alone, that he was moving and not the world beneath his feet, that he could go in any direction at all, that the furrow he ploughed – his own, unique life – was only visible behind him, in the tracks left by his laborious steps. He had not yet understood that the same furrow ran as deeply and pitilessly ahead of him.

That's how it was before, thought Ante Valdemar Roos. That was how I used to visualize my life. As deep incisions or inscriptions on a gravestone that was already standing. As if . . . as if that gravestone – and the interminably slow reading of its inscriptions – was the aim and purpose in itself.

He was not sure if that was precisely what Cărtărescu was driving at, but he didn't care, he thought in a sudden burst of cheerfulness as he kicked a deflating red beach ball, sending it a good way out into the water. He didn't care and it didn't matter! Once upon a time he had played inside right for Future Stars boys' football club and the clip was still there in his right foot. It's the feeling and the road taken that make it worth the trouble, not the words and the potential solution of the equation.

Yesterday evening she had sung for him, just the two songs because the fatigue had come over her again. One was 'Colours', an old Donovan song – he thought it was amazing that she had picked up so much from the distant sixties – and the other she had composed herself, and it was about him.

'Valdemar the Penguin'. He didn't realize until afterwards that he had been crying as he listened.

And he had felt gratitude. A deep gratitude that they had not succumbed to panic and fear after that grotesque turn of events at Lograna – but gave themselves time to think and pack a few things in the car. Her guitar, for example. Most of her possessions, too, the idea being to expunge all trace of her from the house, but when they had been on the road for a few hours that night, she remembered she had left a plastic bag of dirty washing under the worktop in the kitchen.

So they would definitely be able to tell that a girl had been living there, too. Lograna had not just been Ante Valdemar Roos's place in the world.

Assuming they got as far as finding Lograna. There was still nothing to indicate that they had, but it was bound to happen sooner or later. Sooner or later, he was under no illusion about that.

For the first couple of days he had anxiously listened to every radio news bulletin and skimmed through every newspaper he came across, but her calmness gradually rubbed off on him. And when they decided the wound on her head was starting to look better after all, and they wouldn't have to go to a hospital, that was another turning point. It meant they had no need to stay in the country. They drove across the Øresund Bridge just over a week after they had left Lograna, the sunshine of an autumn morning accompanying them, and it gave them a deafening sense of freedom to leave Sweden behind. Valdemar thought so, anyway; a confined little world closed behind them, a vast space opened up ahead of them.

He said it to her, too, in exactly those words. She laughed and put her hand on his arm.

'When someone closes a door, God opens a window,' she said.

'What do you mean by that?' he asked.

'It's what my mother used to say,' she replied. 'To my father, when I was younger. I liked it a lot. I used to lie in bed in the evening after they'd had a row and think about it.'

'I like it too,' he admitted. 'When someone closes a door, God opens a window. Do you miss your mum?'

'A bit.'

'How's your head feeling?'

Those first few days he had asked too often.

'Does it hurt? Do you want to lie down on the back seat for a while? Shall I help you change the bandage?'

Far too often, but it was hardly surprising he was worried. She had been lying unconscious on the grass when he found her and it had taken him several minutes to bring her round. The whole left side of her head was covered in sticky blood, and he cleaned her up with wet towels to reveal a gash almost ten centimetres long. Above her left ear, a swelling and a crude crescent shape that extended right across to her temple, just below the hairline; the rusty iron bar with which she had been attacked lay a few metres to one side, just under the apple tree.

The swelling persisted for several days, but she had soon got the hang of doing her hair slightly differently so nothing really showed. They were lucky: at the first hotel, that second night, they had managed to pass themselves off as Mr Eriksson and daughter. She'd had a blinding headache when they were at the reception desk signing in, but the injury and the bandage were hidden by her thick, dark-brown hair.

They stayed in Halmstad for three days. She stayed in bed most of the time, and he looked after her as if he really were a good father with a poorly daughter. He made sure she drank plenty and ate the occasional little something. He bought pain-killers at the chemist's, along with plasters, compresses and vitamins. He sat at her bedside and watched over her.

Asked her if she needed anything. Asked if she was in pain.

Way too often. On the morning of the fourth day, she got up, had a shower, told him to stop fussing and asked if it was about time they moved on.

For a moment he felt he barely recognized her. It was as if he didn't really know who it was, standing there at the narrow door of the en suite bathroom, wrapped in the hotel's white bath towels – one round her body and one round her head – and addressing him almost as if she were Signe or Wilma. The way they sounded when he had once again and for obscure reasons failed to live up to their expectations.

But then she saw that she had upset him, took three steps across the room and gave him a big hug.

'Sorry, I didn't mean to snap at you. But don't you agree it's time we got out of here?'

It had scared him, that moment, and it wasn't easy to put behind him. It lingered in one corner of his mind like an evil omen or sense of foreboding.

He drove on to Karlskrona, though he wasn't sure why. Perhaps because it would take a bit longer. In the car, on the road, was where they belonged, at least for these few days. As if motion itself was the only conceivable board on which the game could play out. But they only spent a single night in Blekinge province, where she slept for thirteen hours solid, and then they went on to Hotel Baltzar in Malmö.

Her headache came and went. She was sick a few times. He bought a variety of painkillers. Treo, Ipren, Alvedon. She said she found Treo worked best and when they drove across the Sound they had twelve tubes of it in stock.

But the swelling gradually went down and the gash began to look better. By the time they got to Malmö on the Saturday, they decided not to bother with any more plasters or compresses; they took a long walk in the Pildamm Park and it wore her out, of course, but afterwards she promised to follow him to the end of the world, as long as he had enough money for petrol and a few provisions for the journey.

He had withdrawn 500,000 in Halmstad; at the bank they asked what on earth he needed so much cash for, and he told them he was buying a boat. Eccentric seller, but he just had to go with the flow.

He knew he'd got that out of some book, the boat-buying story, and it made him grateful that he was an avid reader. He wouldn't have come up with it by himself.

But they definitely had the money for petrol and provisions. In Malmö he exchanged some of the Swedish notes for thirty thousand euros and twenty thousand Danish kronor, and that didn't seem to present any problems.

There was no need to bring up a boat or anything else.

He stopped and looked at his watch.

Half past six. The sun had come up properly now, but the beach was still deserted. He hadn't met another soul, so perhaps the Danes were a people who preferred a bit more time in bed in the morning.

They did have a certain reputation, after all, thought Ante Valdemar Roos, yawning and turning his steps back towards the main part of town. Or perhaps they had more important things to do, he corrected himself a few moments later. Work and so on. No time for wandering along beautiful beaches at sunrise, even if they were right outside your door?

They hadn't stolen his shoes and socks, at any event.

'I had such a strange dream.'

He nodded. She had described her dreams to him a few times before. Usually while they were having breakfast; it had almost become a habit of theirs.

'It seemed totally real, it was hard to believe it was just a dream when I woke up.'

He thought that if life consisted of just one day, he would be very happy for it to start like this. First an hour's walk along an empty sandy beach. Then breakfast in a seaside boarding house garden and a dream from this singular young woman's lips.

'What was it about?' he asked.

She drank some tea and started spreading jam on another slice of bread. Good, he thought, she's getting her appetite back.

'I think it was actually about death. And how we needn't be scared of it.'

'Oh?' he said. 'No, of course we needn't.'

'You were in it. My little brother and my mum were, too, but I had the main part. I was death.'

'You were death?' he exclaimed, involuntarily dismayed. 'Now I truly don't think—'

'Oh yes,' she assured him. 'I was death, and the one everyone had to come back to sooner or later. I knew that, and it meant there was no hurry about anything. You and Mum and Marek were in a boat, out on a river—'

'Marek, your little brother?'

'Yes. You were all in that boat and it was being carried towards a waterfall and you'd all, like, lost control of everything. But none of you realized, because the current wasn't especially strong to start with, you just thought it was an exciting adventure. And I was waiting for you further on, where the current got stronger, where I knew it would dawn on you that this was serious and you really were in danger.'

'Did we know each other?' he asked. 'Me and your mum and your brother?'

'Oh yes, and I was looking forward to being reunited with you all, because I'd been dead for a long time and the last time I'd seen you was at my funeral and you'd all been so sad and forsaken, somehow.'

'Forsaken?'

'Yes, that's how it feels when the dead leave the living behind.'

'How do you know?'

'It came home to me in the dream and it's something you just kind of know, anyway.' She nodded as if to confirm this to herself before she went on. 'The whole dream basically revolved round me just sitting and waiting for you all to come to me in the rapids. I knew you'd all be terrified at first, but then when it was over and you were with me at last, everything would be fine again.'

'Me and your mum and your little brother?'

'Yes.'

'What happened then? Did we go down the waterfall?'

'No, the strange thing was that you didn't. I don't know

what happened, in fact. I mean, you didn't have oars or anything, but somehow the boat was able to find its own current and come ashore instead. I sat there waiting and felt a bit disappointed, really, but it wasn't too bad. I knew you'd all be coming another day. And then he came instead.'

'He? Who do you mean?'

'Him.'

'Steffo?'

'Yes. And I absolutely didn't want to see *him*. He came speeding through the water on his scooter and just before he reached me, you were suddenly there after all, Valdemar. Maybe Marek and Mum were too, I don't know, but you blew on him and then he was gone.'

'I blew on him?'

'Yes, kind of breathed on him. And that was all it took. You leant down from Heaven, I think – I could see your upside-down head, at any rate – and then you breathed on Steffo and suddenly he didn't exist any more. I kissed you and then I woke up.'

'My God, Anna. You're making me . . .'

'Making you what?'

'Embarrassed.'

'You feel embarrassed because I kissed you in a dream?'

'Well yes, I do.'

'All right then, I'll try to control myself better next time.'

She laughed. He laughed. It felt to him like the happiest morning of his life.

Never better than this.

That afternoon they sat in deckchairs on the beach. The sun was coming from the right direction now.

'You still can't remember?' he asked.

She shook her head. 'No.'

'Are you getting any closer?'

'No. I rushed out, grabbed up the knife from the draining board as I went. I heard him coming after me. I caught my foot on that root in the grass and tripped over. Then . . . well, then it's a blank.'

'Good,' he said. 'It's probably just as well you don't remember any more.'

'I don't know. Maybe, but I would like to remember.' She paused and racked her brains. 'But I must have killed him, however you look at it. Just as he hit me with that iron bar. That must be what happened, mustn't it?'

'There's no way of being sure. Anna?'

'Yes?'

'Whatever happened, you don't need to feel guilty about it.'

'I know that's what you think. I think the same, but we can't control our consciences.'

He looked at her in silence for a while. Two joggers, a man and a woman in red and black tracksuits, ran past them further down the beach.

'Is it hurting? Shall we go back so you can have a proper rest?'

She pulled a sudden face, hard for him to interpret. 'How long are we going to stay here, Valdemar?'

'When do you want us to move on?'

'I don't know. Tomorrow perhaps. Or the day after.'

'Well let's say we'll make our minds up tomorrow.'

She nodded and put her hand on his for a moment.

'There's something up with my arm, Valdemar.'

'What? Your arm?'

'Yes, my right arm. It feels heavy and weird.'

'Have you . . . I mean, how long has it felt like that?'

'I noticed it yesterday evening when I was playing the guitar. My fingers felt so thick and clumsy.'

'Do you think it's anything serious? Do you think it could have anything to do with . . . ?'

'No, I'm sure it'll pass if I just rest up. Look, what's that over there? Swans?'

He peered towards the sun.

'Herons, I think they're herons.'

'They look like some kind of mirage.'

'Yes, almost.'

33

'Has he done something?' asked Espen Lund. 'I mean, do you suspect him of some crime?'

Eva Backman shook her head and fastened her seatbelt with a resolute click.

'He's been missing for two weeks,' Inspector Barbarotti informed him from the back seat. 'You don't happen to have any idea where he might have got to?'

He tucked a small cushion under his leg and thought that once he finally got rid of the plaster and could walk like a normal human being, he would never spare that sodding foot another thought. It had already monopolized far more of his attention than it deserved.

'Me?' said Espen Lund. 'Why on earth would I know where Valdemar Roos has gone?'

'You sold him that house,' Eva Backman reminded him. 'Nobody else seems to have known about it.'

'Discretion guaranteed,' said Barbarotti.

'For heaven's sake,' groaned Espen Lund. 'I sell thirty houses and flats a month. I didn't know I was also responsible for how my buyers choose to spend their time.'

'Steady on,' said Barbarotti. 'We're just trying to get to the bottom of this. You were old friends, you and Valdemar Roos.

He must have told you what he wanted the old place for. And why he didn't want his wife knowing about it?'

Espen Lund hesitated for a moment.

'He was a bit secretive about it.'

'Secretive?' said Backman.

'Yes. He wanted it all handled discreetly . . . just like you . . . what's your name again?'

'Barbarotti,' said Barbarotti.

'Oh, so that's you? What have you done to your foot?'

'Fight with a gangster,' said Barbarotti.

Espen Lund gave a strained laugh. 'And the other guy's in hospital, I suppose?'

'The cemetery,' said Eva Backman. 'Why was he so secretive about it, then? You must have been a bit curious, surely?'

Espen Lund sighed. 'Valdemar's as dull as ditchwater,' he said. 'I don't really know him all that well, but there was a period in our lives when we saw a fair amount of each other. After his divorce and so on. We were playmates as children, I can't help that. These past fifteen years I haven't seen him more than four or five times.'

'So you were surprised when he rang and said he wanted to buy a house from you?'

'Well not surprised, exactly,' said Espen Lund, inserting a portion of snus under his top lip. 'Nothing much surprises you after a few years in this business. Valdemar Roos wanted to buy a cottage for some peace and quiet. What's so remarkable about that?'

Eva Backman shrugged and pulled out onto the Rocksta roundabout. Barbarotti thought that, for his part, he would never buy anything from this jaded estate agent. But on the other hand, if you were already the owner of 350 square metres of property in need of renovation, you probably didn't require any more houses.

'Did you have any contact with him afterwards?' he asked. 'Once the sale had gone through, I mean?'

Espen Lund shook his head. 'Nope. We signed the contracts, the previous owner was there, too, and since then I've seen neither hide nor hair of him.'

'And when was that exactly?' asked Backman.

'We signed on the twenty-seventh of August,' said Espen Lund. 'He picked up the keys on the first of September. I saw him then, of course, but only for ten seconds. I checked the date after you rang yesterday.'

'All right then,' said Barbarotti. 'You don't know his wife, do you?'

'Never met her,' said Espen Lund.

'His first wife?'

'Nor her,' said Espen Lund.

'Hmm. OK,' said Eva Backman. 'It's starting to rain now, as well.'

Gunnar Barbarotti looked out of the window and saw that she was right. Then he checked his watch.

It was twenty past nine. It was Monday 29 September and they still knew nothing about the further adventures of Ante Valdemar Roos.

But in half an hour they would be at his cottage in the woods. At least that was something, thought Barbarotti.

At least that was something.

They hadn't brought a search warrant with them, but it turned out not to matter. It only took them a minute or two to come across the body, and at that moment the smallholding in the forest became a crime scene and all their assumptions were radically altered.

Despite the plaster cast on his leg, Barbarotti succeeded in forcing the door open at the first attempt; perhaps the more correct procedure would have been to sit in the car in the rain and wait for backup, but what the hell, he thought, and he was sure Eva Backman agreed with him, he could tell from the look of her; she certainly offered no protest. Some rules were made to be broken.

'Nice to get under cover, at any rate,' he declared, looking round the simply furnished kitchen.

Eva Backman located a switch and put on the overhead light. It was only mid-morning but the rain had brought with it a crepuscular gloom. She took out her phone and requested reinforcements. She gave a terse outline of the situation and ended the call.

Barbarotti looked at her and realized neither of them much fancied going out to stand guard over the body.

'Why does it always have to be raining when we find a dead body?' he grumbled. 'It's always the same.'

'It's Heaven, shedding tears,' said Eva Backman. 'Let's stay in here for now, eh?'

He nodded.

'No point standing out there getting soaked to the skin.'

'No.'

Espen Lund gave a sob. The good estate agent had gone extremely pale at the sight of the dead body and was now slumped over the kitchen table, resting his head on his arms. Backman and Barbarotti did a quick scout round inside the cottage. A kitchen and one other room, that was all. Simply furnished, certainly, but it looked lived in, thought Barbarotti.

There was bedding on the bed and food in the fridge. Newspapers a couple of weeks old, various items of clothing and a clock radio in working order.

But nothing to offer any pointers to why there was a dead body outside.

What the hell happened here? thought Gunnar Barbarotti. This is getting weirder and weirder.

Backup arrived about half an hour later, with the police doctor and CSI team two minutes behind them.

The rain had turned into a downpour in the meantime and Espen Lund had smoked three cigarettes outside, getting drenched in the process.

'Snus *and* cigarettes?' Barbarotti asked, but got no answer.

Espen Lund had not uttered a single word since they found the body; Barbarotti assumed this was a symptom of shock, but supposed it would be safest not to try to do anything about it.

The victim was lying behind the earth cellar, right on the forest margins but fairly clearly visible to anyone venturing onto the plot of land round the cottage. A young man somewhere between twenty and thirty, as far as they could tell, but the forest creatures had come and eaten parts of his face, so it was hard to judge precisely. He was lying on his back, at any rate, with his arms at his sides, and although it was debatable how he had died, the dried blood encrusting his jacket from his navel up to roughly nipple level provided a pretty good indication. It looked as though the wildlife had been feasting on that part of him, too, and when Barbarotti came back and tried to examine the body a little more closely, he could easily understand why Espen Lund had gone so pale and quiet.

'The stab wound to the stomach, what do you reckon?' said Eva Backman as the photographer snapped away from every conceivable angle and the CSI technicians shifted their feet impatiently, waiting to get their plastic canopy up so they could at least avoid a total soaking as they went about their delicate task.

'Not exactly a wild guess,' said Barbarotti. 'He's been lying here for quite a while, too.'

'No doubt about that,' said Eva Backman. 'It's two weeks since Valdemar Roos went missing. And if there's any logic in this business, this fellow's been dead for about the same length of time.'

'Logic?' said Barbarotti. 'You don't mean to say you can see any logic in all this?'

'It's not him, anyway,' said Backman, accepting the umbrella that one of the technicians passed to her.

'What?'

'That's not Valdemar Roos.'

Barbarotti looked again at the ill-treated corpse. 'You're right,' he said. 'His wife didn't say anything about him having a pierced eyebrow.'

Three hours later they were in the car again, on their way back to Kymlinge. Lund the estate agent had been taken home earlier, so at least they were spared that bother. The rain had stopped, too, but in all likelihood only temporarily. The sky above the strip of forest to the south-west looked an ill-tempered blueish-black; further heavy showers were surely on their way.

'All right then,' said Eva Backman. 'Shall we try to recap?'

'By all means,' said Barbarotti. 'You go first.'

'Man of around twenty-five,' said Backman. 'Murdered. Stab wound to the stomach.'

'The aorta,' said Barbarotti. 'Right on target, huge loss of blood. Probably dead within a minute.'

'Unconscious in thirty seconds,' said Backman. 'But he could have staggered a few metres before he collapsed.'

'No sign of his being dragged or carried to the scene.'

'But somebody pulled out the knife. The murder weapon hasn't been found.'

'Looks to have been a big kitchen knife or, like, a carving knife.'

'Must you use that expression?' said Backman.

'Like?' said Barbarotti. 'I know you don't like it. Anyway, never mind the lectures on modern Swedish language usage, let's get on. Identity unknown. No wallet. Probably murdered at the scene, probably twelve to eighteen days ago.'

'We'll call it a fortnight,' said Backman, 'for logical reasons.'

'As discussed,' said Barbarotti.

'That Sunday evening, then,' continued Backman. 'It seems pretty plausible to imagine that's when something happened. But what? And who is he?'

'Good questions,' said Barbarotti. 'What else do we have?'

'We have a red scooter, a Puch,' said Backman. 'Registration number SSC 161. Found by the road, a hundred metres from the house. We still don't know who the thing belongs to but if we're lucky that's how we'll find out the victim's name.'

'You think so?' said Barbarotti.

'Sorrysen should be ringing about that before long,' said Backman. 'He's had half an hour.'

Their colleague DI Borgsen back at HQ went by the nickname of Sorrysen because of his generally mournful demeanour.

'Expect he'll call shortly,' said Barbarotti. 'What can we say about the house?'

'Roos was living there,' said Eva Backman. 'He's been using the place as some kind of retreat, instead of going to work. No doubt about it.'

'But why?' said Barbarotti.

'Search me,' said Backman.

'Anything else?' said Barbarotti.

'There seems to have been a woman living there too. Or should we say a girl? Those panties and cami tops in the bag of washing point to someone pretty young.'

'About twenty?' said Barbarotti.

'Like, yes,' said Backman, putting her finger to her temple.

'And therefore?'

'And therefore we can assume that the account of Wissman, the witness at Ljungman's that Friday, was accurate. Can't we?'

'Exactly,' said Barbarotti. 'But who the heck is she?'

'And where have they gone?' said Backman.

Barbarotti thought for a moment. 'What's to say they aren't lying somewhere in the forest with fatal stab wounds to the stomach as well?' he suggested. 'Nothing, as far as I can see.'

'Lay off,' said Backman. 'One corpse is quite enough.'

'OK,' said Barbarotti. 'Where are they then?'

'You can get a fair way in a fortnight,' said Backman.

'The far side of the moon, if you want to,' said Barbarotti.

Backman was silent for a while, chewing on her bottom lip. 'A lot of question marks,' was her eventual conclusion.

'A lot,' Barbarotti agreed with a sigh. 'I think I've got water in my plaster cast as well. It feels like a meringue after all that bloody rain out there.'

Eva Backman glanced over her shoulder and saw him slouched uncomfortably in the back seat. 'Shall I take you straight to the hospital?' she asked.

'Yes please,' said Gunnar Barbarotti. 'I promised to be there at two and it's half past now.'

Eva Backman nodded.

'We'll have to sit down and give some proper structure to this later. Sylvenius is going to lead the preliminary investigation, and the case is going to be mine. Do you think you could come to HQ when you're done?'

'Of course,' said Barbarotti. 'Just got to guzzle some new plaster, it won't take a jiffy. But . . .'

'Yes?'

'I've got a date with Asunander to discuss the graffiti as well, hope I can put it off.'

'Stabbing trumps graffiti, surely?'

'I hope so,' said Barbarotti. 'But I can't be sure.'

In the event, he was stuck at the hospital for most of the afternoon – with several long periods of waiting – and had plenty of time to reflect on that morning's find at Lograna.

That was the name of the property, Espen Lund had told them before the power of speech deserted him – *Lograna* – but it remained unclear whether the name was attached to the land or only to the house itself. The previous owner's name was Anita Lindblom, anyway, just like the celebrated singer, the one who had a hit with 'Such is Life', and the purchase price had been 375,000 kronor.

Just before they got to the cottage that morning, Barbarotti had again asked if Valdemar Roos had mentioned another woman, and Lund had again denied this was the case.

'And you didn't suspect anything along those lines, either?' Backman had tried.

Not at all. The estate agent had been categorical. Admittedly he didn't know Valdemar Roos all that well nowadays, but for him to have started chasing women at his age seemed as unthinkable as . . . well, words failed him.

We've heard that before, thought Barbarotti as he made sure his meringue foot was propped up nice and high in the waiting room. Every single person to express a view on this Ante Valdemar Roos had said the same. Stressing how unlikely it would be for him to have a lover.

And yet it was so. He'd had a girl at his secret cottage. All the signs pointed to it. It wasn't just the bag of dirty washing that indicated her existence, there were other things too. A couple of long black hairs in the bed, for example, and some sanitary towels in a sack of rubbish in the outhouse.

Was there any room for uncertainty?

Could it be that she didn't exist, in spite of everything?

Conceivably, thought Barbarotti – a shadow of a doubt, as the saying went – but he found it hard to believe. The witness at Ljungman's, the evidence at Lograna, everything about Valdemar Roos's recent behaviour, as reported by his wife and others . . . no, decided Inspector Barbarotti, everything argued for there being a young woman involved in this strange story.

But who was she?

Where was she from and where had he found her?

And the victim, who was he? The young man knifed in the stomach, who bled to death and then lay undiscovered behind an earth cellar for two weeks?

He hadn't been carrying any ID. No particular distinguishing features, or at any rate none they had discovered so far. Jeans, trainers, a polo-neck sweater and a pale jacket.

That was all. The secondary injuries inflicted on him by the birds and animals were disgusting. His eyes had been eaten; Barbarotti remembered his ex-wife carrying one of those organ donor cards in her purse, an undertaking to donate her organs to whoever happened to need them if she suffered a fatal accident, but her eyes were not to be touched.

Had he come to Lograna on the scooter? They now had details of the registered owner, Backman had told him over the phone. But it appeared to be a dead end: the vehicle belonged to one Johannes Augustsson in Lindesberg, but it had been reported stolen at the start of June. Johannes Augustsson was eighteen, Inspector Sorrysen had spoken to him on the phone, and there was no reason to doubt the information he had given. The scooter was taken from the car park of the big Gustavsvik water park on the outskirts of Örebro, and he never saw it again.

The cottage and garden had been painstakingly searched, of course. Or the search was in progress, at any rate. Looking for fingerprints and so on, and a number of bags containing a range of items had been sent to the National Forensic Centre in Linköping for analysis. So that aspect was covered. Where some things were concerned it was best to stick to the accepted procedures.

Inspector Barbarotti was not feeling particularly optimistic, however, and he wondered why. Perhaps it was really only because his foot hurt, and because Marianne had looked sad when he left home.

Only?

He rang her number from his mobile but there was no answer.

Oh well, he thought. This evening I shall tell her I love her and would rather be dead than be without her – and as for the mystery of Valdemar Roos, at least we've made a few steps in the right direction. Haven't we?

They had found a cottage and they had found a dead body. It could have been worse.

Barbarotti glanced at his watch. Quarter past three. Dr Parvus was running half an hour late now. The waiting room was a greyish green and he had been sitting alone in it for forty-five minutes. He picked up a well-thumbed copy of *Women's Weekly*. It dated from June 2003 and had a blithely smiling Swedish princess in folk costume on the front cover.

Fascinating, thought DI Barbarotti, and started leafing through it.

It was half past five by the time he got back to the police station. He went straight in to Inspector Backman for an update. In the doorway he coincided with Sorrysen, who was on his way out.

'Peculiar business,' said Sorrysen. 'A lot of people we know nothing about.'

'Two,' said Barbarotti, 'if I've counted right. We know about Valdemar Roos, at any rate?'

'But he's missing,' said Sorrysen. 'Right, I must get off home. We'll carry on with this in the morning.'

He nodded to Backman and Barbarotti and left.

'What's up with him?' said Barbarotti. 'He's not usually in a hurry to get home, is he?'

'His wife's heavily pregnant,' said Backman. 'Smart plaster cast you've got there.'

But she sounded glum. 'What are you thinking about?' asked Barbarotti.

Eva Backman sighed and sank down behind her desk. 'All sorts of things,' she said. 'That boy, for example. I can't get that picture out of my mind, somehow. Nobody should have to die like that – just think if we never find out who he was.'

'Of course we will,' said Barbarotti, propping his crutches against the radiator and parking himself on the yellow plastic chair. 'You'll have to update me, I'm several hours behind.'

Inspector Backman's eyes rested on him for a while with that same mournful expression. 'You know what,' she said, 'apart from the fact that we've sent out enquiries in all directions and issued a few press releases, absolutely nothing of interest has been going on. The only thing that's happened is Alice Ekman-Roos going to look at the body.'

'And she didn't recognize him?' asked Barbarotti.

'No,' said Backman, 'but she threw up over him.'

She's right, thought Barbarotti. This is a day that seems completely devoid of silver linings.

Eva Backman woke with a start. She looked at the clock. The red numerals showed 05.14.

Oh God, she thought. What am I doing waking up at quarter past five in the morning?

Ville had his back to her and was breathing heavily. It was pitch black in the bedroom and the rain was rustling the foliage outside the window. She turned her pillow over and decided to try getting back to sleep. It was an hour and a half until she actually needed to be up, so what was the point in lying here and . . . ?

But before the numerals had time to flash onto 05.15, it came back to her.

She had remembered something in a dream, and that

memory had flung her up out of the well of sleep. It was something important. It was to do with . . . with Valdemar and . . . her father.

What he'd said.

What he'd said on the phone that time, when was it? About two weeks ago.

Yes, that was right. They hadn't talked since, and she hadn't been in touch with her brother or sister-in-law either. She'd been thinking about them, of course, out at Lograna yesterday. In the car on the way there she'd realized Valdemar's cottage must be close to Rödmossen, but she hadn't mentioned it to Barbarotti. The fact that her father, and her brother and his family, lived no more than a kilometre from where they found a man who had been stabbed to death just hadn't seemed . . . relevant.

Except in her own private system of coordinates.

Until now, that was. She pushed back the duvet and went to the bathroom. She put on the light, slipped out of her nightie and had a shower.

What on earth was it her father had said? How had the conversation started?

He had claimed he'd seen a murder, that was the gist, wasn't it?

He had been out for a walk and had witnessed someone killing someone else. Surely that was what he'd said? And blood, he'd talked about the colour of the blood, she remembered that.

Then the account had veered off in other directions, the way it usually did when Sture Backman embarked on a story. She had only been listening with half an ear, but he *had* started with something about a murder, hadn't he?

He said he'd seen something dreadful and that was why he'd rung Eva.

Because she was a police officer.

Yes, that was definitely it.

And two weeks after that day they found a body about a kilometre from where he lived.

Why didn't this come back to me yesterday? wondered Eva Backman as she turned the water to cold for a moment – she needed to kick-start her brain, apparently. Why has this suddenly surfaced hours later, in a dream? she asked herself irritably. I must be losing my touch.

Or maybe that was simply what dreams were for?

She went to the kitchen and put some coffee on.

Poor old Dad, she mumbled to herself. You must have been so scared, so scared.

Because that was how things stood. Sture Backman would often be anxious and upset when he couldn't understand the reality around him. When the dark cloud forced its way inside him, casting a blanket of shadow over his mental capacities. When he realized he was losing control of everything he had – effortlessly – been able to control all his life.

Like an eclipse of the sun, he would say. It's like an eclipse of the sun.

What should she do?

Interview him? Question him about what he had actually seen that day?

Was that a good idea? There was every risk of his having forgotten the whole thing. She would probably just worry him. He wouldn't understand what she was talking about, and the tears would come. It felt . . . well, *indecent*, in some obscure way she couldn't really explain to herself.

347

But on the other hand: what if he really had seen something vital? What if it might after all be possible to fish up something from that confused memory of his?

Take him to the scene of the crime?

Eva Backman started on her first coffee of the day and felt a sudden wave of nausea.

34

They left Grærup around lunchtime on Tuesday 30 September. She had slept right through to ten and woken with a headache.

She took three Treo and slept for another half hour. She had a strange dream about dead fish washing ashore on a little palm-fringed island, where she was abandoned all alone. Her dreams had been getting odder and odder since they first set off, and more vivid, too. They seemed more real than real life, somehow.

Valdemar had been out to buy her coffee and fresh Danish pastries, but she found it hard to get anything down. As usual they had shared a pipe on the little balcony outside, but that hadn't tasted very good, either. She decided to ask him to get her some cigarettes instead. Not right then, but later in the day. She was well aware that sharing a pipe with her felt special to him, but it made no difference. She was tired of it.

Tired in general. She had slept for almost twelve hours solid again. That had never happened before in her entire life; seven to eight had been her usual dose, possibly rising to ten if she needed to catch up. But twelve? Thirteen, even? Never.

Something's wrong, she thought. Something happened to my head back there at Lograna. I don't know what, but something must have come apart.

★

She struggled with the pictures in her mind. Whether she was awake or asleep.

But anything from that day which found its way into her dreams was never as clear as the rest. She couldn't bring it up to the surface with her, except very occasionally, when she was sitting in the passenger seat beside Valdemar, or lying tucked up on the back seat . . . then an image would come to her, or a short film sequence; for a second or two it would swirl through her consciousness and then vanish.

Steffo's face. His fucked-up, deep-set eyes. His arm goes up, he's got some long object in his hand, there's no time to see what. Her own hand gripping the handle of the knife . . .

But nothing stays with her. She can't hold on to the images; it's as if the headache drives them away, pushes them aside and takes their place as soon as they appear.

Maybe she doesn't want them to be clear, either?

Maybe she doesn't want to know what happened?

What use would the knowledge be?

But every now and then there were periods of lucidity. A different sort of truth.

Moments of sudden clarity and sober, justified questions.

What is happening? What am I doing?

I'm sitting in a car with a man of almost sixty, who I've known for less than a month.

We're travelling south, staying at a succession of boarding houses and hotels, and we've killed somebody. We're on the run.

I've killed somebody.

I was running away from the centre at Elvafors, now I'm running away from something else entirely. With this man who's old enough to be my father. My grandfather, almost. We have no particular destination in mind.

Where are you going, Anna Gambowska? Young girl, dumb girl.

Do you really believe this can end well?

But they were short, these moments of clarity. They were thinly spread over days and nights ruled by another disposition. A dreamlike, slightly unreal state, the past and future giving way to events unfolding in the present, meaning the only thing that existed was the here and now. The space they occupied, the growl of the engine, the cows grazing out there in the sunlit fields and the longing for a cup of coffee at the next stop. As if she was inside a glass bubble. Yes, that was exactly how it felt. Frosted glass, not entirely transparent, through which you couldn't really get a clear idea of what was happening in the world around you. And nor did you want to.

And there were good moments, plenty of good moments.

When he was telling her stories from his younger years. He was reluctant to talk about them, she had to coax it out of him. He was that sort of person; a crabby old grumblebear whose tummy you had to tickle to get him on the right wavelength.

You do see, don't you Anna? he would say sometimes. I've kept mum all my life and then I go and meet a little rascal like you. You've got to forgive me being a bit slow.

As slow as the elk, he said. The one standing out at Gråmyren. Never better than this.

Hemming, she prompted him, because she didn't really understand that bit about the elk. Your cousin Hemming, the one who died young when he was on military service. Why did the two of you raid Pålman's garden centre?

He sighed, dug about in his memory, and began the story.

Your teacher Mr Mutti and his Volkswagen? she asked him a while later.

Haven't I already told you I wasn't involved in that? he protested.

I think I must have dropped off before the end, she begged him.

Hmm. Well, Mutti's VW was a right old saga, he admitted. If they'd got caught they'd have been expelled, all three of them.

Some good moments. Valdemar Roos had no stories of any great note to tell – sometimes they were no more than trivia, for which he apologized – but they came from a forgotten world that was all but lost.

Maybe his father, for example, would have done better in his suicide's heaven to remain untouched and undisturbed on his pillow of cloud, and contemplate eternity from the viewpoint he had reserved for himself, or had been allocated by wiser and more senior decision makers. That was exactly the way he put it – *been allocated by wiser and more senior decision makers*. Sometimes she had to laugh at his slow and ponderous words.

But Valdemar subjected his father to endless scrutiny. He returned to him with a doggedness that Anna could not always understand. Can you imagine, my girl, he said, I can still see his eyes in front of me. They were blue, so very blue, and my mother used to say those eyes were their misfortune, his and hers. And mine. They should have been in someone else's head, and without them I would never have come into this world. That was what she said and I had no conception of what it really meant, I was only a little child. But I remembered the words and gradually, as I grew up, they took on some sort of meaning . . . right, that's enough, I'm talking too much. It's your turn now, your grandma in Poland, I'd like to hear more about her.

And she told him. About Babcia and pierogi and beetroot soup, the smell of coal in Warsaw and the ducks in her grandmother's backyard; Anna didn't even know if she was still alive, because they no longer had a mobile phone. It got broken when Valdemar hurled it into the glove compartment that Sunday, and it was just as well, really. Just as well to be without.

So they couldn't be tracked down that way.

She told Valdemar about her mother, too, her touchiness and bouts of depression. The sudden swings between light and dark, her moodiness. She had always loved her mother but there had been times when it wasn't easy. She told him about Marek, her little brother, and in the end about herself, too: how she came to slip further away from home life and that school up in Örebro; how she became a kind of mall rat at a local shopping centre and started truanting and smoking hash and drinking stronger beer, a second-generation-immigrant mall rat in a no-man's-land that . . .

Mall rat? Valdemar asked. Whatever is one of those? She laughed at him. Oh, they didn't exist in your time, Valdemar.

Some good moments.

But something else had happened. The good moments were surrounded by others. They were green islands in a swamp. Something was wrong with her head. She was constantly taking painkillers and sleeping away half the day.

And her hand, the whole of her right arm in fact, wasn't obeying her as it should. It felt strangely heavy and stiff. If she clenched her hand and closed her eyes, she couldn't tell after a while whether the hand was still clenched or not.

But it would pass. Hospital was out of the question, she and Valdemar were in agreement on that. They had left a dead body behind them at Lograna and they were on the run.

It was something they scarcely spoke of.

Valdemar told her, that first day in Halmstad, that he had found her in the grass, brought her round and carried her into the house. He had pulled the knife out of Steffo's stomach and buried the bloodstained weapon out in the forest. Along with the iron bar.

After that, they didn't return to the subject. She could not remember what had happened; her memory was blank from the point where she caught her foot on that root and fell over on the grass. Occasionally he asked her directly whether any memories had come back, and she answered that they hadn't. He seemed content to leave it at that.

No point digging about unnecessarily.

By evening they were in Germany. They crossed the border while she was asleep, so now there was a whole country between them and the dead body at Lograna.

Valdemar drove into a town called Neumünster and they checked into a hotel in the centre. From their window they could see a cobbled market square, some attractive gabled roofs, a town hall, a church. The peal of the church clock sounded every quarter of an hour and she liked it very much. Valdemar went out to buy them a few little treats.

A few little treats, he said that virtually every time.

Yes, they had put a whole country between themselves, Steffo and Lograna, and she didn't really know how he had managed to get hold of a Swedish newspaper. Perhaps he had bought it at the railway station; she had an idea they tended to sell foreign papers at stations.

At any event, he was pale in the face as he showed her.

'Look,' he said. 'They've found him. They'll be looking for us now.'

She was barely awake and there was a persistent dull ache in her head, but even so she could hear that he sounded rather worked up. *They'll be looking for us now.*

'Do you want me to read it out to you?' he asked.

No, she thought. No, I don't want to know.

'Yes, Valdemar,' she said. 'Would you, please?'

35

'We can't have DIs in plaster mixed up in murder investigations,' said Asunander. 'Barbarotti, you're to keep your focus on the graffiti.'

'Of course,' said Barbarotti.

'I might need to call on him for assistance,' said Eva Backman. 'It's a complicated business.'

'Use him sparingly,' said Asunander. 'You have DI Borgsen at your disposal. And Toivonen. And masses of back-room assistance and foot soldiers. Got that?'

'Got it,' said Eva Backman. 'Gerald's wife is expecting a baby any day now, but I understand the situation.'

'Gerald?'

'DI Borgsen.'

'Well he's not the one who's pregnant, is he?'

'No, indeed,' said Backman, closing her notebook. 'It's his wife. Was there anything else?'

'Not for the moment,' said DCI Asunander. 'But I'd be bloody surprised if we didn't get a bit of help from the newspaper-reading public on this one.'

'We've every reason to be optimistic,' agreed Barbarotti.

Asunander's surmise proved more or less right. When Eva Backman called them all together at 3 p.m. on the Tuesday afternoon – present: herself, DI Sorrysen (whose confinement was still awaited), DI Toivonen, assisted by Tillgren and Wennergren-Olofsson, plus DI Barbarotti (who had temporarily escaped from the graffiti case) – she opened the meeting with a summary of what had come to light as a result of the appeal for information in several of the major dailies and on radio and TV.

The first thing she was able to confirm was that Valdemar Roos really was in the company of a young woman and that they had evidently left the cottage at Lograna on the evening of Sunday 14 September, or on the morning of the following day.

They had checked into Hotel Amadeus in Halmstad around 2 p.m. on Monday the fifteenth. Under the names Evert and Amelia Eriksson. Father and daughter, the receptionist reported with ill-concealed excitement – but he had the newspaper open in front of him at the page with Valdemar Roos's picture and there was absolutely no doubt it was him. No doubt at all. The receptionist said his name was Lundgren and he had a good memory for faces.

They had stayed in Halmstad for three days and taken the opportunity of withdrawing half a million kronor from a bank account Valdemar Roos had opened six weeks earlier, of which his wife Alice said she was totally unaware. Despite the size of the withdrawal there were still 600,000 kronor in it. Where Valdemar had got the money was also completely beyond her, Alice informed the police with tears catching in her throat.

Where Valdemar Roos and his female companion had spent the night of the eighteenth was unclear, but on the nineteenth they had checked into Hotel Baltzar in Malmö and stayed for three nights. After that date, there was no further sign of them.

'Denmark?' said Eva Backman. 'It's not too wild a supposition that they crossed the Sound, is it?'

DI Sorrysen flicked through his diary. 'Last Monday,' he noted. 'They could have got as far as Malaga by now.'

Eva Backman nodded. 'It's one of those times when I wish we still had a few passport controls in Europe. But we are where we are.'

'No chance of tracing them via their mobile phones, then?' asked Wennergren-Olofsson.

'Afraid not,' said Eva Backman. 'The last time Valdemar Roos used his mobile seems to have been when his wife called him on that Sunday.'

'Smart,' said Wennergren-Olofsson. 'They're not using mobiles or plastic. That means we can't trace them. Was it half a million he took out?'

'Correct,' said Backman.

'How the hell must that feel?' Wennergren-Olofsson wondered aloud. 'Having so much cash, I mean.'

'Let's get on,' said Barbarotti, a touch impatiently. 'What do we know about the girl and the victim?'

'Not much,' conceded Eva Backman. 'Naturally we're trying to match them both up with people reported missing, but we've had no luck so far. We haven't got good descriptions, either. We know next to nothing about the girl's appearance. Karin Wissman, the witness who saw her at Ljungman's, says she has no clear recollection. The girl was thin, not particularly tall, dark-brown hair, around twenty and . . . well, that's basically all she can remember. But the guy from the hotel in Halmstad is coming here tomorrow, and we'll try to get an identikit picture done.'

'The victim?' said Barbarotti.

'As for him, we've got any amount of data of course: height, weight, blood group, dental status . . . but his face isn't in a fit state for us to give the papers a photograph.'

'I don't really follow you,' said Wennergren-Olofsson.

'Hungry wildlife,' said Backman.

'God, no, ugh,' spluttered Wennergren-Olofsson.

Barbarotti scraped his club foot irritably across the floor. 'Örebro?' he said. 'That scooter was stolen in Örebro, wasn't it? That's some indication, surely?'

'Absolutely,' said Backman. 'Perhaps he has some kind of link to the place, and possibly the girl does, too. It's likely of course that there's some link between the two of them, but remember this is just speculation. We've no idea what lies behind this murder; all we can do is carry on with our enquiries and hope things become clearer. Establishing the identity of the victim is our number one priority, of course.'

'And the identity of the girl,' said Sorrysen.

'And the identity of the girl,' sighed Backman.

DI Toivonen, who tended not to open his mouth unless the subject was fly-fishing or Greco-Roman wrestling, cleared his throat and adjusted his spectacles.

'I heard,' he said, 'that our dead man had puncture marks. Have we been able to confirm whether he was an addict?'

'You're right there,' said Eva Backman. 'Various substances were found in his blood . . . what was left of it. Yes, he was a user, I forgot to mention that.'

'Were there any other signs of drugs out at the cottage?' asked Toivonen.

Eva Backman shook her head. 'No, nothing.' She paused and leafed through some papers. 'We've also put out an alert for the car, of course. We can probably assume they're still driving around in his Volvo. But as they could basically be anywhere in Europe, we ought not to pin too many hopes on finding them that way.'

'They stayed in Sweden for a whole week before they went over to Denmark,' Sorrysen pointed out. 'Pretty risky, don't you think? I mean, they can't have reckoned it would be all that long before the body was found.'

'Hm,' said Eva Backman. 'I think we need to be clear that we're not dealing with out-and-out professionals here. A lot of what's happened seems have been irrational or pure chance . . . or maybe it just seems that way inside my head. OK then, can we leave it there, or does anyone want to say anything else?'

Tillgren, who had only been in the assistant role for a month, plucked up his courage and summed up the situation:

'This is a pretty tricky case, isn't it?'

Yes, thought Inspector Barbarotti once he was back in his office with his foot propped on the desk. He's not wrong there, young Tillgren.

A tricky case.

Ultra-dull fifty-nine-year-old bales out of his life.

Goes missing with an unknown young woman.

Leaves behind an unknown young man, stabbed.

It was all in a kind of haiku format, you might say. He actually sat there for a few minutes, trying to make it into a formally correct haiku – seven syllables, five syllables, seven syllables, if he remembered rightly – but when he realized what he was doing, he scrunched up the sheet of paper and threw it in the bin.

It was just a question of patience, presumably. Give it time, and the reports would start to pour in. Witnesses would come forward. They would speak to people who could provide snippets of information about one thing and another, and gradually things would become clear and comprehensible. That was usually the way, and in fact the process was not at all as tricky as the reality it could potentially uncover.

And while he waited for those mills to finish grinding, there were other things to be getting on with.

The graffiti investigation, for instance.

The problem – the acute problem – was that he happened to have settled his plastered foot on top of the file he needed.

That's a pity, thought Inspector Barbarotti, closing his eyes and leaning back in his desk chair. A damn pity, but a little nap was always a passable alternative.

While he waited for those mills to grind.

Inspector Backman had just decided to clock off for the day when the call came in via the switchboard.

'Is that the police? Am I still through to Kymlinge police station?'

Eva Backman confirmed this was the case.

'And you're the one dealing with that murder over in Vreten?'

She confirmed that, too. She introduced herself, and the woman at the other end of the phone gave her name as Sonja Svensson.

'I apologize if I'm barking up the wrong tree here, but I think I might have some information that could be useful to you.'

'Oh? What's that?'

'I'm the manager of the Elvafors residential centre, perhaps you know it?'

'Elvafors?' said Eva Backman. 'Yes, I think I do, actually. Near Dalby, isn't it?'

'That's right,' said Sonja Svensson. 'We've been running it since 1998, my husband and I. We look after young girls who've taken a wrong turn, you might say. Young addicts. We give them a chance to get their lives back on track.'

'Ah yes,' said Eva Backman. 'I think I've seen your centre, actually. I've driven past it once or twice.'

'Sixty-five kilometres from Kymlinge,' said Sonja Svensson. 'Though that doesn't take you round the same way as Vreten, of course.'

'I see,' said Backman. 'So what did you want to tell me?'

Sonja Svensson cleared her throat at some length. 'The thing is,' she said, 'we get all sorts of girls coming to us. We cope pretty well with the majority of them. We keep them off the drugs, get to grips with their problems, give them a new belief in themselves and . . . well, we prepare them for a fresh start in life, essentially. We succeed with almost all of them; our policy is firm but fair. If you're not prepared to set standards, you don't get anywhere with that sort of young lady. They gradually come to appreciate it. No mollycoddling, that doesn't help anybody.'

'I think I see,' said Eva Backman, feeling she was repeating herself. 'If we could just . . . ?'

'I'm only saying this to fill you in on the background,' Sonja Svensson went on. 'A bit of insight into our philosophy, you might say. The twelve-step programme is an important component, of course, and as I say it works well for most of our girls. But one or two decide to go their own way, of course. They think they know best and that can sometimes have an unfortunate effect on the other girls. We don't see it often, but occasionally it happens.'

'Of course,' said Eva Backman. 'I do understand all this, but . . .'

'Good,' said Sonja Svensson. 'No point making things unnecessarily complicated. Now we come to what I wanted to tell you. About a month ago, one of the girls ran away from the centre. One of those problematic girls, that is. We don't go in for locked doors or anything like that. Everyone's here of their own free will, and they all sign a contract to say they undertake to stay at the centre and observe our rules. If they don't want to stay, in principal they're free to cut short their treatment whenever they want. I said "ran away", but that isn't really the right expression in this context, of course. Anyway, I started thinking about this girl you're looking for . . . and it occurred to me that it could be her, that's all.'

Eva Backman hesitated for a second. 'What makes you think it could be her?' she asked.

'Not much,' admitted Sonja Svensson. 'The time matches, roughly speaking . . . and the geography. She could have set off along the Dalby road, and she hasn't been seen since.'

'Hasn't been seen?' queried Backman. 'When did the centre report her missing, then?'

'Only recently,' said Sonja Svensson.

'Recently?' asked Backman. 'What do you mean by that, exactly?'

'A couple of days ago,' said Sonja Svensson.

'But she'd been missing for a month, right?'

'Yes.'

'Why did you wait so long?'

Sonja Svensson cleared her throat again. 'We always like to give the girls a chance,' she explained. 'Sometimes they go, but come back after a few days. They have second thoughts.

If we report it to social services right away, they've burnt their boats.'

'Ah, all right then,' said Eva Backman, thinking there was something in all this that she didn't really get. But this clearly wasn't the time or place to poke around in it any more. 'What's the girl's name?' she asked instead.

'Anna Gambowska.'

'Can you spell that?'

Sonja Svensson did so and Backman wrote it down.

'I imagine you've got all her particulars?'

'Yes, every detail,' said Sonja Svensson.

'And you say she's been keeping out of sight ever since she left?'

'As far as I know,' said Sonja Svensson. 'The usual thing when they run away, of course, is for them to head for some large town or city. Stockholm, Gothenburg, that sort of place. That's where the drugs are, and it's fairly easy for them to keep their heads down for a while. So I can't say anything for certain, of course . . . she just came to mind when I read about that murder.'

'What about her parents?' asked Backman.

'Haven't been able to get in touch with them,' replied Sonja Svensson. 'I don't know anything about her dad, and her mum isn't answering the phone.'

'Who did you report it to, the fact that she'd run away?'

'Social services in Örebro. They were the ones who sent her here.'

Örebro? Eva Backman heard the name and gave a start. Things were starting to come together.

'A photograph?' she asked. 'Have you got a decent photograph of this Anna Gambowska?'

'I have an excellent photograph of Anna,' Sonja Svensson assured her.

'Can you email it over?'

'I can try, but the scanner has been playing up for the past couple of days. If I can't get it to work, can I make another suggestion?'

'Go ahead,' said Backman.

'I need to come into Kymlinge tomorrow for something else. I could come in and see you, and bring all the particulars you need. And the picture.'

Inspector Backman considered this for two seconds. 'Great,' she said. 'Let's do that. What time can you get here?'

'About ten?' suggested Sonja Svensson. 'Would that suit you?'

Eva Backman said it would, thanked her for calling in and rang off.

She had no sooner done so than it struck her that Lundgren, the receptionist from Halmstad, had also promised to be there at ten.

Well so much the better, she thought. He was certainly the right person to look at a photograph.

Things are progressing, she thought, switching off her desk lamp. I really believe they are, all of a sudden.

36

On Tuesday 2 October, Ante Valdemar Roos woke up at half past five in the morning and had no idea where he was.

At first he didn't even know what kind of room he was in. It had a high ceiling, and a street lamp or some other source of light was casting yellowish rays through the gap between the thick curtains onto the mirror on the opposite wall, which in turn spread a cobwebby pattern, paler but still yellow, across the bed and the big wardrobe.

Hotel. It came to him after a few seconds. We're at a hotel.

We? Yes, he and Anna, of course. For a few blank seconds, she too had been absent from his consciousness and that had never happened before. Not since they left Lograna; if there was one thing monopolizing his thoughts and cares, she was definitely it.

Anna, his Anna.

He turned his head and looked at her. She lay there only half a metre from him, in the same big bed; she had her back to him and was curled up in her usual way, barely visible under the puffy feather quilt.

My baby bird, he thought, and gave a laugh. Because that was exactly as it should be. A baby bird tucked up in down. Safe and secure.

And it was the puffy quilt that made him realize they were

in Germany; he had stayed at German hotels a few times before in his life. But he couldn't remember the name of this town, however he racked his brains. He remembered they had arrived and checked in late last night; they had spent the last few hours on smaller roads, avoiding the autobahn. It was their second night in Germany, he had forgotten to buy a map at the last petrol station again and . . . and if the truth be told, he hadn't been very sure where they had ended up last night, either. He had never really known, and therefore he had forgotten.

But what difference did it make, he thought, if they were in one German town or another? Here they were in a huge double bed, snuggled amongst downy bolsters and pillows that were equally huge and seemed to be full of whipped cream or shaving foam, so beautifully soft. Could they wish for anything more? Could life be better than this?

But even so, he had woken up. There had been a succession of mornings like that now. Anna readily slept until nine or ten, even if she had gone to bed early – it was something to do with that blow to the head – but he was finding it harder and harder to hang on to his sleep. The fatigue in his body and soul cried out in vain for a few more hours, for an extra hour or even a half, but it did not help. He bobbed up to wakefulness like a cork and then it was impossible to find his way back.

Twenty to six. Anna was sure to sleep for another three or four hours. He realized there was an armchair with a little standard lamp by the window; in fact, if he drew back the curtains a tiny bit more, he needn't even bother with the lamp. He could make do with the dirty yellow illumination of the street lamp and the dawn light that couldn't be far off now.

He went over to the chair, where he found his half-finished crossword from the day before, the one in the Swedish women's magazine he had got hold of the day before yesterday. The magazine in which there was also a report of a young man found murdered in the Vreten area between Kymlinge and the Norwegian border, with a picture of a man sought in connection with the case.

He wondered if it was Alice who had supplied them with the photograph. He presumed it was and he presumed she had had to go to some effort to find it. He leafed through to the relevant page and looked at it again. It was one of the worst pictures of himself he had ever seen. He could not for the life of him work out where it had been taken, but he was unshaven and looked sweaty, had his mouth half open and an expression in his eyes that made him look as if he was about to have a stroke. Or was straining to go to the toilet. Bloody hell, thought Ante Valdemar Roos gloomily, as if it's not enough to be wanted for murder, I have to look like some drunken slob as well.

He sighed and turned his attention to the crossword. Seven down. *Nabokov scandal.* Six letters, the second *o*, the fourth *i*.

Doping, thought Valdemar Roos. It was obvious, even though the Swedish word was actually *dopning* with an *n*, but crossword compilers didn't always do their homework properly. Nabokov was a Russian skier, anyway; he had won an Olympic gold medal and then been found to have banned substances in his blood. It was some years ago now, but the name had stuck in his mind.

He filled in the word, yawned and went on.

He must have dropped off in the armchair after all, because he was roused by the sound of the church clock striking seven. This time he was instantly aware of where he was – that was to say, in an unspecified old hotel in an unspecified old German town – and as he assumed the restaurant on the ground floor would now be open, he got dressed and went down for some breakfast.

He had quite enjoyed his early morning time upstairs, but when he got to the empty, drab-brown dining room – which proved to be down in the basement – and was met by a tired, middle-aged waitress with a sour expression who besieged him with questions about his room number and whether he wanted tea or coffee, his spirits sank. He would have liked to explain to her that he preferred not to have his coffee right away but only once he'd had some yogurt, cereal and a soft-boiled egg, if these were on the menu, but his imperfect linguistic knowledge raised insuperable barriers to such requests, so he merely said 'Vier ein sechs. Kafee, bitte', and sat down at the corner table to which he had been directed. He had picked up a paper on the way in, *Welt am Sonntag*, which was as thick as a novel and several days old, but he started flicking through it just to have somewhere to park his eyes.

Durch, für, gegen, ohne, um, wider, thought Ante Valdemar Roos as the coffee thumped down in front of him. Prepositions taking some case or another, he couldn't remember which and in any case he was rather hazy about what a case was. 'Danke schön,' he said, and the weary waitress shuffled off, leaving him to his fate with the newspaper and coffee.

Well, what *is* my fate? he wondered. How have I ended up here?

Good questions, without a doubt, and as the contents of the newspaper were refusing to penetrate his consciousness, he started looking for appropriate answers. Without demanding any great depth or precision, but even so.

He had long since realized that the events of these days and weeks were the point of his whole life. His encounter with Anna Gambowska had been written into some kind of musical score of the hereafter, etched deep into his gravestone, and it had been as inevitable as destiny and Alice's verrucas. I know, he thought, still with his eyes on the paper, that this is the moment my life is alight. It's what I make of these circumstances that is going to count on Judgement Day. This and nothing else.

And yet I feel so dispirited and tired and fragile this morning in this unfamiliar hotel dining room, he thought. I have Anna's life and future in my hands, and it is her fate that she met me just as much as the reverse, of course, but sometimes . . . sometimes I feel she doesn't understand that. She's so young, and perhaps she just needs time. Time and recuperation, she really does sleep away most of our days, it isn't fair, or perhaps it is . . . and I, I alone, am the one bearing the burden and taking responsibility in this hardest period in our relationship. It weighs me down so much, this albatross, this millstone round my neck . . . but what the hell? What the hell am I doing, drivelling on in my pathetic and enfeebled state? Albatrosses and millstones? No, by God, decided Ante Valdemar Roos, it's up to me now to make sure . . . everything hangs together. Hangs together, hangs together, I should have brought the Romanian to breakfast instead of this indecipherable newspaper, of course I should . . . as long as we can find the right words for the circumstances in which we find ourselves, we can usually see the light at the end of the tunnel.

He drank some of his rapidly cooling coffee and reprised that last thought.

As long as we can find the right words for the circumstances in which we find ourselves, we can usually see the light at the end of the tunnel.

Good, thought Ante Valdemar Roos. Damn good – that can be today's aphorism. I shall remember to write it in my book as soon as I get back upstairs.

And he did. Then he sat in the armchair for a while and read through everything he had written since he started three weeks before – and these words, all these abstract but well-formulated thoughts on the subject of life and its labyrinth, slowly improved his mood. To the point, at least, where he could undertake some practical planning. It was certainly needed, and if nothing else he felt as if Anna demanded it of him. Or as if her condition did, at any rate. Whatever the difference was.

She was sleeping just as before, in the same position as she had been when he left the room. It was quarter past eight now, but she was unlikely to stir for another hour. I wish, thought Ante Valdemar Roos, I really wish she didn't sleep so much. It feels as though she's absent most of the time, and this is time that's so important.

But he had to be patient, he knew that. Healing takes time and care, and not that much more really. In a few days, a week or two, she was bound to be back to normal. By then they would be some way further south. Perhaps in France or Italy, he didn't know exactly; perhaps some mountain air was what she needed to get better, or the sea.

Then another thought struck him. He'd had to show his ID when they checked in last night. The weedy receptionist with the leather waistcoat and long, horsy face had accepted the excuse that their passports had been stolen, but he still needed some form of ID, he informed them. Even if they paid cash in advance these were different times, and it was not that kind of establishment.

That kind of establishment? Oh well, he assessed the risk as quite small. Of course it would be documented for all time that they had checked into this little hotel in this particular little German town, whichever it was – but it seemed pretty unlikely that this would come to the attention of the Swedish police. And if it eventually did, and he was proved wrong, they would be far, far away by then. There was no great risk of them being tracked down, he thought, even if he had to show his driving licence now and again. It wouldn't have worked in Sweden, it would have been madness, but down here on the continent it was a different matter, noted Valdemar Roos. Completely different. And when your homeland closes a door, the world opens a window.

They would stay in this hotel in this town for another twenty-four hours. He had paid for two nights and he would make sure to use the day well. First of all he would buy a decent road map and find out the name of the town and its exact location.

Then he would find a chemist's; Anna's stocks of painkillers were running low. After that, with these chores out of the way, perhaps they could spend a bit of time at some nice cafe. The weather on the other side of the heavy curtains did not look bad at all; the yellow street lamp had gone out and been replaced by a generous sun.

They could sit there and talk about life, make a few plans together. Most of all he would like her to play the guitar and sing something for him. It was a few days since she had last done so, but he didn't want to press her if she didn't feel like it.

It has to come from an actual desire, he thought. The same applies to things in general but that hasn't been the way in my life so far, that's been the missing component. Not the only one, but the most important.

And if she didn't feel like singing, or telling him about her life, then he had a couple of stories up his sleeve. They had come into his mind yesterday evening after she was asleep, and although they were strictly speaking about other people, in completely different circumstances, with a few adjustments he could easily put himself in the leading role.

And this, he thought, was how she not only held his future in her fragile hands but also changed what had already taken place in his life. He was not entirely sure of the real implications of this, and whether it was a good idea in the long run to rewrite his own story. But maybe there wasn't going to be a long run, as far as the rest of his life was concerned. Maybe it would only be a matter of a year or two, or even just a few months.

Whereas the present, Ante Valdemar Roos formulated it to himself in silent satisfaction, is above all a matter of *now* and *today*. You had to be present exactly where you were in time and space, the next day it could be too late, and if you didn't—

A sound and a movement from the bed broke the flow of his thoughts, and a second later he was out of the armchair and across the room.

She had fallen out of bed and was lying on the floor, and something had happened.

She was shaking. Her body was taut and arched while her nightdress, really just a big white T-shirt, had ruckled up under her arms, leaving one breast exposed, and he could see her pubic hair through her thin briefs. He cursed himself for not being able to avert his eyes from this unwanted intimacy, but that's the male gaze, like it or lump it, he thought apologetically as he tried to fight back the sense of horror suddenly pumping through his chest and threatening to choke him. What's happening, dearest Anna? What on earth is happening?

He tried awkwardly to stop the shudders that were running through her body. He grasped the tops of her arms and attempted to at least make eye contact with her, but her face was twisted back and away from him. Her throat was emitting a jerky sort of gurgling sound and the shaking seemed to transmit itself into his own body – at the same time as it grew less violent, thank heaven, and gradually ebbed away before finally stopping.

The whole sequence, from her fall out of bed to the end of the shaking, could not have taken more than a minute, but afterwards, as he sat there with her relaxed body in his arms, he thought it had felt like the longest minute in his life.

Her breath was still coming in gasps and when he felt her pulse it was racing. Her eyes were darting restlessly, as he had seen the eyes of blind people do . . . Oh my God, Anna, he thought, what's happening to you?

And he caught himself actually praying to God.

He straightened out her T-shirt and prayed to God.

A few minutes later – five or fifteen or maybe only three, he had no idea – she opened her eyes and smiled at him. It was a little bewildered and feeble, but it was a smile.

'Valdemar,' she whispered. 'Valdemar, why are we sitting on the floor?'

37

'I thought you were going to be working on the graffiti problem,' said Marianne. 'Not that Valdemar Roos.'

'And so I am,' said Gunnar Barbarotti. 'That is, I'm working flat out on the graffiti question, but there's something about Valdemar Roos I just can't let go.'

'So I've come to realize,' said Marianne. 'And to be honest, it worries me slightly that you find him so interesting.'

'Why's that?' asked Barbarotti in surprise, putting two more slices of bread in the toaster. 'What's wrong with being interested in your work?'

Marianne sighed, regarding him across the kitchen table and the debris of four children's breakfasts. For the time being they really were only a quartet, Sara and Jorge having made their flat on Kavaljersgatan habitable enough for them to start spending the nights there. It could be permanent, but it was hard to tell.

And Brother-in-law Roger was a mere memory. It was half past eight, and Marianne wasn't on duty that morning. Gunnar worked flexitime.

And here she was, worrying about him.

'Some people will always be hard to understand,' he said, trying to give her something specific. 'That makes them interesting. I think Valdemar Roos is one of those people.'

Marianne gave a snort of derision. 'Interesting? He's just your average dirty old man in his sixties, as far as I can make out. Thinks a lot of himself, slightly nuts. He leaves his wife without a word of explanation and you reckon that makes him special?'

'Hm,' said Gunnar Barbarotti.

'This is a girl of twenty, if I've understood correctly. They killed a young man and now they're on the run. You must see that it worries me when you call something like that interesting?'

Barbarotti thought about it.

'A junkie girl and an old lecher,' summarized Marianne when he failed to come up with a good answer. 'To put it rather coarsely.'

Barbarotti cleared his throat in an attempt to overcome his vacillation. 'What . . . what are you imagining exactly?' he said. 'That I have some secret wet dream of driving off into the blue with a teenage girl? Is that what you think? In that case let me assure you that . . .'

He faltered and felt a twinge of pain from his foot.

'That what?' said Marianne.

'That I love my wife more than anything on earth and that my interest in Ante Valdemar Roos is exclusively to do with its . . . psychological and universally human aspects.'

'Bravo,' said Marianne, bringing her palms together and making him feel for a moment as if the whole conversation was the seventh take of a hopeless scene from some even more hopeless low-budget reality show for morning TV. Did such things exist? And if they did, surely there was no time for retakes?

'But tell me one thing,' his wife went on. 'If this noble

and universally human policeman really loves his wife as much as he claims, how can she really be sure things are as he says? Mightn't he just be trying to provide some window dressing?'

'What the heck is up with you?' said Barbarotti, and gave his plaster an anxious scratch. 'I just don't get how you can . . .'

But then he saw she was smiling, and that her dressing gown had fallen open in the sort of way that changes things entirely and leads to places radically unlike, say, a low-budget daytime reality TV show.

'Come with me,' he said, holding out his hand.

'What do you mean?' said Marianne.

'So you've made it at last?' said Eva Backman, looking up from her computer.

Running a bit late, thought Barbarotti. My wife and I shagged for two hours this morning. Sorry, it takes longer when you're in plaster.

He might have said it out loud, too, if it hadn't been for Inspector Sorrysen, who was all too sensitive when it came to that sort of frankness and who also had a heavily pregnant wife.

Was the latter fact even remotely relevant?

'There was a graffiti lead I had to follow up,' he said, sitting down. 'How's it going?'

Eva Backman looked at him with a suspicious frown. 'Well,' she said, 'it's going well. I think we can say with a fair degree of certainty that we've found the girl.'

'It was her?'

'That's right,' said Backman. 'Our little Polish friend. Sonja

Svensson the Elvafors manager and Mr Lundgren from Halmstad were in complete agreement.'

Inspector Sorrysen nodded and read from a sheet of paper. 'Anna Gambowska. Born in Arboga on first August 1987. Mother Polish, came to Sweden in 1981. Grew up in Örebro . . . the girl, that is. Completed her years of compulsory schooling and started an upper secondary course but left in 2003. Taken into the care of local authority social services in Örebro at the end of July this year at the request of the girl's mother. Obvious addiction problems, admitted to the Elvafors residential centre on first August.'

'On her birthday?' said Barbarotti.

'Correct,' said Sorrysen.

'We're awaiting further particulars from Örebro,' explained Backman. 'But we have a good photo of her, and Sonja Svensson was able to give us quite a lot of information.'

'Such as?' asked Barbarotti.

'Ahem,' went Backman. 'Such as she's evidently a tough nut. Impaired empathy, seemingly, and not inclined to cooperate. Refuses to stick to rules, self-willed, keeps herself to herself rather than joining in communal activities. Difficult to deal with, in Sonja Svensson's view. After she ran away, the atmosphere at the centre improved right away.'

'I see,' said Barbarotti. 'And when was it she ran away?'

'The start of September,' said Backman.

'And they waited nearly a month to report that she'd gone?'

'Yes.'

'That's odd, isn't it?'

'I didn't press her on that point,' said Backman. 'But I agree with you, it is a bit odd.'

'And how the hell did she get wind of Valdemar Roos?' Barbarotti went on.

'We don't know,' said Backman.

'There's no previous link between them?'

Eva Backman shook her head. 'It seems not. Why should there be? But we don't know that definitely yet, of course.'

'I don't suppose Roos has a record where narcotics are concerned?'

'Clean as a whistle,' said Sorrysen. 'They're an odd couple and no mistake.'

'And the victim?' asked Barbarotti. 'Have we got anything to give us a lead on who he might be? He had substances in his blood, didn't he?'

'Could they all have lived at the cottage together?' suggested Sorrysen.

'The girl certainly did,' said Backman. 'There are loads of fingerprints that are presumably hers. But none of the victim's, as far as we know.'

'And the relationship between the two?' asked Barbarotti. 'The victim and the girl, that is.'

'We haven't got that far yet,' Backman reiterated. 'But when we get the material from Örebro, we can start pulling it all together. We've established a police contact up there. DCI Schwerin, if you remember him?'

Gunnar Barbarotti smiled. 'Schwerin? Excellent, then we needn't worry.'

'Just so,' said Backman. 'It might take a while, but we needn't worry.'

Inspector Borgsen looked quizzically from one colleague to another.

'Last autumn,' Backman filled him in. 'Dead Man's Field outside Kumla.'

'Oh yes,' said Sorrysen. 'Right, I'm with you.'

'Precisely,' said Barbarotti.

He stayed on for a while in Backman's office after Sorrysen had departed.

'So what do you really make of all this?' he asked.

'I don't know,' said Backman. 'What *is* one to make of it?'

'Was the girl a prostitute?'

Backman sighed. 'That's unclear. Nothing on record to indicate it, at any rate, but why should there be?'

'Yes, why should there be?' said Barbarotti.

'There aren't that many ways a girl can get money for drugs,' Backman observed gloomily. 'Though she's only twenty-one and her addiction seems mainly to have been to hash, some smack, too, but she seems to have gone into rehab before she was reduced to that. Maybe she hadn't been reduced to that; she'd had a few jobs since she opted out of college. So it could be she was managing financially, somehow.'

'Could be,' said Barbarotti.

'She could have been dealing, too, but Sonja Svensson didn't actually know very much about her background. Their focus at that place is looking to the future, she claims. Not digging into the past. It's all part of their philosophy.'

'Philosophy?' queried Barbarotti.

'That was the term she used,' said Backman.

'And we're dealing with some tough little nut, that was what she told you?'

'Yes, that was what she told me. But that's par for the course, wouldn't you say? Toughness is a precondition in that world.

If they haven't got a hard shell they fall apart, you know that, surely? Christ, sometimes I feel grateful I've only got boys.'

'Yes,' said Barbarotti. 'It's easier being a man. But only half as interesting.'

'A quarter,' countered Eva Backman, unable to suppress a smile. 'Why do you always have to exaggerate every damn thing, you males?'

'Sorry,' said Barbarotti. 'I got a bit carried away. But now she's going to get her picture in the paper too, our tough cookie Anna. Don't you reckon?'

'Of course,' said Backman. 'And they are an interesting couple, as we said. I can imagine the tabloids making a splash with this tomorrow. They're not exactly Bonnie and Clyde, but a sixty-year-old man and a twenty-year-old girl on the run together . . . well, that ought to shift a few copies.'

'Especially as they've left a corpse in their wake,' Barbarotti added. 'Yes, I fear you're absolutely right. Though . . .'

'Yes?'

'Though we're scarcely going to find them with the help of our press, magnificent though they are. I imagine people down in Europe don't give a toss what's in our papers. But what's your view? Because I've only got a quarter of a brain, as we agreed.'

Eva Backman laughed. 'There's nothing as attractive as a modest guy. What size brain do you think Valdemar Roos has got, incidentally?'

'Good question,' said Barbarotti.

'Certainly is. Half a million in cash and a twenty-year-old female addict as a sidekick. A fatal stabbing at a secret cottage and then a getaway down through Europe . . . he's losing his reputation for dullness, that's for sure.'

Barbarotti was thinking. 'He must have bought the cottage first,' he said. 'I mean, quitting his job and starting on a secret life and all that . . . you don't think it had anything to do with Anna Gambowska from the start, do you? Could he have got to know her when she was being treated at Elvafors . . . or even earlier?'

'No, I don't think so,' said Eva Backman. 'Sonja Svensson had no idea who he was, at any rate. It all seems so improbable. Maybe . . . well maybe they met by sheer chance.'

'Yes, that's how we rationalize it, I suppose,' said Barbarotti. 'How do you mean?'

'When we can't grasp how things fit together, that's when we put the blame on sheer chance.'

'You're so smart sometimes,' said Eva Backman. 'I'm almost inclined to believe God equipped you with two quarters of a brain.'

'Thank you,' said Barbarotti. 'Right, I must get to my office and put the final touches to the graffiti mystery. Let me know if there are any developments.'

'Final touches?'' said Eva Backman. 'You don't mean to say . . . ?'

'I've got a theory,' said Gunnar Barbarotti. 'Now where the heck did I leave my crutches?'

Her father looked older than ever.

And so he was, of course, but when she saw his ashen face and sunken cheeks and met his anxious eyes, she really felt it could not be long now.

She tried to work out when she had seen him last. June, she decided, the weekend before midsummer. Almost four months had gone by.

Shameful, it was the only word she could find. Of course she had talked to him on the phone five or six times since then, but Erik and family had him with them every day. Every hour of every day.

Feeling that sense of shame did not render it any easier to make contact with him. Ellen had the day off, evidently, and they exchanged a few words when her sister-in-law arrived, but not many. Then she left them alone in the kitchen and shut the door.

Alone with a pot of coffee and a plate of freshly baked cinnamon buns.

When did I last bake cinnamon buns for my family? thought Eva Backman. What sort of person am I, when it comes down to it?

She pushed aside the self-criticism and poured some coffee for her father. Cinnamon buns had nothing to do with human qualities, did they?

'No sugar,' he said. 'I've given up sugar.'

'I know that, Dad,' she said. 'You gave up sugar forty years ago.'

'Too much sugar isn't good for you,' he declared. 'Dr Söderqvist told me to give it up, so I did.'

'How are you keeping these days, Dad?' she asked.

'Fine,' he said, looking anxiously about him as if it were some kind of trick question. 'I'm doing fine. I live here with Erik and . . . Ellen.'

'Yes, it's very nice for you here, Dad,' she said. 'Do you still go for walks in the forest?'

'Every day,' he said, sitting up straight. 'You have to do something to keep your brain going . . . or your body, anyway.'

As if he realized his brain wasn't up to much any longer.

She swallowed and decided to get straight to the point. He was always clearer in the head at the start of a conversation; as soon as he tired, his concentration went, his ability to focus on what they were actually talking about.

'You rang me a couple of weeks ago to tell me you'd seen something awful, Dad. Do you remember that? You said you'd seen a murder.'

He raised his coffee cup and put it down again. Suddenly there was a new expression in his eyes, and she could have sworn the colour of his face changed. A healthy sort of flush spread across his cheeks and forehead. Good, she thought. He remembers. Keep it in your head now, dear Dad.

'Oh yes,' he said, 'of course I remember. I rang you to tell you about it because you're in the police. Have you started investigating it?'

'Yes Dad, we have. But I could do with . . .'

'Are you on the track of anybody?'

'What? Well yes, you could say that. But I'd like to hear again exactly what it was you saw.'

He raised his cup and this time he drank. He put the cup back on the saucer and smacked his lips.

'I used to like it better with sugar,' he said. 'I think I'll start putting some in again when I get old.'

'And what was it you'd seen, that day you rang me?' she prompted him. 'It was over by that old crofter's cottage, wasn't it? The one they call Lograna.'

'I don't know what it's called,' said Sture Backman, 'but I know what I saw.'

He fell silent. Go on, Dad, please go on, she thought. Don't let it sink back into darkness.

He coughed and thumped his chest a couple of times with

his fist. 'Damn nuisance, this cough,' he said. 'You want me to tell you about the murder?'

'Yes please, Dad.'

He cleared his throat and prepared himself.

'I came out onto the road,' he said. 'Do you know which road I mean?'

'Yes Dad.'

'Right. Well then, I was walking along, whistling to myself, I do that sometimes when I'm out for a stroll . . . or I sing if the weather's fine, I'm not embarrassed to tell you that. Old tunes, usually, the ones that were popular when I was young. Mum and I used to dance—'

'What did you see at the cottage?' she broke in.

'I'm just telling you,' he replied a little indignantly. 'Don't you interrupt me, my girl. They came running out of the house, her first, but he died.'

'He died?'

'He died. They flew at each other, and he had some kind of cudgel that he hit her with, but she stuck the knife in his stomach.'

'Did you see it happen?'

'Of course I did. He was bleeding like a pig. He staggered round in the currant bushes and then he collapsed. I'm sure he must have died, because . . . because the blood was pouring out of him, it was bright red and I was scared stiff. Can you understand that I was scared stiff, Eva?'

'What happened to the girl?' she asked.

'Eh?'

'The girl. The one who stabbed him with the knife, what happened to her?'

Sture Backman gave a shrug.

'I don't damn well know. I could only see him, staggering about and bleeding like a stuck pig. Then I took to my heels, I thought I ought to get away. Anyone would have done the same.'

'Did you see an elderly man?'

'What's that?'

'An elderly man. Was there anyone there apart from the two you told me about, at the cottage . . . or nearby?'

Sture Backman thrust out his lower lip; she could not tell if he was thinking or if it was an indication the memories were fading away. She sat quietly, waiting.

'There was only one elderly man,' he said finally. 'But that was me, and I was standing out on the road.'

'Thank you, Dad,' she said, realizing she had tears in her eyes.

Sture Backman put out a hand to take a cinnamon bun. 'What year did that happen?' he asked.

'What?'

'What we're sitting here talking about, of course. What year was it?'

'It was a little while ago,' she said. 'Quite recently, in fact.'

'Yes, well, I don't go past that house any more. It's a shame because I used to like doing that circuit. Do you think . . . ?'

'Yes?'

'Do you think things have calmed down, so I could go round that way again?'

'I think so, Dad,' she said. 'Yes, I'm absolutely sure you can go round that way if you want.'

His face brightened. 'Oh good,' he said. 'Thank you for coming to explain the situation, Eva.'

'I'm the one who should say thank you, Dad,' said Eva

Backman. 'And I promise to come back very soon and go out for a walk with you. How are things looking next week?'

Sture Backman drank some coffee and considered the matter.

'I could make sure to keep a day free next week,' he said, and stretched out a hand to her across the table. 'But why on earth are you crying, my girl? That's nothing to blub about, is it?'

38

They were on the road again.

This is what I like best of all, she thought. Being on the road.

Just think if we could live our lives like this. Always on the road.

He was in a good mood too, she could tell. There was something about his posture, the rhythm his fingers drummed on the steering wheel, and the way he was keeping watch on her from the corner of his eye. He had been terribly worried after what happened to her yesterday in the hotel room. She could remember nothing about it at all, and she tried to convince him it was just a dream. She had dreamt something and fallen out of bed, what was so strange about that?

But it wasn't a dream, she knew that. She slept for the rest of the day, more or less. She did not venture out of the room, and her arm was as numb as ever. Her headache came and went, but he went out to get her some new painkillers. She had taken three of them this morning before they set off and they were helping a bit. They seemed to work better than the old Swedish Treo, which she must have taken by the hundred.

There was something about her thoughts, too, though that had been the case all along, ever since they set off. They fluttered like butterflies, coming and going, their content changing faster than a pig can blink. Where did that expression come from? Faster than a pig can blink? Something she had read long ago, wasn't it? She decided to ask him, in case he knew.

'Faster than a pig can blink, where does that come from, Valdemar? I like that expression, don't you?'

'Yes I do,' he said, scratching his chin and pondering. 'I think it's Astrid Lindgren, you know. *Emil in Lönneberga* or something like that.'

'Can you tell me a story, Valdemar?' she asked. 'We can pretend you're Astrid Lindgren and I'm a child who's keen to hear something exciting.'

'Astrid Lindgren?' he said, and laughed. 'I can't measure up to her. You're asking too much there. But maybe I could tell you some other kind of story.'

'Oh please do, Valdemar.'

'What would you like it to be about?'

'You decide, Valdemar.'

He drummed his fingers on the steering wheel for a few moments. 'I could tell you about Signe Hitler. What do you reckon?'

'Signe Hitler?'

'Yes. Would you like to hear that?'

'Oh yes.'

'Although it's a bit gruesome.'

'That doesn't matter, Valdemar.'

'Or perhaps not gruesome. Cruel would be a better word.'

'I see. Well, you start telling it and maybe I can decide if it's gruesome or cruel.'

He cleared his throat and launched into it. 'I don't think I've told anyone about this before. And there are reasons for that, as you'll find out. Signe Hitler was a teacher of mine at elementary school. Her real name was Hiller, but we called her Hitler because she was so utterly horrible to us.'

'Really?'

'Yes, really,' said Valdemar. 'It's not often you come across people who are out-and-out malicious, or not in my experience, anyway. But Signe Hitler was one of those, I think I can fairly say. A devil, she was. And above all she hated children and everything they like doing – running, laughing, squabbling, playing rounders – though when I think back on it, I reckon she loathed adults just as much.'

'She doesn't sound much fun,' said Anna.

'No, she wasn't. She was single, of course, a real old maid, though she can't have been more than forty-five when we got her as our form teacher. And my God we were scared of her. From first thing in the morning, when we were singing our hymn, she would fix her yellow look on us, her gimlet eyes would scan each and every one of us, and we would know we were goners. We didn't stand a chance. If you looked away, it meant you felt guilty about something, but if you held her gaze it meant you were obstinate. There was this boy Bengt, and initial eye contact with her used to make him wet himself, so then we had the smell of urine in the classroom all day, but for some reason it didn't bother her. Maybe she wanted us all to be so scared of her that we wet ourselves, too.'

'Obstinate?' Anna put in. 'Did that mean, like, cheeky, or what?'

'I think so,' said Valdemar. 'Anyway, it was a complete reign of terror she imposed on the class. She never hit us, but she would poke her sharp nails into the back of your neck and twist them until you cried, or into the very top of your ear – it's extra sensitive there, I don't know if you've ever noticed.

And she never had a kind word for any of us. If you got full marks for an arithmetic test or your spelling there was never any praise. She kept you back after school just for getting hiccups or giving the wrong answer to a question, and she once sent a girl home and banned her from school for three days because her neck wasn't clean.'

'But you can't just . . .' protested Anna.

'Not these days, no,' said Valdemar. 'But back then, in the 1950s, or it could have been the early 60s, it was acceptable. Parents never interfered in what happened at school, as long as everything was kept in good order. And there was never any goddamn shortage of good order with Signe Hitler at the helm. Eventually we just couldn't take it any more.'

He inserted a dramatic pause and Anna filled it, realizing this was expected of her.

'You couldn't take it any more? So what did you do?'

'We decided to kill her,' said Valdemar.

'Kill her?' said Anna. 'You don't really mean that?'

'Oh yes I do,' said Valdemar, straightening his back and pulling out into the outside lane. 'We thought it was the only way out, and I think the same today. Hitler had been terrorizing kids for twenty years, and if we didn't do something about it, she'd go on for twenty more.'

'How old were you?' asked Anna.

'Ten or eleven, or thereabouts,' said Valdemar rather vaguely. 'Old enough to be able to plan a murder, but not old enough to go to prison. What did we have to lose?'

'But still,' said Anna. 'So what happened?'

Valdemar scratched the back of his neck and thought for a moment. Not because he had to dredge his memory, she felt, but because he wanted to get the words right.

'We had a club,' he said. 'The Secret Six. We were four boys and two girls, and we offered to take – what's it called? – collective responsibility. But the whole class was in on it, you have to understand that Anna.'

'I understand,' she said.

'Good. Well, one of the boys in the club – his name was Henry – had a dad who stored lots of dynamite in their base-ment. I don't know where it came from and you're not supposed to leave dynamite lying about in your basement, but there it was. I think he was a former rock-blaster or something. It was a simple plan: we, the Secret Six, drew lots for who was going to do the deed, and it fell to me and Henry. That was practical, as it happened, seeing as he was the one who had to get us the dynamite anyway.'

'Oh my God,' said Anna. 'Astrid Lindgren would never tell this kind of story.'

'I'm not so sure of that,' said Valdemar. 'But this is all true, that's the great thing about it, the beauty of it, you might say.'

'Well, not beauty exactly,' said Anna.

'I suppose you're right. But in any case, we made our move one dark and rainy evening in November. Henry and I headed off to Trumpetgatan on the north side of town, where Signe Hitler lived on the top floor of a three-storey block. We'd convinced ourselves it was an advantage she was on the top floor, because the force of the explosion would travel upwards and nobody else would get hurt. We went in through the front entrance and up the stairs. Outside her door, Henry got out the sticks of dynamite he'd hidden under his jacket, I lit the fuses and he pushed the sticks through the letterbox. Then we rang the doorbell and ran like hell down the stairs, out of the block and away. We hadn't gone more than a few metres when we heard a hell of a bang.'

'You're crazy, Valdemar. Do you mean you kids really did that?'

'You bet we did,' said Valdemar. 'But you're virtually the first person to know the details . . . apart from the rest of the Secret Six, of course. There was a police investigation and all that sort of stuff, but nobody ever found out how it had happened. Well, they worked out the mechanics, but not who was behind it.'

'And how did things turn out for . . . for Hitler?'

Valdemar cleared his throat and hunted for words again.

'They turned out well,' he said at last. 'Yes, that's how you have to see it, nothing to do with regret or exoneration or anything like that.'

'I don't really understand,' said Anna.

'Well this was how it went,' said Valdemar. 'The blast didn't kill her, but it did leave her blind and deaf, or almost deaf, anyway, and afterwards it was as if she'd become an entirely different person. When she got out of hospital she was the gentlest, kindest individual you can imagine. She couldn't carry on as a teacher, of course. She started work for the Salvation Army instead, looking after poor children and homeless cats and God knows what. She stood in the square every Saturday, sang uplifting songs and collected money for the needy in less developed countries. It was a kind of miracle; the doctors couldn't explain what had happened to her and nor could anybody else. She died two days before her eight-ieth birthday, got run over by the snow plough because she couldn't see or hear. The funeral was so packed that people had to stand.'

'Valdemar,' said Anna, 'do you expect me to believe this? How could she sing if she was deaf?'

'Almost deaf, I said,' replied Valdemar a little truculently. 'There's a long newspaper article about her in the library in Kramfors. Of course it says nothing about what a terrible old witch she was before the explosion, or who was behind it, but I promise every single word is true. Why would I lie to you?'

'I don't know,' said Anna. 'You've . . . you've always said your life was so dull. But the things you're telling me don't seem dull at all. What happened to your life?'

'What happened?' answered Valdemar pensively. 'I only wish I knew.'

Then he was silent for a long time. She started to feel drowsy and realized she would soon be asleep. I've got to talk to him about Steffo this time, she thought. I really must.

But I don't know if he'll want to hear it. We've barely exchanged a word about what happened at Lograna, at the end. I've simply got to.

But she didn't this time, either.

Maybe it was for the best, she thought. He had asked her just once who that Steffo was, and she had told him the truth. That she'd been with him for a few months before she was admitted to Elvafors, and that she was scared stiff of him.

With him, he'd asked.

Yes, she'd replied.

Scared stiff?

Yes.

Was that why he had told her that peculiar story about Signe Hitler? So she would understand you had the right to kill wicked people? Or that he thought so, at least? *Try* to kill them.

He's strange, she thought. I ought to find a way of . . .

This can't go on any longer, I've simply got to . . .

But her thoughts could find nothing to hold them in place. What could she do on her own? In her state? Before she took any decisions about determining her own fate, she would at least have to get well. Her right arm felt completely lifeless now and her headache was back. She looked at him cautiously; he had gone quiet and was slumped slightly over the wheel, as if the storytelling had taken it out of him. Has this morning's hopefulness already evaporated? Or is it just me who feels that way? she thought. Am I trying to transmit my own hopelessness to him? What am I doing here? Why . . . why am I sharing a car across Europe with this old man? I'll never be able to explain it to myself afterwards. No, not ever.

If there is an *afterwards*.

Why should we always imagine an *afterwards*?

There was a ticking in her head and her thoughts kept slipping off course. He said something, but she couldn't hear what. Signe Hitler? she thought, closed her eyes and fell asleep.

Around six in the evening they reached another hotel in another town. He claimed it was called Emden. It was raining and the grubby twilight erased all the colours; they had to walk several blocks from the car park to the hotel, and as they stood in the lift on their way up to the room, she suddenly felt she was about to faint. Her field of vision shrank to a narrow tunnel, a dull, rhythmic throbbing seemed to engulf her, she could barely breathe and then everything went white.

She woke up to find herself lying in a bed. She realized she must have been sick; there was a nasty taste in her mouth. He was sitting on a chair beside the bed and holding her hand in his.

She couldn't feel it, because it was her right hand, but she saw it when she turned her head a little. She saw, too, that he was horror-stricken. He was not immediately aware that she had opened her eyes, and there were a few seconds in which she could study his face before he had time to adjust it. There could be no doubt that it mirrored a deep sense of despair within.

He looked like someone sitting at his own deathbed.

Initially that was all she could see and take in. She did not know who he was. She did not know where she was. She was in a bed in an unfamiliar room, and there was a desperate old man beside her, holding her hand.

Perhaps I'm actually dead, she thought. Perhaps this old guy is God himself and perhaps this is how it feels. I shall never have the strength to move again.

But why would God be frightened? Why would God look so desperate?

Then he registered that she was awake.

Anna? he whispered.

Hitler? she thought. No, that wasn't right either.

Valdemar? Of course, that was his name. And he was neither God nor Hitler.

39

'I'm afraid I have to ask you if you recognize this girl,' said Barbarotti, pushing the photograph gently across the table.

'No, I don't,' answered Alice Ekman-Roos without a glance at it. 'And I don't need to look at it again.'

'You saw it in the paper?' asked Barbarotti.

She made a minimal head movement which he interpreted as confirmation. 'I know this is painful for you,' he said, 'but I'm afraid we have to talk to you again. So we are aware of all possibilities.'

'What possibilities?' said Alice Ekman-Roos. 'I don't care about this any more.'

'I can understand that's how you may feel about your husband,' said Barbarotti. 'But it isn't only his disappearance we have to take into account now. We have a murder investigation to consider as well.'

'Yes, I know that,' said Alice Ekman-Roos. 'But I have no idea who that girl is. I don't want to hear anything about her. We've started getting rid of his things; he needn't think he can come back and ask us to forgive him after all this.'

'Your reaction is entirely natural,' said Barbarotti.

'We're having his clothes burnt,' she elaborated. 'And sending his books and other possessions to the charity shop.'

'Oh?' said Barbarotti.

'I want the girls to forget him as soon as possible.'

'I see,' said Barbarotti.

He considered his reply and wondered if he really did see. Well yes, he decided. Perhaps even more than that; her resolve in getting on with things in this situation was understandable and even somewhat admirable. Although the urge to take action could go off at its own tangents sometimes.

No, it wasn't Alice Ekman-Roos's behaviour that was incomprehensible, he thought as he absent-mindedly scratched his plaster, it was her husband's.

'And you have no idea where he is?'

'None at all.'

'If you were to guess? Is there anywhere in Sweden, or in Europe, that you think he would choose to go . . . for any reason?'

'No,' said Alice Ekman-Roos.

'He's made no attempt to contact you?'

'No.'

He wondered why he hadn't done this interview over the phone instead, but there were procedures one had to follow.

'I had absolutely no idea events would unfold this way when you came to see me at the hospital,' he said. 'I really am sorry.'

She regarded him gravely for a few seconds. 'Thank you,' she said. 'I know you're a first-rate policeman, but there's really no point in being sorry. The girls and I have got to get on with our lives, that's what matters now.'

'I'm glad you have the resilience to feel that way,' said Barbarotti. 'It's best for all parties.'

What the hell do I mean by all parties? he thought, but she showed no sign of reacting to it.

'Is there anything else?' was all she said.

'No, that's all,' declared Inspector Barbarotti.

Once she had gone he looked at his watch. The interview had taken exactly four minutes.

'Schwerin's got a lead up in Örebro,' said Sorrysen. 'A girl called Marja-Liisa Grönwall, who claims she may know who the victim is.'

Eva Backman smartly closed the folder in front of her. 'Not before time,' she said. 'He's been dead nearly three weeks.'

'Only five days since we found him, though,' Sorrysen reminded her before reading from the piece of paper he had in his hand: 'Stefan Ljubomir Rakic. Born in Zagreb in 1982. Came to Sweden at the age of five and not unknown to the Örebro police. If it's him, that is.'

'And why should it be him?' asked Backman.

'The informant said they were a couple,' said Sorrysen. 'Miss Gambowska and Rakic, that is. He apparently lived at her place, at least periodically. Last summer, for example . . . and, well, that's all I can tell you.'

'And he's disappeared?' said Backman.

Sorrysen shrugged his shoulders. 'That's the presumption. Nobody's reported him missing, but he evidently has – or had – a pretty chaotic and irregular lifestyle. Schwerin's looking into it and he'll get back to us as soon as he has anything more.'

'Good,' said Eva Backman. 'Make sure you stay in touch to keep him at it. He sometimes goes off to play golf instead of getting on with the job. Right, I've got a different sort of interview to do now.'

'A different sort?' enquired Sorrysen.

She nodded and got to her feet. 'It's to try to get some

insight into Anna Gambowska's character. From a man who'd apparently met the girl. How's your wife doing?'

'I'm sure it won't be long now,' said Sorrysen with a weak smile.

The name of the character witness was Johan Johansson.

'They call me Double Johan,' was his opening remark. 'Can't imagine why.'

Have you by any chance used that line before? thought Eva Backman, but she made no comment.

Instead she observed him as she pretended to leaf through her notepad to an important page. He was a fairly tall, slightly bloated man of around sixty. Round-shouldered, slightly hunched. He was wearing jeans, a checked shirt and a leather jacket. Adidas trainers that looked new; he was clearly trying to give a youthful impression, thought Eva Backman.

But not succeeding very well. She switched on the tape, spoke the standard formalities and leant back.

'All right,' she said. 'What have you got to tell me?'

Johan Johansson adjusted his heavy glasses and cleared his throat.

'I think I've got some information about that girl which might be of interest to you.'

'Oh yes?' said Backman.

'The thing is, I fell foul of her about a month ago.'

'Fell foul of?' said Backman.

'I chose my words with care,' said Johan Johansson. 'I can't think of a better way of putting it.'

'Can you tell me what happened?'

'Of course,' said Johan Johansson. 'That's why I'm here. It was like this, see: I live out in Dalby, I've been retired for two years because of my health, you know the way it can go. These damn back problems.'

He flexed himself gingerly in his chair to demonstrate the fact.

'That's the way it can go,' said Backman. 'Backs are no laughing matter.'

'Exactly. Not everybody understands that, but it's so true. Sometimes I can't sleep in the mornings, so I go for a drive. Sometimes I carry on all the way to Kymlinge and do some shopping out at Billundsberg, otherwise I take a different route round . . .'

'I see,' said Backman. 'Are you married?'

'No,' said Johan Johansson. 'I was, but not any longer.'

'Go on,' said Backman.

'Yes, of course,' said Johansson. 'That morning, I think it was the sixth of September but I'm not a hundred per cent sure, I was heading south on the 242. I suppose I'd passed Elvafors about ten or fifteen minutes before, and then I saw a girl walking along the edge of the road. In the same direction as I was going. I think she put out her hand to ask for a lift, but again I'm not sure. But either way, I thought I could take her a little way. It looked as if it was going to rain and I felt a bit sorry for her.'

He paused. Inspector Backman nodded to him to go on.

'So I stopped and picked her up. And it was this girl you're looking for, no doubt about it. I recognized her in the paper straight away. The drug addict girl, you get me?'

'There's nothing about drug addiction in the paper,' said Backman.

'No, but I can work it out for myself,' said Johansson.

'I follow you,' confirmed Backman. 'Do you know roughly what time you picked her up?'

'I'm not sure,' repeated Johan Johansson. 'But around half six I should think, could have been a bit later, could have been a bit earlier.'

'That early in the morning?' queried Backman.

'Yes. I suppose I didn't think about it. Maybe I reckoned she'd missed the school bus or something. Though it was a Saturday . . . and I soon twigged that she'd run away from the centre.'

'The Elvafors centre?'

'Yes.'

'Did she tell you that?'

'I asked her and she said she had.'

'So what did you do then?' asked Backman.

Johan Johansson spent a few seconds adjusting his back and his glasses before he answered.

'It was like this,' he said. 'I didn't want to help a girl run away. I don't know anything about that centre, but I'm sure it's good for them. So I thought the best thing would be for her to get out of the car. And besides . . . well, it might be illegal too, I thought, to help her on her way, so to speak. So I stopped and asked her to get out.'

'How far had you gone by then?'

'Not far. A couple of kilometres, I suppose. And that was when it happened. I'd barely pulled in and stopped the car when she attacked me.'

'Attacked?' said Backman.

'There's no other word for it,' said Johannson.

'Can you describe it in detail?'

'I didn't really have time to register what happened,' said Johan Johansson, 'because I passed out. But she must have had some kind of weapon, a hammer or something . . . I don't fucking know. She whacked me on the head, anyhow, and I passed out. When I came round she was gone and there was blood all over the place. She nicked two thousand kronor off me as well.'

'Your wallet?' said Backman.

'Yep. It was in my inside pocket as usual. I suppose she found it and took the money. It was lying there on the seat, empty as a Biafra tit.'

'Biafra tit?' said Backman. 'What's that?'

'Oh, you know,' said Johan Johansson. 'Just an expression. The thing was empty and the girl had scarpered. It cost me two thousand to get the blood cleaned out of my car, too, so you could say I'm four thousand down all told. But they mended my glasses for nothing at the optician's, and I suppose I should be grateful I'm still alive. I mean considering . . . well, what it said in the paper.'

Eva Backman nodded and thought for a moment.

'You didn't report this incident?' she asked.

'Incident?' said Johansson.

'The attack,' said Backman.

He shook his head. 'No, I didn't. I should have done, of course, but you read about all these unsolved crimes. Suppose I thought there was no point. It taught me a lesson, too – that bitch was lethal, I can tell you. It's not worth being a hero in this country.'

'Maybe not always,' said Eva Backman. 'If I've understood this correctly, you didn't have much time to talk to her.'

'She wasn't in the car more than three minutes,' said Johan Johansson. 'But I still thought I should come and tell you about it. So you know what sort of person you're dealing with.'

'We're grateful for that,' said Eva Backman. 'You didn't get any idea of where she was going, for instance?'

Johan Johansson shook his head. 'None at all,' he said.

'What her plans were and why she'd run away?'

'Short answer: no.'

Eva Backman turned off the tape recorder. 'Right then, Mr Johansson. I'd like to thank you for taking the time to come in. I might get back to you at a later stage.'

'Are we done already?'

'Yes.'

He cleared his throat and placed his hands on his knees. 'And if I wanted to pursue the matter of some kind of compensation, how would I . . . ?'

'You'd need to follow procedures for making a formal report to the police,' said Eva Backman. 'And talk to your insurance company, too.'

'I'll have to think about it,' said Johan Johansson, getting laboriously to his feet. 'Have you caught her yet?'

Eva Backman did not answer his question, instead ushering him politely but firmly out of the room.

It was quarter to five on Friday afternoon when Inspector Backman knocked on Barbarotti's door and put her head round it.

'Graffiti?' she asked.

'Graffiti,' said Barbarotti. 'I'm snowed under at the moment.'

'I thought you had a theory?'

'I can't quite stand it up yet.'

'Ah. I assume you won't have time for a beer at the Elk, then? What with your extended family and your foot and everything. Plus the graffiti.'

'You're right there, I'm afraid,' sighed Barbarotti with a harried look. 'But a quick cup of coffee at our genius bar in here, how about that?'

'The Elk can wait,' agreed Backman. 'I really could do with talking a few things over. I just can't get my head round this case.'

'Nor me,' said Barbarotti. 'Could you fetch the coffee, and an almond tart? You can see I'm handicapped.'

Eva Backman was straight out of the door and back three minutes later with a tray. 'They'd run out of the tarts,' she said. 'You'll have to make do with a chocolate truffle ball.'

'Fair enough,' said Barbarotti. 'Life never turns out quite the way you imagine. So what's been going round and round in that mind of yours, then?'

'That bloody Roos,' said Eva Backman with a sigh. 'I know men are the way they are, but how can you get yourself into that kind of mess?'

'What do you mean?' said Barbarotti.

'Well, that girl he's got with him seems to be some little psychopath, or verging on it.'

'Was it this afternoon's witness who told you that?'

Eva Backman nodded. 'Yes, him, and the head of the Elvafors centre. Anna Gambowska seems to be a nasty piece of work, though we can't be sure of course. How could a sixty-year-old man be so naive that he doesn't realize? How could he fall for her? That's the question I want you to answer for me.'

'From my male point of view?' asked Barbarotti.

'For instance,' said Backman.

'There's only one answer,' said Barbarotti. 'The well-worn one.'

'And what's that?'

'It isn't easy being a randy old tomcat.'

'Fuck,' said Eva Backman.

'What makes you say that?'

'Well I know no one's really had anything good to say about Valdemar Roos,' she declared, 'but you're the first one to describe him specifically in those terms.'

'Steady on,' said Barbarotti, putting up his hands. 'It was only a suggestion. You wanted the masculine take on it, didn't you?'

Eva Backman bit into her truffle and reserved judgement.

'Which of them did it, do you think?' said Barbarotti after a few moments' silence. 'We've barely talked about that.'

'I've no idea,' said Eva Backman.

'They can hardly both have been holding the knife.'

'No, hardly,' said Backman, and he could see that for some reason she was reluctant to discuss the matter.

'Either way, it certainly looks as though she's exploiting him,' he said. 'Don't you think? She must have been staying at his cottage before this happened. I don't know how long for, but it must have been a few days, mustn't it?'

'Double Johan claims he picked her up on the morning of September sixth.'

'Double Johan?'

'That's how he's known in Dalby. This witness of mine, I mean. So she could very well have been at Roos's cottage ever since then, and it was the fourteenth when they took off. Or the fifteenth.'

'Almost ten days,' said Barbarotti.

'Roughly, yes,' said Eva Backman. 'And now two weeks more have gone by. Our friend Double Johan claims she bashed him on the head and tried to kill him after three minutes. She took his money as well, two thousand.'

'Tried to kill him?'

'Knocked him out, anyway.'

Barbarotti nodded and said nothing. He glanced sideways out of the window at Lundholm & Son's closed-down shoe factory, now undergoing demolition, and tried to fend off the rhetorical conclusion he was expected to draw. In the end he gave up.

'I can see where you're going with this,' he said. 'Valdemar Roos took out half a million. When did we last have any sign of life from him?'

'The twenty-second of September,' said Eva Backman. 'Hotel Baltzar in Malmö.'

'Do you know if the girl's got a driving licence?'

'She hasn't.'

'But she could know how to drive anyway.'

'She might have given him the time to teach her.'

Barbarotti pondered. 'It's a fortnight since they were in Malmö,' he said. 'We're looking for two people, when in fact it might only be one. Is that what you're getting at?'

'One alive and one dead,' said Eva Backman. 'I know that still makes two, but no, that wasn't what I was getting at. I really would prefer . . .'

She trailed off. Barbarotti shifted his eyes from the ruin of the shoe factory and looked at her. 'Prefer what?' he said.

'Prefer things not to be that way,' said Eva Backman. 'To put it simply. Is that so odd?'

'It's not odd at all,' said Barbarotti. 'If Valdemar Roos is dead, we'll never get the chance to talk to him. And if there's one thing I'd like to do, it's to hear what he's got to say.'

'Why?' said Eva Backman. 'Why is it so important to you to talk to Valdemar Roos?'

'I'm not really sure,' said Gunnar Barbarotti. 'But Marianne's wondering the same thing. She thinks it's because I've got a screw loose.'

'You as well?' said Eva Backman. 'Not just him?'

'Me as well,' said Barbarotti.

Eva Backman was silent for a while. Then she got to her feet. 'I think that's enough for today,' she concluded, and left the room.

40

The rain came lashing down.

He could not remember when he had last driven in such foul weather. Of course it had rained hundreds of times on all his commuter runs between Kymlinge and Svartö, but this was something else. The fury of the elements, that was the phrase, wasn't it? And the precipitation seemed to be coming from all directions at once, not just from the angry sky; the lorries – one of which they were currently stuck behind – were sending up cascades of dirty water from the soaking road surface.

And this even though they were travelling at low speed, no more than fifty to sixty kilometres an hour. Don't they have mudflaps? thought Valdemar Roos, turning his windscreen wipers to their fastest setting. There I was thinking they'd achieved at least some degree of civilization down here.

It was impossible to make out the number plates of the filthy vehicles but he assumed they must come from somewhere in southern Europe. Or eastern, maybe, but they certainly weren't Scandinavian or German. There was no point trying to overtake them, either, because visibility in his rear-view mirror was so poor that it would have been far too risky. Every now and then some crazy Mercedes came swishing past in the outside lane, sending a cascade over him from the other side, too; no, there was nothing for it but to stay up the arse of this monster truck. If that was the technical term. He liked the phrase, anyway. It would make a good book title: *Up the Arse of a Monster Truck: My Motorway Memories*.

Jesus, was his next thought. What is all this crap? I need a break. My eyes aren't focusing properly, either, and these road conditions are well nigh lethal. He had decided some time back to pull in at the next services or petrol station, but twenty minutes had passed and he hadn't come to any. It was typical; whatever you were looking for always kept its distance, that was a truth he'd learnt as a child. If I count to 128, he decided – it was one of his favourite numbers, although he could no longer remember why – and if I can't even find a lay-by, because a pee wouldn't come amiss either, then I shall just have to overtake this monster after all, do or die.

And all these thoughts, this halting but never-ending supply of words, as empty of life as they were of real content and meaning, flocking in his head like doomed stray birds, had no other purpose than to keep the abyss and the panic at bay. He knew this, and it felt constantly as if a flood of tears was dammed up inside him, behind his brow bone, behind the rampart of words, yes, right there, waiting to break out, nothing could be clearer.

But I don't want to give way, he thought. *I am not going to give way.*

Anna was asleep in the back seat. He checked the time and saw they had been on the road for over four hours. Apart from a short spell when they set off she had been asleep the whole time; she had tossed and turned uneasily a couple of times, probably dreaming, but in the main she had seemed peaceful. If she can just sleep, he thought, she'll get well. There's no better doctor than good, revitalizing sleep. And anyway, what alternatives do we have?

What alternatives indeed? Taking her to a hospital would be tantamount to giving up. That was the plain fact of the matter; naturally they wouldn't be seen anywhere without showing their ID and saying something about their circumstances, and then . . . well then mills would start to turn, no, grind was the word, mills would start to *grind*, and sooner or later, somehow or other, it would come out that they were on the run and wanted for murder in Sweden.

No, thought Ante Valdemar Roos, and realized he had well and truly abandoned counting to 128, because you can't think and count at the same time . . . no, that alternative simply wasn't an option. She'll get well, she'll get well. It's just a question of sleep and care and love, and I'll make sure she has all those.

The best care in the world, but I wish . . .

'Well, what is it I wish?' he mumbled almost inaudibly to himself, just as the south- or east-European lorry sluiced yet more water over his windscreen, momentarily reducing his visibility to zero.

Stupid question. He wished she would open her eyes, of course. Look at him, smile at him in that slightly impish way she'd had when they were still at Lograna, before disaster struck. Say she felt much better, tell him about her life, about Grandma's ducks or her remarkable Uncle Pavel or anything at all, and . . . that she was hungry.

That would be a good sign. If she felt like something to eat. She'd barely eaten anything for two days now; he'd made sure she had enough liquid, but that was basically all. Water and juice and a couple of cans of Coca-Cola; he'd heard that this dubious fizzy drink was beneficial for various things, stomach ache and screws that had rusted in place and assorted other complaints, but he wasn't entirely convinced.

But what if . . . what if she didn't get better?

Well, there was an emergency plan. Plan B, the last resort.

It had been swishing around in his head for a while now. Like a jellyfish washed in by the waves, which he didn't want to bring ashore or to study too closely. But it was floating there, dismal and transparent. As it had been since that morning, to be precise, when she fell out of bed and scared the living daylights out of him. But he was damned if he was going to acknowledge its presence.

Yet there it was, nonetheless. Like some subterranean secret passage.

He pushed it aside; they hadn't reached that point. Nor would they, not for a long time to come. What's all this about jellyfish? he thought. Secret passages? What a load of bullshit.

Only an emergency solution if . . . if she didn't get better, basically.

Plan B.

Despite the slow speed of the traffic, he almost missed the turning, but at the last instant he signalled right and turned off for the services. The car park was full of wet cars and he saw that it looked like all other motorway services the world over. Or all over Europe, at least; he couldn't honestly say he had any conception of the rest of the world.

He parked as close to the entrance to the cafe as he could, switched off the engine and checked Anna was still sound asleep in the back seat. He adjusted her blanket, gently stroked her cheek and left the car.

Although he ran the twenty or thirty metres to the entrance, he still got drenched. He stood in the coffee queue behind two young girls who were chattering enthusiastically to one another in a language he didn't recognize. They were Anna's age, maybe a bit younger; how I wish Anna could sound that enthusiastic, he thought. Good God, don't let the dam burst while I'm here in this queue.

The dam? he thought. What dam? What am I talking about? I'm making no sense to myself any more.

But as he sat at a red plastic table by the wall, right next to the toilets, he started worrying whether he'd locked the car or not. He presumed he had – it was one of those automatic moves, those familiar little actions you'd performed so many times that your brain no longer needed to get involved. Your hand and the car key were enough.

But it wouldn't be good news if he *had* locked it. If Anna started shifting about in the back seat she could set off the alarm, and the car would start honking and flashing and drawing attention to itself. They didn't need any attention just at the moment, thought Ante Valdemar Roos. In fact, if they were really unlucky, it could prove disastrous.

For a few seconds he was poised to get up and go out into the rain to check, but in the end he didn't. Would it be that much better to leave her in an unlocked car? Anybody at all could open one of the back doors and abduct her. She could be a defenceless victim of – what was it called – trafficking?

The devil and the deep blue sea then, thought Ante Valdemar Roos. Car locked or unlocked, they were both equally bad.

No, he corrected himself. Of course they weren't. Anna being abducted was much worse than her setting off the car alarm, of course.

But there was still no need to hang around in this noisy and tedious roadside diner, he decided. He bolted down the last of his cheese and ham sandwich, finished his coffee and went to the gents. Must go while I'm here, he thought, this is a different sort of dam that might just burst. And I don't particularly want to stand in the rain at the side of the road.

And as he was peeing into the smelly metal trough, that day's aphorism came into his mind.

The worst that can happen to a person is to lose his memory at a petrol station in a foreign land.

Perhaps that sounded a bit too categorical, he thought, and rephrased it slightly:

It is no fun to lose one's memory at a petrol station in a foreign land.

Then he shivered for some reason, perhaps because of his wet clothes. Or perhaps it was the aphorism. He hurried out of the service station and ran over to the car.

It was gone.

For a few sodden seconds he was sure he was going to pass out.

Or die.

The wet tarmac under his feet felt as if it was starting to dissolve, or perhaps he himself was starting to dissolve, and when the process was complete, whichever of them it was, he would be sucked into a swirling black maelstrom and down into the depths of the earth forever. Like pee in a urinal, exit Valdemar Roos, missed and grieved for by no one, what a fucking way to end . . .

But as the seconds passed, a thin ray of reflective thought found its way into his brain and he realized what had happened.

He had dashed off in the wrong direction. It was as simple as that: he had cut across to the right rather than the left when he came out of the cafe.

How thick can anyone be? thought Valdemar Roos, and just as he caught sight of the car, parked on the very spot where he now registered he had left it, he realized the expression was borrowed from Wilma. *How thick can anyone be?* That was exactly what she would say to him seven times a week, rolling her eyes and looking as if she wondered where her mother had dredged him up from, this repulsive old man, and had the bad taste to marry him into the bargain.

Well, Wilma dear, that's one annoyance I've freed you from, at any rate.

He had in fact locked the car, but Anna appeared not to have moved in her bed on the back seat. She had not set the alarm off, anyway. Once he had climbed into the driver's seat and pulled the door shut, he reached back to feel her forehead.

It was cold and wet. Well, OK, he thought, I assume that's better than dry and hot. She mumbled something and shifted position, but did not wake. He tucked her in again, started the car and backed out carefully from the cramped parking space. He headed out of the services to rejoin the motorway.

But he had only covered a hundred metres when he realized something was amiss. The car was behaving oddly. There was a problem with the front right wheel, and he had to steer hard to the left to keep the car going straight. It was jolting and bumping slightly, too, and he soon worked out what was wrong.

A puncture.

Jesus wept, thought Ante Valdemar Roos. Modern cars don't get punctures.

In the rain.

In a foreign land. On the run.

He hadn't got as far as the motorway but was still on the gently curving slip road from the service station. He pulled as far over to the right as he could, switched on the warning lights and stopped.

He felt the floodwaters lapping once and then twice against his dam, but gritted his teeth and tried to remember when he had last had a puncture.

Thirty years ago, he reckoned. Twenty-five at least. Long before he met Alice, anyway. Long before he started at Wrigman's Electrical.

Modern cars don't get punctures.

Then he had one of those thought sequences he had been prone to when he was ten years old or thereabouts. He remembered them coming in for a lot of use after his father hanged himself.

If I reverse the car and go back into the cafe – ran this thought sequence – and sit down at the same table, that red one over by the wall, and pretend this hasn't happened – pretend I haven't even left the table or peed in the smelly trough or left the building or turned the wrong way to get back to the car – well, then it will be in perfect working order when I pull away. No puncture, and for something like that to happen twice in one day simply isn't possible.

He sat there for quite a while, weighing up this alternative, but in the end he abandoned it. A man's gotta do what a man's gotta do, he thought. He felt Anna's forehead again – it was still cold and wet – and rummaged in the glove compartment for the instruction manual.

*

The slip road was wide enough for him to stay where he was. Especially as the problem was with the front right wheel, so he would be tucked away in the protection of the car as he worked.

But he had no protection from the rain. The whole damned process must have taken him half an hour: extracting the spare wheel from the boot, finding the jack and the wrench, getting the stiff wheel nuts to budge (*Coca-Cola, Coca-Cola*, he thought as he tugged with all his might), removing the punctured wheel and fixing the new one in place, and all the while, all the while, it kept on raining.

But he carried out the task with a kind of stoical, mechanical calm. Step by step, operation by operation, wheel nut by wheel nut. Once he thought he heard Anna call out from inside the car, but he decided it must just be his imagination and did not go over to check. The cars leaving the services drove past him at intervals, some of them flashing their lights at him but most not, and it was just as he had got the car back down on four wheels and worked the jack loose that he realized a police car had stopped right behind him. The blue light on its roof was flashing and a policeman in a greenish uniform was approaching him with a greenish umbrella.

He straightened up, still with the jack in his hand, and it struck him that he had never before seen a policeman with an umbrella.

'Do you have a problem?' the policeman asked him in English.

Valdemar assumed he had seen that the car was Swedish and answered, also in English, that he had had a problem but that he had now fixed it.

'Can I see your driving licence?' asked the policeman. 'Parking is not allowed here.'

Valdemar tried to sound friendly but firm and told him shit happens and the licence was in the car. The policeman asked him to get it. He sounded unnecessarily stern, Valdemar thought. Stern and bossy and full of himself. A real pig.

'Fucking awful weather to get a puncture in,' said Valdemar, to lighten the mood a little.

The policeman did not reply. He nodded to him to go and find the licence. Valdemar opened the passenger-side door and reached in to get his licence. As the light came on in the car, the policeman took two steps closer and looked in.

'What is wrong with the girl?' he asked.

'Nothing is wrong with the girl,' said Valdemar. 'She's asleep.'

But when he glanced her way he saw that she was at a strange angle halfway to the floor, and that there really did seem to be something wrong. Her face was twisted upwards, she looked sweaty and pallid and had something at the corners of her mouth that Valdemar could not make out. Little bubbles of some kind, perhaps it was just saliva. And one of her legs was twitching.

'Come out of the car,' said the policeman. 'Put your hands on the roof and don't move.'

As he said it he took a radio from his breast pocket and pressed some buttons. Valdemar backed out of the passenger seat and noticed he still had the folded jack in his hand.

He thought for maybe half a second before bringing the metal object down with full force on the policeman's head.

A minute later they were out on the motorway again.

FOUR

FOUR

41

It basically took a week to complete the identification – from the moment Barbarotti and Backman found themselves staring down at the dead body by the earth cellar out at Lograna to when Miroslav Rakic made his resolute but tearful declaration that it was indeed the body of his son lying in front of him on the cold steel table and that he would personally see to putting a bullet through the brain of the fucking Swedish bastard who had killed him.

Miroslav Rakic was fifty-four years old. He had lived in Sweden since 1989 and had been brought from the prisoner detention facility in Österåker, where he was currently serving an eight-year sentence for armed robbery, attempted murder, actual bodily harm and assorted other breaches of the law. Stefan Rakic's mother had died three years previously, and there were no siblings or other close relatives.

In addition to this identification, which took place on the morning of Monday 6 October, they also had a match to dental records, so there could no longer be any doubt who it was they had found out there in the rain with a gaping knife wound to the stomach.

The residual doubts they had were attached entirely and exclusively to the perpetrators. Or at any rate to the odd couple whose departure from the old crofter's cottage at Lograna had occurred at the time of the murder of Stefan Rakic – it was impossible to know if the crime had been committed by some other person of whom the police were unaware, but no one in the investigation group led by DI Eva Backman was inclined to think it likely.

Ante Valdemar Roos and Anna Gambowska, they were who this was all about. They were the ones who had to be found.

But where the hell had they got to?

And how could they be tracked down?

'Anyone reckon they could have changed to another vehicle?' asked Eva Backman.

Nobody did.

'Good,' said Eva Backman. 'Nor do I. So they are travelling in a blue Volvo S80 with registration number UYJ 067. They could essentially be anywhere in Europe, and as they are using neither credit cards nor mobile phones they can keep out of our way for a long time if they want.'

'They've got plenty of cash, too,' pointed out assisting officer Wennergren-Olofsson.

'Yes, that ought to last them a good while,' said Eva Backman.

'Masses of the bloody stuff,' elaborated Wennergren-Olofsson.

'But there's a warrant out for their arrest,' his fellow assistant Tillgren reminded them. 'Presumably all we have to do is wait for them to be found?'

'How many cars do you think there are in Europe?' asked Backman.

'Masses of the bloody things,' supplied Wennergren-Olofsson.

'And if they've, say, hidden it in some barn down in Skåne

and continued by train,' suggested Barbarotti, hoisting his leg onto a chair, 'it could take a long time for anyone to find it. But it's true there's not a lot we can do. How many of us do we need sitting here waiting? Two? Five? Ten?'

'Sooner or later they're going to run out of money,' said Wennergren-Olofsson.

'Or they'll slip up and use a card,' said Tillgren.

'You reckon?' said Barbarotti.

'Maybe not,' said Tillgren.

'Well we can keep refreshing our alert,' sighed Backman. 'So our colleagues on the continent get that we mean business. The EU is all well and good, but it hasn't made Europe any smaller in a geographical sense.'

'Er, you've lost me,' said Wennergren-Olofsson.

'I'll explain afterwards,' said Backman.

'Hm,' said Barbarotti. 'Where's Sorrysen? Has it . . . ?'

'Not yet,' said Backman. 'But they went in early this morning, so sometime during the day, I expect.'

'A kid?' said Wennergren-Olofsson.

'You've got it,' said Eva Backman. 'A baby.'

Barbarotti stayed on in Eva Backman's office after the assistants had trooped out.

'You've got something else,' he said. 'I can tell.'

'We-ell,' said Eva Backman, 'I don't really know.'

'What don't you really know?'

'How to evaluate it. I talked to that girl up in Örebro this morning. Marja-Liisa Grönwall, the one who rang in about Anna Gambowska. Schwerin has interviewed her, too, of course, and her picture of the girl is rather different.'

'A different picture of Anna Gambowska?'

'Yes. Though she's a sort of friend, so I'm not sure how impartial she is.'

'And what does she say?'

'She says Anna's a kind, gentle girl, a bit soft, not at all the tough type we've been hearing about.'

'A sort of friend . . . was that what you called her? What does that mean?'

'It means I don't think they knew each other all that well. But Miss Grönwall has clearly been in a relationship with our victim, too. And she had a good deal to say about that.'

'Let's hear it,' said Barbarotti.

'I'm waiting for Schwerin to send down his interview with her, I only got to talk to her for ten minutes . . .'

'It's a start. What did she have to say about Stefan Rakic? You must have got some kind of impression, anyway?'

Eva Backman initially said nothing, her face expressing ambivalence, Barbarotti thought. Or maybe it was just fatigue. 'She said he was a complete arsehole,' she said eventually. 'That was the gist of it. She used words like scary, dangerous, psychopath . . . the whole caboodle. The problem's just that . . . well, you know.'

'That she's his former girlfriend.'

'Exactly. It's hard to say how credible she is.'

Inspector Barbarotti thought about it.

'What does this essentially change?' he asked. 'If she turns out to be telling the truth, that is.'

Eva Backman went on looking ambivalent/tired.

'Everything and nothing,' she said. 'Purely clinically, it perhaps doesn't make much difference. I mean as far as work on our investigation goes. But for anyone interested in psychology, it makes a huge difference. I'm right, aren't I?

I thought you were keen on thrashing out this sort of problem?'

'Yes I am,' said Barbarotti. 'But the manageress and that double guy the girl attacked in the car, they were both singing from the same hymn sheet . . . weren't they?'

'Undoubtedly,' said Eva Backman. 'Yes, there's something that doesn't quite fit here, and it seems likeliest Marja-Liisa Grönwall is the shaky one.'

Gunnar Barbarotti nodded. 'Let me know when the interview comes in from Schwerin. There must be other people who could give us their take on the girl's character, mustn't there?'

'Let's hope so,' said Eva Backman.

There was a knock at the door and Tillgren put his head into the room.

'Sorry to barge in, but we've just tracked down her mum.'

'Anna Gambowska's mum?' asked Barbarotti.

'That's right,' said Tillgren. 'She's at a hospital in Warsaw. Her mother – that's Anna's grandmother – has just died, apparently.'

'Oh God,' said Eva Backman.

It took them fifteen minutes to get a phone number for her to call Krystyna Gambowska on, but she sat there at her desk for a further ten minutes before she could bring herself to do so.

As far as Backman could ascertain, no one had told Krystyna Gambowska about her daughter's current situation, and given that she had just lost her mother there was good reason to think over what one was going to say. And very carefully, at that.

But Anna's mother had a right to know, of course; keeping the truth from her out of some kind of misguided humanitarian consideration would merely postpone the problem. Eva Backman had misjudged such situations in the past, and she knew there were no comfortable solutions.

Of course, it was not only Eva Backman's duty to provide information that made her want to talk to this Polish-Swedish woman. There was indubitably a legitimate investigative interest too.

Although telling someone who had just lost her mother that her daughter was on the run and wanted in connection with a murder case . . . well that was a scenario requiring a certain amount of mental preparation.

It was a very crackly line.

'Krystyna Gambowska?'

'Yes, that's me. Krystyna.'

Backman explained who she was and where she was ringing from.

'I can't hear you very well,' said Krystyna Gambowska. 'So you're from the police?'

She had a faint but unmistakable Slav accent. Eva Backman cleared her throat.

'Yes, I'm a police officer. I know you've just lost your mother but there's something I've got to tell you.'

'I don't understand,' said Krystyna.

'We've been trying to get hold of you for quite a while. How long have you been in Poland?'

'Oh,' said Krystyna. 'Several weeks. I was told my mum was in a bad way and might not live much longer, so I came here on . . . well I think it was the tenth of September. My mum died early this morning.'

'Yes, I heard,' said Eva Backman. 'I'm really sorry.'

'She was old and sick,' said Krystyna. 'I'm glad I was able to be with her for these last days.'

'I can understand that,' said Eva Backman. 'I'm ringing you now about your daughter. Have you been in touch with her recently?'

'Anna?' Her voice was suddenly filled with anxiety and apprehension.

'Anna, yes. When did you last hear from her?'

There was a long silence at the other end of the line.

'I haven't had much time to devote to my daughter these past few months,' explained Krystyna, her voice sounding close to tears. 'What's happened?'

'We don't really know,' said Eva Backman. 'But we'd very much like to get hold of her. There's been a death here in the Kymlinge area, it seems she might have been involved.'

'Involved?' gasped Krystyna. 'In somebody's death? How? I don't understand what you're saying.'

'Stefan Rakic?' said Eva Backman. 'Do you know the name?'

Another silence. Then a tentative: 'I think so.'

'He's dead,' said Eva Backman. 'He was found a week ago, but he's been dead longer. You recognize the name?'

'Dead?' whispered Krystyna, her voice now barely audible. 'Did you say he was dead?'

'Yes,' said Eva Backman. 'Stefan Rakic is dead. So you didn't know that?'

'No, of course not,' declared Krystyna in a slightly stronger voice. 'How would I know that? How . . . how did he die?'

Eva Backman decided not to go into detail. 'How do you know Stefan Rakic?' she asked instead.

Krystyna took so long to answer that Eva Backman thought for a few moments that she'd lost the connection.

'Hello?' she said.

'I'm still here,' said Krystyna. 'I'm sorry, this just doesn't seem real. First my mother and now . . . yes, he was Anna's boyfriend, this Steffo. I think he was, anyway, but not any more. That was before . . . well, they haven't been together for quite a while.'

'We know Anna had been admitted to a residential centre,' said Eva Backman.

'Yes,' said Krystyna. 'That's right, she was at a home—'

'*Was?*' asked Backman. 'You say *was*.'

'Yes, she . . . I think she ran away from there.'

'How do you know this?'

'She rang and told me.'

'When?' asked Backman.

'Why . . . why are you asking all this?' asked Krystyna. 'Has anything happened?'

Eva Backman found she was clearing her throat again. 'We don't exactly know what happened. But Stefan Rakic is dead, as I said, and your daughter has disappeared, and we think there's a connection.'

'Disappeared?' said Krystyna.

'Yes, it seems that way,' said Backman.

'Oh . . . ?'

Eva Backman waited, but nothing more came. Just silence and a slight crackle on the line. Why isn't she asking more questions? thought Backman. Wouldn't that be natural?

'I shall need to speak to you face to face,' she said in the end. 'I'm terribly sorry I had to ring you up at a time like this, but I only got your phone number a few minutes ago. What

I primarily want to know is when you were last in touch with your daughter. I mean I'd like you to tell me now – we can leave all the rest until later.'

'I see,' said Krystyna after another pause. 'Well, I spoke to Anna just after I got to Warsaw. That's about three weeks ago . . . just over three weeks.'

'And since then you haven't heard from her?'

'No.'

'The two of you spoke on the phone, is that right?'

'Yes, she rang and told me . . .'

'Yes?'

'She told me she wasn't at that home any more.'

'All right,' said Eva Backman. 'Did she say where she was?'

Krystyna Gambowska took some time to think about it.

'I think she said she was at a place called Lo– something.'

'Lograna?'

'Yes, that was it. Lograna. I don't know where it is.'

'And when was that, would you say? When she rang . . . it was just one call, was it?'

'Yes, she only rang me once. It must have been some time in the middle of September, when I'd just arrived in Poland. My son Marek, Anna's brother, came out to join me a week later. We're staying with some relatives down here . . . he's only eight.'

'Did Anna say anything else when she called you?' asked Backman. 'Where she was living or anything?'

'She said she was living at somebody's house . . . and that she could stay there for a while.'

'Did she give you the name of the person whose house it was?'

'No.'

'Or say if it was a man or a woman?'

'I think it was a man. No, wait . . . she didn't say that . . . maybe I just assumed.'

'Did she say anything else?'

'No, nothing else.'

'Not how she was or anything like that?'

'She . . . she said she was fine. But she told me she didn't like it at that home, and that . . .'

'Yes?'

'She said that I . . . wasn't to worry.'

Here Krystyna's voice suddenly broke and she started to cry. Eva Backman apologized again for having called about this on such a day, but she had had no choice.

A few seconds went by and then Krystyna apologized, too, blew her nose and came back on the line.

'Can I ring you later?' she asked. 'This evening or maybe tomorrow? I feel as if I've got to pull myself together a bit first.'

Eva Backman said she should feel free to call any time, gave her mobile number and said goodbye.

After that she hunted out a paper tissue from the bottom drawer of her desk – it was her turn to blow her nose.

And then she just sat there staring out of the window for ten minutes. She could see two pollarded limes; they were the ones she always looked out at and it struck her that after she was dead, someone else would sit in this very chair and look at them.

Or perhaps a different chair, but the window and the trees would be the same.

It was not a particularly profound thought but it stuck in her mind. The transitory nature of things and the accumulation of passing days. It probably wasn't her turn to leave life yet, but her father might not have long. He was eighty-one, and even if he lived on for a number of years, there was another kind of darkness waiting for him. His mind had been unusually clear when she went to see him the other day – as if what he had seen at Lograna was a memory he needed to tell someone about before it could disappear. It really seemed that way; he had rung her late last night and seemed more muddled than ever, with no recollection of seeing her just a few days ago.

But she would drive out there and go for a walk with him; she had made that promise to him and to herself.

She wondered why she had not told Barbarotti about her father's testimony. It was a matter of boundaries, she supposed. Boundaries between the private and the public. Should she drag her father to town and let someone else interview him, or what? It would be pointless in terms of helping the investigation. He wouldn't remember, but just sit there overwhelmed by anxiety and shame at not knowing what was going on. What was being demanded of him. It would be . . . humiliating for him? Yes, *humiliating* was exactly the right word.

But she might have to tell Barbarotti about it eventually. Just him, no one else. Her father was a witness to murder, when all was said and done, or manslaughter at the very least, but for now it was sufficient for this knowledge to stay inside his daughter's head. Whether it still existed in his own was less certain.

Now what was that thought she had decided to chew over with Barbarotti?

Why do people have to age so much quicker than the imprints they leave behind them?

That perhaps wasn't a particularly original question either, she realized, but she would still have liked to talk it over with Barbarotti. Was it an optimistic reflection or a pessimistic one, for example?

And then another question presented itself, unannounced. How come I would never even consider discussing these things with my husband?

That was more serious, considerably more serious.

42

The pictures would come and go.

At first she felt there were lots of them, but she gradually realized there were only three. More like film sequences than pictures, in fact, but it somehow always started with a still image. As if she was leafing through a photo album, stopped and let her eyes rest on one of the pictures, and as she did so, it started to move and come to life.

To come and go.

The first one was the sea. She was looking out over an immensely long sandy beach, over a calm, greyish-blue sea, and there was something small and white swirling in the air, almost like snowflakes, although they never landed; initially she didn't know what she was seeing, but they must have been somewhere along Poland's Baltic coast. *Nad morzem.* She was sitting on her father's shoulders, which she hadn't realized at first, but it must have been that way. He took her down to the water's edge. She was about four or five, had not yet started school, and her parents were still together, at least from time to time.

It was summer, or early autumn rather, and they had taken the ferry from Nynäshamn to Gdansk – she had a clear memory of the ferry – then they carried on westwards by car and crammed themselves and their bags and baggage into a tall, pointy house set amongst others all the same in a beech forest at some kind of camp. That was how they would spend those summers. For a few brief seconds she saw the tall, triangular brown house, too, and the campfire they would light outside it in the evenings, and the other children at play, laughing and shouting, and funny fizzy drinks in garish colours with different tastes from those she was used to; and ice creams, *lody, lody, dla uchłody*, but then she tore her gaze from all this and turned it on the beach again. It was almost deserted and the sand was so white and fine-grained. Her dad was singing something as he walked and she held onto his ears so as not to fall off; they came to Mum, who was a bit further up, in the shelter of the dunes, lying on her stomach on a big red bath towel, sunbathing naked.

And her father lifted her down and they lay down beside Mum, one on each side, and she made a fuss because she wanted to be in the middle, but eventually, and because they give her a sweet to suck, she settled down. They lay there on their stomachs, all three of them, and Mum and Dad whispered to each other and it was lovely and warm. It makes you feel really happy, she thought, and after a while she fell asleep.

But then she suddenly sat up again with her knees drawn up, looking out over the sea at the air full of thousands of little white butterflies making for the shore. Thousands and thousands of them, she could see now that they were butterflies, they were tiny, so tiny, carried on the wind, and she woke her mum and dad who were still lying close together and seemed to be asleep although they weren't, and she asked what kind of butterflies they were and where they'd come from.

Her father propped himself up on his elbow and looked out for a while at the featherweight invasion from the sea, then he said: don't take any notice of them, Ania *kochana*, they are the butterflies of death and they've come over the sea from Sweden.

Butterflies of death from Sweden, he actually said that and she has never forgotten it. Even though she didn't really understand what it meant she was going to remember it, she decided right there and then, on the beach.

The second film sequence was shorter. It had a sort of sepia tinge, as if the images were old or had suffered some kind of damage. She was sitting at her school desk, the school in Varberg that she went to for a term or a term and a half. They sat in twos, but because her desk-mate Julia from Argentina was off sick, she was by herself that day. The teacher's name was Susanne but she was known as Snusanne because she used snus; maybe she'd popped along to the staff room to tuck a new one under her top lip – she did that every so often.

Things were fairly quiet in the classroom even though the teacher wasn't there, because they were all doing exercises in their workbooks. But then one of the boys in the double desk in front of her turned round, the one with piggy little eyes and unnaturally white hair. He gave her a nervous sneer of a grin and whispered: 'I know your cunt goes crossways, that's the way they have them where you come from. My dad often goes over there to screw birds, so don't try to tell me otherwise!'

He gabbled it all in one breath, as if he had sat there practising it first, and when he had finished he turned quickly back round again. Presumably only she and Pig-Eyes' deskmate heard what he said, but she still picked up her pencil and jabbed it as hard as she could into his back. She pushed it in and gave it a twist, and he yelled his head off just as Snusanne came back into the room.

Jimmy – yes, that was his name – threw himself onto the floor and whimpered and generally carried on, bawling: She's out of her tiny mind; She's dead dangerous; She tried to kill me; She's a fucking Polish retard; and Fuck, am I bleeding, am I?

But mainly he just yelped and moaned, and the teacher pulled his shirt out of his trousers and inspected the wound, and the whole time, because all this took quite a while, Anna just carried on calmly filling in her workbook. She was using a different pencil by then, because the point of the first one was stuck in the back of Jimmy Pig-Eyes.

And when she was asked afterwards to explain why she had done it, because Snusanne and the school counsellor in the sandals and the study advisor and all sorts of people wanted to know, she said nothing. Nothing; not a single word passed her lips. She didn't even tell Mum, but seeing these yellowed images now, she couldn't really comprehend how she had done that. She couldn't have been more than ten, and she had no recollection of ever having been as tough as she was on that occasion. Neither before nor since.

And Jimmy Pig-Eyes kept well away from her at playtimes, as did his mates, and a few weeks after the incident she changed school, because Mum had once again found something that was both cheaper and better.

The third film was the strangest of all.

Her little brother was sick again, and lying in bed in a room she at first didn't recognize, but she soon saw that it must be the cottage at Lograna. She had just finished painting the walls; for some reason it was important for her to finish the job so

Marek could get well. He looked so small and pitiful lying there in the bed, and she realized he was changing size. Whenever she approached the bed, he shrank, but when she stayed at a slight distance he seemed more or less normal.

She tried to go right up to her brother, because she wanted to touch him, of course, but when she put out her hand he was suddenly so tiny that he was invisible, and she whispered to him not to be afraid, it was only her, his sister Anna, wanting to stroke him and help him get better, but not being able to see him frightened her out of her wits and she hastily retreated to a corner of the room. And then, although not right away, he grew larger and was visible again.

This film was the scariest and was a constant repetition of this one thing: she approached her little brother, he shrank and vanished and she backed away from the bed, terrified. Worst of all were those seconds after she got back to her corner and couldn't be sure if he was going to appear again. Perhaps it was too late, perhaps she should never have tried to touch him one last time.

Sometimes, between the film sequences, she was awake. Or almost awake, anyway, because Valdemar was with her and he was neither a memory nor a dream. He was reality, sheer reality, and part of what was actually happening.

They were in the car all the time, he in the front seat and she in the back. Sometimes they stopped, sometimes they were on the move; from time to time he helped her out so she could pee beside the road, and she felt freezing cold as she squatted behind some bush, and afterwards she always got the headache.

He talked to her, said things to her, but she understood hardly any of what he was trying to say. It was simpler to go back to sleep and watch the dream sequences unfold, though she did wish there could be other pictures. But it was always just those three. The beach, Jimmy Pig-Eyes, Marek.

He listened to the car radio, too, and she could hear it. Usually just music, but now and then there was a news bulletin; she didn't understand the language they were speaking, but it could be Swedish even so, she thought. She didn't understand what Valdemar said to her, did she, but he must surely be talking Swedish? Maybe they'd soon be home.

Home. It was a strange word, meaning different things to everybody in the whole world, yet they all knew what it meant and for her part . . . no, wait, there was one person who didn't know, and that was her.

It worried her for a few moments, but then it occurred to her that Valdemar was bound to know. Yes, he definitely would, and she wanted to say it to him, tell him she appreciated it, and that she liked him, and as soon as she got well, she thought, she would explain all that to him and play the guitar and sing to him so he really understood that she meant it.

Young girl, dumb girl . . . no, not that song, and anyway it wasn't really a song but just a silly sort of chant. It had to be something else that he'd recognize and like. Maybe 'Valdemar the Penguin', that one she wrote for him.

But if she died instead, she would come and visit him in his dreams. So whichever way it turned out, there could only be a happy ending.

She could see the butterflies again now, it was amazing that there were so many of them and they could fly so far without having to touch down. She held on tightly to her dad's ears so she wouldn't have to get her feet wet, either.

43

'Explain,' said Asunander.

It was Tuesday afternoon and six of them were assembled in the chief inspector's office. Prosecutor Sylvenius was sitting on a chair in front of the window, looking as if he had just bitten into a lemon. Asunander himself was enthroned behind his desk. Backman, Barbarotti and assistant Tillgren were squeezed together on the leather sofa while Wennergren-Olofsson preferred to stand. Possibly because there were no other seats in the room.

'We don't know if this is right,' said Backman.

'What *do* you know, in fact, the lot of you?'

'It was just an idea,' said Backman.

'Stop talking drivel,' said Asunander.

Inspector Backman cleared her throat. 'It could be them, but it could be someone else. It's much more likely to be someone else, really.'

'Where's DI Borgsen?' asked Asunander, as if everything would have been as clear as day if only Sorrysen were present.

'Fatherhood has intervened,' said Backman. 'His wife had a little girl last night.'

'Hrrmm,' said Asunander. 'I see. Well?'

Eva Backman sighed and went on. 'The German police are

looking for an unidentified Volvo. Probably an S80, probably dark blue or dark green, possibly Swedish . . .'

'Possibly, possibly, possibly?' said Sylvenius. 'What the hell does that mean?'

'It means exactly what it usually does,' said Backman. 'So what's happened is that a German police officer was brutally attacked at some motorway services . . . on the slip road at the exit from the services, to be precise. He's on a respirator, unconscious, and they don't know if he'll pull through or not.'

'Attacked how?' asked Sylvenius.

'With some kind of blunt object, apparently,' said Backman. 'Could be anything, basically. This all happened yesterday afternoon and a Europe-wide alert has been put out for this car, of course, but they've no more specific description than the one I just gave you.'

'Possibly, possibly, possibly?' repeated Prosecutor Sylvenius crossly, and began polishing his spectacles on his tie.

'Yes, it's all we've got,' said Backman. 'I'll let you all have a copy of the details so you can read them for yourselves. It's a pretty basic translation from the German, but the gist is—'

'What's the gist?' asked Sylvenius.

'Could you please stop interrupting, Mr Sylvenius?' said Asunander. 'We haven't got unlimited time here.'

'Thank you,' said Backman. 'Well, the details are roughly these: the police officer in question, who unfortunately was alone in his car at the time because some sort of emergency had prevented his colleague coming with him – they're normally in pairs – was found at the edge of the road by his car, just at the exit from a service station. Knocked unconscious by some heavy blunt instrument. They've heard from various witnesses that they passed the police car, which was parked there with its blue light flashing, and that . . . that there was another vehicle parked there too. Other witnesses say they passed this Volvo earlier – if we assume it was a Volvo – so before the police car arrived, and the driver evidently had a puncture. It was pouring with rain at the time, and he seems to have taken quite a while over changing the wheel. The car was parked in a rather awkward place and that might have been why the police officer decided to stop and check up on it. His name is Klaus Meyer, by the way.'

'Where did this happen?' asked Asunander.

'Near Emden,' said Backman.

'And where's that?' said Sylvenius.

'In Germany,' said Barbarotti.

'But why . . . why should it be them?' asked Tillgren tentatively. 'I mean there must be thousands of cars fitting this description. Tens of thousands.'

'That's just what we're here to decide,' said Asunander.

'Whether to give them the registration number or not,' clarified Backman.

'I don't like this,' said Sylvenius.

'But there's already a warrant out for Roos and Gambowska's arrest,' said Wennergren-Olofsson. 'Isn't there?'

'There certainly is,' said Backman. 'But the attempted murder of a police officer on the autobahn carries more weight with the Germans than a couple of runaways from Sweden . . . if you get my drift?'

'Oh, right,' said Wennergren-Olofsson.

'Do we *believe* it could be them?' asked Barbarotti. 'I mean, why on earth would he club down a police officer?'

'That's a good question,' said Backman. 'But a moment of panic can be all it takes.'

'Plus happening to have an appropriate weapon to hand,' said Barbarotti. 'But yes, that's possible. How do things stand? Could there be more witnesses coming forward who might have seen the registration number and so on? Or be able to confirm the car is Swedish, at least?'

'Could well be,' said Backman. 'They're working flat out on this down there. A lot of people saw that car on the slip road. They're issuing repeated appeals for witnesses on radio and television, but of course it's difficult to make out any details if you just go swooshing past in the rain. What shall we do? Release Valdemar Roos's number to the Germans, or wait a bit?'

'Why would we wait?' asked Wennergren-Olofsson.

'Because,' said Asunander, glaring at the assistant, 'if the Germans think there's a police killer in that car, they'll fire the grenade launcher the minute they locate the vehicle. And ask questions afterwards. That's how it is, so we'll have to wait at least until we get confirmation the Volvo is registered in Sweden. Backman, keep me updated.'

'Of course,' said Backman.

'On a continuing basis,' said Asunander.

'On a continuing basis,' said Backman.

'Do you want to bet on it?' asked Barbarotti.

'By all means,' said Backman. 'It's them, I don't know how I know, but I've got this feeling.'

'There could be fifty thousand dark-coloured Volvos in Europe.'

'Could be,' said Backman.

'The chances are awfully slim.'

'Argue back, then. You wanted a bet.'

Barbarotti sighed and lifted his leg onto the desk. 'Sorry,' he said. 'Can't do it. I think the same as you. Although . . .'

'Although?'

'I still think we're doing the right thing in keeping the information to ourselves for a while. Don't ask me why.'

'Why?' said Backman.

'Hang on a minute,' said Barbarotti. 'I've just thought of something. Don't they have CCTV at German petrol stations? To stop people making off without paying.'

'Yes,' said Backman. 'On the autobahn I'm sure they do.'

'And if this driver filled up before he drove on and got a puncture . . . well, they'll have the car on camera? All they need to do is check.'

'I don't know how it works,' said Eva Backman. 'They haven't given us a list of numbers to check up on, at any rate.'

Barbarotti thought about this. 'Would they need to?' he said. 'Would they have to go via the Swedish police if they're looking for a Swedish car? Couldn't they just ring the vehicle registration authority direct . . . ours, I mean?'

'Well yes, I should think so,' said Backman. 'If they've got anyone who can speak Swedish, that is. And . . . well, there's already an alert out for our getaway Volvo, so as soon as they find it, and if they've got a CCTV image as well, they can . . .'

'Get out the grenade thrower without any reference to us,' supplied Barbarotti.

'Exactly,' said Backman. 'That could happen. But perhaps they didn't fill up. They might have just stopped for a coffee, mightn't they? And then they wouldn't be on camera.'

'You're right,' said Barbarotti. 'And we mustn't forget that it's still only a one-in-fifty-thousand chance.'

Inspector Backman nodded and sat there looking glum. Then she glanced at the clock.

'Lunchtime,' she said. 'Do you think you could drag that foot as far as the King's Grill?'

'I'm prepared to give it a go,' said Barbarotti.

After lunch he got down to the final act of the graffiti case. The files filled two carrier bags. A bin bag would have been more appropriate, thought Barbarotti, but they were destined for the archives of course. Even though no one would ever open them again. Perhaps they would be thrown out in fifteen or twenty years' time, when more space was needed on the shelves. For yet more files.

He stuck a yellow sticky note on one of the bags – *Archives* – and put them out in the corridor. Then he rang down to the switchboard to find out if the individuals he had asked to come in had arrived.

He was told they were waiting for him, so he picked up a tape recorder, pad and pen and left the room.

Hope I can pull this off, he thought.

Because if I can't, Asunander's going to throw me to the wolves.

Just before five he looked in on Backman again.

'Anything new?'

She shook her head.

'You look tired.'

'Thanks.'

'Sorry, that wasn't how I meant it. It's a bloody awful business.'

'It's not that,' said Eva Backman.

'Not that? What do you mean?'

She hesitated. 'Have you got five minutes?'

He came in, closed the door behind him and sat down. 'What's the matter?' he said.

She did not answer. Did not look at him at all but sat staring out of the window instead. It was what she had been doing ever since he stuck his head round the door. Christ, he thought. Something's happened. I've never seen her like this before.

He lifted his foot onto the other visitor chair and waited.

'It's Ville,' she said in the end, still not turning her head. 'Gunnar, I just can't stand it any longer.'

He cleared his throat but said nothing.

'I . . . can't . . . stand . . . it.'

She pronounced each word, each letter, as if it were a matter of chiselling her announcement into a rune stone.

Which presumably it was.

Irrevocable. The thought ran through his mind that if this were a charade, he would have guessed the word straight away.

'Ouch,' he said. 'I mean . . .'

She finally turned her head and looked at him. 'I'm still here because I don't want to go home,' she said. 'Can you believe it?'

'Yes, I think so. What's wrong, then?'

'Everything,' she said.

'Everything?' he said.

'I can give you a list if you like, but telling you what isn't would be quicker.'

'What isn't?' he asked.

She thought about it. 'Neither of us has been unfaithful,' she said, adding, 'I don't think so, anyway. And we both love the children. And, well, I guess that's all.'

'Hm,' said Barbarotti. 'Not a great deal to build on, I suppose. A lot of sport too, am I right?'

'So . . . much . . . sodding . . . sport,' said Backman, chiselling her rune stone again. 'I'm living with four fundamentalists. As if it wasn't enough for them to be out training and playing in their blessed unihockey matches eight days a week, they have to watch every single bit of sport on TV as well. Whether it's football or hockey or handball or athletics or swimming, and now they've started watching golf and trotting races as well . . . NHL hockey from America in the middle of the night. Boxing! We've got a hundred channels on our TV, and sixty of them are showing sport round the clock. And they work out bets together, I mean on ATG . . . sit there coming up with systems, talking about odds and doubles and Harry Boy and God knows what. Gunnar, I . . . can't . . . stand . . . it! Not one second longer!'

'Have you talked to Ville about this?' Barbarotti asked cautiously.

'For fifteen years,' said Eva Backman. 'But now I've had enough of talking.'

'You mean you're actually . . . ?'

'. . .'

'. . . going to leave him.'

'Yes.'

'Have you told him?'

She seemed to falter for a moment. Then she gave a laugh.

'No,' she said. 'I thought I ought to tell you first.'

'I . . . I appreciate the confidence,' said Barbarotti. 'But . . . ?'

'I'm going to call and tell him now,' said Eva Backman.

'Now?'

'Yes. I'm composing myself.'

'Oughtn't you to go home and do it face to face?'

She shook her head. 'No way. There's every risk of me whacking him over the head with a frying pan. I'm going to sleep here tonight.'

'Here?' said Gunnar Barbarotti. 'You can't sleep in the bloody police station.'

'It'll be absolutely fine,' declared Eva Backman. 'I've slept on that couch in the quiet room before and I think you have, too, haven't you? Don't worry, I know what I'm doing.'

'Have you really thought this through properly?' asked Barbarotti.

'For ten years, do you think that'll do?'

'OK,' sighed Barbarotti. 'But can't you come and spend the night at ours instead? It wouldn't be any trouble at all, you know that.'

'Thanks,' said Eva Backman. 'Another day, perhaps. But for now I just want to do it this way, and then we'll see. It . . .'

'Yes?'

'It feels good to have made my mind up. And to have told you . . . there's no way back now.'

'Oh surely there is? I mean, you can always—'

'But don't you get it? I don't damn well want there to be any way back.'

'Aha? Yes, I see.'

'I might go and stay with my brother and sister-in-law, actually . . . and my father. I haven't asked them yet it if would be all right, but I think it ought to work, on a temporary basis.'

'OK then,' said Barbarotti. 'OK, I'll go along with that, as long as you bear in mind that our house is half-empty. Marianne likes you, you know that.'

447

'All right,' said Eva Backman. 'It's good of you to say that. But off you hobble now, I've got an important call to make.'

'Good luck,' said Gunnar Barbarotti. 'I'll ring you later on this evening and see how you're doing.'

'Thank you,' said Inspector Backman. 'And I mean that.'

44

It was the cold that woke Ante Valdemar Roos.

He was lying in the front seat of the car, it was pitch black outside and a tree branch was scraping persistently against the windscreen. The rain had stopped, but a fierce wind came in strong gusts, intermittently rocking the car.

Or perhaps it was just his imagination. Perhaps it was his own internal movements that somehow corresponded to the whining rise and fall of the night's sounds. He did not know where they were and recalled only that he had turned off into a parking area after almost falling asleep at the wheel. Some time around midnight, just after twelve it must have been. Before surrendering to sleep he had got out of the car and buried the plastic bag with the jack in it. Deep in a ditch, he hadn't been able to see a thing, it had been as dark then as it was now and he had dug with his bare hands. It had been mostly twigs and leaf mould, but he thought he had buried it well enough. Who would go rooting around in a ditch behind a car park?

If we get another puncture we won't have a jack, he had thought just before he dozed off. And the thought came back to him now, which was rather odd, but perhaps it had followed him into his sleep.

On the other hand, they had no spare tyre either, he had

gone on to think, and he remembered it had made him laugh. It was a good sign that he could still laugh.

Anna was asleep, lying across the back seat, and he reached out a hand to feel her pulse. It was faint but seemed normal, he thought. Neither too fast nor too slow. Her wrist was so thin, almost like a young child's. He gave a shiver and pulled himself more upright in his seat. He could feel his lower back aching. Of course it damn well aches, he thought, sixty-year-old backs aren't meant to sleep all scrunched up in the front seat of a car.

He started the engine to create a little warmth. He left it running while he went out to pee against a tree. Like a dog, he noted. Here I am peeing against a tree like a dog without a master.

He got back into the car and scrabbled around for the map. Sometime during the night they had come to a motorway junction and he had turned without even knowing which point of the compass he was heading in. Then he had driven for a further two hours until exhaustion suddenly caught up with him. An image of a road sign came into his mind, presumably from just before he turned into this parking area:

AARLACH 49

He had never heard of the place and he couldn't find it on the map. Oh well, that didn't mean anything. There were lots of places in Europe he had never heard of.

He looked at his watch. It was half past four. Nearly morning then, he told himself, rubbing his eyes. Time to get to grips with a new day.

He was aware of his own smell. A persistent odour of stale

sweat and dirty clothes; he hadn't changed for two days now. Nor had Anna, so she probably didn't smell as fresh as a daisy either, lying there in the back seat rolled up in blankets, towels and other stuff. All in an attempt to keep her warm; as for him, all he had was his flannel shirt and thin windcheater to rely on, so it was no wonder he was freezing.

He angled the rear-view mirror so he could see his face for a moment. Good grief, he thought. That bloke there looks like a tramp. A real down-and-out. His hands are dirty, too, from his nocturnal excavations in the ditch. He sniffed them, and they smelt of earth and decay.

He moved the mirror back into its normal position so he wouldn't have to look at himself. He sat there, still and silent with his hands on the steering wheel, as he felt the warmth slowly start to seep into his body. After a while he started looking for some chewing gum to get the nasty taste out of his mouth, but he couldn't find any. There must be a packet somewhere, he knew, because he had bought it at that petrol station last night.

He had bought a newspaper at the same time and read about that policeman who had been bludgeoned at another petrol station. His condition was critical, evidently. Klaus Meyer, wife and two children, there was a picture of him too, but he didn't really recognize him. There was a warrant out for the perpetrator and there was a full-scale police operation in progress across the country. *Der Täter*; that meant perpetrator, didn't it?

Me? he had asked himself when he read it. Can it be me, Ante Valdemar Roos, tied up in all that?

Der Täter.

There must be some mistake. That wasn't how it happened,

he thought, not at all, and if only he hadn't been so bloody nosy, that Klaus Meyer, it wouldn't have had to happen. If you had a wife and two children you ought to be a bit careful, anyway, but there was such . . . such an injustice to it all, decided Valdemar Roos angrily, some goddamned kind of injustice that he couldn't quite put into words. But expressed in words or not, it was still crucial. He had Anna's life and future fate in his hands, that was the crux of it all, and that Klaus Meyer had tried to get in his way. He'd had no right to come and interfere . . . bloody idiot.

Valdemar shook his head and his hands clenched round the steering wheel. Banish these pictures from my head, he thought. Along with the doubts and trivial annoyances, the main thing now . . . the main thing now was to look forward. What was top priority at this moment?

To get indoors, he thought. Of course.

Find a hotel room where they could have a shower, change their clothes and have a decent sleep in a proper bed. Admittedly neither of them had any clean clothes to change into; they had been able to do some washing at that boarding house in Denmark, but a long time had passed since then. He'd lost track of quite how long.

But if he could only get her into a bed, he could have a hot shower and then go out and buy a few things, whatever they needed. And then . . . then he would wake her, she could have a shower . . . or a bath, a bath would be even better, he could buy some scented bath foam, something nice and feminine, while he was out getting supplies . . . they could eat a proper breakfast . . . or lunch, or anything . . . and while they were sitting over their second cup of coffee afterwards, replete and content . . . he with his pipe, she with her cigarette . . . they could decide how they were going to continue their journey. Yes, that was exactly how they would do it.

Italy maybe? France?

Satisfied with this simple bit of planning – and with this simple scenario in his mind's eye – he put on his seatbelt and drove out of the car park.

The dawn light brought some kind of insight.

Perhaps that was the true task of dawn light? he thought. That was the why it existed, for better or worse, and the worse in this case consisted of the idea of arriving in a new town, parking somewhere, finding a hotel, going to the front desk and . . .

In this state? he thought, taking a mouthful of tepid water from his plastic bottle. Looking like this? I just can't, we'd never get away with it. If Anna was a bit livelier and on her feet then maybe, but having to drag her across a lobby, explain that she was his daughter and they needed a room for one or two nights, that they had unfortunately had their passports stolen, that they wanted to pay in cash . . . their smell, their grimy appearance and their . . . no, it was impossible.

On the other hand, they simply had to get out of the car. They had to find some kind of lodging; that bed and shower and clean clothes stuff was an absolute necessity. An imminent necessity, thought Ante Valdemar Roos. Could you say that? Could necessities be *imminent*? Or were they by definition always imminent?

Another question to sit there brooding about. Why couldn't he just . . . ?

'Valdemar?'

He gave a start and the car veered onto the rumble strip along the side of the road.

'What's that noise?'

It was the first thing she had said for twelve hours or more. Her voice was as thin as rice paper.

'Anna?' he said, steering the car back on course and slowing down. 'How are you?'

'Where are we? Will we be there soon?'

'Yes, we will,' he said. 'Before long. How are you feeling? Do you want something to drink?'

She was breathing heavily and trying to pull herself a little more upright. 'I feel so funny, Valdemar. I'm all kind of . . . numb.'

He reached back and patted her on the arm. 'We'll stop soon,' he said. 'We'll get ourselves somewhere so you can have a proper bed and a proper rest.'

'Rest?' she said. 'But I've . . .'

'Yes?'

'Valdemar, I've done nothing *but* rest.'

'You'll be better soon,' he said. 'You ought to eat something as well. Aren't you hungry?'

Her answer took a while to come, as if she was really considering how she felt.

'No, Valdemar,' she said. 'I'm not hungry . . . not a bit.'

'We've got to take care of you Anna,' he said. 'Is it hurting anywhere?'

She considered again.

'No, not hurting . . . there's no feeling at all.'

'No feeling?'

'No.'

'I see. Do you need to stop for a pee?'

'I don't think so. How much longer will it be?'

'Only an hour,' he said. 'You go back to sleep and I'll wake you when we get there.'

'All right,' she said.

She curled up again with her back to him and pulled the blanket over her head. He sighed and turned his attention to the road ahead. Another sign came into view at the roadside.

MAARDAM 129

Excellent, thought Ante Valdemar Roos. That's what I was counting on. Plan B.

The woman at the desk had something wrong with one of her eyes. The eyelid drooped, covering half her eye, and he assumed she was blind on that side.

She would have been pretty nice looking otherwise, he thought. Forty-five perhaps, dark-haired, maybe a little too dolled up, but if you worked at reception in a motorway hotel, maybe you were expected to look like that?

'You speak English?' he asked.

She said she did. Some, at least. Her voice bore witness to whisky and a forty-a-day smoking habit. Over many years.

Good, he thought, here's a woman who won't ask unnecessary questions.

'Been driving all night,' he explained. 'We wanted to get on, but my daughter is feeling car sick, so . . .'

'You can't check-in until two o'clock,' said the woman.

'I could pay a bit extra,' said Valdemar.

'Let me see what I can do,' said the woman. 'One night, yes?'

'One night,' said Valdemar.

She leafed through a folder.

'You can have number twelve,' she said. 'An extra fifty for early check-in.'

'That's fine,' said Valdemar.

'Payment in advance. You can park the car just outside here.'

'Thank you,' said Valdemar. 'Thank you so much.'

'You're welcome,' said the woman.

He was just paying when he remembered something else.

'How far is it to Maardam from here?'

'Fifty-five kilometres,' said the woman.

'Is there anywhere closer?' he asked.

'There's Kerran,' said the woman.

'How far is that?

'Six or seven kilometres. You'll see the sign for it in about five hundred metres.'

She pointed along the road. He nodded and finished paying.

He thanked the woman again, she repeated that he was welcome, and he went out to the car.

Once he had tucked her up he sat on the edge of the bed for a while, stroking her cheek with the back of his hand. She was not really asleep but she didn't seem entirely awake either. She muttered things now and then, but he could never work out what she was trying to say.

Perhaps it wasn't anything important and she was just talking to herself. He found himself thinking of a baby bird he tried to save when he was a child. It had a broken wing and other injuries and he kept it under his bed in a shoebox filled with cotton wool, grass and a few other things. It was somehow like Anna and he remembered the tenderness he'd felt as he gently touched it with his fingers. Just like now.

But one afternoon when he got home from school the baby bird was dead, so it wasn't really the same.

'I'm popping out for a while,' he said. 'Going in the car to get us a few little treats. I'll be back in a couple of hours.'

She did not answer.

'Anna, do you understand what I'm saying?'

She mumbled something that he interpreted as a yes. An indication that she thought it was a good idea.

'Three hours at most. There's water and cola and stuff here on the table. No need to worry about anything.'

She sighed and turned on her side. Great, that's great, he thought, she'll sleep for a couple of hours now, and she can have a shower when I get back.

'I'll get you some cigarettes, too. And some clean undies. Do you want any particular size? Or colour?'

No reply. He stood up, felt another stab of discomfort in his lower back and crept quietly out of the room.

45

DI Barbarotti was reading the Bible.

Or at any rate he had it on his lap, but it was just lying there waiting for the impulse to strike. It was still Tuesday 7 October and although it was ten in the evening, he was sitting out on the terrace. With a rug over his knees, admittedly, but even so. Marianne was sitting beside him with a rug over her knees, too, and she had just remarked on there being something funny about the weather. The unnatural warmth. Apocalyptic, she called it. It feels apocalyptic, don't you think? As if the whole world is waiting for some great change to happen.

'A catastrophe?' he asked her. 'To me it just seems nice and warm.'

'I think so, too,' she said. 'I'm just trying to inject a bit of drama. Do you want a drop more wine?'

He did. If catastrophe was coming anyway, it was as well to have some warmth in your veins. Marianne's not on duty tomorrow, he thought. A little lovemaking might be in order once all the kids are in bed.

Maybe not right here, but we could go down to the jetty.

The jetty her brother had built. Making love outdoors in October, he thought. In a plaster cast, on a jetty – the world is definitely out of kilter.

The weather certainly is. But seriously: thank you, Brother-in-law Roger.

It was only a thought, of course, the jetty idea. There still seemed to be plenty of kids awake. They came and went, intermittently passing their rug-furled parents on the terrace with questions about this and that, including why they were hanging about out there.

Not all the children asked that question, only some of them. But their parents chose not to move, for once.

'It feels rather magical this evening, don't you think?' Marianne asked one of them, but the child just responded, 'Sure, magical, whatever', and announced that she had a maths test the next morning.

Her parents smiled, quietly raised their glasses and couldn't quite keep their hands off each other. Then Gunnar Barbarotti decided the time had come, put his index finger into the Bible at random, opened the page and read:

They shall eat every man the flesh of his own arm:
Manasseh, Ephraim; and Ephraim, Manasseh.

'Manasseh and Ephraim?' he exclaimed, nonplussed. 'How on earth am I supposed to interpret this? The flesh of my own arm?'

'You know what,' said Marianne, 'I'm not sure the good Lord always appreciates your way of reading the Bible.'

'You think so?' said Barbarotti in surprise. 'You mean He finds my approach a bit . . . unsystematic?'

'Sometimes, yes,' said Marianne.

'And maybe there's a line or two in here that isn't exactly the peak of perfection either?' suggested Barbarotti.

'One or two, yes.'

'Eva Backman's getting divorced,' he told her half an hour

later, once Ephraim and Manasseh had been set aside and the kids seemed to have gone to bed. But before they had made any move towards the jetty. He realized it was very unclear whether they would ever get there, but he didn't want to dismiss the idea out of hand.

'Divorced?' said Marianne. 'High time, too.'

'Eh?' said Gunnar Barbarotti. 'What do you mean?'

'I mean she's doing exactly the right thing, of course,' answered Marianne. 'If she'd left it another couple of years it could have been too late.'

'You've only met her once, haven't you?'

'Yes,' said Marianne. 'But sometimes once is enough.'

'I didn't think there was any serious problem with him.'

'There isn't any serious problem with a glass of water, either.'

Gunnar Barbarotti pondered this.

'She's left it quite a long time, as it is,' he said.

'That's what I'm saying,' said Marianne. 'So do you think she needs some help?'

'I . . . I don't know. Of course she wants to talk about it . . . I told her she could come here if she wanted, but she thought the couch at work would be the best place to spend the night.'

'Tonight?' said Marianne with a glance at her watch.

'Yes.'

'And when did she tell him?'

'This evening. By phone. And then she was planning to bed down at the police station, as I say.'

Marianne sat bolt upright. 'Gunnar, presumably you told her we had loads of room here?'

'Of course I did.'

'And said how much I like her?'

'Yes, I said all of that, but she insisted . . . I suppose she wants to be on her own. So she can . . .'

'So she can what?'

'Test out what it feels like and so on. I called her mid-evening and she said everything was OK.'

'Hm.'

Marianne was quiet for a long time, twirling her glass in her hand. 'Yes, maybe that's sensible,' she said finally. 'No point applying a sticking plaster until it really starts bleeding. Do you know what?'

'What?' said Gunnar Barbarotti.

'I think we're in a state of grace, you and I, being able to sit here like this. We must never start thinking we've earned it. A state of supreme grace, do you hear that?'

'You mean the house and garden and lake?' asked Barbarotti.

'No, you idiot,' said Marianne. 'I mean you and me and the children. The house and garden and lake are lovely, too, but that's not the important part.'

'I get you,' said Barbarotti.

'Are you quite sure of that?'

'Absolutely,' said Barbarotti. 'And we can't ask for nights like these, either. It must be twenty degrees, don't you think? In mid-October. You don't . . . you don't feel like going down to the jetty for a while?'

'The jetty?' said Marianne.

'Yes.'

'Why not?' said Marianne.

He gave Eva Backman another call as soon as he woke up.

She assured him everything was under control, she'd slept for at least five hours and after work she was going to see her family to discuss the future. This would require them to miss an important unihockey training session, but after a certain amount of negotiation, all parties had agreed to the arrangement.

'You're joking?' asked Barbarotti.

'I'm afraid not,' she replied. 'And it doesn't surprise me. In fact, I'm just glad they're all making time to come.'

'Bloody hell,' said Barbarotti.

'Let's not talk about it any more,' said Inspector Backman firmly. 'I shall be staying with my brother for a few days, starting tonight, and then we'll have to see.'

'I explained the situation to Marianne last night,' he said. 'She thinks, as I do, that you should come to us.'

'I appreciate it,' said Eva Backman. 'I might take you up on that in due course, but we don't need to decide anything now, do we?'

'Of course not,' said Barbarotti. 'Talking of your brother, by the way, I had a thought.'

'Oh yes?'

'Doesn't he live pretty close to Lograna?'

'Er, yes. Why are you asking?'

'Well, I just wondered if we ought to ask them about . . . they might have heard and seen things. I don't mean the actual murder, of course, but they might have come across Valdemar or the girl, earlier on?'

'I've already checked that,' said Eva Backman. 'I'm afraid none of them saw anything.'

'OK,' said Barbarotti. 'It was just a thought. And no news from Germany?'

'I know I'm in the building,' said Eva Backman, 'but I'm not on duty yet.'

'I'll be there in an hour,' promised Barbarotti. 'I expect you to be on duty by then, at any rate. We're going to find that damn Valdemar Roos today, I've got this feeling.'

'We'll put our faith in your male intuition then,' said Eva Backman, and ended the call.

46

Suddenly it was the voices, not the pictures, which were jostling for position in her head. Sometimes she could identify them, work out who was talking, but sometimes she couldn't.

Lie absolutely still, if you move you're a goner! for example. Who was saying that? It was a man, there was no doubt about that, she could hear it, an abrasive sort of voice that seemed a long way off, and it didn't sound as bad as it had first seemed. It was more like advice he was trying to give her: she was to stay put, or something along those lines.

I'm so tired, Anna, you'll have to take Marek to nursery today, I've been throwing up all night! That was her mum, of course. *Come on, hurry up, they're going on an outing today, he's got to be there in fifteen minutes!* And after a short pause for her to light a cigarette: *I know I've had a bit too much to drink, Anna, but we've got to sit down and talk. Your father isn't a good person, I hate having to say it, but it's a fact. Keep away from him.*

Yes, there was a lot her mother had to say to her and she was perpetually on that fine knife-edge between pleading and threatening. No, not threatening, that was something else, it was more that you never really knew who was the one that needed looking after.

And you knew it would all end badly, you could absolutely depend on that. It was just a matter of time.

But Valdemar's voice was there, too. *Little Anna, how nice you've made it look. Where did you learn to play so beautifully? Haste is a concept God didn't see fit to create, let's have a nap.* With Valdemar it sounded more like an old radio play. He was playing the good dad, or even granddad, while she took the role of . . . well, she never heard her own voice, but maybe she was just the good, silent daughter, or maybe she wasn't even in the play but just listening to the radio.

And Steffo. She wanted to put her hands over her ears whenever Steffo started up, and she assumed she actually did, too, trying to press her head into the pillow and make herself deaf, but it didn't help because the voices came from within her, not from outside.

You're mine, he said, Steffo. *No one else's. Now get your clothes off and show me that tattoo, it's your birthday present and I paid for it.*

Yes, Steffo was as distinct as he was evil, but who was it she could hear saying: *You've given away your heart, Anna, and anyone who gives away their heart is lost?*

And: *We have weighed you on these scales, but the needle registers nothing. How do you explain that?*

She didn't know. Even though exactly the same voices and exactly the same words kept coming back, over and over again. But gradually it all got messier, the voices jumbled together, talking over each other, squabbling and jockeying to have their say. Even though none of them actually shouted out their message, they somehow upped the tempo, spoke ever faster and ever more insistently as if they were not only competing for her attention but also demanding some sort of answer from her, and even Valdemar sounded irritable. In the end, someone shouted: *My name's not Hitler, my name's not Hitler, I'm a good person!* and that was probably what woke her up.

But the boundary between dream and waking felt blurred and viscous. She opened her eyes and stared at a bedside table with a clock radio and a window with the blinds down, but the voices didn't fade away entirely as she did so. They were still there, murmuring away quietly at the back of her head, and when it dawned on her that she was awake and dreaming at the same time, she was scared. Hearing voices? A sort of ice-cold, goosebumpy fear came over her because she realized, of course, that it was Death making his presence felt again, but this time he wasn't gentle and kindly, but ominous and terrifying.

But where was she to find the strength to resist him? For he had to be resisted, there was no question of doing anything else. Her head was aching as usual – a dull, nagging ache – and her right arm was numb, also as usual. A vague queasiness was starting to develop and suddenly there was another voice that didn't sound at all like the others; it was located somewhere deep inside her chest and after a while it dawned on her that it was her own.

Find a way out of this room, it said. You have to get to a hospital. You are dying. And it wouldn't shut up. *Find a way out of this room. You have to get to a hospital. You are . . .*

She decided to obey it – almost instantly she decided that, but it wasn't the easiest thing to do. Even just easing herself into a sitting position on the edge of the bed took quite a while. When she tried to stand up she almost fainted, and covering the few metres of floor between her and the door felt like running a marathon. Her exhaustion was like a multi-ton weight, it was a rucksack packed full of paving slabs and horror and lead and anxiety, and she had to shout orders at her legs to get them to move at all.

She had hoped to emerge into a corridor or something like that, to the extent she had hoped anything at all . . . at least a room in which there were people, but instead it was a parking area. The wind seized hold of her and she staggered before she realized with gritted teeth that she had to go on a bit further. She *had* to. She stood there with her hand still gripping the cold door handle, as if trying to draw strength from it in some absurd way, and looked at the cars lined up with their muzzles pointing in her direction, like hungry animals – one blue, one red, another red one and a kind of camper van – and beyond the cars a big road – she could hear the traffic roaring past – and beyond that, improbably, a greenish-yellow strip of forest and some birds flying around beneath a windswept sky. Where am I? she thought. How did I get here? Are these the heron mirages taking flight again? Which way should I go?

But then the voice resumed inside her chest. *You have to get to a hospital. You are dying.*

Well then, she thought, taking as much air into her lungs as she possibly could. Well then . . .

She let go of the handle and took a step forwards.

By the time she opened the door to the hotel reception area – a low little room just a few square metres in size with a counter, two glaringly red plastic chairs and a small display rack for leaflets – her strength was all gone. She fell diagonally forwards, hit her head on the display rack, started to bleed from a gash above her right eyebrow and landed between the chairs like quarry that had just taken a bullet.

The one-eyed woman behind the counter rose halfway to her feet, put her hand to her mouth and stubbed out her cigarette.

Then she picked up the phone and rang for an ambulance.

47

'How are you feeling?' asked Barbarotti.

'As I deserve to,' said Eva Backman. 'But we haven't got time to discuss our private lives, I'm afraid.'

'Why's that?' said Barbarotti.

She gave a sort of shrug and looked at the clock.

'We have a date with Asunander in five minutes.'

'With Asunander? Again? Has anything happened?'

'You could say that,' said Eva Backman. 'The son called in half an hour ago.'

'The son?' said Barbarotti. 'Do you think you could clarify just slightly?'

'Sure thing,' said Eva Backman. 'Greger Roos called us, here, this morning. It was Toivonen who took the call, but he passed it to me after a minute. Our man's down there, evidently.'

'Hang on,' said Barbarotti. 'You're saying that Greger Roos, who I assume to be Valdemar Roos's son, rang here? Remind me where he lives again?'

'Maardam,' said Backman. 'He's lived in Maardam for fifteen years, works at a bank or something.'

'I didn't think they were in touch with each other,' said Barbarotti. 'But never mind that, what did he want?'

'He wanted to tell us he'd had a visit from his father.'

'His father?' said Barbarotti. 'So . . . so we've got him, then.'

'Not exactly,' said Backman. 'He apparently just dropped by and then went away again.'

'Fuck.'

'You could say that.'

'Did he have the girl with him?'

'No, he didn't. But he left a letter.'

'A letter?'

'Yes.'

'And what does it say?'

'We don't know. His son hasn't opened it. But it's addressed to us, it seems.'

'What the hell are you saying?' said Barbarotti, and groaned. 'Valdemar Roos went to see his son down in Maardam, left a letter for us and pushed off?'

'Correct on every point,' said Eva Backman. 'Shall we go in to Asunander now? We might as well continue with this in there.'

'Pass me my crutches,' said Barbarotti.

Asunander looked like the cat who, even if he hadn't quite eaten the canary yet, had bitten off its wings and trapped it in a corner.

Not entirely displeased, in other words.

And we are the canary, thought Barbarotti. They sat down and Inspector Backman opened her notepad.

'How is it,' said the chief inspector with studied slowness, 'how is it that we haven't looked into this aspect any sooner?'

'Er, I'm sure we—' ventured Gunnar Barbarotti, but Asunander held up his hand and cut off what might have followed. Just as well, thought Barbarotti. Seeing as I hadn't anything to finish the sentence with.

'You,' said Asunander, 'are a graffiti investigator. I would prefer to hear DI Backman's account of this.'

'Of course,' said Eva Backman, and cleared her throat before continuing. 'But I'm afraid you've got the wrong end of the stick, Chief Inspector. I contacted Greger Roos the day after we found the body out at Lograna. My note of the conversation is included in the report I wrote the same day. I have it here, if you'd like to refresh your memory.'

That woman, thought Barbarotti, biting the inside of his cheek so as not to smile.

'What?' demanded Asunander. 'I mean . . . really? Well then, why didn't we follow it up?'

'Because there was no need,' explained Eva Backman. 'Valdemar Roos has no contact at all with his son. The last time they saw each other was at a funeral, ten years ago.'

'Whose funeral?' asked Asunander.

'Valdemar's first wife. The boy's mother. It was in Berlin, and father and son only spent four hours together, all told.'

'That wasn't long,' said Asunander.

'The bare minimum, if you ask me,' said Backman. 'So, as I say, there was no reason to expect Greger Roos was going to have any involvement in this. But he promised to call if he thought of even the slightest bit of information to pass on. And now he has.'

DCI Asunander leant back in his chair and let this sink in for five seconds.

'Three questions,' he said.

'Shoot,' said Eva Backman.

'First: where is Valdemar Roos as we speak? Second: where's the girl? And third: what the hell does that letter say?'

'Those are precisely the questions I've got written on my

notepad,' declared DI Backman. 'Plus one more: shall we call him and ask him to read it out to us?'

Asunander frowned as he pondered. 'God knows,' he said. 'Obviously that would be the quickest way . . . but just to be clear, we haven't had confirmation yet that they were the ones behind the petrol station business, have we?'

'No,' said Backman. 'We haven't. And there's no news on the condition of the police officer, either. I think the doctors are keeping him in a medically induced coma – you'd expect that in these circumstances. It's to do with swelling round the brain, from what I understand.'

'I'm aware of similar cases', Asunander concurred. 'But be that as it may, we need to decide whether—'

He was interrupted by the ringing of one of the telephones on his desk. He scowled at it, but lifted the receiver and answered. A few seconds later his eyebrows rocketed upwards, but he made no clear comment on what was being said at the other end. He just mumbled the occasional 'yes', a 'no' or two and then a 'really?' shortly before he hung up.

He clasped his hands in front of him and his eyes moved back and forth between Barbarotti and Backman.

'We can cross out question number two,' he said. 'The girl has been found. She's in the Gemejnte Hospital in Maardam.'

'What?' said Backman.

'What?' said Barbarotti.

'Exactly what I said,' muttered the chief inspector. 'She was admitted yesterday afternoon, apparently. She's in quite a bad way.'

'A bad way?' said Barbarotti. 'What does that mean, in a bad way?'

'I didn't get any details,' said Asunander. 'But I've just decided how we're going to find out.'

'How?' said Backman.

'You two,' said Asunander, leaning forward over his desk. 'You're to fly down pronto and look into this. Not just the girl. The letter and this damned Roos as well. I want his head on a plate; don't come home without him.'

'Right . . .' said Barbarotti. 'But—'

'Is there anything you're not clear about?' asked Asunander.

'No, nothing,' declared DI Backman. 'It's all as clear as a bell.'

In the car on the way to Gothenburg's Landvetter airport, she thought of yet another question.

'How come he let you tag along?' she asked. 'I thought you were on special graffiti duties? He's gone on about nothing else lately.'

DI Barbarotti gave a modest little cough. 'Hrrm, I think it might be because that case is solved,' he said. 'Might be, at any rate.'

'You've solved it?' exclaimed Eva Backman. 'You know who PIZ and ZIP are, then?'

'I'm not certain,' said Barbarotti. 'But my solution is on Asunander's desk, so you might say the ball's in his court now.'

'What the heck are you on about?' asked Backman.

'Maybe we can leave that until we get back,' suggested Barbarotti. 'I think we ought to concentrate on what's happened down in Maardam.'

'All right,' sighed Eva Backman. 'Oh bollocks!'

'What is it?' said Barbarotti.

'Our family pow-wow,' she groaned, scrabbling for her

mobile. 'I completely forgot to call it off. Pipe down for a minute, I must get hold of Ville and tell him what's happened. If they cancel their training session and I don't show up, I shall lose custody and the house and the whole shebang.'

'Never a dull moment working with you,' said Barbarotti. 'Hardly ever, anyway.'

'Shut up,' said DI Backman.

48

No skimping at the end.

Someone had said that to him long ago, he couldn't remember who. It sounded like something Uncle Leopold would have said, around the time of the funeral, but Valdemar was not entirely sure it had been him.

Whatever the case, he remembered the advice: No skimping.

He was aware of a kind of lightness inside him as he walked round the centre of Maardam, buying the things he needed. There were really only two – a fiendishly sharp knife and a fiendishly expensive whisky – but he took his time. No rushing either, he thought. At the end.

He had lunch at an outdoor cafe. It was beside a canal. The weather was nice and he treated himself to two glasses of red wine with his pasta, and left a generous tip. He stayed on for a while over a cup of coffee, smoking his pipe and watching the dark water, the trees with their branches almost dipping into it and the moored boats bobbing up and down.

The people strolling by. All sorts.

Never better than this.

It took a couple of hours to find a good forest. He drove west, into the sun, and he was still not rushing. He left the motorway at random, at the junction for a place called Linzhuizen, turned onto a narrower road that led south, drove on through a small place with a name he couldn't pronounce, starting with Sz–, then through an even smaller one called Weid, and eventually eased the car along the base of a tree-covered ridge running parallel to the road, along by a little river.

He crossed the river via a narrow iron bridge and turned left onto a simple dirt road heading up over the ridge. The road wound its way in gentle curves, a couple of hairpins, too, and eventually came to a car park that seemed to be the starting point for a footpath for walkers.

Here, he thought. He turned in, parked and switched off the engine. This is it.

There was still some warmth in the air as he got out of the car. Hardly a breath of wind, and way down in the valley he could hear a dog barking. There were no other vehicles in the parking area, just a rubbish bin and a little noticeboard telling him that there was a choice of three walking routes, marked in red, yellow and white.

He opted for the red one. The noticeboard proclaimed it to be 6.2 km long. It doesn't matter, he thought, I won't be doing the whole thing anyway.

He put what he needed in a plastic carrier bag and set off.

Whisky, knife, notebook and pen.

When he had been walking for about twenty minutes, he could suddenly hear his father's voice. Gruff and a little out of practice after all these years, but still fully recognizable.

Look around you, Valdemar my lad.

He stopped. Wiping his forehead with the arm of his jacket, he realized it was just the right advice. A little to the west he caught sight of a clearing; it was not large, about the size of a circus ring, but there were lots of rocks to sit on and it had a view of the countryside below. He had topped the crest of the ridge now and was on the far side, looking west.

He made his way over to the clearing and sat down on one of the rocks; the sun had warmed it up, although it was well into October. It's different down here on the continent, he thought. The summers and autumns last so much longer. Maybe I should have lived my life here. Like Greger.

He uncorked his whisky and took a mouthful. It was a litre bottle, the stuff was called Balblair and it had cost him €229.

It was smooth and delicious. Thank bloody goodness, thought Ante Valdemar Roos, it's the best spirit I've tasted in my entire life.

Not before time. He got out his pipe and tobacco. Shuffled down onto the ground and leant his back against the rock instead. That was better. Even better.

The afternoon sun in his face. Pure, clear air, still pleasantly warm. Yellowy-green broadleaved trees that were whispering all around him in the lightest of breezes.

He lit his pipe and drank another gulp. Took out his notebook.

Its contents were extremely varied.

As he slowly and purposefully worked his way through the bottle of whisky, and as the sun sank in the west with the same slow pace and firm purpose, allowing the shadows free rein in the clearing, he read everything he had written since he started – in those five or six weeks, or however long it was.

He did not rush this, either. He stopped now and then to think, reflect and make a correction. He replaced one word with another, or found a better expression. Some of the maxims, those that had come from Anna or the Romanian, he left untouched. Got to respect the moral rights of the author, he thought. It was not his business to express an opinion on them.

He had made his last entry the day before, after Anna had left him and he had paid a visit to his son on Keymerstraat. He had spent a long time in that hotel room – it had been the longest night of his life, though by no means the worst – leafing back and forth in the Romanian before he found it.

For when two people travel side by side, this generates the narrative of the love between them, the narrative that is always another and always has a personality which could not have been foreseen, like a child conceived from their minds in passionate embrace, and at the same time the leaden, lacklustre book is not the book itself but the tool by which the book has a chance to be born.

That is not exactly, he had thought – and was thinking again now, as he took another swig of whisky and his eyes scanned the open vista – that is not exactly how my life has panned out. I have none of the prerequisites for understanding this, and yet I do.

And yet I do.

He could feel the whisky starting to play its intended role. He filled his pipe and lit it for a final smoke, turned over to a fresh page and started to apply himself to his closing remarks.

He wanted something short. Pithy, certainly, but also a sort of summing up.

And his own words, not borrowed ones.

No words came into his head. But people did, a whole succession of them:

Alice.

Signe and Wilma. Wrigman, Red Cow and Tapanen.

Espen Lund. Greger and his wife, whatever she was called. He'd only ever seen her in a photo.

His father. His mother. Someone he did not recognize, claiming to be called Nabokov and wanting to make some kind of elucidation. He took no notice of him.

And finally – but only once the others had run riot inside him for a good while – Anna. And when she came, everything else faded into the background.

Yes, everything and everyone else made way for her and he had a sense of his whole life, all these hours and days and years, suddenly assembled at this single point. Just here, just now. And Anna was with him in some unfathomable but at the same time completely natural way; perhaps she was not really aware of it herself, but she would come to realize it, he knew. One day when she was well again she would understand everything, and know that his last thought was of her. She was the one he carried in his arms as he walked through the Twilight Land.

In some goddamned unfathomable way, that is.

With Anna, the final words presented themselves. He took a last swig of whisky as he weighed them in his mind, so they would be absolutely right.

He swallowed, put pen to paper, and wrote.

Events, always so infernally overestimated, are nothing compared to the parentheses around the spaces in between. You do well to bear that in mind, all you people who blindly rush

about the world and think you are on the way somewhere –
everything is in the pauses. It is also worth noting that
expensive whisky tastes significantly better than the cheap kind.
Now I am done and have nothing more to add.

He read it through twice, nodded to himself in confirmation,
and took out the knife.

He suddenly felt doubtful.

49

Barbarotti and Backman landed at Sechshafen airport outside Maardam at half past three in the afternoon, and caught a taxi straight to the Gemejnte Hopsital.

After diverse misunderstandings and wrong turns, they finally found their way to the right ward. There they were met by a ward sister called Sister Vlaander and a detective inspector who introduced himself as Rooth.

The ward sister explained that her patient, Anna Gambowska, had been admitted to the hospital the previous day and undergone an operation later that evening, and was not yet in a fit state to answer questions. But the operation had gone well, Dr Moewenroede who had performed it would be coming round in an hour or so, and if the police officers would like a brief word with him, having travelled so far, that would be fine.

Then she left Barbarotti and Backman with DI Rooth in the waiting room.

'So why are you sitting here, exactly?' asked Eva Backman once a helpful nursing assistant had brought them all cups of coffee.

'Orders,' said Rooth genially. 'That's the way it usually is in the force here. You get an order and you obey it. Isn't that what happens up in your country, then?'

Backman conceded that it did. More often than not, anyway.

'Oh, and she's a murder suspect as well,' added Rooth. 'That's the impression I got, at any rate. But I expect you two know more about that than I do.'

Backman conceded this, too.

'Do you know how she's doing?' asked Barbarotti. 'Beyond what Sister Vlaander told us, I mean?'

Rooth nodded and popped a biscuit in his mouth. 'They seem pretty sure she's going to be all right,' he said. 'But surely she can't have murdered anybody, that little thing?'

'That isn't entirely clear yet,' said Barbarotti. 'She was involved, though. In some way.'

'And what are your orders?' Rooth asked them.

'To interview her as soon as possible,' said Backman. 'Take her back home with us if we can. But we ought not to stay more than a couple of days.'

'Maardam isn't a bad town,' said Rooth. 'There are a few nice pubs if you get the chance. And autumn's the best time of year.'

Barbarotti nodded and studied his colleague. He looked to be in his fifties, powerfully built with a square face and thinning hair. There was something familiar about him, but Barbarotti could not put his finger on it.

'Are you going to sit here and wait for Dr Moewenroede?' asked Rooth. 'Because if you are . . . ?'

'You can go off for a couple of hours,' said Backman. 'How about if we call you when it's time for us to think about leaving?'

'Great,' said DI Rooth. 'There are a couple of things I need to sort out in town. I'll be back within two hours.'

They exchanged mobile numbers and Rooth left them on their own.

'I thought I recognized him,' said Barbarotti.

'Me too,' said Backman. 'OK then, we'll sit here, I suppose.'

'I suppose so,' said Barbarotti. 'Maybe I should ask them to take a look at my foot? What do you reckon?'

'I reckon that would be pushing it,' said Backman.

When Dr Moewenroede turned up, he asked them if they preferred a brief or a full description of Anna Gambowska's condition and Backman said they would be happy with the condensed version. Moewenroede told them she had been suffering from a subdural haematoma, quite common after a head injury, and although the operation had proved slightly complicated, it had gone well. The patient now needed plenty of sleep, and would probably have to spend a week in hospital, but unless there were any unforeseen developments it should be perfectly all right for them to have a short conversation with her the following day.

Barbarotti and Backman thanked him and handed over to DI Rooth, who had returned to the ward.

They ordered a taxi at the front desk and went to Keymerstraat to speak to Greger Roos, hoping that he, at least, would be able to talk to them.

He was a tall, spare man of about forty, possibly a little younger. Barbarotti immediately looked to see if he had any features in common with pictures of his father, but could detect no resemblance. He was wearing cords and a white shirt unbuttoned at the neck, and made a vaguely sophisticated impression. None of those they had spoken to had ever used the word 'sophisticated' when attempting to describe Ante Valdemar Roos, and Barbarotti began to appreciate that the indications they had very little in common were evidently true.

Though they must share a few deeply buried genes, he supposed.

A wife and two children in the six-to-eight bracket said hello and withdrew to some corner of the big flat with its tastefully minimalist décor, leaving them in the living room with three beers and a bowl of nuts.

'So we gather you were surprised when he turned up?' began Backman.

'Surprised is an understatement,' observed Greger Roos. 'He rang me from the cafe downstairs and two minutes later he was in the hall. We haven't met since Mum's funeral.'

'Ten years ago?'

'That's right,' said Greger Roos. 'It's a shame to have to say it, but there have never been very strong ties between my father and me.'

'How old were you when they got divorced?'

'Five. From then on I lived with my mother all the time. He – my father – kind of wasn't even on the map.'

'He vanished off the scene entirely?' asked Barbarotti. 'I mean . . . ?'

'There were a couple of summers when we spent a few weeks together. To be honest, we both found it rather difficult. Unfortunate, but that was simply how it was. He didn't make any efforts to foster the relationship, either.'

'And your mother?'

'As regards him, you mean?'

'Yes.'

'I don't think she actively disliked him. But we never talked about him. She just thought . . . well, I think she just found him terribly boring.'

Here we go again, thought Barbarotti.

'I remember she once described him as a glass of water. Tepid water.'

Barbarotti gave Backman a quick glance and thought about what Marianne had said.

'What did he say while he was here?' asked Backman. 'How did he seem and how long did he stay?'

Greger Roos gave a laugh. 'The oddest thing was how well dressed he was . . . that is, I don't mean in the sense of super-smart. But he had new clothes. A suit, shirt and tie, and it looked as if he'd bought the whole outfit just that day.'

'Maybe he had,' suggested Backman with a quick little smile. 'He's been on the run for several weeks, after all.'

'Possibly,' said Greger Roos. 'Anyway, he apologized for barging in, but said he needed my help with something. Two things, in fact.'

'Two things?' said Barbarotti.

'Yes. First this letter I told you about. He wanted me to make sure it reached you. It was incredibly important, he said. It would explain everything and he solemnly swore its contents were true.'

'Solemnly swore?'

'That's what he said,' said Greger Roos. 'He used exactly those words.'

'Why couldn't he just have posted it to us?' asked Backman.

Greger Roos shrugged his shoulders. 'I don't know. I didn't ask and he didn't offer any explanation. I was so taken aback by seeing him that I couldn't quite think what to say.'

'What else did he want help with?' asked Barbarotti.

Greger Roos sipped his beer and wiped the corners of his mouth before answering. 'He wanted me to forgive him.'

'Forgive him?'

'Yes, precisely that. I said he had nothing to ask forgiveness for, but he persisted and said that I was wrong. And that of course I knew what he was talking about.'

'The fact that he had failed you as a father?' said Backman.

'I assume that's what he was thinking of, yes. He was very insistent and in the end I said that I did. That I forgave him. He only stayed half a minute after that, gave me the letter and left. It was . . .'

'Yes?'

'It was almost like a dream. I happened to be alone here, as well, and I almost wondered if I'd imagined the whole thing. But I pinched my arm and I – anyway, there was the envelope, so I knew it must actually have happened.'

'How long was he here?'

'Five minutes at most.'

'And he didn't say anything about where he was going?'

'No.'

'Nothing about a young girl?'

'No. And I didn't pull myself together in time to ask him anything, either. Your phone call was in the back of my mind, of course, but it all happened too fast.'

Eva Backman sighed. 'I can understand that,' she said. 'This whole business is pretty out of the ordinary. Can we see the letter?'

Greger Roos went to get it from the next room. He came back and laid it on the table. It was a big, fat envelope. Barbarotti had unconsciously been imagining something smaller, but this looked more like a document wallet of some kind.

'All right,' said Eva Backman. 'I think we'll take this with us. We'll be in town for a couple of days. We'll need to talk to you again, I'm sure. You'll be contactable?'

'No problem,' Greger Roos assured them, handing her his card. 'You can ring me any time.'

They thanked him, shook his hand and left Keymerstraat.

They were sitting in Backman's hotel room when they opened the letter.

Barbarotti was aware of his heart beating overtime and he could see that Eva Backman felt equally tense.

The large envelope, addressed to 'The Kymlinge Police', contained two smaller ones. One of them was thick and sealed and had 'Anna Gambowska. By hand' written on it. The other, thinner envelope only had its flap tucked in and was not addressed to anyone.

Eva Backman glanced at Barbarotti. He nodded, she opened the flap and took out a folded sheet of paper. The letter was handwritten and almost covered both sides of the paper.

'Read it out loud,' said Barbarotti.

Eva Backman cleared her throat and did so:

'I am writing this in full possession of my mental faculties so that everything is clear and there can be no misunderstanding.

As a human being I have been rather a failure. Since my father died, I don't think anyone has liked me, and I was twelve then. There has been no good reason to like me, I know, and I have not had any great fondness for other people, either, so there is no more to be said on that subject.

But I have three lives on my conscience and they must be declared. The first is that boy at Lograna. He was a bastard, threatened Anna and bashed her on the head with an iron bar, I don't know where he found it. I got there in the nick of time, stabbed him because I had no choice, and I don't regret it.

The second life is that policeman at the motorway services near Emden. I lashed out in panic, he would not leave us alone and was trying to take the girl away from me. It happened in an instant and I know I did wrong. It was an unforgivable act.

The third life is my own. I am sick and tired of it. I have lived for almost sixty years, and it's only very recently I have been able to see any meaning to it at all. But I realize that this good time is over and have chosen to die by my own hand, as they so poetically say. Knowing now what this past month has brought me, I am glad I put the decision off for so long.

And I also have a fourth life on my conscience, but in an entirely different way. From my heaven, because I believe there is a heaven for everyone, I will always hold a protective hand over Anna Gambowska, that figure of light. The money in the other envelope is for her. It is my own money, won on the football pools, and I am completely within my rights to do what I want with it. Also in the envelope are the keys to two left luggage lockers at Maardam central station, where I have put her guitar and other belongings.

I also want the girl to have Lograna – she can sell it if she wants so she can afford to carry on studying and get on in life as best she can. She is the only person since my father who has meant anything to me.

I expect Alice and the girls will lay claim to my other assets, and they deserve them. Perhaps Greger should have a small share, too. They will have to discuss it.

I am writing this in a hotel room in Maardam on the night of 7 October and it is my last will and testament.

Yours faithfully,

Ante Valdemar Roos'

She passed the letter to Barbarotti and he read it through to himself again. As he got to the end he saw that Backman was standing over by the window, looking out. It was dark now, and a thin drizzle was falling on the town; she had her hands clasped behind her back and was rocking slowly back and forth on her heels and toes.

He cast about for something to say, but for some reason failed to find any words.

She was clearly in the same boat, and they just stayed there like that for quite a long time, she at the window with her back to him, he sitting on the edge of the bed with Ante Valdemar Roos's letter in his hands and in his head, thinking that he would always – for reasons he did not fully understand – remember this moment. An imprint or tableau was slowly but inexorably etching itself in his memory, and it would never allow itself to be forgotten.

Eventually she turned round. She gave him a mournful look and said: 'One of those nice pubs Inspector Rooth mentioned, what do you say?'

'Sounds good,' said Gunnar Barbarotti. 'We should probably try to analyse this.'

50

The one-eyed woman did not like the police.

This was made abundantly clear, and he wished he had introduced himself as a family member instead.

'So what?' she said. 'I could see the girl was sick, so I rang for an ambulance. What's it got to do with you?'

'We're really more interested in the man,' explained Barbarotti. 'He said he was her father when he checked in, is that right?'

'That was what he said, yes,' the woman agreed truculently, and lit a cigarette.

'How did he behave when he got back? After the girl had been taken off to hospital, I mean?'

'Behave?'

'Yes,' said Barbarotti. 'What did he say? What did he do?'

'Has he broken the law? Why are you asking me this?'

Barbarotti thought for a moment. 'He's dead,' he said. 'We're looking into the circumstances of his death and some others. Please just answer my questions. This will only take five minutes if we do it here and now, four hours if I have to take you to the police station.'

That did the trick. To some extent, anyway. 'You don't say?' she said irritably, taking a couple of drags on her cigarette. She tapped the ash into a sort of bowl on the desk in front of her.

The bowl looked like half a shrivelled brain and Barbarotti hoped it was an imitation, but couldn't be entirely sure.

'Yeah well, he came storming in here,' she went on. 'He was in a right state. He shouted: where's the girl? Luckily there was another client in here – a retired boxer, his name's Bausten, he sleeps here now and then. He strong-armed the old guy into a corner and told him to shut up.'

'I see,' said Barbarotti. 'And what then?'

She took another drag on her cigarette and shrugged.

'Well, then he went off to their room. I thought it would be best to leave him alone. Half an hour later I saw him drive off.'

'And he didn't come back?'

'No, he didn't. I checked the room a bit later. There was no one there, but he'd paid in advance, so I wasn't worried.'

'And you've no idea where he was heading next?'

'None at all.'

Barbarotti paused for thought again.

'And the girl?' he asked. 'Can you tell me anything about her?'

'She was completely out of it,' said the one-eyed woman. 'An overdose or something, I don't know.'

'It wasn't an overdose,' said Barbarotti. 'Did the man ask which hospital they took her to?'

'No.'

'He didn't say where he was going?'

'No.'

'Is there anything else you want to add?'

'Not a word.'

Bloody hell, thought Gunnar Barbarotti. I hope Backman is having better luck.

*

Eva Backman observed the girl, who had just opened her eyes. The thought ran through her mind that she looked like a sparrow.

'So this is you?' she said.

'What?' said the girl.

Her voice was just a whisper and Backman took the cup of water that was on the bedside table and helped her drink a little.

'So you're Anna Gambowska?'

'Yes . . . yes, I am. Who are you?'

'My name's Eva Backman,' said Backman. 'I'm a police inspector from Kymlinge in Sweden. Do you know where you are?'

'Police?'

'Yes. Do you know where you are?'

Anna Gambowska looked around cautiously. 'I . . . I must be in hospital.'

Backman nodded. 'Quite right. Do you know which one?'

She shook her head.

'You're in the Gemejnte Hospital in a town called Maardam.'

'Maardam . . .' whispered the girl. 'He talked about Maardam.'

'Who?'

No answer.

'Who talked about Maardam?'

'Valdemar.'

'Valdemar Roos?'

'Yes . . .' An anxious, restless look came into Anna's eyes. 'Where is he?'

Eva Backman put a hand on her arm. She made eye contact and held it for a few seconds before she replied, deciding not to beat about the bush.

'We think he's dead, Anna.'

'Dead? Valdemar's . . . dead?'

'Yes, it looks quite likely.'

'How . . . I mean . . . how did he die?'

'If he is dead, he chose that path himself.'

At first she did not seem to fully understand, but then she nodded. She closed her eyes and seemed to be clenching her jaw. Backman waited quietly. When the girl opened her eyes again they were brimming over with tears, and she did nothing to stop them. She simply let them flow, keeping her hands clasped on her chest as she lay there. She looked almost as if she was praying. After a while, Backman passed the girl some tissues, and she dabbed at her eyes and blew her nose.

'I . . . I can understand it,' she said. 'Yes, I really can.'

'You mean you can understand Valdemar doing that?'

'Yes.'

'Can you tell me why you're in hospital?' asked Eva Backman. 'What's wrong with you?'

The girl thought about this, her eyes scanning Backman's face as if looking for something. Some kind of reassurance . . . or confirmation.

'You can trust me,' said Eva Backman. 'I know almost everything that's happened, but I'd just like hear it from you, as well.'

Anna Gambowska nodded again and dried her eyes.

'He hit me on the head,' she said. 'Steffo did, I can't remember it but that must have been what happened. Then, when I woke up, Steffo was dead, it was just Valdemar and me, and we . . . well, we ran away, you could say. I mean, we couldn't stay there . . . we just couldn't.'

'But Steffo hit you over the head with an iron bar?'

'Yes . . . yes, I'm sure of that bit. Even if I don't remember the actual blow.'

'How did he die?' asked Backman.

She looked as if she was thinking and then she cautiously shook her head.

'I don't know. I've tried and tried, but it won't come back. He chases me out of the house with that iron bar in his hand . . . I've got this dim picture of him putting his hand up ready, but it keeps fading away . . .'

'Do you know how he died?' asked Backman.

'A knife,' said Anna Gambowska. 'Valdemar said he was stabbed in the stomach and bled to death.'

'Who was holding the knife?'

'Valdemar said he did it.'

'But?'

'But I don't know. I've got this feeling I had a knife in my hand . . . so maybe . . . it's all so fuzzy, sometimes I think I just dreamt it all, but of course that can't be—'

Eva Backman cut in, taking hold of her hand.

'Anna,' she said. 'You can forget that. It was Valdemar who killed Steffo, just like he said.'

'Are you sure?' the girl asked.

'I'm sure,' Eva Backman confirmed. 'Are you tired?'

She nodded and attempted a smile. 'Yes, quite tired.'

'I just need to ask you one more thing. Do you remember anything about getting a puncture, you and Valdemar?'

'A puncture?'

'Yes.'

'No, I don't remember that. But we drove such a long way and I . . . I was asleep a lot of the time. It's because of my head, I think . . .'

'You don't remember Valdemar talking to a police officer while he was changing the wheel?'

Another shake of the head. 'No . . . no, I'm sorry . . .'

'Tell you what,' said Backman, releasing her hand. 'I think you need to rest now. If I come back this afternoon or tomorrow to talk to you a bit more, would that be OK?'

'That'll be OK,' said Anna Gambowska. 'Am I going to . . .'

'Yes?'

'Am I going to get better?'

Eva Backman smiled at her. 'The doctor says you will.'

'Does my mum know I'm here?'

'We're trying to arrange for your mum to come tomorrow. Your little brother, too. Then you can all fly home together when you're strong enough.'

'Thank you,' said Anna Gambowska, and closed her eyes. 'Thank you so much. And I'm so sorry that Valdemar . . .'

Then she ran out of words.

Backman stood up. A tough junkie bitch? she thought. Pull the other one.

51

They found a nice place to eat the second night, too. It was beside one of the canals and was called Grote Flick. They were given a table tucked away under a whitewashed arch and the thought ran through Barbarotti's mind that Inspector Rooth was absolutely right. Maardam was a very livable town.

'So we've still got a few question marks to straighten out,' he said once they had ordered their food and had a carafe of red wine on the table. 'Haven't we?'

'Yes,' said Backman, 'I suppose we have. Which ones are you thinking of?'

'Whether it really was Valdemar Roos who stuck the knife into Stefan Rakic, that's probably the first one.'

'It was him,' said Eva Backman.

'I don't see how you can be so sure of it,' said Barbarotti.

Eva Backman made no reply.

'The girl doesn't remember and he said he did it so she won't have to carry the can,' he went on. 'She could very well have done it. And she'd very likely get off; it must count as self-defence.'

'I think you should stop digging,' said Eva Backman. 'He's confessed; she can't remember. Why can't you be content with that?'

'I don't know,' said Barbarotti. 'My passion for the truth, perhaps?'

'There's no need to air your luxury problems,' said Backman with a sudden hint of annoyance. 'There's another aspect, too, but you haven't thought about that, of course.'

'And what's that?' said Barbarotti.

'Stefan Rakic's father,' said Backman. 'He's currently in jail, I know, but he's sworn to kill whoever killed his son. I wouldn't say I picked up any good vibes when I went to see him.'

Gunnar Barbarotti sipped his wine and mulled this over for a while.

'I see,' he said. 'You're right, and I won't bring it up again.'

'Great,' said Eva Backman. 'Any more question marks?'

'Why didn't he take the girl to hospital?' said Barbarotti. 'Did it really not dawn on him what a terrible state she was in?'

Backman hesitated. 'I don't know,' she said. 'The girl says she's sure it didn't, but if she was asleep nearly all the time and had some kind of epileptic fit into the bargain, he really ought to have realized. But you can choose not to see things when you don't want to, of course.'

'Yes, indeed,' said Barbarotti. 'He was pretty good at that . . . or *is*?'

'What do you mean by that?'

Barbarotti shrugged. 'How convinced are you that he really is dead?'

'Pretty much convinced,' said Eva Backman. 'But they'll surely find him in any case, whether he's alive or dead. His letter felt genuine though, didn't you think?'

'Yes,' said Barbarotti. 'All too sodding genuine and all too sodding tragic.'

'Exactly,' said Backman. 'And Klaus Meyer's out of his coma, so that's one life he won't have on his conscience. But unless Valdemar Roos has driven his car into some deep lake or river, they'll find him sooner or later . . . as I said. It's strange, but it doesn't feel particularly important, somehow.'

'If he's alive it's important,' said Barbarotti.

'He's not alive,' she said. 'Can we decide that, too?'

'Fine by me,' said Barbarotti. 'Well then, I've only got one more problem.'

'Go ahead,' said Eva Backman.

'The girl,' said Barbarotti.

'And what's your problem with her?'

'The witness statements about her character,' said Barbarotti. 'I've scarcely ever come across a meeker, gentler girl than her. I was only with her for a short while of course, but don't you agree? A junkie as hard as nails? That's total crap.'

'It certainly is,' said Backman. 'One hundred per cent. So that's one thing to look into before we close the case . . . well two things, to be more accurate.'

'And they are?' said Barbarotti.

'That residential centre and that Double Johan. Assuming he did actually have the girl in his car, what happened was something very different from what he told me . . . I'll ask Anna about it in due course. And it'll certainly be worth taking a closer look at Sonja Svensson and her Elvafors, while we're at it.'

'Excellent,' said Barbarotti. 'Let me know if you need any help.'

'You can be sure I will,' said Eva Backman.

They sat in silence for a while. A pianist started playing somewhere at the back and the lights dimmed slightly. Eva Backman suddenly thought of something.

'Oh, I forgot to ask,' she said. 'You solved the graffiti case, didn't you say?'

Gunnar Barbarotti shuffled in his seat. 'Well yes, possibly I have. But the ball's in Asunander's court now.'

'Yes, you said. So be my guest, it's your turn to straighten out a question mark for me.'

'Hm,' said Barbarotti.

'Go ahead,' said Backman.

'OK then,' said Gunnar Barbarotti. 'If it's as I think, it isn't complicated at all. You recall that graffiti remover I told you about?'

'The Cerberus Cleaning Company?'

'That's the one. Its owner is a Kent Blomgren. I reckon it's his two sons who are PIZ and ZIP.'

'Wha-at?' spluttered Backman as her wine went down the wrong way. 'What the heck are you saying?'

'Well that's the way it looks,' said Barbarotti. 'It was Sara who hit on it, not me . . . if I'm honest.'

'Sara?'

'Yes, she's in the same class as one of the brothers, and we happened to be talking about it at home one evening. And then she came out with the fact he was a real bad apple at school, that Jimmy.'

Eva Backman burst out laughing. 'So you're telling me . . . you're telling me the sons see to it that their dad doesn't go out of business? They do the graffiti and he cleans it up. It's bloody brilliant!'

'That's debatable,' said Gunnar Barbarotti. 'Asunander certainly didn't use quite those words, but I think . . . well I'm not entirely sure about this, of course.'

'About what?' said Backman.

'I thought I detected a smile as I put my solution to him.'

'Asunander? A smile?'

'I think so.'

'Well I'll be damned,' said Eva Backman.

'And there's another intriguing connection,' said Barbarotti.

'What's that?'

'Well, this Kent Blomgren – Mr Cerberus, that is – was a classmate of Lars-Lennart Brahmin of local paper fame. Thirty-five to forty years ago. The front of his apartment building has come off worse in the graffiti attacks than anywhere else in town. There's something simmering away there, clearly – upper-class versus lower-class and probably more besides. But it's as old as the hills and I haven't looked into it properly.'

Eva Backman nodded with interest.

'Some long-held grudge,' she said. 'It sounds a bit sick, wouldn't you say?'

'Yes. And then there's another problem.'

'What's that?'

'They deny it point blank.'

'Aha?' said Backman. 'All three?'

'All three. And we're on dodgy ground when it comes to evidence. If the sons *are* the ones committing these crimes, their dad has effectively erased all traces.'

'Incredible,' snorted Eva Backman. She had been on the point of drinking some more wine but was obliged to put the glass back down on the table. 'And Sturegård spent almost a year working on this?'

'Yes,' said Barbarotti. 'But I'm not casting any aspersions on her. It was just Sara's flash of genius, and as I say, we've no firm evidence.'

'So what's the next step?' asked Backman.

Barbarotti wiped something out of the corner of his eye

with his serviette before he answered. Backman waited patiently.

'Third degree,' he said. 'Asunander's going to interrogate all three of them. I suppose the idea is to reach some sort of . . . deal.'

'A deal?'

Barbarotti nodded. 'On the quiet, yes. Asunander scares the whole family shitless, the graffiti stops. No perpetrators are apprehended, but the problem goes away.'

'And everything in the garden's rosy?'

'Everything in the garden's rosy,' said Barbarotti. 'Though Cerberus might be for the chop. Let's drink to that.'

'Cheers,' said Backman.

They drank, and their food arrived. They ate in silence for a while. The pianist moved on from 'Take the "A" Train' to 'Smoke Gets in Your Eyes'. Then Eva Backman put down her knife and fork.

'You know what?' she said. 'And I'm straying into my private life now. It's been three whole days since I told my husband I didn't want to live with him any more. Since then I've spoken to him just once, when I rang to postpone our family council – don't you thing it's a bit strange? He hasn't tried to ring me even once.'

Barbarotti nodded. 'Perhaps he's struck dumb with grief?'

'I doubt it,' said Eva Backman. 'It's more likely they're out training or watching the TV sport round the clock, now they've got the chance.'

For a moment he saw a touch of bitterness in her face. It was the first time, if so.

The very first time in all those years.

'What is it with you men?' she said. 'Valdemar Roos. My

husband. Johan Johansson . . . and Cerberus. You get what I'm talking about?'

'I think so,' said Gunnar Barbarotti cautiously. 'But I haven't got a good answer. Perhaps . . . no . . .'

'Please go on,' said Eva Backman.

'It's as if we were born with a hole.'

'A hole? I had the idea it was us women who—'

'A different kind of hole,' said Barbarotti.

'Explain,' said Backman.

'Well, it's a kind of imperfection or vacuum that has to be compensated for. Or at any rate some kind of built-in defect that you women don't have. A question mark . . . Some of us simply try to iron it out through sport, because there's nothing as uncomplicated as sport . . . No, it's no good, I'm not making any kind of job of expressing this.'

He lapsed into silence and looked at Eva Backman, who was watching him from the other side of the table with an ambiguous smile on her lips. 'You've thought about this before,' she said.

'Only since I was thirteen,' admitted Barbarotti. 'Anyway, there's a kind of gender flaw we all have in common, you're quite right about that. A lot of us are able to cope with it, but not all.'

Backman raised her glass. 'I like that phrase,' she said. 'Gender flaw. We're getting into some pretty deep things here, don't you think?'

'Yes,' said Barbarotti. 'But we've hit the bottom now, at least where I'm concerned. There are more words than there are thoughts, too, and that's another problem . . . though that's true of both sexes, when I come to think about it.'

Eva Backman laughed. 'Sorry,' she said. 'I shouldn't have

brought it up. It's a shame you sold your flat, to move on to the next subject.'

'Why?' said Barbarotti.

'I could have bought it,' said Eva Backman. 'Now I'm going to be a single-person household. I liked that balcony.'

'So did I,' said Barbarotti. 'But I'm pretty sure there are other balconies in town.'

'You reckon?' said Eva Backman.

'I'd swear to it,' said Gunnar Barbarotti.

But before the evening was over they returned once more to Ante Valdemar Roos. It was when they were each sitting over an espresso and a small cognac.

Gunnar Barbarotti was aware of being pleasantly inebriated and he thought that this was one of those moments he would be very happy to sustain for a little while. Lie at anchor and just float there in the stream of time. He was about to put that thought into words, too, when Eva Backman said:

'What would be the best ending to this business, do you think? Valdemar Roos, I mean.'

'I'm not sure I understand the question,' said Barbarotti.

'We've agreed that he's dead,' said Eva Backman. 'But it grieves you a bit, doesn't it? Admit it.'

Gunnar Barbarotti raised his glass and took a sniff at the splendid spirit.

'Did you know,' he said, 'that cognac is the only drink enjoyed to best advantage through the nose?'

'Now you're just playing for time,' said Eva Backman. 'Well, it grieves you that you never got to meet boring old Valdemar, I know that. Marianne's quite right; you've got a screw missing there.'

'Hm,' said Barbarotti. 'Maybe. But if he's written a fake suicide note, I have to say he'll sink in my estimation. Are you with me on that?'

'Of course,' said Backman. 'So what would be the best ending, then? That was my question.'

Gunnar Barbarotti savoured a small amount of cognac – through his mouth – before he answered.

'The best ending is that we never find out,' he said. 'Regardless of whether he actually took his own life or not, we never find out. He can lie at the bottom of a lake from now until judgement day, or die a natural death in Barcelona in twenty-five years' time – it makes no odds, the important thing is that I don't find out which.'

'Do you really mean that?' said Eva Backman.

'Yes,' said Gunnar Barbarotti. 'I really mean it.'

Backman pondered this for a while, and then smiled.

'You're right, Gunnar,' she said. 'It's a shame I'm drunk, because I think you said something unusually wise there. If I were sober I would be able to elaborate on it, absolutely I would.'

And Gunnar Barbarotti smiled too, as he allowed himself to be slowly filled with the present – the jazz piano, the drop of cognac still trembling in the bottom of his glass, Eva Backman's familiar laugh lines and the diminutive birthmark above her right eyebrow, the slumbering but ever-present thoughts of Marianne, of the children, of the state of harmony and fulfilled needs that had arrived in his life without warning, the quiet, civilized murmur beneath the vaulted ceiling in this foreign town – and the singular inner satisfaction a blind chicken feels when she finally thinks she has found a grain of corn.